HOPE

WOLVES OF WALKER COUNTY

KIKI BURRELLI

CONNECT WITH KIKI

Join my newsletter!
And stay up to date on my newest titles, giveaways and news!
Want a free—full length— wolf shifter Mpreg novel? Join my newsletter when you get Finding Finn!

———

Join the Pack! Awooooo!
Come hang out with your pack mates!
Visit Kiki's Den and join the pack! Enjoy exclusive access to behind the scenes excerpts, cover reveals and surprise giveaways!

EXPERIENCE THE WOLVES OF WORLD

Wolves of Walker County (Wolf Shifter Mpreg)

Truth

Hope

Faith

Love

Wolves of Royal Paynes (Wolf Shifter Mpreg)

Hero

Ruler

Lovers

Outlaw

1

NASH

I NEEDED TO GET LAID.

That was the thought that carried with me as I jumped over a long log, covered in moss, that must have fallen between my run the day before and now. Every day, my runs got longer. My regular five turned into my regular ten, and now I was up before the baby—if it happened to sleep at all that night—putting in fifteen miles before most people were even awake.

My tennis shoe landed in mud, and I cursed but kept moving forward. These shoes were circling the drain anyhow. Maybe I'd take the ferry off Walker and go to Seattle for the weekend. I'd find a larger selection out there.

Of shoes and of willing men to bury myself in. It was clear I needed a break, something to help work the edge off.

I broke through the line of trees to the yard of my house, experiencing that familiar wave of pride when I looked at the sturdy walls and windows that gleamed in the morning sun. The sprawling, modern log cabin sat directly where the Lynx River emptied into Walker Bay. We'd made that, the four Walker cousins. It had been our first home away from the only home we'd ever known. Branson and Aver had done most of the planning and preparing, leaving Wyatt and myself to do the grunt work, but that didn't change anything.

We'd built that home when we'd had nothing but each other—and Nana.

It looked big, but not when you considered everyone who lived inside: four grown alpha shifters, a newly changed omega mate, and a baby.

A baby who had caused a lot of whispers on the other side of the bay.

I didn't need some asshole with a memo pad and a pencil, asking me how I felt to figure out that was the root of my recent excess energy. The nearer I got to the end of my run, the closer I was to the wraparound porch. Already, I could see a small pile forming on the mat in front of the door.

I snarled at the collection of baked goods, homemade baby toys, and clothing.

The influx of visitors and gifts was mostly Nana's doing, with all that talk of Riley, my cousin Branson's chosen omega, being *blessed*. According to her, Riley was blessed, his pregnancy was blessed, his spontaneous transformation from normal human to wolf shifter was blessed, and the wiggling bundle of poopy diapers and around-the-clock screams was blessed as well.

I supposed baby Branson wasn't so bad. He was the only child I knew to be birthed by a man via some kind of spontaneous shifter osmosis—though I was the only one who called it that. We'd all wondered *where* Riley's baby would exit his body when it became clear that the impossible was true and he was with child. As alpha wolf shifters who had been born at the same time and been tasked with battling each other to the death to discover who the pack's new leader was, the four of us cousins were used to strange. But picturing which of Riley's orifices the baby would make his debut out of had been a cause for squeamish, yet heated, debate. Whenever Riley had been out of earshot, of course.

I was glad we'd all been wrong. Even if we still didn't understand completely how it had all happened.

But now, the pack that we'd done a fan-fucking-tastic job of avoiding for ten years was in our faces again. Not so much the elders or our grandfather, Alpha Walker, but the other shifters that belonged to the pack. They believed in that blessed business more than anyone and hadn't stopped dropping off gifts for the *blessed Walker baby* since his birth.

Ha. I was forsaken because I'd made the choice not to murder my cousins and brother, but the baby was blessed.

Jealous of a baby before seven, a new record.

I stepped over the pile of gifts instead of stomping on them. I'd have to remember I did that for the next time Aver accused me of being a selfish narcissist. I preferred the term "unarguably gorgeous" to narcissist anyway. I couldn't be selfish and be a fireman. Aver knew that. He just forgot every time I was forced to use the rest of his shitty almond milk when we were out of regular.

"Hey, Rye," I said, passing him in the living room on my way to the kitchen. I grabbed a bottle of water from the fridge and meandered back to where Riley was giving Bran Jr. his bottle. The baby suckled happily, his eyes closed.

"You're sweaty," Riley replied, eye-fucking me from top to bottom.

Maybe he wasn't eye-fucking me, since he seemed to see something in my cousin, but let's be honest, he was enjoying the show. I stuck up my foot and struck a pose.

Riley snorted. "How many miles today, Nash?" he asked as if the number would worry him.

I shrugged. I knew the number but didn't like the way the wrinkles formed between his eyebrows. He didn't need to be worrying about me when he had so much more to concern himself with. "I better shower." I spun around.

"Nash?"

My feet froze against the wood. The smarter thing would've been to go and leave Riley to care about the things that were important at the moment. But he was clearly upset, and that wouldn't change if I avoided the conversation. If anything, it would just get me yelled at later when Branson attempted to bust my balls for upsetting his mate. And I'd hate to have to kick his ass when he was just defending his mate. "Yeah?" I asked without turning.

"Are you sure you're okay with this party we're planning?"

He and Branson had decided the best way to celebrate their union and the baby was with a huge get-together. So far, the guest list was a hodgepodge of people Riley used to know, people around town, and certain shifters. "Of course."

Riley's pause told me he wasn't convinced. "Would it be easier for you if I divided our time more, some nights here, some at my apartment?"

He still had a few months left on his lease. He'd barely unpacked the first box when he'd met Branson, and the rest was history. Shame filled me. I'd made him feel unwelcome. I deserved to be yelled at. "No, Riley, you're one of us now. Not just a shifter, but a part of the family."

"So you have to endure me and the baby? That doesn't sound fair. I know you're not as on board with having an infant around."

That wasn't fair. I pitched in as often as any of the other

guys—maybe not as much as Nana. But I'd changed as many diapers, fed as many bottles, and experienced as many wet burps as the other guys. I didn't have any problem with Bran Jr. Only with the attention he brought.

"I'm not saying you don't help. Branson and I couldn't do this without you guys."

"I thought you could only hear my thoughts when you touched me." I made a lame attempt at joking to change the subject.

"I don't hear your thoughts. You speak your truth, and you're right, it is only when I touch you. You're safe from my curse, Nash."

That was a relief. I attempted to not allow that to show on my face, though. "I don't want you or the baby moving. Ever. You're staying here. Okay?"

Riley's frown didn't budge. "But..."

"No buts, and don't ask again. You'll send Branson into a tizzy. Poor fragile guy. We're out of smelling salts."

Riley snorted again while Branson walked up behind me. "What will send me into a tizzy?" he asked, passing me without a glance and making a beeline to his mate and son. He kissed both, his boxers hanging indecently low on his hips as he whispered something I was glad I couldn't hear.

I didn't need nor want someone to whisper endless declarations of love. Now, if they wanted to whisper all the dirty things they wanted me to do to them, that was a different story. "I'm going to Seattle this weekend. Try not to freak out."

Branson just stared at me. "So? Go to Seattle. Have fun. Don't get arrested."

"There's another pile of gifts from the pack outside," I said, watching a meaningful look pass between Riley and Branson. "That's all I'm saying." I lifted my hands in surrender. "There is no judgment assigned to the message. Just they are there. Okay?"

I left for my room before those two could put their heads together and decide more things that might be wrong with me. I had no problem with the baby. I never brought my dates home anyway. But I hated how much more the pack across the bay was in our lives now because they believed Bran Jr. was blessed. We'd left those people, as well as our way of life, behind when the four of us had left the pack.

Now, I couldn't turn without the pack inserting itself back into my life in some way—without my consent.

My happy place was wherever the pack wasn't.

I reached for my towel when my department-issued cell beeped, alerting me to a recent call. I scanned the information on the screen. This was way easier than those beepers we'd been using until a few weeks ago. I hadn't realized how behind our department was in that regard. But we had new phones, with a built-in app that dispersed call information, and we were even getting a new fireman to come help with how busy things were becoming.

He wasn't set to come until tomorrow. I knew the guys had been on shift for over forty-eight hours, and they were nearing the end of that time period. It wasn't odd for me to take on extra calls that came through the Walkerton station. In exchange, they allowed me to avoid the majority of the calls that came through the station closer to pack lands. None of my crew knew why I avoided that part of the island. They understood that I'd grown up there, though, and likely had figured it was some sort of familial parting of ways.

The location of the call was familiar, and ironic. The same apartment building Riley was waiting out his lease for.

Thanks to Branson and Aver and their construction company, I knew the apartment building contained twenty units, so I wasn't in a rush to let Riley know. He couldn't do anything at this stage anyway but worry and get in the way.

I changed direction, heading back out to the foyer, where I grabbed my coat and keys. "Got a call, need to run," I said over my shoulder, shutting the door gently on my way out.

I hopped in my car and sped down the winding roads toward town. By the time I got to the building, the truck was there, and Paster and Krat were already applying first aid to those of the occupants that needed it.

From the size of the crowd shivering in their robes on the sidewalk, I'd say they had everyone evacuated. Including a tiny dog that wouldn't stop yapping.

"What's the situation?" I asked Paster as he cleaned a nasty-looking cut on an elderly woman's face.

Paster looked up, frowning. "Small appliance fire inside Mrs. Boxer's bathroom."

"Hairdryer?" I asked, looking up at the apartments. There was no smoke or damage visible from the outside.

Paster's lips twitched. "Charcoal barbecue."

"Inside?"

"I just wanted my sausages," the old woman mumbled.

I looked to Paster.

"Mrs. Boxer had sausages gifted to her that she wanted to grill," he explained slowly, somehow managing to not let it be heard in his tone how idiotic of an idea that was.

"It is cold outside," I agreed, sending Mrs. Boxer a wink. Paster could reprimand her after.

She smiled, but it quickly faded. "I didn't mean to get anyone hurt. Where's Phin? I must apologize."

I followed her gaze up to the crowd, but she didn't seem

to spot the person she was looking for. "You don't see Phin?" I asked, the hairs on my nape standing up. "Paster?"

"Krat did the sweep," Paster said. "Krat, you cleared it, right?" he called out.

This sort of thing wouldn't happen with a larger crew. But with only five of us to cover all the calls for Walkerton including the surrounding Walker County, there were times when things slid through.

Not normally people.

"I'll check it. What's the number?" I asked Mrs. Boxer.

"309, right next door. I don't see him." Her voice had risen with alarm.

I was already on my way to the entrance, strapping my ventilator over my face. The fire had been contained and extinguished, but if she was grilling indoors, that meant there could be carbon monoxide issues as well. By the time I climbed to the third floor, taking three steps at a time, I'd prepared myself to find the worst possible scenario.

The apartment door was already open, likely from when Krat had swept the rooms. The room looked clear, but I supposed it had when Krat came through as well. I went inside, opening the door to the bedroom. All these units were constructed mostly the same, and I knew from being in Riley's apartment roughly where the rooms were. The bed was unmade, the flannel sheets twisted at the foot like whoever had slept there hadn't done so comfortably.

There were a few posters on the wall for movies and games I wasn't familiar with and a desk with two monitors. I might have thought the room empty as well if it weren't for my shifter senses. I could hear someone breathing—softly, slowly, but they were here. Hurrying around to the other side of the bed, I lunged forward toward the mostly naked man who lay crumpled on the carpet.

I grabbed him, and he lifted his head, opening his lids to reveal soft gray eyes. "Monster?" he mumbled.

For the span of half of a second, I froze, paranoid that this young man had seen through my human facade to the wolf lurking below. But then I remembered my mask and ripped it off, pressing the mouthpiece against his face. That would've been a dangerous maneuver for anyone who wasn't also a shifter. "I'm a fireman. I'm here to rescue you. Don't be alarmed."

The man, Phin I assumed, mumbled something that sounded like, "Mkay," and passed out.

I tucked his unconscious body against my chest and rushed for the door, flying down the steps to the outside. I didn't like how slow his breathing had become, decreasing rapidly even as I sprinted.

Outside, the crowd pressed in when they saw me.

"Fuck," Krat spat. "Stay back, please, give him some room."

"I need the oxygen," I told him, laying Phin out on the grass. Poor guy would wake up freezing. I'd just be happy if he woke up. He was thin and pale. His arm fell open, revealing a tattoo on his inner wrist. The silhouette of a crow mid-flight.

His chest rose with each shallow breath.

"Fuck!" My gut clenched. This was hitting me harder than normal, and I had to take a moment to keep my head clear. He looked so helpless, fragile. They always looked that way, but this guy was so pale. His cartoon rocket ship boxers only made him look more precious. And there was so much of him on display. I found myself wanting to curl over him both for warmth and to keep his body out of view.

I spotted a matching tattoo on the inside of the man's other wrist. A second crow, its wings spread as if it were seconds from lifting from his skin. I needed to know why he chose that tattoo, what it meant to him.

Krat rushed over with the gurney and the oxygen. I fit the mouthpiece over Phin's mouth and told him to breathe deeply. He inhaled, his eyes fluttering. Krat got into position to help me lift him up on the gurney, but I disobeyed protocol and lifted the young man myself. There wasn't any reason more people had to touch him at a time like this.

He stirred when his back hit the gurney, almost like he was trying to climb off.

"Just wait a second," I told him quietly. "Take in a few more big breaths. You passed out for a while there." I pushed his dark brown hair back off his forehead.

He mumbled something that I couldn't understand. I wouldn't let him take off the mask yet, so whatever it was would have to wait.

"Phin!" Mrs. Boxer rushed over. Paster hadn't bandaged her forehead yet, but the wound had stopped bleeding. "I'm so sorry, son." Her wrinkled hands fluttered in front of her. "I know you told me it was dangerous to keep grilling, but I didn't think anyone would notice if I cooked up a few. They were a gift." She seemed to add the last part as a reason that would explain everything else.

Meanwhile, I was biting back my growls. Mrs. Boxer was sorry; that much was clear. Her eyes were watery, and her hands still shook. "We generally frown against people using charcoal grills inside, Mrs. Boxers. Is there something wrong with your stove?"

"No, but the smoky flavor is what brings out the seasonings."

I didn't think that was true but wasn't going to argue with the old woman. "If you do it again, you may receive a ticket. Even if it doesn't end with having to evacuate your entire building." We should've given her a ticket immediately. I'd made up my mind to do just that when Phin's hand collided with my arm.

I looked down at where we'd touched. He'd shoved me. Because I wouldn't tell Mrs. Boxer everything was fine? Fuck that. He could've been killed. I wouldn't think about what might've happened if I'd gone to the firehouse at the beginning of my shift instead of rushing in early to help.

Mrs. Boxer went back to where she'd been waiting. Except now her frail shoulders shook. I'd probably feel horrible about that later.

"You didn't have to be so rough with her," Phin croaked.

My joy that he looked like he was responding well to the oxygen faded with his tone. "Did you want me to tell her it's okay? Let her burn down the whole place next time?" I put the mask back over his mouth.

He lifted it immediately. "She's a lonely old woman. She didn't mean anything by it."

"And yet you're still sitting there sucking down pure oxygen in nothing but your rocket boxers because a lonely old woman *didn't mean anything by it.*" Anger flashed a second time.

Phin pushed up off the gurney, and I moved, landing between his legs in my effort to stop him. His bare thighs cradled my hips. A few seconds longer and I'd spring the most inappropriate boner in the history of boners. I didn't get it. Phin wasn't my type at all. For one, he wasn't falling at my feet for saving his life. I didn't require the gratitude, but it felt nice when most people were appropriately thankful. Judging from his physique and coloring, he wasn't a big outdoors type either. I remembered the setup he had upstairs, and while I didn't know heads or tails about computers, it had certainly seemed impressive. That made him more Aver's type than anything. Aver liked those quiet nerdy ones. When he wasn't pretending he wasn't gay anyway.

But Aver was too diplomatic to tell it like it was to Phin. And apparently, he needed a big dose of reality. "You realize you were almost dead there, right?"

"We all die." He shrugged.

That just made me angrier. "Is that what you want on your tombstone? Suffocated to death in pursuit of smoky wieners?" I shoved the mask in his face, knowing I needed to relax. More than that, I needed to step back from where our bodies pressed together, but I could do neither.

"What do I care? I won't be around to read it."

"Well, *someone* will care. Worry about them." I should've just dropped it. Why did it matter to me that this guy seemed to care so little about himself? Perhaps because he seemed so very blasé about the whole topic. Like he lived in constant danger and had come to terms with the idea that he might not live the day every morning he woke up. He wasn't a cop. I knew all the police in Walker County. "Where did you come from?"

"I moved here a few weeks ago from Spokane."

That explained why I'd never seen the man before.

He frowned. "I should probably let my friends know I am okay."

Thank the lord, the guy had friends. So maybe a lot of what he was saying was just the shock talking. I lifted my face to the crowd of other tenants. They'd stopped focusing on us. Some had left, while those with no place to go lingered on the sidewalk. "I'll bring them over. Point them out."

"Online," he clarified.

I groaned. He was one of *those*.

"What?" Phin snapped.

One thing was for sure, he didn't take shit. But what had I expected? Him to open his eyes and immediately begin worshiping me?

Kind of.

"Nothing," I said, and I really, really, *really* should've left it at that, but I couldn't. "Just—I meant real friends."

Phin's face twisted into a glorious mask of anger. I felt his ferocity like a challenge that I was more than eager to meet. My heart pounded as my senses sharpened as if danger were nearby. "You know, thank you so much. I'm so glad that I know now. It is possible to save people while also being a complete and utter asshole."

2

PHINEAS

"You NEED to sit there and continue breathing. You should go to the hospital and get checked, blood tests—"

"Nope." I hopped off the gurney. I already didn't feel as dizzy as I had when this guy had burst into my room, making me sure I was finally living a scene in *Close Encounters*.

I was lucky, really, that the gladiator who had rescued me was such a jerk. At least now, there was no possibility of us becoming friends. It was always a problem when I moved to a new town. Well-meaning neighbors, mothers who lived down the street who have a son I *would just love.* I'd already gotten too close to Mrs. Boxer.

We'd done no more than exchange pleasantries, maybe stopped to chat when our paths crossed. Now she was out here in her pink nightgown.

I shivered. Now that He-Man wasn't next to me, I could feel the cold morning air.

Something draped over my shoulders, startling me. It was *that guy* with one of those shiny blankets they pass out at disaster relief centers. I thought about yanking it off me, throwing it in his face, and standing up to bullies everywhere—but that didn't exactly make sense since he'd given me the blanket, likely to keep me warm. He wasn't a bully, he was...

Gorgeous.

But he knew it too. As foreign as the concept was, I had nothing against people who were self-confident. What I hated were people who thought they were *better* than other people. "Thanks," I mumbled, grabbing the two edges of the blanket and drawing them together. I finally looked down at his name tag. I didn't think he'd been wearing it the whole time. Had he snuck it on when I wasn't looking? "Thanks, Walker."

"Nash," he grunted. "You can call me Nash."

"Phineas." I stuck my hand out. Nash just looked at it until I slowly let it begin to drop.

He lunged forward and grabbed my hand like he was falling from a great height and my hand was the only thing left that could save him.

"Okay, that was weird," I mumbled as our joined arms pumped once. First, he'd taken forever to accept my hand; now, he wouldn't let go. A few seconds later, I tugged my hand out of his. How were his hands as sexy as the rest of him? Because he was perfect, that was how. Perfectly chiseled body, perfect lips, perfect glossy black hair that shone despite the close military-style cut. I appreciated how he wore it a little longer. I imagined him at the barbers. *Military, but make it fashion.* Smirking at the mental image, I found Nash's gaze directed at my lips. "What?"

"Phineas, I..."

I leaned forward, thinking at first he'd spoken too quietly for me to hear, but no, he'd just stopped talking after that. Was this guy okay? Was he even a firefighter? The

other two wore gear. Other than the mask and the mysterious nametag, this guy looked like he'd been out jogging.
Maybe he ran by and thought, *I'll save someone today.*

"...Well at least now everyone can't see your... *everything.*" He finished strong, sounding like an upset father
who had caught sight of what their daughter was wearing
before a date.

"O-kay." I stepped back to the apartment. As a writer, I
was physically unable to be away from my computer for so
long. What if the smoke had somehow damaged my hard
drive? Sure, my stuff was backed up in three other places,
but what if all those places had failed as well? The firemen
hadn't been back in, and the alarms had stopped. It was
probably safe enough for me—

"What are you doing?" Nash asked, blocking my path.

I looked around the sidewalk. "Is there no one else for
you to help?"

"No, you were the only one hurt," Nash said as if that
made him angry.

"Mrs. Boxer's forehead doesn't look so good." I frowned.
This was the first time my curse had hurt someone so old.
Mrs. Boxer was at least ninety and still lived alone. Her children had all moved out of Walkerton a long time ago, and
she looked forward to the care packages they sent her. I'd
learned she also had a penchant for online shopping. She
got so excited every time something was delivered.

Yes, I had warned her about grilling inside when I saw
the barbecue delivered, but I wasn't going to tell Nash that.
He already seemed ready to string the poor woman up on
the stocks.

"Can I just go grab my phone then? Tablet? Laptop?"

Nash shook his head each time, throwing kindling on
the fires of my frustration. "It isn't clear. You can't go in."

"But the barbecue is out! Her apartment vents into mine sometimes, which is probably how I ended up passing out anyway. I'll turn on a fan. Open the window!" Every time I offered a perfectly reasonable suggestion, this stone gargoyle just shook his head. I tried to keep calm, but I only felt stuck. I shouldn't have been out where there were so many people. "Please, they'll worry. I was at my computer, complaining about a headache, and moved to the bed. I must have passed out there."

Nash's face never changed, and I was sure my attempts were useless when he suddenly stabbed his hand into his pocket and pulled out a cell phone. "Here, use mine." His fingers tightened over the phone just as he was handing it to me. "If someone texts—"

"I'll take a message. Don't worry, you won't miss out on any hot dates because of me, big boy." *Where the ever-loving fuck had that come from. Big Boy?!*

Thankfully, Nash didn't comment on it and released his fingers. "It isn't that. My cousins might text. Don't read it. Just tell your friends you're okay."

I had no desire to uncover Nash Walker's secrets—hold on. "Nash *Walker?* Like Walkerton, Walker County, Walker Bay?"

Nash grimaced, but the expression did nothing to hide his appeal. "Yes, and there's a Walker street. It goes right down the middle."

I'd been so curious about these guys. Since moving, the people I'd interacted with spoke about them like royalty. "You're a big deal in this town."

"Wrong Walkers," Nash bit out. "You want the ones on the other side of the bay. They're the Walkers responsible for naming everything the same stupid name."

All right then. Touchy subject. Got it. "Thanks for this." I

17

waved his phone near my face before opening the screen. "You don't have GeekGab?" I asked, looking at the apps available.

"No, I don't have..." He exhaled sharply. "Just download it. It's fine."

I certainly wasn't going to ask twice. I tapped through the screens to download the app and signed in, breathing a fresh breath of air at the familiar screen. As I'd suspected, I had several mention notifications. Scrolling through what was said, my worries were confirmed. I tapped out a message.

GoblinKing: *Hey, I'm fine. There was a fire, and the fumes knocked me out. No worries, guys.*

As if the conversation would be left at that.

Xcept4Bunnies: *WTF?!?!1*

ChuckShurley: *A fire? Have you called your insurance? Do that now, man. Check your Loss of Use policy.*

Despite being my regular chat companions for most of my young adult life, I'd never met any of my friends face to face. Things were safer that way. Without chat, I wouldn't be able to have any friends at all. Besides, I knew them as well as I would anyone else. Better. Chuck had recently gone through a divorce. He'd been in the military until recently, and it turned out she'd only been there for the benefits and prestige of being an Army wife.

Chuck was happier in his life now, though, so that all ended up being more of a good thing.

Registered_Companion: *A fire? Were the firemen hot?*

Xcept4Bunnies: *Fuck that, did Hot Neighbor burst in and save you?*

I rolled my eyes. Telling these guys about the attractive

man who lived on the other side of the hall had been a bad idea. Ever since my first day, when I'd been hauling in boxes, walked by his door, and spotted him stark naked, I'd had an unhealthy attraction. It was a lost cause, though. I knew a guy like that, a perfect male specimen, would never want me. And, if by some miracle, he did, it wouldn't be for long.

ChuckShurley: *Guys, I don't think he wants to talk about that. He should be focusing on minimizing his losses at the moment.*

There was Chuck, always the mediator.

GoblinKing: *I haven't seen Hot Neighbor. He must have left early for the gym.*

I checked the space around me, finding Nash nearby but sitting down on his haunches, where he was entertaining a small toddler. My stomach did a somersault, and I looked away angrily.

GoblinKing: *The fireman was hot. But he knows it. Head the size of Jupiter.*

Registered_Companion: *Confidence isn't a sin!*

Xcept4Bunnies: *Yeah, but did he make your secret garden flood?*

My lip curled with disgust.

GoblinKing: *I'm a dude, Bun. I don't have a secret garden, and it definitely doesn't flood.*

Xcept4Bunnies: *Fine, then does he make your little soldier stand at attention?*

My gaze drifted back to Nash, where he'd lifted the little girl in his arms and was now dancing with her, much to the toddler's amusement and joy. The girl's mother watched him as well, the look on her face saying she was in a Lifetime movie of her own making, *Seduced by the Fire-*

man. Now starring anyone who gets near Nash Walker because his animal magnetism spared no one.

GoblinKing: *He'd make a dead soldier come back to life and stand at attention. Believe me, he's a lost cause.*

Registered_Companion: *Yeah, cause you've made so much headway with Hot Neighbor. Does he at least call you by your name now?*

He'd called me Glenn the other day, which was a step up from not calling me anything at all.

GoblinKing: *Baby steps.*

A quiet moan of pain lifted my attention from the screen to where Mrs. Boxer had gone to sit. She held her head, a grimace of pain stretching her lips. I didn't spot the other firemen and assumed they were in the building inspecting the damage to clear the scene. I typed out a quick message, letting the others know where I was going. I tiptoed to Mrs. Boxer, tapping her gently on the shoulder.

"How are you feeling?" I asked.

Her face brightened, but her eyes were still tight. "Oh, I'm fine. How are you, dear?" She noticed what I was wearing and immediately tried to take off her robe. "You'll catch a cold!"

"No, Mrs. Boxer, I'm fine. This is one of those special thermal blankets," I assured her. "I'm worried about you, though. Are you in pain? Please tell me honestly."

"It just hurts a little. The nice fireman said to sit, and if it feels worse when they're done, they'll take me to the doctor."

It was probably just a bump, and the incident that had led up to her injury had been her responsibility, but I still couldn't shake that same feeling that I was to blame. At least I knew how to help her.

I knew how to take away her headache, anyway.

"Can I see?"

Mrs. Boxer lifted her face up to me. "If it will make you feel better, dear. It's not even bleeding anymore."

She told the truth. Her cut wasn't bleeding, but it was red and looked painful. I checked around us to see if anyone was looking. No one was, and I quickly cupped my hand over her cut. I closed my eyes, letting the heat travel down my arm to my palm. I grimaced, my arm burning almost too hot for me to bear. It did every time, but no matter who was at the other end, they never seemed to feel it, only the release from pain that came from healing.

"What did you do? It feels so much better!"

I pulled my hand away before her cut could heal completely. Judging from the headache I now had, I assumed the injury under the skin was worse than anyone had thought. It was healed now, though. My skull would pound for a while longer. The exchange was always different. If I healed someone with a broken leg, my leg would feel as if someone had taken a sledgehammer to the bone. My pain wasn't ever as intense as what the injured had felt when they got hurt initially but a fraction of it, but it was an unpleasant side effect. "I just said some healing words," I mumbled through my pounding headache. "It was mostly healed already."

The cut was smaller and the redness gone. Maybe I'd gone too long, made it too noticeable, but I'd been worried about her pain. And the fact that it would take a team of CIA interrogators to get the truth out of her if she was hurting.

"My phone?" Nash's shadow enveloped us both.

I spun, trying not to look guilty. "Here, sorry. I wanted to check on Mrs. Boxer."

Nash took his cell back and slid it in his pocket without

looking. His tough expression melted a little. "What would you rate the pain, Mrs. Boxer?" he asked, not unkindly.

"Nothing now. It feels great."

Nash looked from Mrs. Boxer to me like he already knew my secret. If he was about to guess, he'd be the first person in my life who'd put two and two together. I almost wanted him to guess, but that was a selfish desire. Being able to do what I did didn't come without a cost, both at the moment of healing as well as initially.

"Hey, Glenn, what's going on here?"

Of course Hot Neighbor would come now. "Hey, Zach. The apartment caught on fire."

"What?" Zach looked up at the building and frowned, almost like he was confused by the lack of flames. His blue tank was wet with sweat, and he used the bottom of his shirt to wipe his face. My eyes dropped to his briefly exposed waist, his shorts hanging on his hips like they were clinging to life. Hot Neighbor was everything I wasn't. Tall, fit, blond, blue-eyed, and with a dimple in his chin that I wanted to dip my tongue in. Except... had he always been so short? I looked down at his shoes, but he wore his normal trainers.

Had he run here?

"Is my apartment okay?" he asked.

I shrugged, and Nash cleared his throat. "The building is being cleared. Looks like some indoor grilling sparked a small fire. It also caused several carbon monoxide alarms to go off in the hallway. We've got the team in testing everything. You should be able to enter shortly. If you want to wait with the others." Nash swept his arm toward where the majority of the renters waited.

Zach walked off in the direction Nash had pointed. Couldn't he have waited with us? I longingly watched him walk away. Sure, the guy focused so much on the gym and staying in shape that he probably dreamed of lifting weights, and the few times I'd tried to spark a conversation had been painful, but a man could dream.

"Friend of yours?" Nash asked, his eyes narrowed on my face.

My cheeks blazed red. "He's my neighbor."

I'd been frowning at Nash's question, but as Zach turned around and came back toward us, my face lit up. Nash followed my gaze and let out a low noise that made my stomach flip. My eyes jerked up to him. What was wrong with me? Had it been so long that my standards had been reduced to just *are they insanely hot?*

"Hey, Glenn, they're really boring over there. I'm gonna go get a few more reps in. Will you text me when they open the place up?"

My lips felt light, and I had to concentrate on damp-ening my smile. If I let my mouth stretch as wide as I wanted, the result would only be terrifying. "Sure! Yeah! Totally. I just..."

"What?" Zach asked while Nash remained where he was, standing so close he looked like he was part of the conversation.

"I don't have your number."

"Oh yeah, where's your phone?"

I didn't have that either. Or a pen. My hands grew sweaty. I was *this close* to getting Hot Neighbor's phone number. I knew nothing would be able to come of us before I'd be forced to pack up and move on, but I wouldn't say no to the distraction while I was here. "I don't have anything..." I looked around my person, letting the thermal blanket fall from my shoulders.

"Keep the blanket on. You need your body heat to stay

where it is," Nash grunted. "I've got a pen." He passed it over, looking as unhappy as any guy could.

Why offer for me to borrow it then?

I accepted it, but only because I *really* wanted Hot Neighbor's number. I set the tip against my palm and looked up at Zach expectantly.

He grabbed my hand and pulled it closer. My fingers pressed against his chest. His shirt was wet and cold, but the flesh beneath it was hard. The pen tickled against my skin. When he was finished, I had his number on my palm and the feel of his fingers lingering on my skin. I hardly noticed him jog off the same way he'd come.

I stared after him, barely daring to breathe for fear it would wipe the numbers away.

"You're a good friend, *Glenn*," Nash deadpanned.

I spun back to him, my tongue flexing, prepared to tell him exactly what he could do with his muscles and attitude. But when our gazes collided, he looked expectant, ready, and most of all eager. Did he want me to scream at him? I would oblige. "And you're a—"

"Okay everyone," one of the firemen yelled to the crowd from the entrance. A guy with a jacket that said City of Walkerton was with him, likely making sure things were safe. "You can go back inside. We'll be sending maintenance around to check all emergency alert devices and make sure they continue to work as they are meant to. Thank you for your patience."

The crowd groaned and moved forward as one as if their time on the sidewalk had lumped them together into a single, massive, disgruntled monster.

"You were saying something?" Nash prompted.

I'd been about to call him a stream of mean things, but now that I knew I could retreat back into the safe hole of my apartment, it no longer seemed important. Still, he looked excited to hear what I'd been about to say. "You're a dick," I told him without any real passion.

He frowned, but when I went up the steps to my apartment, helping Mrs. Boxer as I did, he couldn't say anything to stop me. I felt something tug at my chest, urging me to turn back around.

Nash Walker, while pretty to look at, was a blip in my life, and it was time for him to go back to wherever perfect people lived.

3

NASH

I DUG the rusted spines of Nana's tiller into the frozen ground. She'd asked me over at the perfect time. After the residents all went back into their homes, Phineas included, the chief had dropped by with a new fireman to join our ranks. He'd made a point of mentioning he was new to the area, not to the job.

Chief had wanted to show the new guy the ropes, and he was eager to start, so I got sent away to stay on call while they remained at the station.

I'd been lost for what to do—for exactly thirty seconds—until Nana had called. I didn't know how she knew I had free time, but I'd been at her property since then, tearing through the top layer of frozen dirt to help control the pest population that Nana spent the rest of the year battling.

"Baaa," the demon goat bleated at me from through the fence. It hadn't stepped away from the moment I'd taken up position next to its paddock. Even after the others had grown bored and wandered away, that bulb-eyed bastard never blinked, watching my every move.

"I could eat you," I told it, spinning the tiller around to

go back up the next strip of land. Most animals knew well enough to leave me alone. They sensed the beast that lurked beneath my skin. Occasionally, I met the animal, or man, who was immune. Beelzebub here would get along swimmingly with one annoyingly adorable, rocket boxer-wearing nerd.

I growled, shoving the spines into the dirt. I was doing the best sort of work for the mood I was in. As I stomped forward through the mud I was creating, I spotted a tiller spine that had snapped off in the process. My head ducked between my shoulders, and I looked back at Nana, knitting something together on her porch.

She was looking at her project, not me. She couldn't have—

"You break my tools, you fix 'em, Nash Walker."

The woman had eyes on top of her eyes. Of course, she'd say the spirits told her things. As a kid, I'd believed that nonsense, until I'd set traps, done things that should have gotten me in trouble. I'd learned only when Nana was around did she know what I'd been up to. There weren't spirits telling Nana my deeds; she was just an incredibly observant shifter who had picked up all the tricks that kids got up to through her decades of caring for her family.

Just like it wasn't spirits that told her Riley or the baby were blessed and that they'd be responsible for bringing the pack to its former glory. It was only the hopes of an old woman.

"I see—and hear—more than you think, son," Nana said, peering at me from over her yarn.

This was another one of her tricks. Say something all vague and knowing and let the person she's talking to dig their own hole. I wasn't going to fall for it. Not anymore.

"Yeah, what do you hear about how to get the pack off our backs? Anything on that?"

She pursed her lips together and looked back at her knitting needles.

Just like I thought.

Feeling extra cocky, I stepped forward into a pile of something squishy that I refused to examine further, and my ankle twisted out from under me. Luckily, I had the tiller handle to grab on to and save some of my pride.

I didn't hear Nana's knitting needles clack together until *after* I found my footing again. *She didn't make you fall.*

It would be a whole heck of a lot easier to believe Nana didn't have extra special powers when stuff like this happened. I shook my head and pressed on, noticing the back of my nametag stabbing through my undershirt.

I'd forgotten I'd hastily put it on while Phin had been looking the other direction. I'd wanted him to know my name, who I was. Though now, I felt foolish. He wasn't interested in me. He was interested in Zach No-Brains Ballard. I knew Zach from the gym—the only place anyone knew Zach from. I hadn't known Zach could utter a sentence that didn't include the words *protein shake* or *reps.*

It had been painful to watch Phin melt in his presence as well.

I stomped forward, my feet landing so heavily I nearly packed down the dirt I'd just tilled. Why should I care what the nerd did? He wasn't the last man in Walkerton.

You should've shaken his hand faster.

When he'd lifted his arm to me, I'd had flashes of Riley. His touch compelled the person at the other end to tell the truth. According to him, that truth could be anything but was normally the thing a person wanted to keep hidden the most. Riley had no idea why he could do what he did. And luckily for him, Branson was an open book. What you saw was what you got.

But I'd looked at Phin's hand and had panicked. I didn't want my skeletons popping up for a quick chat. Phin wasn't Riley, though. And thank goodness. Branson would kick my asshole into my nostrils if I'd thought the same inappropriate thoughts about Riley as I was with Phin. What about Phin was so amazing anyway? His pasty white skin?

I winced at a sharp pain in my chest. The feeling was so sudden and blinding it was gone before I could grab my shirt.

Phin wasn't pasty—he was creamy. Like a bowl of milk waiting for me to lap up.

Except he was already in someone else's fridge.

I spun around, ready to tear down the next strip of land, but the spines hit pebbles. I looked up, shocked that I'd done the whole space in such a short amount of time. I found Nana on the porch still, this time with one of her huge cookbooks open in front of her. She hardly ever followed the recipes, instead saying they were starting points. Then, when she'd made the meal, she would go back and make corrections.

"Feel better?" she asked without ever looking up.

I did, and I didn't. I no longer felt like smashing Zach's face in. Maybe I'd just knock his teeth out, see how amazing Phin thought he was with nothing but gums for a smile. "What's next?" I asked in a low voice.

"Wood needs chopping and stacking," Nana said, again without ever looking up.

I growled as I grabbed the ax handle. The wood stack was closer to the goat pen, near the gate. I steadied the first piece and swung my ax down, relishing the way the wood split beneath my power. This wasn't like me. I didn't need to worry about other guys being more appealing than me. What was more appealing than over six feet of solid muscle? I glanced over at the goat right as he was taking a crap, staring at me the entire time. I didn't need to take this sort of treatment. I was a highly sought-after guy.

I shoved my hand in my pocket, pulling out my phone. I'd just find someone to spend the evening with, and most of the night. All I needed to do was fuck this feeling out of my system. But, as I scrolled to my contacts, I spotted an icon I wasn't familiar with, a smiling green alien head.

I frowned. Phin forgot to delete that nerdy app he used to talk to his fake friends. Why was I being such a dick about that? I hadn't teased my twin brother Wyatt once when he'd gone through his chat phase after we'd left pack lands. And he'd gone on and on every day, telling me about their lives. I'd listened patiently until it had become too annoying and I'd hit him in the head to start fighting instead. For some reason, when Phin did it...

My finger hovered over the X icon that would delete the app from my phone. As I stared at it, a number appeared. A notification? My lips curled, and I tapped the alien. Sure enough, Phin had logged in, but he hadn't logged off. I scanned the lines of text, most of it stuff I had no idea what they were talking about.

This is an invasion of privacy.

Technically, yes. The right thing would've been to click out, delete the app, and forget about it.

However...

Phin had been the one to stay logged in—maybe he wanted me to know? Or maybe a reason didn't really matter since I was so desperate to learn more about this guy and why the fuck he didn't want me. I probably wouldn't find out anything anyway. Wyatt used to lie all the time to his little chat friends. That was the main reason why I didn't see the point. He could be anyone he wanted online; so could the people he spoke with. No one was real, so how could any of it mean anything? Maybe I'd at least learn why he was so connected to that neighbor who had caused the whole mess in the first place. Something about the two of them still plucked at my ball hairs. And was I going insane, or had the old lady healed really quickly?

I was about to close the stupid thing when I spotted the word *fireman*. Had Phin been talking about me? To his friends? My lips curled.

The fireman was hot. But he knows it. Head the size of Jupiter.

That line had been written by the goblin king. Was that Phin? I scowled at the mention of Hot Neighbor. Yep, the goblin guy was Phin. At least it looked like some of his friends were more understanding. Confidence *wasn't* a sin.

He'd make a dead soldier come back to life and stand at attention. Believe me, he's a lost cause.

So he wasn't immune to my charms. Or he wasn't immune to my looks and thought I had no charms.

I didn't feel any better now that I'd looked. He knew I was hot and still wanted to talk about Zach. I shoved my phone back in my pocket and concentrated on the task at hand: slaughtering these dead wood chunks so they would know how annoyed Phin made me. The stack of wood took me no time at all. I loaded what I'd split in the wheelbarrow, using my usual style of stacking the wood until it teetered over my head as I rolled it up to the porch.

Nana closed the book she'd been *fixing*. "Still in a rush to finish."

"That's a weird way to say thank you," I grumped.

Moments later, there was a sharp pain at my backside. I rubbed my buttcheek and looked back at Nana.

She held a handful of acorns. "Want to sass me again?"

"No." Damn. She might've been showing her age recently, all the color nearly gone from her silver hair, but her flicking finger was as strong as ever. "I'm sorry, Nana. I'm going through something, and it's making me an ass."

"Language," she scolded me. She brushed aside the papers that covered the second chair on the porch and patted the seat. "Sit with me, now that you've got your energy out. Tell me about it."

Sighing with relief, I sat down. "I saved this guy today." I kicked my legs out so they were unbent but crossed in front of me and folded my hands over my chest while the chair groaned beneath me.

"It's what you were made to do, my boy. Save people. I'm glad you found an answer to your calling."

That was saying it kindly. After the four of us, Aver, Branson, Wyatt and me, left pack lands with just the clothes on our backs, we'd been thrust into an unfamiliar world. Living off pack lands was nearly almost the same, except no one cared about your birthright. Sure, we got some extra attention because of the whole Walker thing, but on the pack lands, even as a child, I'd recognized how they'd treated us like gods.

I'd searched for that feeling again when I was eighteen and without a job. I'd been drawn to the physical demands of firefighting, as well as the natural competition that cropped up between firefighters. I currently held every timed record but one, the ladder climb. I'd graciously pretended to miss a rung during the trial and let Paster hold that particular title.

That had kept my attention until I'd gone on my first

call. I loved the adrenaline and anticipation. On the scene, I loved the clarity of figuring out what to do and in what order. And then there was the actual saving, being the thing that separated a life from possible death, helping those who couldn't help themselves. Nana was right that firefighting was the best job for me, but I was glad she didn't know exactly why. She'd be disappointed in me if she understood how shallow I really was.

"The pack is going to need you and your skills when—"

I jumped to my feet, heading for the stairs. "Nana, stop it." She'd always been unable to turn from the pack as my cousins and I had. "Maybe you've got Branson drinking your Kool-Aid, which means Aver isn't far behind, but leave Wyatt and me out of it. We don't want to go back. Ever. Not after what they did."

"I'm not forgiving your parents for what they did," Nana said sternly. Today, her eyes were an icy blue and spooky as all hell. "They are what caused this mess, them and the other elder families. But it's your job to fix it. Already, the pack has been blessed. What's happened with Riley and the babe, it is a sign. The pack's savior is here, my boy. I'm sure of it."

Why should it be my responsibility to help the same people who had asked me to murder my cousins? My own brother? To me, the pack crumbling around their heads was the perfect punishment. It sucked for the other shifters, the ones who relied on the pack. There were three elder families, not including Alpha Walker, but hundreds of shifters lived on the other side of the island who had sworn loyalty to the pack. They would be the ones to suffer, and if I thought too long about that, it would just make me angry, so I didn't. Except, now, Nana had planted the seed in my brain, and dammit if it wasn't growing like a weed.

"There are other packs in this country. Better ones, probably." Other than the spare pack representative that came to visit—spy—now and again, I hadn't had a lot of experience dealing with other packs. I knew Paul had come from one in Texas, and according to him, that pack was the ninth circle of hell. Maybe shifters just weren't meant to live in packs.

I knew that wasn't true, though. When the four of us had left pack lands, we'd clung to each other. Shifters were social creatures, not in the sense that they were outgoing or extroverted, but in the way a shifter was always happiest when they had someone to care for and protect, as well as someone they thought did the same for them.

"I wish you could've seen the pack in the days of my beloved," she said wistfully.

I turned, wincing from her sorrowful tone, and grabbed her hand. She clung to my fingers so desperately I sat back down. "I'm sorry, Nana. I'm sure the pack of your memories is something else entirely." She was our great-grandmother, our parent's grandmother, Alpha Walker's mother, and the widow to the former Alpha Walker, our great-grandfather. A Walker had led the pack since its creation. Generations of Walkers, until now.

"It isn't just the pack of my memories, Nash. It's the pack of my dreams. It's gonna happen. Something is already happening." She sounded so different than she had even moments before that I was suspicious of her earlier sorrow.

"Well, as long as whatever that is stays confined to Branson and Riley, that's fine. They're grown-ups. They can choose to step in whatever pile of shi—poop that they want. But my boots are staying clean." Ironic, considering my boots were currently caked with mud. I had my own reasons for wanting to stay away from the pack. As usual, they were selfish. I remembered almost every day of my childhood. I'd grown up wanting for nothing, told I was everything, and believed it. Namely, I'd been a little shit. I didn't like who I'd been in the packs.

Nana kept hold of my hand but let her gaze wander. She looked at the devil goat, the two of them likely conspiring a plan against me. "When you boys were little, you were always the one who stood on your own, Nash. People said it was Aver who held that silver spoon tightest in his mouth,'but you've thought you were the world's gift since you uttered your first sound."

All true, but damn. Nothing like a dose of Nana honesty.

"You put up walls, my child. You always kept to yourself separate from the rest of the pack. Wyatt's been by your side since he came out of your mother with you standing on his shoulders. No one had ever seen such a thing before," she said with a smile. "He couldn't wait. Couldn't bear to be parted from you for even a moment. I was thankful you had him then, even if you still stepped away first. Always." Nana let my hand go and looked at me with bright eyes. "Now, the man I see is in the thick of it. Knee-deep. You're there not just for your brother, but your cousins, this town. These ten years have been good for you, boy. It's taught you that you might need help. And that you can help others."

She was right, of course. I'd been a judgmental dick in the past. Now, I tried to be just a dick. But accepting help from my cousins was nothing like accepting anything from the packs. "Why ruin a good thing then, Nana? Maybe this is how we are supposed to live, separate. You still have us, and you get to visit the packs. We'd never ask you to stop."

She gave me a look that said she'd very much like to see us try.

I cleared my throat. "Empires rise and fall. Ask the Romans. If every elder house suddenly sunk into the ground or was wiped out by a volcano, I'd be happy."

"You're gonna need your pack one day, Nash Walker. Both of 'em."

I stood, rubbing her shoulder to try and help lighten the sting of what I had to say. I didn't want to hurt my great-grandmother. If anyone tried to hurt her in front of me, I'd rip their arms off without blinking, but I needed to be clear. "If the moment comes where I am standing between accepting help from the pack or dying, I'll choose death. Every time."

Nana didn't explode or make an outburst. She just sighed, quietly, tiredly. "Hold on a minute, boy. I've got a care box for Riley and the babe." She ducked inside, coming back out with a box I hurried to take from her. "Just some meals for the week and the blanket I finished. Tell Riley I put in that calming cream for him to practice his shifts. He's getting faster every day."

Nana didn't mention what I said. Even she understood a lost cause.

4

_____

PHINEAS

THE BELL TINKLED SOFTLY, indicating a new patron to Walkerton's only cafe, Rise and Grind. The selection wasn't quite what I was used to. Spokane was a larger city than most people realized, and I'd had no trouble finding several places to set up my laptop and camp.

I was a walking cliché. A writer in a coffee shop.

But they had decent Wi-Fi and outlets on every wall, and coming here got me out of my apartment and let me be around people without actually being around people. Plus, the cafe was on the way to the gym so I sometimes spotted Zach on his way to or from.

I hadn't seen him today. In fact, I hadn't even thought of Zach. Oh no, my every waking thought, and most of my sleeping ones, had been focused on one rude, gorgeous, arrogant, perfect man. Why couldn't I get him out of my head? I already had a designated piece of unobtainable eye candy to drool over in this town. I didn't need two.

I hadn't seen Nash since the day before, and I was trying to convince myself I should feel thankful for that. I'd been in Walkerton for weeks without spotting him. That was probably the norm. Unless Mrs. Boxer decided to grill up some more sausages.

A dark head caught my eye, hair the exact color of Nash's, but longer. The man walking outside, crossing the street in the other direction, looked so much like Nash, I leaned forward as he stepped onto the sidewalk in front of a bar called The Greasy Stump.

It wasn't Nash, though. Unless he wore a wig or his hair grew like grass overnight.

The bell tinkled again, and my head drifted that direction, seeing two guys. One looked to be in his late twenties, around the same age as me, while the other was younger. The older one held a baby, and there was something about the way he cradled the baby in his arms that made me smile.

I was still smiling when our eyes met, and the man offered me a timid smile in return. He had kind eyes, but I guessed my run-in with Nash had let me forget that I was supposed to be staying away from people. For their benefit.

Bringing my attention back to the screen, I stared at the blinking cursor. My books were never very serious, and they weren't very popular either. I had a small fanbase that happened to love reading about quiet gay men solving mysteries in small towns. It kept me busy and, along with my parent's monthly inheritance money, gave me enough to live on.

"Delia hasn't shown her face since Branson took over," the younger of the two men said. I didn't mean to eavesdrop. My table wasn't even that close to where they stood in line.

"If she knows what's good for her, she'll keep it that way," the other said, but not in an angry tone. More tired than anything.

It was their turn next, and both walked up to the counter. I frowned, insanely curious by what I'd heard, but also angry that I couldn't seem to mind my own business. I supposed this was a sure-fire way to make sure I didn't accidentally make friends. No one liked a snoop.

They ordered and then arranged themselves, the diaper bag, and the baby at the table right next to mine. I learned as the barista called out their names that they were called Riley and Paul. Were they together? They seemed comfortable with each other, but not in a way that made me think there was something sexual going on. Maybe they were brothers. The baby probably belonged to Riley's wife, and he stayed home instead. This was really just my own gender bias being confronted, and I should have been thankful for the moment to learn and grow.

Instead, I was angling my head so that I could hear their conversation better. My eyes landed on a sign hanging on the opposite wall. *Feelin' depresso? Have an espresso.* I snorted. My weakness had always been puns, and the sudden noise brought my table neighbors' attention.

"Hi there, I noticed you earlier. A new face," the older one, Riley said. His smile was back, and there was no malice in his words. He wasn't angry that I was obviously listening in.

"Sorry, hi. I am new. I didn't mean to bother you guys."

"No, it's okay. I'm new to Walkerton too," Riley said. He gestured between himself and the other guy, Paul. "We both are, actually. I'm Riley, this is Paul, and this is Bran Jr."

Because they traveled here together? I looked at the baby again, this time for hints of his parentage. He had a mess of brown hair, just like Riley's, but his eyes were closed. I couldn't tell if they were blue like Paul's or brown like Riley's. That wouldn't tell me much anyway.

"Figured it out yet?" Riley asked with a twinkle.

My cheeks burned. "I'm that obvious?"

"Nah, you just aren't the first," Riley said.

Paul rose to snag their prepared drinks from the counter. "Or the last," he said over his shoulder. I wasn't sure how old he was. His expressions made him seem young, and he had a slim build that offered no real additional clues.

Riley turned his chair so that it angled more my direction. "I moved here for work. I'm with social services. If you ever need any help in that department."

"I'm good right now. But, actually, do you guys have any programs for the elderly?" I didn't think Mrs. Boxer was in need of outside help at the moment, but maybe they had a program where people came to visit. I wouldn't be in Walkerton forever. If my pattern held, I'd be here for a few more months maximum.

The baby gurgled, bringing Riley's attention away while Paul returned.

I leaned not quite so far in their direction, looking awkwardly at my screen. Talking with people was so much easier online. There, I had the safety of a screen for one, and these pauses in conversation were never so odd to navigate.

Riley thanked Paul for grabbing the coffees and took a sip. "Mmm, you aren't to tell Branson," he said sternly. To me, he added, "Branson is my husband. He's been getting on me about how much caffeine I take in during a day. I tried to explain I consume the bare minimum I need to function, but it does make me jittery. I've been working on... staying calm, recently."

The odd pause made me think there was a story there. "Your secret is safe with me. I don't know anyone in town anyway, except my neighbors."

"Is that why you were wondering about services for the elderly? We have the usual programs—Meals on Wheels, a shuttle service. Let me make some calls, and I'll get back to you on what else we can offer." He tapped his forehead sharply. "I keep forgetting I'm on leave." He smiled at his child, and my heart thumped at the obvious love this man held for his offspring. "I'll still make the calls. Apparently, leave only means I answer emails from home instead of the office."

The baby was clearly his. Now that I knew he wasn't with Paul, I could see so much of Riley in the baby's face. But if he was married, to his husband... had they contacted a surrogate? "It's okay. She survived before I got here. She'll survive after. I just worry. Mrs. Boxer is a sweet woman."

"Elise Boxer?" Paul asked. "She's friends with Nana."

He said Mrs. Boxer's friend's name like I was supposed to understand who that was.

"Are you planning on moving so soon?" Riley asked. The baby fussed, despite the way Riley rocked. He fished around in his diaper bag, pulling out a pacifier he slipped in the baby's mouth. Bran Jr. quieted immediately.

"No plans yet, but it usually happens like that. I can stay pretty mobile with my work and tend to take advantage of that." At least, that was the story I told people. No one knew about my curse, my ability to heal. Most of the people I'd had an occasion to heal had probably only been harmed because of my presence in the first place. I didn't know how bad things always happened to those around me, just that they did. Both Paul and Riley were still looking at me, making me think I was supposed to say more. "I've got to get somewhere in time to make friends for my birthday anyway." That sounded dumb.

"Oh, your birthday is soon?" Paul asked.

"No."

Riley snorted without malice, and my lips tugged up in the corners.

"It's in June."

"Mine too!" Riley exclaimed. "You have a while." He looked from me to Paul. I got the feeling something silent passed between them, a message I wasn't privy to. "You know, we're having a get-together, tomorrow, at my house. Some of my old coworkers and people I used to know are visiting for the first time."

"I couldn't impose. That sounds like a pretty big moment."

"It would be no imposition. They are just part of the guest list. A lot of people from Walkerton are coming too. It's sort of this baby shower, housewarming, wedding reception, getting to know your neighbors kind of thing."

"A Franken-party," I said.

Paul laughed, and it felt nice to hear laughter instead of reading it on the screen.

"Pretty much. Paul will be there along with some others from the pa—"

"Backpack," Paul nearly shouted.

"From the backpack?" I asked with a smile that fell when neither smiled back. I knew a secret when I saw one and understood forgetting for a moment that something wasn't meant to be shared. "It's cool. I've thought about backpacking."

Riley laughed nervously. A, L-N-OL. "Yeah, well, if you are into it, it's the Walker place where the river—"

"Did you say *Walker*?" I asked, my head swiveling back across the street where the Nash lookalike had disappeared to.

"Uh-oh, what did Wyatt do?" Paul asked sharply. His question held a proprietary edge.

"I don't know a Wyatt," I rushed to explain. Had Paul's nails gotten sharper? Maybe the smoke from the day before was causing hallucinations. Chuck had warned me of that. "There was a fire yesterday, and I met—"

"Nash," both Riley and Paul said at the same time.

Paul's worry cleared instantly, but not Riley's.

"You must live in my old apartment building," Riley said. "Nash and Wyatt are twins. Wyatt owns the bar across the street there." He pointed to The Greasy Stump. "Nash mentioned a fire at the apartments. Are you okay? Were you displaced?"

That was definitely social worker speak. "No. We were let back in pretty soon after. Nash and I just bumped heads." I'd have to hope they knew I meant metaphorically and not literally.

"Probably because his is so big," Paul muttered.

If it had been anything else, I might have defended Nash simply because he wasn't here to defend himself, but Paul seemed to know him better than I did. Had they dated? I didn't think so, only because it seemed Paul had a thing for his twin.

I understood. Though I preferred the way Nash had his hair a little shorter, more manicured. "He saved my life, for which I am very appreciative."

Riley looked to Paul, Bran Jr., and then back to me. "But?"

What a choosy beggar I was. Complaining about the attitude of the man who had saved me.

"It's okay. You can't say anything either of us hasn't thought," Paul said.

"You both have eyes. You know he's gorgeous. He'd also be just fine if the world began calling him by the title he believes he is owed, Master and Commander."

"You're too nice." Paul reached for Bran Jr., and Riley handed him over, pacifier and all. "At the party, I'll get a few drinks in you, and then you can really let how you feel out. In front of him."

The idea was appealing. It also sounded like a nightmare. "I don't know about that. But, yeah, why not. I'll come." Nash most likely being there had *nothing* to do with my decision.

"There will be other guys there too. You might find one you like better. Not Wyatt," Paul added quickly, sighing immediately after. "I don't even believe they are twins anymore. Wyatt is so..." He fanned his face with his free hand.

"You'll get no complaints from me," I assured him while mentally calculating the danger I'd be putting everyone in if I went to the party. Sometimes, my curse seemed to focus on only those people in my immediate life: favorite teachers, friends I'd made. Others, it felt random. But, normally, smaller functions held outside of the public eye were safe. I could reasonably expect to go to the party and get home without a major event.

It would be nice to get out. At least, that's what I told myself. Reg would be thrilled when I told her in chat later on. Chuck would probably send me a thousand links on how to detect if your drink had been drugged, while Bun would quiz me on blowjob techniques.

"Great! I'm glad," Riley said, reaching for the baby after he cleared off their table. They were taking the rest of their drinks to go. "I'll let Branson know." He frowned and then asked, "Should I let Nash know?"

I shrugged. I didn't need Riley or Paul going back to Nash telling him I was claiming we had more history between us than we did. Nash had probably already forgotten all about the people he'd saved yesterday. He had a whole different list of people to save today. "If you did, he might ask 'who?' It isn't necessary. But thank you for the invitation, really. I'm excited. What should I bring?"

Riley shook his head. "Just yourself. We have everything handled. You're sure you don't need a ride to the house?"

I'd have to take a taxi. I didn't know if Walkerton even had a taxi service. "I'll figure it out."

"Well, if you drink, you're welcome to spend the night. I think a few might end up staying."

The way he spoke, his house sounded like a dorm more than anything else. Riley must have understood my expression because he explained, "The four Walker cousins live together. They built that house. I recently moved in with Branson."

"It couldn't have been too recent, eh?" I asked with a second smile that wasn't reciprocated. How did I keep saying the wrong things?

Riley laughed, but it sounded too bright and a little forced. "Why wait when you know you have a good thing? Anyway, Paul lives with friends on the other side of the bay, and I happen to know he likes to hit the Midori a little hard—"

"Hey!" Paul protested.

"—so you won't be the only one who needs a ride if you don't want to stay," Riley finished while laughing.

"You're crazy if you think I'm leaving. Wyatt will need to snuggle with someone at the end of the night." Paul batted his eyes. He had to be in his early twenties, if that. I wouldn't be surprised if he was nineteen. But he was a likable nineteen, if that made sense.

"We should get going. We've got a checkup to get to," Riley said. He fished for a pen and handed it to me along with a napkin. "Write down your number. That way I can text you if something happens."

"Is the party still a maybe?" I asked as I jotted down my number.

"No, it's a for-sure, but we never know," Riley said, the tips of his ears going as red as his cheeks. He put my number in his pocket.

I waved as they gathered the rest of their stuff and made it for the door. "See you tomorrow." I was surprised by how nice it felt to be able to say that. The concept of someone counting on your presence, or being alarmed when you weren't around, was comforting. It was part of the reason why I kept up with my friends online, even if they got a little weird and wacky. The simple act of knowing someone would at least be worried if you didn't show up one day was nice. And until I had them, I hadn't had that feeling.

A flash of blond caught my eye, and I smiled as Zach passed by. Leaving my computer, I rushed out, catching him as he passed the door. "Zach! Hey!"

Zach jumped back like I was a troll who had popped out at him from under a bridge. "Jesus, little buddy, you scared me. Do you work here?"

Awesome. I'd been demoted from Glenn to *little buddy*. Was it possible that Zach didn't know who I was because he wasn't seeing me in the place he normally did? He needed the hallway and apartment doors to recognize me? "No. I mean, I am working here—"

Zach scratched his head. "Oh cool. Do you know if they have protein boosters like they have at Jamba?"

What had I been thinking? Why had I rushed out? Every other time when I spotted him, I watched him pass like a normal person. Talking to Riley and Paul, getting invited to do something with people face to face had made me cocky. I'd thought I was some sort of Lothario with a knack for seduction.

I was no longer under any such delusions. Zach was still waiting for my answer. "No. They don't, sorry."

He shrugged. "Thanks for the info, pal," he said before continuing down the sidewalk.

I watched him walk away. He had a nice ass, so sue me. But as I watched him, I wallowed. I didn't need to bother moving around. Apparently, I wasn't memorable for even my own neighbors to recognize me.

5

NASH

"NEED ANOTHER BEER?" one of Riley's friends asked. I knew this one wasn't his friend from work. That man I'd met at the beginning of the night, Hal. He'd made the journey from Seattle with his wife, and both would be staying in the guest house at the end of this evening. At first, the two seemed unlikely friends. Riley was in his late twenties, a new shifter, and father. Hal was a black man in his sixties, circling in on retirement. But Hal had seemed overjoyed to meet Bran Jr., and both men were crazy about DIY. They'd started talking about glue stick sizes and favorite spray paint brands, and, if Hal's wife's face was any indication, the two still hadn't stopped.

But the rest of Riley's friends were different. He'd confessed right before the party that the rest of his friends were people he'd met from a new gay father's group on Facebook. He'd met each face to face in various baby classes or playgroups, but we still had Riley shake each of their hands in a semi-private location.

Riley's touch, specifically when he put his hand on your hand or wrist area, forced people to blurt out a truth. If they meant us harm, Riley would've found out. But he and Branson—who had stood with him the whole time—seemed convinced that they were all just here to party.

Which meant I got tasked with fending off single-for-the-night, horny, gay dads.

"No, thank you. I've still got half left," I replied, trying to remember the name he'd given me. "Linus."

The man winked. "You seem like the kind of guy to really *suck it down.*"

Was that what I sounded like? I frowned, trying to clear the unpleasant thought. "The party has just begun. I've got to pace myself." I didn't want to be rude to Riley's friends, but I also wasn't interested in the slightest.

Which was pretty fucking annoying since the whole day leading to the party, I'd told myself that I would use the night to get Phin out of my head. We all had invited people. I waved at the chief as well as Krat. They'd brought the new fireman, Charles. So far, he seemed like an intense but quiet type of guy. Wyatt had asked a few of his regulars from the bar. Most of the twenty to thirty-aged crowd that lived in Walkerton was here, which meant I had the pick of the litter. Except I could still only think about the runt, in his rocket boxers.

I'd almost bought a pair online that looked exactly the same. Thankfully, I'd stopped myself before I took the first step down the path of complete insanity.

"Good thing I'm going to be here *all night,*" Linus replied.

Normally, I loved a guy on a hall pass. No muss, no fuss. But whenever I tried to convince myself to just take the plunge, I kept seeing Phineas. Like now. The man walking from the foyer to the kitchen looked exactly like—Hold up.

That was Phineas walking past the living room with a gift bag.

What was Phineas doing here?

I pushed off the wall, emerging from the corner I'd attempted to hide in. Passing Wyatt on the couch, I smirked. He had no problem accepting the love and affection that Riley's dads were keen to offer him. As well as Paul and a few other shifters from the pack who Paul had vetted. I'd been against them coming but had been overruled. Again.

Paul seemed nice. I had nothing against the kid. But he was a part of the pack and had sworn loyalty to my grandfather and the elder houses. I could never trust him.

I slipped in behind Phin, passing my firemen buddies. Krat flashed me a double thumbs-up, making me snort. The chief was looking the other way, and Charles suddenly seemed upset to be there. Maybe he wasn't a party type of guy. That was fine. We didn't need to be friends as long as he pulled his weight at the station.

I paused in the kitchen, watching Phin say hello to Riley. How did they know each other? It felt like ants crawling across my chest. What was this feeling? Jealousy? Was I jealous that Phin had a friend? A real-life one? I should've been glad it was Riley.

"Hey," I said when Riley caught sight of me lingering behind them.

"Oh, hey, Nash. I think you actually know—"

"Phineas," I said, giving him a nod. A nod? What was wrong with me?

"Hey. I hope this isn't... I mean, I bumped into Riley at the..." His face went red as his lips, pressed into a straight line. He wore glasses now, ones that he hadn't been wearing before. I liked the way they magnified his eyes, making them brighter and easier to read. But his face was good without glasses too.

I lifted my hands as if in surrender. "No worries. Any friend of Rye's is a friend of mine." No, that wasn't what I meant to say at all. Phin was *my friend* first. I saved him! I should have been introducing him to Riley!

"Thanks," Phineas said with a nervous laugh. "And thanks for saving me the other day. I don't remember if I did. Those hours are kind of fuzzy."

I scowled, hating the idea that Phin might not remember every single second that passed between us. I did.

"I know you said not to bring anything," Phin said to Riley, setting the gift bag on the marble counter. "I didn't really. There wasn't time to order anything, but here, for the house and the baby."

Riley beamed. He hadn't been expecting gifts, even though Hal and his wife had brought loads of baby stuff, both homemade and purchased. I thought he was more appreciative of the gesture. Before us, Riley hadn't had a lot of people in his life. He pulled out a toy first, an action figure of a tyrannosaurus rex.

"It's from the *Jurassic World* movies. I know everyone is all about the Indominus Rex, but I'm a classics guy myself. There aren't any little pieces, so he shouldn't choke on anything. Though, now that I am thinking about it, maybe a hard plastic toy isn't best for a baby."

"I love it. Thank you," Riley said, enveloping Phineas in a hug that I ordered myself not to be jealous of.

"There's one more..." Phin said, and Riley stuck his hand back in the bag, pulling out a packet of seeds.

"Sage?"

"For the housewarming party. It's a pretty good plant to

have around for digestion or memory. Or for warding off evil spirits," he added with a smirk.

"Thank you. This is amazing." Riley turned to show Hal the gifts, and he launched into a story about the time he'd made sage-infused lotions for his wife to pass out at a luncheon.

Except, when Riley got to the part where a normal person would be glad the story was over, he asked, "Did you use a double boiler?"

"How's Mrs. Boxer?" I asked Phin quietly, partly because I still felt guilty about how I'd snapped at her and partly because I was trying to prove to Phineas that I remembered every moment.

Phineas smiled, and it was as if the light in the room shone thirty times brighter. "She's feeling better, thank you. I checked on her right before taking the cab here." He frowned. "Not sure if I'll get one to go back. It took him about an hour to get to me after I called."

He'd come in a cab? Did that mean he could possibly stay? I set my beer down, the trajectory of my night changing dramatically with this one bit of information. "I bet she's business as usual already. Tough old girl. Even her forehead had looked way better by the time the building was cleared."

Phin's gaze darted out of the kitchen like he'd heard his name. "Yeah, well, I hear old people heal quick." His words were rushed and higher in pitch. "I should go mingle."

Never mind the fact that old people definitely did not heal quickly—Phin was pretty much running from me, leaving me with Riley and Hal around the kitchen island.

Be nice, Riley mouthed.

I turned before growling in response. I was being nice! It was Phineas who had run from me. It crossed my mind that perhaps I was responding to the love of the chase, that each time Phin rejected me, it made me want him more. Except that had never been my sort of thing before. If I asked, *do you want to kiss*, and the person said no, I didn't waste my time convincing them. I moved to the next. Phin hadn't said no, though. He'd just run into the dining room.

I'd nearly caught up to him when Linus slid in front of me, draping his left arm over my shoulder as he leaned heavily against me. His breath smelled of liquor, and he was wobbly on his feet. I'd have to check in with Riley to make sure this one had a safe ride home. Or a spot on the floor. "Looks like you need one now," he said, gesturing with his head at my beer-free hands.

Phineas chose that moment to look back. He took in the sight, Linus draped over me like a scarf, and smirked, shaking his head slightly.

I wanted to howl at the moon I was so frustrated.

Wyatt had moved from the couch to the kitchen table. He sat at one end, his long hair ruffled and sticking out like someone had just finished running their hands through it. Considering he had a different guy perched on each of his knees, I figured the new style was due to one of them. Aver sat at the other end of the table, Wyatt's complete opposite.

I could never understand Aver's desire to maintain a relationship with his parents despite what they'd all done to us. Even before recent events had intertwined our lives with the pack's, Aver had regularly visited his parents—off pack lands. He spoke to them almost weekly, and despite being a grown man who co-owned a successful construction company with Branson, he couldn't seem to figure out how to come out to them. As far as the pack, Walkerton, and Walker County were concerned, Aver was the sole straight man in a house of homosexual awesomeness.

There was no one perched on his knee, but Phin did look like he was about to take the vacant seat directly next to them.

No way. Aver was just the type of guy to let Phin hide behind him for the rest of the night. I knew he wouldn't make moves on Phin, not with everyone watching, but I'd been around Aver enough to know that the whole straight guy routine was like catnip to a gay man.

I grabbed the last empty chair from next to Wyatt and carried it around the table, setting it at the table's corner between Phin and Aver.

Phin scooted his chair over when it was clear that I was putting mine there whether there was room or not. "So," I said brightly. "What are we playing?" There were a few boxes of games on the table. Most of them wouldn't work for a party like this because they required being able to hear each other and to pay attention. I grabbed Jenga and slid it toward me.

"We hadn't decided," Aver said. "Phineas was just telling me that he moved here recently."

They'd been sitting next to each other for seconds.

"Good. Now that you know each other, we can play Jenga." I slid the blocks out of the box so that they were mostly stacked on the table.

Aver looked to Phin, and my chest rumbled. Thankfully, the sound was too quiet for Phin to hear over the party sounds, but not Aver. His eyebrow arched as his lips turned down in a frown. He could frown all he wanted as long as he knew Phineas was off-limits. "What would you like to play, Phineas?" Aver asked, ignoring me entirely.

Had he not heard my growl? I didn't expect anyone else to know what that meant, but my own cousin should understand me.

"Jenga is fine. Should be easy to play and keep talking."

Keep talking? What more did they have to talk about? I was right there!

Aver nodded. "Cool, why don't you go first?"

Phineas leaned forward, took a moment to ponder his move, and slid the first block out. When he leaned back, I half-expected Aver to skip right over me, since he seemed so intent on pretending I wasn't there. But he looked at me expectantly.

I made my move without even looking. As a shifter, I had tremendous dexterity. Aver snorted and, at his turn, looked at the tower up and down. "So Phineas, how are you finding Walkerton? I'm always curious what the town seems like from an outside perspective."

"Small, quiet, but beautiful," Phineas replied. "I can do my work from anywhere, though the cell service leaves something to be desired."

"Get a signal booster," I said, meaning for it to sound like a wise suggestion from his older, hotter friend. Instead, it sounded like an order. "For your phone."

"I understand what signal boosters do," Phin shot back.

Aver's eyes flicked between us. "I could help you shop for one," he said. "We recently got one for Riley when he moved here. Branson had me researching the best brands for hours."

"I don't really have anyone to call anyway." Phineas shrugged while I crowed with joy on the inside. Not about the part where Phineas didn't have anyone to call, but the part where he rejected Aver. "Most of my *friends* I can contact as long as I have Wi-Fi."

Would I never live that down? "He means online friends," I said to Aver. There, let Phin see I wasn't the only one who—

"Oh, cool, I had a pen pal growing up. He lived in Manchester, England. Always meant to visit him one day."

That time, both men heard my growl.

"Do you need some water, Nash?" Aver asked. He knew exactly what he was doing, and when this party was done, I was going to settle this with my fist in his face. Branson and I went at it all the time. It had been too long since Aver had been on the other end.

"If you're getting a cold, try not to breathe on me," Phin said. He smirked at Aver as if the two of them shared some secret.

Fucking great. I was bombing, for the first time ever. Okay, it wasn't the first time, but it was the only time that mattered to me. "Whose turn is it?"

"Yours," Phin and Aver said at the same time.

In my anger, my hand shot out with more force than I'd intended, knocking the entire tower over. The pieces scattered noisily over the table, drawing everyone's attention while also making a mess. Aver and Phin jumped up to clean, but when they reached for the same block, I pushed between them. "Let's play a new game."

"How about Twister?" Wyatt suggested, waggling his eyebrows at the men on his knees. They giggled just as Paul came into the room with fresh drinks. His eyebrows furrowed at the sight.

"No Twister." I couldn't stand the mental image of Phineas's body twining with anyone else at this party but me.

At my tone, Wyatt's smile disappeared. The guy on his left knee leaned in, whispering something in his ear while pretending to need to balance his hand directly on Wyatt's dick. Whatever was whispered—I didn't even try to pick his words out through the din—had Wyatt smirking again. "A drinking game then," he suggested.

"Yeah!"

"That sounds fun." Those around him seemed all too eager.

"One we play in our own chairs," Paul added, but no one agreed with his idea.

"Truth or dare?" Linus suggested before blowing me a kiss.

"Why not spin the bottle?" I suggested sarcastically. There wasn't a teenager among us besides Paul, and I got the feeling he was trying to seem as mature as possible.

"Just dare then," Linus said, though I wasn't sure how that made it better.

But Wyatt was already on board. He shimmied, shedding off his hangers-on like drops of water off a dog. "You dare. If you refuse, you drink."

"What about Walker-ball?" Aver suggested while looking at Phineas.

Phin's eyes had gone round with worry, and he nibbled at his bottom lip. "Things are getting exciting. Maybe I should step back and let you guys—"

"Nonsense," Wyatt said, shooting me a not-so-subtle wink. "Walker-ball is the best game."

I wouldn't go that far. Walker-ball was something we'd made up as eighteen-year-olds, freshly separated from the pack with more energy than we knew what to do with. Half dodgeball, half Jackass stunt, it was fun—if you didn't mind the idea of people throwing all sorts of balls at you while they were blindfolded.

I knew why Wyatt would be eager to play the game, but not Aver. Not until I remembered which position he often played when we'd been younger.

With just four of us, one had acted as the catcher, two of us were blindfolded and were throwers, and that left one to stand on the sideline and judge. Having judges was especially important since the throwers couldn't know if their balls hit their target while blindfolded. We'd added the blindfolded bit because, as shifters, just throwing a ball at a target wasn't all that difficult.

From there, the game evolved. Sometimes, we made the area where the catchers stood more treacherous. On hot days, we'd all played in the bay. But it was dark and cold out now, something no one seemed to mind as we marched through the kitchen to the back patio.

"What's going on?" Riley asked.

"Walker-ball," Wyatt replied, but Riley just frowned at Branson.

I knew Branson would have something to say about this from the wrinkles that were already on his face. "I don't know that Walker-ball is such a good game with a big group of... mixed talents."

He meant the humans among the shifters. Yes, shifters had the upper hand, but that had only made me like the game more.

"Should we be worried?" Riley whispered to Branson.

He shrugged, but the frown never left his face. "Everyone's an adult here. If they want to play Walker-ball..." He sounded as though he had no idea why any of us would, but at least he wasn't going to turn into Daddy Walker like he sometimes did.

I stayed close to Phineas, who in turn stayed close to Aver. I tried to convince myself that he'd just latched on to the safest-seeming person at the party, but that thought did little to comfort me. I saved him. He should think I was safe.

Pretty soon, I'd have to stop holding onto that thought so hard.

On the way out, I bumped into Charles, the new fireman, as he came inside. "Amazing view out there," he grunted. With as friendly as he'd seemed until now, that was dang near an invitation to be besties.

"Yeah," I grunted in reply.

Charles continued back in, and I smirked. That was how communication should be: no one getting the wrong idea, no one saying something they hadn't meant to.

Once outside, we lost several players just due to how cold it was. Wyatt's entourage remained, as well as Phin and Aver. Wyatt cupped his hands over his mouth, taking charge. "This is how it goes. We need two teams: catchers and throwers. Catchers, you will get hit if the throwers are any good, so keep that in mind."

At his announcement, most of the men who'd been keeping close to Wyatt on the catcher side skittered across the line to the thrower side, where Aver was dragging the tubs of various balls we'd collected over the years.

"The teams don't have to be even, and if you don't want to catch or throw, stand over here next to Phin, and you can judge."

Phin looked relieved to have been named a judge instead of having to choose it, though I was pretty positive he would have anyway. Aver headed toward him.

"We need one of us on the throwing side, or Wyatt and I will win too easily," I told him, knowing he'd know I meant *one of us shifters*.

His mouth turned down, but he went to stand with the throwers.

"Throwers need to find something to tie over their eyes,"

Wyatt said before turning to Phin. "Judge chooses the handicap."

"What's the point of all this?" Phin asked. "How does anyone win?"

A valid question without an easy answer.

"You can win in several ways. As throwers, if you hit the catchers, they are out. Throwers can only win as a team. As catchers, if you last until all the balls are gone without bleeding, you win."

"Without bleeding?" Phin repeated. "The object of the game is to not get hurt?"

"Isn't that the object to life?" Wyatt asked playfully. "Now get ready. Let's play some Walker-ball!"

The others whooped. I went to stand near Wyatt in the grassy portion between the patio and the shore while the others found things to tie around their eyes. Wyatt whipped his shirt off, moving behind Paul to wrap it around his eyes. Paul's cheeks burned, and he smirked, much to the displeasure of the rest of Wyatt's posse. I'd be surprised if Wyatt got that shirt back. Linus gave me a look like he wanted the same treatment, but I pretended not to see it, checking in on Phin instead.

"Can you see from there?"

Phin stood on some decorative boulders. He brought his hands up to his hips and shrugged. "I wait to see if someone gets hit, right?"

I smiled. "That's about the whole of it."

"This game is insane," he said, but there was an excitement to his voice. To be part of the game? Or just to be out in general?

"Nash!" Wyatt screamed my name. "Let's go! Round One!" He pointed at Phin with double finger guns. "What's the handicap?"

"Uhhh..." Phin looked to Aver.

"Why not hop on one leg?" I whispered so only Phin could hear me.

"Hop on one leg," Phin replied, seeming relieved to say the thing that would get people to stop looking at him.

"I heard that, Nash," Wyatt barked. "But I will allow it. Okay. Are the throwers ready?"

There was a halfhearted chorus of yeses.

I took my spot a few feet to the side of Wyatt and lifted my left leg. We were the only catchers. That was probably for the best. Walker-ball was stupidly dangerous. I'd broken more fingers than I could count, a fact that only cropped back up while I stared down the other team of blind, mostly horny men who wanted to sink their claws—and teeth—into my brother.

"On your go, Phinster," Wyatt said without looking.

Phin beamed at the nickname and raised his arm into the air. "Go!" he shouted, slicing his hand downward.

I had to swerve immediately to avoid the first of the balls. The throwers giggled more than they did anything, and when they did manage to grab hold of a ball from the bins, they mostly threw them to the sides or over our heads. Aver was a thrower, though, and he seemed to have forgotten that Wyatt existed at all.

I hopped, jumped, and spun, twisting my ankle more than once as I balanced on one leg. I should have suggested a handicap I was better at. When it had been just us, we often played *mouths only,* where the catch only counted if it was between our teeth. A baseball zoomed directly for my face, and I heard a gasp just as I dodged out of the way. The sound had come from the side. From Phin.

I looked for the next ball to fly my way, waiting until I was nearly struck before moving. Again, Phin made a sharp noise, one that he did not make whenever Wyatt almost got hit. My chest pounded, not from exertion—this was easy—but from the thought that Phin cared if I was pegged in the face. It wasn't much, but I'd cling to it with all I had.

I was feeling especially cocky as Aver threw a football. He aimed low—because he was smart—but I jumped on one leg, rising several feet in the air. I had less control on the way down, which became a problem as Wyatt maneuvered somewhat beneath me.

"Look—!" Phin shouted, but he didn't have time to say any more than that.

I fell, managing to catch my upper half with my hands while my legs tangled with Wyatt. I wasn't a light man and had been falling fast. My heart leapt into my throat when I heard a snap, followed by the scent of blood and then Wyatt's groan of pain. I rolled off him, tucking my feet under my body to rise into a stand. His leg had to be broken. I thought I'd spotted a shard of bloody bone.

Phin was already beside Wyatt before most people realized they needed to take their blindfolds off. I dropped to my knees beside him just as Phin sat back, removing his hands from Wyatt's leg. His forehead was sweaty, and his lips twisted with something that looked like pain, but Phin had been standing along the sidelines. He couldn't have gotten hurt.

Aver stood over us. "Everything okay? I thought I..."

I knew he'd been about to say *I thought I smelled blood* but couldn't exactly claim such a thing in mixed company. Meanwhile, Wyatt's fan club was helping him to his feet, each more eager than the next to be the one Wyatt leaned on. Normally, at these sorts of events, I was Wyatt. Seeing it from the other side was startling.

But I wasn't envious. Not in the slightest. Not now that Phin was beside me. Still sitting in the grass.

"Here, let me help." I offered him my hand, but he waved it away.

"I twisted my leg funny. Let me sit for a second."

I bent down and picked him up, much like I had the first time I set eyes on him. I sighed silently at the contentment that washed over me having Phin in my arms again. Carrying him through the crowd, I didn't slow until we were in the kitchen and I could set him down on one of the cushioned chairs.

"What happened?" Riley rushed forward.

"Nothing, I'm fine," Phin hurried to say. "Wyatt's the one who was hurt."

Just then, Wyatt came into the kitchen, an arm over the shoulders of the men on either side of him. They were all laughing, while Wyatt walked without even a limp. I'd heard a snap, though. I'd smelled blood.

Was it a coincidence? If not, what was the real answer? Phin refused to look at my face, making me more suspicious. What the hell could he be hiding? I thought briefly of asking Riley to touch him. That was something I refused to do myself. I wasn't going to foist that fate on Phin. He wasn't like the horny new gay dads. He was...

Different.

That was the best word I could come up with at the moment.

Riley returned with a pack of ice which Phin declined and a drink that he accepted. It smelled fruity, but with a subtle burn of alcohol. Phin tipped the bottle back, taking several large gulps. "That's the stuff," he said before he burped. Immediately, his cheeks burned red.

He was fucking adorable.

He was also still clearly in pain. Why? How? Maybe Wyatt had rolled on him accidentally? It hadn't looked like that had happened, but I knew I hadn't touched him.

Everyone had come in from outside, most of them deciding that Walker-ball wasn't quite the type of game they were hoping for. I regretted it now too.

"You don't have to sit with me," Phin mumbled a few minutes later. In all the excitement, I hadn't noticed what he was wearing. I could say without a doubt it was the most clothes I'd ever seen him in, but he was no less enticing for it. His jeans were faded and worn. He wore a blue hoodie, with white stripes down the sleeves. The zipper had fallen down, revealing a light blue t-shirt with the formula $E = mc^2$, and, beneath it, the words, *Energy equals milk times coffee²*.

"I like your shirt," I said. "And I want to sit with you. Is your leg feeling better?"

Phin looked in every direction but at me. "It's okay. Probably just a cramp. You really don't have to stay with me. I should probably go soon anyway, and you seem pretty popular. A lot of people seem eager for you to return to the party."

If he meant Linus, then I was going to murder Riley the next time we played poker. The first time, I'd been nice, letting him win. But it was his fault Linus was here in the first place.

"I'm right where I want to be." I sat down. The two of us weren't just the only people at the small table, but the only two in this corner of the kitchen. "Unless you want me to go? I mean, I'm no hot neighbor..."

Phin's head whipped my way. "How did you know about him?"

I couldn't be upset that I'd let the information slip, not

when it had cause Phin to look at me again. "I must've heard you use it."

He frowned but didn't question me further.

I searched my mind for a different topic. "You know, I'm not into any of these people."

Phin let out a burst of air followed by a sarcastic, "My condolences." He reached for his bottle, and when he spoke again, his breath smelled like a fruit salad.

Was that a good enough excuse for me to lick his tongue? I wanted to. And I didn't want to stop there. I didn't want to stop *anywhere* on Phin's body.

"How do you do it?" Phin asked.

He didn't know what was in my head, the dirty movies playing in my mind, each starring him. He couldn't know, but it felt like he did, and I coughed, clearing my throat and my thoughts. "Do what?" I asked, suddenly nervous.

"I don't know... how do you... be you? Be so cool and sure of yourself."

Was he looking at the right Nash? With any other guy, on any other night, I might have preened and strutted around after that sort of question, but with Phineas I could only sit dumbfounded.

"You think I'm stupid for asking," Phin grumbled. Clearly, he'd gotten the wrong idea from my silence.

"I don't. Not at all, Phin."

"But you think my friends are dumb? No wait, just fake."

I rubbed my face with my hand. "I shouldn't have said that. I didn't mean fake, like how you are thinking. But Wyatt used to lie to his chat friends—"

"So you just think I'm a liar?"

"No! Not you, but the people you talk to."

"So you think I'm gullible, naive, and *stupid* enough to be tricked?"

"I wasn't saying that either!" I replied so loudly Riley turned around and gave me a look. One of the worried variety. "Just, stop, okay? I'm not ever meaning to say something mean."

Phin stared at me for longer than was polite for a casual conversation. I supposed hollering at someone also wasn't polite in casual conversation. "Fine, okay. Don't get your panties in a bunch."

At the mention of panties, I of course imagined his rocket boxers, which then had me wondering what pair he was wearing now. I readjusted in the chair, swinging my legs under the table.

"I think they're playing charades in the other room if you're interested, Phin," Riley said. Branson stood over his shoulder, glaring at me.

"Thanks, but I think I'll sit here for a bit and then head home, if that's okay?"

"Of course it is. You don't have to ask. I feel bad. I invited you, and we haven't had a lot of time to chat." Riley snagged a chair and sat down. Bran Jr. wasn't with either of them, so I assumed he'd gone to bed. Hal and his wife must have headed over to the guest house.

"I've had a lot of fun. Please don't feel bad. Besides, we both live here. We can always—" He stopped speaking so suddenly my instincts went on high alert. He stared at his folded hands on the table as I took in the sights and smells of our surroundings, attempting to pinpoint what had made him retreat so quickly into himself. I sensed nothing but the smells and sights that were always present. "I've had fun," Phin said with a decisive nod.

"I have your number. Is it okay to text next time Bran Jr.

and I have some free time? Maybe I can even get this guy to babysit." He affectionately elbowed Branson in the gut. "We can have a guys' night or something."

"Yeah, that sounds great." Phin's reply held none of his earlier warmth. He'd either become aware of something or remembered something. "I'm probably just gonna ask Nash a favor and then head out. Thank you again."

I sat up at the mention of my name, and Riley looked between us. From the living room, there came a loud burst of laughter; I assumed someone had mimed something particularly funny. "I'm gonna get in there. I'm an ace at charades," Riley said with real excitement.

Branson followed behind him with that same doofy smile he always had when he was with Riley and they were both safe and happy. I'd made fun of him for following Riley around like a puppy, but I hadn't let Phineas out of my sight from the moment I spotted him walking in.

We were alone once more, and this time, I knew he had something to ask me, so I waited.

And waited.

I scratched my elbow, then the other.

"Willyouteachmehowtoflirt?" Phin blurt out in one breath.

"What's that?"

He scowled, maybe thinking I was making him repeat it again to embarrass him, but really, I hadn't had any idea what he asked. He met my gaze without blinking and spoke slowly and carefully. "Flirt. Will you teach me how to flirt? You're like... a Jedi master or something at it. Even when you don't want attention, you can't help but attract it. I can't seem to get someone to remember my face in more than one setting."

I definitely had more questions on what he meant about

that, but I was too busy fuming to ask them. Teach him how to flirt so he could attract some fucking no-neck like Zach? No fucking way. But at the same time, Phin was asking me to do something. There was a need in his life that he chose me to meet. Ignoring entirely for a moment that flirting was more an inherent skill than a learned one, I didn't want to say no, but I sure as hell didn't want to say yes.

Except... teaching Phin anything would mean more time with Phin.

Still, I didn't want to seem too eager—ironically enough, that would also be one of the first lessons I taught him. I didn't have to hand over my whole arsenal; such power couldn't be handed out willy-nilly. But I could give him some pointers while also learning more about him.

Which gave me my next idea. "I'll do it, if you tell me why you've been so weird since Walker-ball. Don't bother saying you haven't been," I said as his mouth opened. "I'm incredibly observant, Phineas."

His lip twitched in a near smile.

"Nah, I'll just ask Wyatt. He's getting more action than you tonight anyway." Phin stood.

That wily coyote. Maybe he had more skills than I gave him credit for. I jumped to my feet. "No you won't."

He looked down at his feet, where he stood in the doorway, and then back up at me. "Do you not see me? I am."

I quickly sidestepped in front of him. He stopped suddenly, but our chests still bounced. Or, rather, his chin bounced against my chest. When he fell back, his left leg crumpled oddly beneath him, and he began to fall. I caught him, bringing him back to standing and immediately launching back into persuading him. "You need me, Phineas...?"

He licked his lips. "Peters?"

"Really? PP?"

He tugged out of my arms.

"No, wait, I'm sorry." I adopted the same silky tone as I'd had before learning of his unfortunate initials. "You need me, Phineas Peters."

His bottom lip popped out in a pout. "If I was confident enough to ask anyone else, I would, Nash. But, you're right. I need you because right now, I'm able to talk so freely to you because there's nothing going on between us. You don't have to worry about me developing an insane crush or anything." His cheeks burned pink.

Because he was lying? Or nervous that he was telling the truth?

I'd have to cling to the former with all I had. It was the only option I could stomach. "I have no problem teaching you, Phin. All I want is for you to show some good faith. What happened tonight? That sort type of collision, all my weight down on his leg—he shouldn't have walked away so easily."

"Maybe you didn't fall like you think," Phin said, his cheeks glowing that same shade of pink.

Lies. Praise the moon. But also, *what the hell?* What was he saying?

"Fine! I'll tell you. Tomorrow, though, okay? Not tonight. I've had my fill of peopling."

I could wait that long. Plus, that meant I would be seeing him again *tomorrow*. "Deal."

His eyebrows flew up and then settled. "Okay, deal. I'll see you tomorrow." He made to move by, and I grabbed his wrist.

"Where are you going?"

"Home?" he said, but his voice was tight. He'd

mentioned being done peopling, and I was learning that was an actual thing.

"How? You didn't call a taxi." I knew because my attention had been on him almost every moment he'd been here.

"I'll just walk. It was only a fifteen-minute drive, and I'm a pretty fast walker. Used to live in some shady neighborhoods."

Phineas Peters had clearly had some shit friends. I would show him how to flirt and how to expect to be treated. "I'll drive you. I'm stone sober by now. I won't talk on the way or make you people. Just let me get you to your front door safely, okay?"

He looked like he might try to argue so I launched in again.

"Call it the Fireman's Code. Never leave a friend to walk through the coyote-filled forest."

Phineas smirked. "I would've kept to the road."

"Oh, and get home in four hours? Great plan." We were at the front door by then, and I turned to find Wyatt, shooting him a wave. He gave me a bro nod.

Phin followed me to my vehicle but stopped suddenly. "You're nicer than I thought. I'm sorry I misjudged you."

I waved him away like it was nothing when really, it was *everything*. "Happens all the time. Something about my physical perfection and overwhelming charm."

"*And* there you are," Phin said, rolling his eyes. But when he got in and buckled his seat belt, he did it with a smile.

6

PHINEAS

By the time I got home from Riley's party, I was exhausted, but not the kind that let me sleep. I crawled into bed, tingling all over from sitting so close to Nash. The ride back home was shorter than I remembered the ride to Riley's being. More likely, it was shorter than I wanted it to be once Nash was in the car. True to his word, he hadn't spoken the whole night other than to say goodnight and confirm he'd be by the next day.

He'd been so different at the party and yet exactly the same. I'd barely walked in the door before he'd been right there beside me, and though I hadn't let it show, it had been nice to have a buddy. Those sorts of events, where the person who asked me to go was understandably busy, I ended up sitting quietly in a corner until I could slink out. I could say, even with the charlie horse that still throbbed in my leg, that it was the most fun I'd ever had at a social event.

I hadn't been pushed to do more than I was comfortable, and there were plenty of extroverts around to entertain the crowds.

And what had I done? Brought my curse down on them

all. I wasn't stupid or vain. I understood that Walker-ball was probably the most dangerous party game I'd ever heard of, but Nash hadn't been wrong about thinking Wyatt should have been hurt more.

His leg bone had been sticking out of the skin. I'd been able to get my hands on him and heal him enough so that he could walk. The process had taken much less from me than I'd expected—like tapping a ball over the edge of a hill and watching it roll. It almost felt like his body had already begun healing and I was just helping it along.

But the fun had still stopped because of me.

Now, I had to tell Nash something to satisfy his curiosity. Would he know if I made up an answer? I squeezed my BB-8 plushie to my chest and groaned. What if—and this was a wild idea—I told him the truth? I hadn't tried something like that before. Maybe this was like a *Beauty and the Beast* curse situation, and all I needed to do was find the one I trusted enough and the spell would be broken.

Did that make me the beast?

I frowned and rolled over, looking at the clock and reaching for my phone in the same moment. I tapped the green alien face icon. Looking at the chatter list, I saw that Reg and Bun were offline, but Chuck was there.

GoblinKing: *Can't sleep either?*

Three small dots appeared near his name, indicating he was typing. I frowned. Chuck had kept a more regular schedule back when he'd been married. Lately, he was on at all hours. It was nice to know there was always someone there to talk to, but at the same time, the guy needed to get out.

Huh. Well, if that wasn't the pot calling the kettle the same thing everyone always called the pot. *Nerd, geek, go outside for once, make some real friends.*

ChuckShurley: *You know, every night's a big night. /s*

GoblinKing: *lol*

I wasn't actually laughing out loud, but I didn't think anyone had taken that acronym literally in years.

GoblinKing: *Need to talk about anything?*

ChuckShurley: *Depends. Didn't you have your big night tonight?*

I was so introverted, going to a friend's for a casual evening was considered a big night.

GoblinKing: *I went, I saw, I conquered. Now, I'm cowering in bed trying to recharge.*

ChuckShurley: *Doors locked? Windows checked? Neighbor's grill extinguished ;) ?*

GoblinKing: *Yes, Daddy Chuck.*

I frowned the moment I hit enter. This world had killed the word daddy for me used in any context that wasn't sexual. I regretted typing what I did, so I did the only thing that I could think to relieve the awkwardness: flood the screen with emojis.

ChuckShurley: *Okay, okay, I get it. Ack! My eyes! Lol. We can talk tomorrow. Sleep well, GoblinKing.*

GoblinKing: *You too.*

As I rolled back over and tried to at least pretend I was trying to sleep, I didn't feel any better. If anything, the chat with Chuck had made me more antsy. I could feel myself about to fall into the portion of the night that came after every social outing where I evaluated each and every word and action I made so I could pinpoint which moments were the most embarrassing.

But, when I thought of the party, I thought of Nash. And when I thought of Nash, I smiled. He had such a gregarious personality. Not smiling while thinking of Nash would be like not smiling at Star-Lord when he busted a move. And now, he would teach me what he knew.

Under Nash's tutelage, I was sure I'd become, at the least, more memorable. I'd just have to make good on my promise and stop any crushes from cropping up. That had been an easy promise to make before Nash had shown that he could be considerate too. But, if my options were to have a crush that went nowhere and ruined everything or keeping it in my pants where it belonged, then it was an easy choice. I'd tamp my burgeoning loins and concentrate on learning all I could about flirting.

At least I knew one thing for sure: I would be learning from the master.

———

THE FIRST THING I LEARNED: when Nash said *see you tomorrow*, he meant *see you in the earliest hours of the day when no sane person should be awake*. It felt like I'd just closed my eyes when there was a knock. Worried it might be Mrs. Boxer, I dragged myself to the door. Expecting a little old lady but getting a great big Nash was my first surprise of the day.

His bright expression transformed into a frown and then a smirk. "Big night?" he asked.

I groaned.

He walked in, stepping around me.

"Please, come in," I said sarcastically.

He either pretended not to notice or really didn't care. "Did you just get up, sleepyhead?"

"What time is it?"

"Eight."

I was close enough to my couch that I could drop onto the cushion and flop over with another groan. "This is my fault. I wasn't clear. I meant, like, afternoon training—"

"No way, Phinster."

His brother had called me the same nickname the night before. Now, it was almost as if he used it to make a point.

"First lesson is to treat yourself and your body well, so that other people will treat yourself, *and your body* well." He folded his arms behind his head and thrust with his hips, making my groin twitch.

No, no, no, the last thing I needed was delayed morning wood.

"I treat myself well," I said through a yawn.

Nash snorted. "Let's see."

Keeping my head resting against the arm of the couch, I opened one eye to keep track of Nash. He stood in the kitchen and reached for my pantry.

I lurched up into a sit. "You have to open that—"

Nash yanked the door toward him, unleashing a cascade of half-empty bags of food, canned goods, and boxes.

"—carefully."

Nash just stood there as the last of my food made their escape. "Okay. We're gonna backtrack. Step zero point five, your home is your temple. Whether you choose to bring lovers back to it is your choice, but it should always be ready to entertain. You don't want to be getting hot and heavy with some guy, decide to head back to your place, and make him wait in the hallway while you make your home look like less of a hobbit hole."

I squinted at him, needing my glasses to see him clearly. I wasn't sure if I should be offended that he'd called my apartment a hobbit hole or happy that he knew what hobbits were. I could make all my hobbit jokes now. "Yes, but maybe the hobbit-esqueness will let them know I'm a good listener."

Nash blinked once. Then again.

"... Because hobbits are known for being good listeners?"

He'd started combing through the food that had fallen, arranging it neatly on the counter. "Quick question, Phin, do you eat anything that doesn't come with a cartoon character on the packaging?"

Of course I did. I got to my feet and went to stand beside him. *I am a grown-up. I totally eat grown-up—oh my god my food is covered in cartoons.*

That hadn't been a trend I'd noticed. "I guess I'm attracted to bright colors." I shrugged.

"And that's lesson number two. You like bright colors because they catch your eye and make you think happy, confident things. In nature, that's one of the ways animals attract a mate, by flashing bright colors." He shut the cupboard. "We're going out to eat," he announced. "Get dressed."

I looked down at the clothes I was wearing. Mostly the same clothes from the day before, but softer pants. I stuck my hands out like I was a magician performing a trick. "Done."

Nash sighed. "I thought you might try something like that. So I came prepared."

He had? Already, Nash was blowing away my expectations for how much help he'd really be. He produced a paper bag I hadn't noticed.

"I had to guess on your sizes." He pulled out a shirt that was solid black.

"I thought you said colors?"

"We'll work up to that. Try this on now, and these..." He

handed me black shorts with a mesh lining and red stripes down the side. "They're all-terrain, so you should be ready for wherever the day takes us."

I frowned, and my stomach bubbled, not with happy butterflies, but nervous ants. "Where is the day taking us?"

"Don't worry, young grasshopper. I'll be with you every step of the way."

Oddly, that assurance made me feel better. I clung to the clothes he'd passed me. "And this—having breakfast, wearing these shorts—that's all gonna help me flirt?"

Nash's expression faltered, his smile slipping for a moment before he stretched it back into place. "Something like that."

I'D THOUGHT when he said breakfast, he meant real food. Instead, he'd claimed there was a great cafe, other than Rise and Grind, that he wanted to go to. It ended up being the smoothie shack at the gym. I didn't even think I could get in without a membership, but no one questioned Nash as we took our seats at the only table in the small space.

"This is where you eat?" I asked dubiously, looking around. It even smelled healthy in here, like flaxseed and hemp oil or whatever the kids were taking these days.

"Normally for second or third breakfast, yes."

Third breakfast? Now we were talking.

"Mostly I chose this place because people won't bother us as much." He got up to retrieve whatever he'd ordered for us. When he returned, he set a smoothie in front of me as well as an open container of what looked like rice cake sandwiches. I picked one up and sniffed it. The filling was some sort of nut butter, but I couldn't pinpoint which.

At least the smoothie was a bright, appealing orange

color. I reached for it right as my stomach twisted with hunger. I sucked hard on the straw, expecting a fruity flavor.

What I got was something else. Something evil.

The liquid stayed in my mouth, my throat refusing it passage.

"What?" Nash asked, seeing my face. "The sweet potato base is a little hard to get used to, but once you do... Phin, swallow."

I held the sip in my mouth, trying not to move a single muscle for fear that it would spread the taste around. I shook my head.

"You have to swallow."

I wanted to, if only to get this moment behind me, but I was physically unable. The taste was savory but not. It didn't make sense in my mouth and made even less sense in my stomach.

"Phin." Nash said my name like it was a warning, but he couldn't stop his lips from curling into a smirk. "You're being silly. It isn't that bad—" He reached over, drinking from my same drink, using the same straw I'd put in my mouth. He winced but swallowed. "Maybe they changed the recipe."

My eyes bulged, tears forming the longer I kept the disgusting mush in my mouth.

Nash ducked his head so he stared only into my face. "You can't spit it out now. It's become a personal challenge. Swallow it, Phin. Mind over matter. Brain over body. *Swallow*."

The way he spoke the last command, letting his tongue linger on the hard *L* sounds, made me feel like we were in a different situation, like he was commanding me to swallow in a more intimate setting. My throat muscles obeyed.

"There you go. Good boy." Nash winked.

I imagined every disgusting thing I could, reminding

myself of my first few days in my apartment when I'd had to dig someone else's hair clump out of my shower drain. Just thinking about that moment had me gagging for days, and it did the trick now. "I think I'm full."

"You're not. Try the rice cakes. I know they don't taste as bad because they don't taste like a whole lot."

"And this is supposed to help me flirt?"

"It's supposed to lay the foundation."

Foundations were important. I'd never attempt a quest without first acquiring the correct skills and equipment. I bit into the first of the cake sandwiches. How could something with the word *cake* and *sandwich* taste so abysmal? But Nash was right. The flavor wasn't nearly as offensive as the *sweet potato smoothie*. I couldn't wait to tell Reg and Bun about it. They'd react with appropriate levels of repulsion.

I reached for another rice cracker, wishing I had something to wash it down with. I'd guzzle gasoline before I resorted to drinking any more of the smoothie. Nash watched me. His drink was half gone, as were his crackers. I pushed mine toward him but instead of taking one, he grabbed my hand and turned my arm palm-side up. He traced the outline of my crow tattoo while I forgot how to breathe.

"What do these mean?" he asked without looking up from my tattoos. He had both my arms on the table, wrist up.

The stark black shapes against my pale skin were always a shock, but I liked that I'd never gotten used to the sight of them. My tattoos had never become something my brain no longer saw, like the nose on my face.

"Nuh-uh." I went to tug for my sleeve but had taken my jacket off already. "That isn't the secret you asked for last night." What the hell was wrong with me? He was giving me an out. Tell him about the crows and my parents instead of making something up to explain how I'd healed his brother. One was a personal, soul-deep fact about me that might change how he looked at me, and the other was a curse that would likely turn him from me forever.

But, if I was trying to not have a crush, then this was the way to do it.

"Tell me both and we'll keep going. Wyatt's bar opens in a bit. The early morning crew would be the perfect ones for you to practice on."

I didn't understand his reasoning but jumped at the chance to spend more time with him today. My own logic wasn't making much sense anyway. I was going to tell Nash the secret that would make him turn from me so that I wouldn't develop too hard of a crush, all so I could spend a little more time with him today? Or maybe, there was a part inside me that *wanted* Nash to know. I'd come close to telling Reg, Bun, and Chuck a few times over the years, mostly on nights when I broke into the wine and was feeling maudlin. But I'd always held back at the last minute.

I didn't want to hold back now. Mostly. I sort of wanted to hold back.

I was a mess.

"And tomorrow," Nash added, seemingly under the impression that I needed more convincing. Why did he want to know so badly? Maybe it was the chase. I'd expressed not wanting to share, so now that was the only thing he wanted? That meant, if I told him, his interest in me would wane.

So I shouldn't tell him? Urgh, this was confusing.

"Phin." Nash said my name with a laugh. "Your face has got some telenovela-level emotions flitting through. Look, I don't want to know anything you absolutely don't want to tell. But sometimes it's nice to share a secret, you know? So the weight isn't so heavy on your shoulders. Look at my shoulders, Phin. I could crack a walnut with my trapezius muscles." He flexed, making me grin.

"Fine, but can I have some water or something?" I eyed my smoothie with disdain. He slid my drink over to his side of the table and got up, ordering at the bar.

He returned with a bottle of something that I would've assumed was orange juice, if I hadn't already been fooled once before. I must have also shown my suspicion on my face because Nash laughed.

"It's orange juice, I promise." He cracked open the top and set it down in front of me. Before stepping back, he leaned in and said, "At Wyatt's, if you're good, we can have fries."

I sat up straight at that but then slouched with a frown. "French fries with real potatoes? Normal, russet potatoes? Not broccoli or cauliflower fries?"

"One hundred percent fried, greasy, frozen, from a bag straight into the deep fat fryer."

I took a sip of the juice like I was a drug dealer in a vacant warehouse taking a sample of the shipment before accepting it. Pure, unfiltered, orange juice. The good stuff. "Okay," I said with a nod.

Nash sat back down, but I missed his nearness.

"So, um, what do you want to know first?"

"Start with the tattoos," he said with an eager gleam.

I rubbed over the ink on my right wrist. "They represent my parents. They died when I was five, almost six. We lived in Monterey, California, and we were driving home from somewhere. I can't even remember anymore. Maybe it was a movie? A dinner with friends? But it was raining, and the roads were windy. It was like we were driving one minute, spinning through the air the next..."

"And then?" Nash asked, leaning forward.

"Then nothing. We hit. I passed out." I was already there in my mind. The smell of the gasoline leaking had burned my nose. Even as a kid, I'd recognized that smell for the danger it had represented. There'd been broken glass everywhere and, the entire time, the steady thrum of rain pouring all around us. And the blood. So much blood. I couldn't tell Nash what I'd done next. That was a secret I'd take to my grave.

"How were you saved?"

"A Good Samaritan drove by and pulled me out. The officials said he even offered to take me home until things got figured out, but my aunt was already on her way by then. I moved in with them, but I wasn't the same. Or maybe I was. I just know I've never really liked being around people for a very long time. Even before the curse, I moved into their pool house when I was able, and off their property shortly after that. At eighteen, I gained access to my inheritance and have been living off that and my writing ever since." What had he asked again? Oh yeah, about my tattoos. And I'd gone right into the whole tragic story.

Most of the whole tragic story, anyway.

"Anyway, when I moved out, the tattoos were the first thing I bought with their inheritance." I swiped my finger over each crow. "It feels like my parents are with me sometimes, when I look at the crows. But they also remind me how quickly everything can change." That was a lesson I'd kept learning. In the beginning, I'd tried to settle, find a hole and stick to it. But as more and more people got hurt around me, that became impossible. So I'd left for a new hole, until the same thing had happened. Now, I just didn't stay very long in one place, and that seemed to work.

"Can I see them?" Nash asked, his question a low murmur.

I frowned, but laid my arms on the table, wrist up. He'd already seen them. What could he...

I bit hard on my bottom lip the moment Nash's finger brushed over the outline of my left tat. He traced the entire image, his finger leaving behind a trail of fire on my skin. I'd nearly moaned at that first touch, and as long as I kept my teeth digging into my lip, I could hold back. I was glad for the table and the air conditioning in the small space. Even when it was cold outside, it was a refreshing temperature in here and kept my body from melting off the chair.

I wasn't sure what information he was gleaning, but I waited, too afraid to move, as he inspected both arms.

"And about last night?" he asked with no preamble. He'd just sat back and launched into more questions.

I scratched my head as I tried to arrange what happened into a shape that made a little more sense.

"The truth, Phin," Nash warned me. Had he seen I was about to lie? He'd proven himself extraordinarily observant. I wasn't told often that I showed my emotions so plainly, but he seemed to read every twitch my face muscles made.

"I can—well, when I... sometimes I... It can happen that I—"

Nash leaned over the tabletop, pressing his index finger over my mouth. "Start with Wyatt's leg. There'd been blood."

"I healed him," I said, staring at my hands as the room began to feel very small. It was as if the walls had shrunk to a size that could include only us two. "With my hands."

"Like massage therapy?"

I caught his gaze. My eyes stared into his, and I refused to blink. "No, not like that. I've—since the accident, I have been able to heal people. I can't cure someone who is sick or anything. My abilities can do nothing against cancer or a cold, but with injuries, accidents, I'm able to heal a person. If I get there in time." Because I wasn't a horrible person, I hadn't done a whole lot of experimenting, but I'd always healed those around me who got hurt, if I was able. These were the rules I'd gleaned from those times. Broken bones, cuts, bumps, bruises—I could handle all of that and had learned that, in most cases, any extra blood, bone, or skin present was reabsorbed into the body during the process. Handy, since I couldn't exactly rush in and heal people only for them to get up and see a pool of blood beneath them.

I waited for him to freak out or for his face to move at all. He looked frozen.

"Look, if you don't want to keep doing this now that you know, that's okay. I won't make you." I got up and reached for my jacket. "I understand."

"You clearly don't," he said, finally shaking from his stupor. "You're telling me that your hands can—that *you* can heal people who are hurt? Just like that? So Wyatt was more injured."

"His leg was badly broken. I was surprised he didn't howl more than he did."

Nash's upper lip twitched at that. "He's got some extra talents as well."

There wasn't disgust or fear in Nash's expression, but I didn't understand what I was seeing. He seemed... excited? I hadn't told him everything, but this felt like enough. I didn't want to tell him about the exchange, the pain I felt when I healed. That was my burden to bear. "I've never told anyone this, Nash. I always thought it would make a person run screaming the other way."

He smiled brightly. "I'm not running or screaming, but maybe it's for the best that you haven't told anyone. This sort of thing, people might want to use for their own benefit."

Obviously, I'd thought of that. But I'd always been less worried about becoming a commodity and more worried about what would happen to the other person once they knew. So why had I told Nash? It wasn't that I didn't care what happened to him. The opposite. Each second in his presence, I was falling harder for him. But he seemed so sturdy, unbreakable. Almost like he was the first person I'd met who I felt could handle the secret.

It looked like I might've been right.

"Mrs. Boxer," Nash said so suddenly I turned expecting to see the old woman behind me. "You healed her, didn't you?"

I ducked my head. "I did. Not all the way, just so it would stop hurting."

"Then why didn't you heal yourself?"

My head felt light, and I was sure my face was a pasty white. "It doesn't work like that." It had, once, and never again.

"You can't heal yourself?" His eyes narrowed, and his mouth turned down.

I shook my head and hoped he'd move to a different topic. But before we did, I needed to make something clear. I couldn't let Nash feel like this was all fun and games. "People get hurt around me, Nash. Like, a lot. The thing with your brother—I'm pretty sure that was my fault too, and I'm sorry."

"I hurt my brother, Phin. Walker-ball is horribly dangerous, and if you think that was even the first time one of us broke something while playing that game, you'd be wrong. You had nothing to do with it. Tell me you understand that." His tone lowered, the command sending a thrill through me that I didn't comprehend all the way.

"I understand," I mumbled.

Nash lifted my face with a finger under my chin and made me look at him. "You healed Wyatt. You didn't hurt him."

I licked my lips. "Okay." I couldn't say more without lying. I certainly didn't believe him.

Nash scowled, and I worried he'd push the issue until he stood suddenly. "Let's get out of here. I'll make Wyatt open early if he isn't already. We both need some real food."

In less than twenty minutes, I was at The Greasy Stump with a fizzy, sugary Coke, tracking Wyatt's movements through the bar as he brought us our fries.

"Do you have steak sauce?" I asked.

Wyatt's eyebrow's dipped into a line. "For French fries?"

"Get the man his steak sauce," Nash commanded, watching me with a small smile.

My mood had improved dramatically. I wanted to blame it all on the gym, but it had been the conversation in the gym that made me uncomfortable as well. Nash hadn't brought it up again. I hoped he wouldn't.

Wyatt returned with the bottle, and I twisted it open, upending the brown, tangy sauce in a pile in the corner. I was being considerate to Nash. Normally, I'd smother every morsel. "See," I said to Nash, holding up a fry. "I can eat food without cartoon characters on it."

Wyatt smirked and disappeared, returning a minute

later with a box. "Not so fast," he said, showing me the front that proclaimed the box was full of flash-frozen Idaho potatoes... with a picture of a cartoon potato next to the words.

"That doesn't count!"

Both brothers laughed. Seeing them side by side, it was too easy to tell them apart. Not only because of their different features and Wyatt's longer hair, but in their mannerisms. Both had a predatory edge to them, but if I had to assign them animals, I would've said Wyatt was more like a panther, smooth and sleek, while Nash was a lion: courageous, strong, and king of all he saw.

"I'm not sure what we should do now," Nash said, letting his head spin as he took in the rest of the place. "I expected there to be some *actual customers.*"

The place was empty, but in Wyatt's defense, Nash had forced him to unlock the doors.

"It's eleven in the morning, bro. You don't want to meet the people who—"

Just then, the bell over the door rang, and Wyatt's voice brightened. "Come on in, Tony! What took you so long?"

Tony was an older, wider gentleman who took a seat at the bar top and grunted. Wyatt understood that to mean he wanted a pint and set it down in front of him.

He seemed a nice enough fellow, but I didn't want to practice my flirting on him. "Maybe I can try on Wyatt?" I suggested.

Instantly, Wyatt appeared with a devilish smirk. "Did someone say they *need* me?" I wasn't sure if it was his longer hair or just his attitude that made him seem younger than Nash. Sillier and more approachable as well.

"No, we don't," Nash replied sharply. He looked from the gentleman at the counter and then back at me. "We'll table that lesson for next time."

"You don't have to," Wyatt insisted, sliding into the seat next to mine. "I don't mind."

Nash must have kicked his chair from under the table because there was a bang that made my fries jump, and then Wyatt's chair toppled to the side. He caught himself before he even looked like he was about to fall. "Fine! Jeez! I'm telling Nana that you—"

The phone at Nash's waist rang sharply, the tone of the ring making me feel like it was urgent call. He looked at the screen. "Shit. There's a fire at the old pumphouse..."

"That's next to pack lands," Wyatt said, all humor gone.

Pack lands? Did he mean like how people used to live in clans?

"It's big. They're worried it will spread through the forest. I have to go. They're calling us all in."

Outside, sirens wailed. "Go. I'll walk home."

"Or he can stay here with me," Wyatt said, leaning in and batting his eyes.

I grinned and rolled my eyes, but Nash didn't look happy. "Do you mind waiting in the car? You won't be in any danger," he added like he would personally see to it.

I hadn't realized that was an option. "I'd love to watch! From a safe distance, of course. People won't mind?"

"I'd like to see someone try to make you leave," Wyatt mumbled. He didn't look too put-out that his suggestions had all been turned down.

I followed Nash to the door, and he held it open for me to go through first. "See you at home," he called over his shoulder to Wyatt.

Before I could step fully out of the way onto the sidewalk, a cop car pulled up, the driver rolling down his window. "You get the call, Walker?" the cops said to Nash.

"Hey, Jake. Just now. We're heading up."

The officer's gaze flicked to me and back. "New fireman?"

"Something like that."

He nodded. "Need a ride to your car?"

We'd driven in his car from the gym to here. "Nah, we'll see you there."

We hurried to his vehicle, and I slipped in, buckling my seatbelt. We weren't in a firetruck, and there were no sirens, but I was still as excited as I'd been as a kid when firemen would whiz by on the street. The rush, the importance, knowing that life and death might linger in the balance—it was infectious, and I found myself as excited to see the scene as I was to keep hanging out with Nash. I knew there was a level of danger, but with Nash with me, it was like I was protected.

How was I supposed to ever walk away from this feeling?

7

NASH

By the time I made it on scene, Phin was vibrating with excitement. Until now, he hadn't given me the idea that this sort of thing excited him. In fact, knowing what I did now about his parents, I wouldn't have expected this sort of response. But I'd been unwilling to leave Phin with Wyatt.

I trusted Wyatt with my life. Phin's safety wasn't the issue. I just knew how persuasive my twin could be. I relied more on my charm and physical appeal, but Wyatt could sweet-talk a shark out of his supper. And Phin and I were still too new. There wasn't even a Phin and I yet. There was just a Phineas and a me.

"There they are!" he shouted with excitement, pointing through the windshield while Krat and Paster operated the water tanker and hose.

Jake Maslow, Walkerton's sheriff, was there, first having changed into his volunteer fireman gear. Most of the police doubled as fire personnel. We were too tiny of a town to have feuds between the two. If the fire did get out of hand and we needed more help, it would take time hauling and shipping everyone and everything in. It looked like they had the fire under control. I still parked and got into my gear, pointing out the safety perimeter to Phin before I rushed to the chief.

"Grab an ax and help the newbie clear out that brush."

The pumphouse looked like a lost cause. It hadn't been in use for decades anyway. But there were blackberries and other bushes growing in around it. Isolating the fire and removing possible fuel was my new priority.

I gave the new guy, Charles, a nod before getting to work. Krat and Paster had already soaked the outside of the pumphouse, and while I couldn't see any flames from inside, dark smoke billowed from every crack. Sheriff Maslow had one of the smaller foam extinguishers and used it to put out the smaller fires that had started around the original.

Without slowing down the task at hand, I checked on Phin every couple of minutes. He never tried to get any closer than the boundary I'd established, and after about fifteen minutes, I found I enjoyed knowing he was there, watching me work.

Maybe I should take off my shirt.

"Friend of yours?" Charles grunted. "He was at that party. Thanks for the invite, by the way."

I'd invited the guys from the station, and he'd come, but I wasn't going to point that out. "No problem. How's the transition? I imagine we're a smaller station than what you're used to." I spun my ax around, using the tapered end to hook a chunk of brambles and rip it from the ground.

"I like the change in pace. And the scenery can't be beat." He looked up into the forest and frowned, drawing my gaze.

He couldn't have seen the shifters skirting just out of sight, but he likely sensed them. I sensed, saw, and—now that the wind had changed direction—smelled them coming. Instantly, I searched for Phineas, finding him the same place he'd stood this whole time. He saw me looking and waved, before thinking twice about the motion and blushing.

He was so fucking adorable.

And I didn't want the pack anywhere near him.

I didn't think whoever was in the woods would come closer. They were probably just checking out the commotion. The pumphouse rode the boundary line. The Lynx River that separated the rest of the island from the pack side wound around at this section, cutting deeper into pack lands.

Continuing to work, I kept an eye on Phin, the shifters lurking in the trees, and the fire. The fire was almost completely out, and Charles and I had cleared out a sizable perimeter around the pumphouse. Sheriff Maslow had already finished his task and was returning to his car. While he was here, that was one less person watching over Walkerton so he often left as soon as the situation would allow.

Chief called Charles and me back a couple of minutes after the sheriff left. "Good job, you two. I'm glad you're getting a chance to work together finally."

I gave him a sharp nod, more eager to get Phin out of here than I was eager to get a pat on the head. "I'm sure we'll have plenty of chances to do the same again." I didn't so much dislike Charles. He seemed like an okay guy. He was older, closer to the chief's age than me or Paster or Krat.

I hurried toward Phin, but before I could get him back to the car, I knew the shifters had come closer. I smelled them and heard them. And when I turned, I saw them, strolling out with a purpose to their steps. I didn't recognize the young man, other than my animal recognizing his. He was a young black man, maybe in his early twenties. His hair was cut close, like a buzz cut, and he wore a white tank top that should've left him freezing. His jeans were muddy and stained. He had the muscular body of a shifter, but with dark, haunted eyes. How did the pack keep getting new members?

First Paul and now this guy, except this guy wasn't alone. There was a woman with him. She looked a few years older than him. Her clothes were as stained as his, and her eyes were wary. She stood behind the bigger guy.

"Where'd you come from?" the chief asked, but the two walked right by him, zeroing in on where I stood.

"We need your help. You're a fireman, right?" the guy asked.

"What's the problem, son?" the chief asked, coming closer.

The guy shook his head. "No, not you, *him*. We want his help." He pointed at me, and I bit back my growl.

This was just what I needed—some new fucking shifters who didn't understand that we all kept a low profile around here. The more he separated me from my crew, the more they would look at me as separate and then wonder why that was. I didn't doubt that he might have needed help, but he wanted me to help solely because he sensed I was like him. Already, Charles looked between me and them as if trying to figure out how we fit together.

"Please, my daughter..." the woman said.

"Did she say daughter?" Phin tugged the back of my jacket.

Fuck.

"Please, we're in a home just over the hill." The young man pointed back the way he came. "It's a five-minute walk. We've put out the fire, but..."

I didn't see any smoke on the horizon. Sure, it was only

five minutes, but it was a five-minute walk I shouldn't have had to take because the pack elders were responsible for caring for the pack. Unfortunately for this guy, the pack elders were my parents and Aver and Branson's. They were also the most manipulative, spiteful group of people I'd ever had the displeasure of knowing.

"My daughter is hurt," the woman whispered, receiving a sharp glare from the guy with her.

Dammit to hell! I stomped toward the engine, pulling out the first aid kit and a travel pack for when we hiked the forests in the summer. I remembered Phin and froze.

"I'll come with you," he said, like he was in my head. Coming to the opposite conclusions.

"Are you okay with this?" the chief asked. As far as they all knew, I'd grown up on the other side of the island and moved out when I was eighteen. Nothing more. The citizens on the human side of Walker County all believed the shifter side to be full of odd extremists or hermits, men and women who preferred living off the grid. Some of them thought the shifters were all in some weird cult—funnily enough, those people weren't too far away from the truth. "I can send Charles with you. Paster needs to get back to the station, and Krat is coming off a shift."

I shook my head. I didn't think these two would let anyone who wasn't a shifter near their problem. They were clearly new to this location, so they didn't know who to talk to in the pack. I'd go, see what was wrong, help anything I could, and then tell Paul that they had newcomers. I didn't want Phin coming with me, but it was better he be with me than wait in the forest. The guys wouldn't hang around much longer now that the emergency had been handled. "It's fine. I'll check it out and radio in if I think I need help."

The woman looked relieved while the younger man

stared me up and down. *You came for my help, buddy. Don't get territorial.*

The car was useless through the thick forest so Phin and I took off on foot. He skipped beside me while I trudged forward feeling like a bear with a thorn in my paw.

"I'll stay out of the way, I promise," he assured me in a whisper that he didn't know the two shifters in front of us had no problem hearing.

I nodded, unsure of how to reply. I couldn't warn him without him having a thousand more questions. He didn't seem at all worried that we'd willingly followed complete strangers into the woods only because they said they needed help. In a book on how not to die, not wandering away with strangers had to be somewhere in the first chapter.

I helped him balance on the rocks while the two shifters simply walked through the cold water. The river was only ankle-deep at the moment.

"There," the man said, pointing at the bottom of the hill we'd just crested. There was a small shack, no larger than the pumphouse had been. I spotted some charring on the outside wall near where it looked like they'd had a firepit.

"You live here?" Phin asked, his worried eyes finding me.

At that moment, our shock was the same. I knew things had gotten rocky with the pack, but not that the people were suffering this much.

"When did you get here?"

"Two days ago," the young man said. "We haven't been approached and weren't sure how..."

In my days on pack lands, there were scouts who were supposed to look out for this exact thing—shifters drawn to so many of us in one area. Some were just curious while passing through, others were looking for a new place to call home, and then a small few came to start trouble. I didn't think these two were here to start trouble, which meant they'd been overlooked, living on pack lands for days.

I also understood the young man's caution. In some packs, you were meant to wait to be addressed by someone higher up the pack pecking order. Not doing so could mean being thrown out or worse.

But they obviously needed help.

I reached for my phone. This couldn't wait.

"Hello?" Paul answered on the third ring.

"It's Nash. You have people near the pumphouse. You know, where you all saw smoke about an hour ago but did nothing to put it out?"

"Whoa, I've been inside Elder Delia's home working on her floor for hours."

"What?" I snarled, my fingers flinching, urging me to hang up.

"She's my pack sponsor, you know that," Paul said with a hushed tone. "I'll come out there right now with a welcome wagon. How many?"

I knew there were three at least. I had a feeling there were a few more people hiding inside that shack, and that wasn't just because I could see a tiny face peering at me through a hole in the siding. "Just bring who you can find." I hung up angry at myself, angry at Paul, angry at the pack.

"Is everything okay?" Phineas asked. I couldn't imagine what this all looked like from his point of view. If I'd brought him along to avoid questions, I'd done it for the wrong reasons.

"This shouldn't happen." I told him as much of the truth as I was able. "When we crossed the river, we crossed into..."

"The backcountry?" he suggested when it was clear I couldn't think of a word to call them.

"Something like that. These people have learned to live

in their own way, and sometimes more people come, drawn to their way of life here." I should've just told him the truth. I wanted to. But, as obsessed as I was with Phin's every breath, word, and motion, this wasn't just my secret. Exposing myself meant exposing Wyatt, Aver, and Branson. Now, that meant exposing Riley and Bran Jr. as well. I couldn't do that to them.

We were at the shack now. I tried to figure out what the small structure had ever been used for. I recalled a time before I was born when there had been a battle between packs. My understanding had been that our Walker County pack had stayed mostly out of the mayhem, protected by our isolation. But the pack had gone into alert all the same. Perhaps this was one of those huts they'd made to provide shelter, safety, or storage for supplies so we wouldn't lose everything in a single attack.

Now, it was breaking apart. The wood had long since splintered and cracked. No wonder they'd tried to build a fire so close to the outside wall; it was probably freezing. *This is Alpha Walker's responsibility.* Ever since Branson's father died, the role of pack Alpha had reverted to our grandfather. I'd known he didn't want the job. Now I knew he clearly wasn't up for it either.

"My daughter," the woman said, holding a girl around the age of five up for inspection.

Her long brown hair was braided back neatly, despite the dirt over her clothes and skin. It allowed me to see her burn clearly, red, shining, and blistering. Shifters already had enhanced healing, and that didn't change because she was a child. If her injury looked this bad now, she'd been burned badly.

"Set her down," I told her, knowing that the moment I suggested taking her to the hospital on the other side of the island, she would whisk her daughter away. "What's your name?"

The girl looked to her mom and then the young man. Both gave her a small nod. "Tanya." She squeezed the dirty stuffed animal that was in her arms. "This is Bonkers. He's Bonkers."

"Nice to meet you, Tanya and Bonkers. Can you tell me how you got hurt?"

Tanya ducked her head between her shoulders. "I was trying to help and make breakfast." She looked over at the scorched wall. "I burnt everything."

I nodded. "You really shouldn't play with fire. And never get near it without your parents around, okay?"

Tanya giggled. "Tutu isn't my dad. He's my uncle. He is bossy like a dad."

I smiled, appreciating the girl's spunk even when she had to be in pain.

Phin lingered back, true to his word. But I felt his worry and concern. There was a tiny wrinkle forming between his eyes, and I had an idea of what he wanted to do. But he couldn't do it here, to these people. Word would get around. After everything that happened with Riley, the shifters would be too interested in Phin.

"We came when we heard about the blessed one," the woman mumbled as I applied first aid.

Case in fucking point.

The shack door opened, revealing an old woman with dark brown, wrinkled skin and a shock of bright white hair.

"How many of you are there here?" I asked Tanya's mother.

"Only us four. There more, but my husband—" She took a deep breath. "We're the ones that made it out."

Fuck, fuck, fuck. I couldn't ask more, even if I wanted to know more.

Behind me came the sound of tires rolling over an overgrown road. We all turned as a van broke through the brush that had grown over the seldom-used gravel road.

"Tyrone," Tanya's mother said sharply. Her voice shook.

I straightened to stand beside her. "It's okay...?"

"Denise."

"It's okay, Denise. I called them. This is Paul. He's with..." I looked over my shoulder, noticing Phin distracting the little girl with some rocks he'd found. "He's with the pack," I whispered.

"Is your human mate the blessed one?" Denise asked.

"No," I said, so sharply Tutu—Tyrone—came over. "He isn't involved in any of this. Just forget you saw him."

The van stopped, and the driver's door opened. I was about to yell at Paul when he rushed around to the sliding van door and opened it, revealing Delia Walker on the other side. She was an elder and, as such, responsible for offering her help, but she was also an evil, conniving bitch who had sent a killer after Riley. Branson, her son, had hurt her in the way he knew she'd feel the most. Money.

But she didn't look like she was scraping to make ends meet. Her cream-colored pantsuit looked ridiculous in the middle of the muddy forest. "Welcome to Walker County," she boomed like she'd rehearsed the line in the van on the way over. "Grab your belongings and come with me, please. We will find you suitable housing, food, and some clean clothes."

Denise breathed a sigh of relief that Tyrone didn't share. He was staring at Paul, judging his every molecule from the looks of it.

With Delia here, that meant I needed to get Phin out

fast. He was still with the girl, and my heart leapt into my throat when I looked back at him, lifting his hand from the girl's face. Her skin was still shining from the burn cream, but the blisters were completely gone, as was much of the redness.

I grabbed my bag and shoved everything back into it.

"Nash Walker," Delia said with that same fake friendly tone. "I am surprised to see you here."

Liar. She'd probably heard Paul receive a call and made him tell her who was on the other end. *This* was why I couldn't trust Paul. And nice as he seemed and as supportive of Riley he was, he'd sworn his loyalty to the pack, just like this group would have to do before much longer. That was the trade-off: become one of us and get our help. These people needed that help, clearly. Tyrone looked like he might do okay on his own, but he wouldn't leave his family behind. I was curious about the type of pack they left behind, but with Phin and now Delia here, my hands were tied.

"Good thing I'm leaving," I replied, tugging Phin to a standing position.

"Who's your friend?" Delia asked.

I searched for Paul and found him helping Tyrone load their backpacks into the van.

"No o—"

"Tanya!" Denise shrieked. She dropped to her daughter and cupped her *healed* face. "Tyrone, look! Mama, look!"

I looped my arm around Phin's waist and lifted him so that his feet just barely skimmed the ground. He gave me a curious look but stayed quiet.

"I knew it. He is blessed," Denise said with happy tears pouring from her eyes.

I felt each of the stares fall on us. My heart pounded as

my limbs filled with an urge to protect and shield Phin from all of this. I'd let him come. I'd brought this danger on him.

"Is there something I should know?" Delia asked. She already knew Riley was the one they called blessed. And she knew this wasn't Riley.

She knew too much already. The kid was healed, and the people would get food and shelter—even if they did get it from a pit viper.

I ignored Delia's question and continued to carry Phin out of sight. I didn't let him walk on his own until we'd crossed the river.

"Nash? Nash? Your fingers are too tight. It's hurting me." I stepped away, letting a foot of air come between us.

"I'm sorry. I shouldn't have brought you. To any of this." My hands shook. This wasn't over. I'd handled that whole thing in the worst way possible, all but ensuring everyone would have more questions. Denise would tell every pack member she met today about the human mate who had healed her child.

Never mind the fact that Phin wasn't my mate. He was a guy I couldn't stop thinking about, who wanted me to teach him how to flirt with *someone else*. My fist slammed into the nearest tree, making the trunk tremble as leaves fell down around me. *And now he thinks you're a psycho with anger problems.*

"Nash?" Phin's voice shook.

"Please don't be afraid of me," I whispered harshly, staring at the smear of blood I'd left on the bark. "I get why you are—that was inexcusable—but please don't be. I made a mistake today."

"With me?"

"Yes."

Phin said nothing for several seconds. I was too

ashamed to look at him. "I understand. Let me at least heal your hand, though. And I guess I'd appreciate a ride back into the city, but you don't have to take me to my apartment. I can walk."

I spun around, my hands outstretched like vending machine claws. "What? No. I don't want you leaving."

"You just said..."

"I shouldn't have brought you *there*," I said, looking back the way we'd come. "I don't like the way that place makes me feel, Phineas. Does that make any sense?"

"It makes a lot of sense. I can't claim to really understand. That lady from the van seemed nice."

"She isn't."

"Okay, I'll believe you."

My lungs thawed a little, letting me breathe more normally. I knew I'd done damage to Phin and myself today, but it wasn't enough for him to stop trusting me. As low as I felt, that fact was everything. "It's complicated, Phineas. I lived over there, and I drank the Kool-Aid right along with everyone else. I held a position of power, when I belonged to the pack."

"Like royalty?"

"Yeah, something like that. It came with a price, though, one myself and my cousins were asked to pay."

"And you didn't?" Phin guessed.

I hadn't. When our parents had come to me and my cousins, explaining that since we were all eligible to become the next Alpha, we had to fight to the death to find the worthy one among us, my first reaction *hadn't* been repulsion. I wasn't like Branson or Aver, who refused from the first second. I'd thought about it. I'd imagined myself as victor. I was going to find a way to save Wyatt and keep him as an adviser or something. But in my mind, I'd made no such provisions for Branson and Aver.

This was my big secret, why I wouldn't touch Riley. My parents had asked me to become a monster, and for the span of a minute, I'd *wanted* to be. Ruling the packs meant being worshiped. It meant having people obey your every command while being looked up to by every member in the pack. I'd been such a spoiled little shit that I'd thought I wanted that.

"I didn't, eventually," I said. "I'm not the best version of me when I'm around *them.*"

"Then let's go," Phin said like the solution was really that simple. "Some guy tried to feed me poison for breakfast, and now I'm starving."

I jogged forward to catch up. I knew I hadn't felt the full ramifications of this day, but for the moment, I'd do just as Phineas suggested and move on.

8

PHINEAS

REGISTERED_COMPANION: *Did you see his dick?*

I choked on my coffee, forcing the liquid down my throat instead of letting it out of my mouth. I'd ruined too many laptops that way, and now my gag reflex was top notch.

I'd considered putting that info on my Grindr profile. However, not only would it be misleading information, but I'd checked when I'd moved to Walkerton. There wasn't a match that wasn't at least a ferry away. I could imagine the conversation.

No gag reflex, eh?

Heck yeah, I deepthroat pure, one hundred percent Colombian roast.

GoblinKing: *We were on a call, nothing sexual.*

Okay, yes, I felt a little important being able to type the words *we were on a call*. I didn't want to be a fireman, but it was still a boyhood dream come to life. Plus, this was all fodder I could use for my next book. Already, I imagined a handsome fireman and the plucky young baker with a mystery to solve.

ChuckShurley: *Is that legal? Are you sure this man is a real fireman?*

Xcept4Bunnies: *Who cares? He sounds smoking. Tell me the swallow story again. Real slow this time.*

She added an emoji of an eggplant and then a sweet potato.

ChuckShurley: *If he's putting you in dangerous situations, you need to be careful around him.*

I frowned. Chuck was always the most cautious one of us. He claimed it was because he was older, wiser, and knew how life worked. But he wasn't normally this negative.

Maybe he wasn't being negative, just realistic. I was the one who had tried not very hard to not have a crush on Nash. Seeing him in action yesterday, arriving on scene and helping where he was needed most, and then how he'd been with that little girl—every moment with Nash had shown me I didn't know who the man was at all. But I liked what I was learning. He didn't feel dangerous, either. The stuff with his family was weird.

But in areas like this, tucked away, people had to rely on each other. It made sense for them to develop a social structure that applied only here. At the same time, I knew there was something that Nash wasn't telling me. Maybe he just needed more time.

Except time wasn't something I had in spades. Mrs. Boxer, Wyatt, and now the little girl had been hurt. I believed Nash when he said Wyatt's injuries were because of the game and not my presence, but it still felt like I was responsible. The injuries would just continue until it became blindly obvious I was the cause. I tried to leave before that point, for other's safety and my own.

It wouldn't be fair to me or Nash to try to become better friends.

GoblinKing: *Maybe you're right. Not about him being dangerous, but that I should limit our time together.*

Xcept4Bunnies: *Whoa, how'd we get to that decision? Dammit, Chuck! Our boy needs to get laid!*

ChuckShurley: *Can't get laid if you're dead.*

I rolled my eyes. That was a little dramatic. I wasn't the one in danger—it was everyone else.

Clearly, I'd gotten caught up in the excitement. Being with Nash seemed to have that effect on me. I'd forgotten that I wasn't just some guy in a new town looking for friends.

Registered_Companion: *If you're done hanging out with him, you should at least return the clothes he gave you.*

That was actually a really reasonable response, for Reg. I side-eyed the comment, looking for her angle.

Xcept4Bunnies: *Yeah, Reg is right. You need to return the clothes. Put them in his hands. It's the only way.*

I frowned.

ChuckShurley: *I don't think you should...*

Before I could reply, Bun and Reg leapt on top of him with their words, demanding to know why I shouldn't. That turned into them accusing Chuck of not taking their advice seriously because they were women, and then Reg just started posting Maya Angelou quotes.

I liked the quotes, but now I had a choice to make.

Whether I liked it or not, I'd made the choice with my heart by liking Nash too much. This had been my decision, the flirting lessons, but it took me seconds into our first one to forget Zach existed entirely. It wasn't about my crush on Hot Neighbor, if I could even claim to still have one. Nash didn't have a hard time remembering me no matter where we bumped into each other.

I'd started this, and now it was time to do the responsible thing and finish it.

———

THE WALKERTON STATION wasn't a long walk from my apartment. Nothing was a long walk within city limits. It might have taken an ark to get here, but the walkability score once in Walkerton was through the roof.

I spotted the station at the end of the street. The wide bay doors were closed, acting more like a display case for the gleaming red trucks within. I didn't see Nash's vehicle. I didn't even know if he was expected at the station today. After deciding the most mature course of action would be to return the clothes he'd let me borrow, I'd quickly chickened out, looking for any option that didn't include telling Nash to his face that he didn't have to teach me anything more.

I was probably making too big of a deal about this. Maybe Nash would be relieved that he'd been let off the hook.

I peered inside the main door. There wasn't an office or anything, just a small empty lobby space. My fingers shook as I pushed the door open. "Hello?"

I heard someone moving around further in, maybe in the garage area.

"Nash?" I hugged the bundle of clothes to my chest. "Is someone here?"

"Nash isn't here," a man said. I spun around with goosebumps on my arms.

"You scared me." I patted my chest right over my pounding heart. I recognized the fireman from the day before. He wasn't the chief, but the one who had worked side by side with Nash.

He stuck his hand out. "Sorry about that. Name is Charles. I'm new here."

"New to being a fireman?" I asked. He had some gray peppering the temples of his black hair. I always enjoyed it when people discovered their calling late in life. It gave me hope.

"No, just new to Walker County. I was a fireman in Monterey where I lived."

"No way! California? I grew up in Monterey!" For as popular of a tourist spot that it was, I didn't meet too many people who had spent a lot of time there. Way out here, we were only two states away, but it felt like the edge of the world.

"Really? It's nice to meet you, Phin."

I frowned, and he added. "I overheard your name at the party, and then yesterday."

He was at Riley's too. Now I remembered where I'd seen him. "Yeah, definitely. Nice to meet you."

His green eyes sparkled. There was something familiar about the shade, like grass at the beginning of spring. He was older, maybe in his fifties. His blue Walker County FD shirt strained over his chest and biceps. A silver fox if there ever was one, except he wasn't quite silver yet, just going that way.

"What brought you here?" he asked

That was a hard question to answer. Thankfully, I had a script. "I went to college in San Jose and stayed there for a bit after graduation. Since then, I've been looking for a place to settle. Spend some time in Sacramento, a bit in San Francisco—before it became clear I wasn't rich enough. I'm a bit of a nomad."

Charles sat down at the black leather couch in the lobby area, and I copied him, suddenly exhausted. This was how I normally felt around people, like every word took Herculean effort. But Charles was just trying to be nice. Clearly, Nash wasn't here.

"I understand you there. Monterey was just as bad by the time I left."

"What prompted your move? This place is pretty different from what you're probably used to."

Charles laughed good-naturedly. "Extremely. My daughter convinced me."

"Oh really? How old is she?" He hadn't had anyone with him at Riley's party. But then, I guessed it would be weird to go to a party with your kid.

"She's about your age, actually. And no, she didn't come with me." He laughed. "Maybe I should've taken that as a sign?"

I smiled right as the door opened and Nash walked in. His hair was wet, and he had a gym bag slung over his shoulder.

My belly flopped at the sight of him, and I stood, forgetting the clothes I'd been hugging. They fell, and I bent over, scrambling to pick them up.

"What's going on here?" Nash asked. He dropped his gym bag and came to my side, looking at the clothes with a wary gaze.

"I needed to talk to you," I rushed to say. "But, um, I..." I looked to Charles. I hadn't planned on having an audience when I did this, and it was throwing me off.

"Say no more..." Charles stood, throwing his hands up in front of his body. "Two's company, three's a crowd. I've got some stuff to do before we switch shifts anyway." He disappeared through the door that led to the garage.

Nash watched him go, prompting me to do the same. When he was gone, he turned to me. "What did you need to tell me? And why do you have those?" He fingered the hem of the shirt I held. What had I come here to do? Suddenly basking in his presence, I couldn't remember.

"Charles is from Monterey," I blurted, buying time.

"Really? I didn't know that. Is that why you came down? Why do you have the clothes I gave you?"

Unlike me, Nash couldn't wait to get to the point. Good. This was good. I should take his lead and get it over with. "I need to give them back." I thrust them toward him, but he didn't take them from me.

"No you don't," Nash said, pushing the clothes and my hands back toward me. "They were a gift. You might want them for our next lesson."

"I don't think we should do any more lessons."

Nash froze, his hands clenched, falling to his sides. "Why?" he asked right before an alarm rang loudly. "Shit."

"An emergency?" I asked.

"Yeah, I'm on shift. I've got to go. Keep the clothes, Phineas. We aren't done."

But we had to be. Not because I wanted it, but because this was the safer, kinder option.

Charles ran by, having changed into his gear. "Are you coming?" he asked Nash.

"Right there," he barked back before turning to me. "I mean it. Take the clothes with you. They're yours. I'll call you later, okay?"

"I—"

Nash frowned. "I have to go," he whispered.

"Go, it's fine. Everything is fine. Go." If I kept him here arguing over a pair of shorts and a shirt, then people might really get hurt, and it would absolutely be my fault.

He hurried into the garage, his gym bag forgotten. The bay doors had already opened, and I went out to the sidewalk, waving bye like an idiot. Nash gave me a short, worried wave through the window before speeding down the street.

I'd come to do the right thing, gotten confused, and now I didn't know what had happened. But I knew Nash wasn't going to let me move on quite so easily.

My biggest question now was why?

9

NASH

I couldn't stop thinking about Phin. I'd been pulled away on a call. A kid had gone missing out by the docks. We found him before having to call the Coast Guard and returned him to his parents, but by the time I'd made it back to the station, it was dark.

And I didn't know what I would say to Phin anyway. In an ironic twist, he'd approached me to learn how to flirt, yet I had no clue how to let him know that I wanted something more.

I'd gotten up that morning without a clue as to what to do. Went on my run without a clue. Showered without a clue. And now I was in the kitchen, with no idea what to do.

I heard the baby gurgle and jumped from the table at the chance to distract myself from my dilemma. I wasn't accustomed to not knowing what to do, especially in matters of love. Besides, Riley had been up since around two in the morning with the baby. Branson had taken the early shift, but he needed to be able to operate heavy machinery today, so Riley had taken over to give his mate time to sleep. And

Bran Jr. had decided he'd gotten enough sleep for his lifetime.

I found Riley asleep on the couch and Bran Jr. on his mat, babbling at the sheep-and-cloud mobile spinning over his head. Riley's mouth opened as he snored deeply. He was kind of cute. Not adorable in the way Phineas was, but cute like a pug with its wrinkly face and booger bubbles.

I bent down and scooped Bran Jr. up. His little mouth turned up in a baby smile as his dark eyes watched me with a knowing gleam. Were all babies so wise when they were born? Looking into that chocolate brown gaze, I felt like I could find the answers to the universe if I just stared hard enough.

A new warmth and rumbling vibration against my palm beneath his diaper told me that the answer to my immediate universe was to find a fresh diaper. We'd transformed part of the living room into a second nursery so Riley wouldn't feel stuck in the bedroom at all hours. With five adults and a baby, we were looking at constructing an addition to the house sooner rather than later.

Funny how the idea of moving out never occurred to any of us. It had been the four of us for so long. Then Branson brought in Riley, and it felt like that had been how we'd lived all those years. He fit in seamlessly. Sometimes, it would have been nice to have more privacy. But how could I be around to help with the little things if I had my own place?

Nana was right about that. This was my pack, and we would stick together until we couldn't.

I set Bran Jr. on the changing table and prepped my materials, checking the clock before I began. My moves were fast and efficient, and from unbuttoning the first button to snapping it back closed, fifty-four seconds had passed.

Ha!

That was a new record. Faster than Aver's time of fifty-six seconds.

No one would believe me, but I would know.

I brought baby Bran with me, setting him in his chair while I washed my hands. I hefted his bouncer to the center of the kitchen table so we could talk face to face, like gentlemen.

"He likes me, Bran. I know he does."

Bran gurgled and drooled. As the first baby that I'd ever met born from a man, he was unique. Nana claimed *blessed* pregnancies had occurred in the past, but there wasn't a lot of documentation, and what she did have was all hand-written and anecdotal. No one had ever heard of it. We knew Bran Jr. was capable of shifting, but after his first shift at birth, he'd remained in his human newborn form. That was lucky. We'd have a much bigger problem hiding what he was if he kept transforming into a puppy. The story we gave people was that he was a son of a tragically deceased relative. I knew it bothered Branson not to be able to publicly claim his offspring, but that didn't change him being an amazing father. Better than any I had, anyway.

Maybe Branson remembered more of Patrick—his father and the former Alpha Walker. From what I remembered and had been told, he'd been the best of the elders. The only alpha out of three sons. He'd had a clear path to the top of the pack.

I sometimes wondered what our lives would've been like if he hadn't died. None of us cousins would have been in the running for becoming the next Alpha. I'd probably still be an asshole.

More of an asshole.

"But I think he was trying to break up with me. I don't know. I've never been broken up with."

Bran farted loudly and then grinned.

"You're right. You've never been broken up with either. We're both perfect male specimens."

The rev of the engine pulling up outside sounded like Wyatt's. He hadn't come home the night before, something that wasn't all that unusual for him. He had a small apartment in his bar that he sometimes crashed in or where he took dates. Judging from the overwhelming scent of cologne, I would've guessed he was coming back from a hookup.

"There you are. I noticed Riley alone in there," Wyatt said. He'd showered, but the cologne lingered on his clothes, which were the same ones he'd left the house in the day before. "What are you doing with Bran?"

"Just explaining who his favorite uncle is."

"Ha!" Wyatt barked. He lifted Bran Jr.'s hand, pretending they were doing a complicated secret handshake while the baby's hand just flopped around. "We're already close. He already knows."

"Hot night?" How long had it been since I'd dated? Days? It felt like years since a hand had touched Mr. Nash, my downstairs neighbor, that wasn't my own.

"Enjoyable. What about you?" Wyatt's eyebrow arched. He wasn't just asking to make small talk—he was curious.

I growled and shook my head.

"Phinster won't give up the goods?"

"Don't talk about him like that," I snapped, my claws growing without my telling them to.

"Whoa there, cowboy. I think Phin is a great guy. He seemed nice. He's got killer hands. You know, we haven't talked about the party, but I think there was something more wrong with my leg, and then Phin came over and just, like, snapped it into place. No more pain." Wyatt's eyes narrowed, and I worried he was going to guess Phin's secret. I told Wyatt everything, but this wasn't my secret to tell. "Is he... a massage therapist? You've been sitting on a man with magic hands for this long without bringing him around?" Wyatt rolled his shoulders like he was working out an ache.

I shared a conspiratorial look with Bran Jr.. "Something like that."

"You can tell me all the juicy details while I make something to put in my stomach. You hungry?"

I shrugged. "I could eat."

Wyatt's head disappeared in the fridge as he rummaged for supplies. He pulled out bacon and a carton of eggs, arranging his materials on the counter. "It was a wild night last night," Wyatt said, slapping bacon on a sheet pan before throwing it in the oven. "You should have been there. You know the Lanser's oldest son graduated law school. He came back last night to celebrate."

"And you helped the celebration continue into the wee hours?"

Wyatt cocked up his right shoulder before letting it drop. "I do what I can. Besides, we might need a lawyer some day. It's good to have one I already have *experience* with."

Under those rules, we were set with any legal, mechanical, medical, business, and hospitality issues. Between the two of us, Wyatt and I'd had many *experiences*. Was it strange that I hadn't thought of a single conquest since rescuing Phin?

I didn't want any more experiences.

And that thought alone should have had me running in

the opposite direction. Maybe I should've let Phin go when he'd wanted to.

A growl sounded low in my chest, and the baby's eyes darted my way curiously. He didn't look afraid but intrigued. Or he was trying to impart some of his baby wisdom on me, and I was too dumb to understand his nonverbal language. "I don't know what to do, Wyatt. Phineas seems under my spell one minute and immune to my charms the next. I lost my temper in front of him, something I never do. That's probably why he was in such a rush yesterday to put me behind him."

Wyatt didn't look away from his egg mixture. "Why did you lose your temper?"

I'd yet to tell anyone about my run-in with the pack. I told Wyatt about the call and then the shifters in the forest. When I got to the part where Delia showed up with Paul, he flicked the whisk out of the bowl on accident.

"Paul is too nice of a kid to be sponsored by Delia."

"So he should ask our parents? Aver's? There isn't a great option."

Wyatt grunted and returned to his task while I made silly faces at the baby.

"What do you think she'll do? Phin is important to you, but there's no reason he has to be important to Delia."

That depended on what Denise ended up telling the rest of the pack. Maybe they'd decide that the girl hadn't been that hurt in the first place. Shifters healed quickly on their own already, though nothing like what Phineas was capable of. It didn't take very long to realize why Delia would be so interested in Phineas if she did find out. Like Riley, he could be used as a tool.

Unlike Riley, Phineas had managed to keep his skill a secret.

"You better tell me whatever it is that's making you make that face." Wyatt spun away from the stove toward me. "Or you're not getting any food."

I considered putting him in a headlock and showing him what would happen if he tried to keep it from me. He must have recognized that look too because he smirked. "Try it. I've been itching for a good scuffle. I have to pull my punches at the bar."

Bran Jr. let out a loud gurgle.

"You've been spared by the baby," I said. "And you won't have customers for long if you keep hitting them."

Wyatt didn't look very bothered by that idea either. He didn't seem bothered by a whole lot. I envied that about him, almost as much as I mourned my ability to do the same. My chill had thawed the moment I'd held Phin in my arms.

"Do you still chat online?" No sooner had I asked the question did I wish I hadn't.

Wyatt made a sharp hissing sound, reminding me of the brakes in a large vehicle or a bus. "I don't. Gave that up when I discovered it was easier to get laid with the person right in front of ya."

Was that why Phineas was so drawn to it? My lip flipped upward in a quiet snarl. If Phin was looking for someone to have sex with from the internet, it would be me. "Would you know how? If I knew where to find him."

"Where to... You mean Phin? He chats? I bet he's kinky."

"He isn't kinky." I bit out the words.

"I really hope you aren't talking about Bran," Riley said, rubbing his eyes with a yawn. "Sorry about that. He was asleep, and I thought I'd wake up when he made a noise. What good are these new shifter senses if I don't hear my own baby wake up?" He leaned in, his nostrils flaring. "I can tell you've been changed, though. And recently. Thanks for that."

"Don't worry about it. You can go take a nap if you want," I offered. "Unless you're hungry."

"Starved." Riley sat down. His timing proved impeccable. Wyatt pulled the bacon out of the oven, portioning a few slices as well as some scrambled eggs.

He separated the rest between two more plates, handing me mine with a fork. It wasn't fancy, but it was greasy and filling—just like his early morning customers would want.

"Who were you two talking about?" Riley asked.

"Phineas," Wyatt blabbed.

I felt Riley's stare on me but I was glaring at Wyatt.

"Phin seems like a sweet guy," Riley said around a bite of bacon.

I bristled at the implication. "And?"

"And you go through dates faster than Bran goes through diapers."

"Junior or senior?" I asked.

The baby made a soft noise, almost like a growl.

I peered into the bouncer. "Did he...?"

"Don't mean-talk his papa," Riley said with a voice as sweet as syrup. He lifted Bran Jr. on his lap, holding him while he ate.

"Look, Phineas is... special. Really special, but it doesn't matter because he tried to break up with me yesterday."

"You're together?"

"No, not together. But he asked me to... help him, and I agreed, and now he doesn't seem to want my help or to even be around me anymore. I don't know. He came by yesterday right when a call came in. I know he frequents GeekGab, and I might actually also have his login information."

"I'm not going to ask how," Riley said.

"Neither am I, but because I don't care." Wyatt returned from the other room with his laptop and set it on the table where we could all see the screen. He'd already navigated to the GeekGab homepage. "You need a chat ID."

"What's wrong with Nash Walker?" I asked.

"Oh nothing, if you want to seem like a grandpa and let Phineas know who you are a mile away. What's his chat ID?"

"GoblinKing." I hadn't opened the app again since that first day, but I remembered his name.

Riley frowned. "I wonder why he chose that?"

I didn't offer an answer despite the fact that I'd spent more time than I wanted to admit researching Phin's name. The best idea I had yet was that in fiction, many goblin kings were cursed, just like Phin had mentioned at the gym. Just like Riley had thought he was. This wasn't the first time I'd found myself comparing Riley and Phin. I also saw Wyatt's point. I couldn't be *me* online. That was the point. Who was I supposed to be? "Is there an option to just have them assign me a name?"

"Probably," Wyatt said. "But then I'd miss out on the fun. Why don't we go with the obvious—WolfBoy?"

"WolfMan, you mean."

Wyatt smirked. "That's the part you have a problem with?" He tapped the keyboard and frowned. "Both are taken anyway. You've got to think wider."

"What about Walker1234?" Riley suggested while preparing Bran Jr. a bottle.

Wyatt shook his head. "Taken."

"And if I can't be Nash Walker, I probably shouldn't be any version of my name."

"Try BuckLondon," Riley said.

"Is that a porn star?" Wyatt asked.

Riley covered the baby's ears. "No, it's the name of—you know what, never mind, yes. It's a porn star."

I didn't think that was true, but I was already frustrated with the entire process, and we'd just started. Why did it have to be so difficult to talk to Phin?

Wyatt took over on the computer, clicking and typing. "Okay, what's his server?"

I didn't have any idea what he was asking.

Wyatt sighed and rolled his eyes. "Give me your phone."

I passed it over while regretting ever bringing any of it up. Not because I wasn't still confused about what to do to keep Phin in my life, but because the situation was speeding out of my control. But, before I could put a stop to anything, Wyatt spun the laptop back around. "You're in, lover boy."

"What do I do?" I asked as Wyatt set the computer in front of me.

Riley stood behind me, feeding the baby his bottle as he swayed from foot to foot. "Say hello."

"Type anyone DTF?" Wyatt said.

"I know what that means, dic—" I looked back at the baby. "*Wyatt*. I just don't know this internet stuff." The chat room was much more intimidating on Wyatt's larger screen. "Crap, I think that one's talking to me."

Registered_Companion: *Hey new face. How'd you stumble in here?*

"What does she mean?"

"Because the server isn't a popular one. It wasn't password-protected, though. That's on them. They probably want to know how you found them. Say you were just passing through."

I thought the words over, arranging them in every configuration I could think of, trying to come up with a way that it was dirty. When I couldn't, I typed the message out and pressed send.

ChuckShurley: *This is a private server.*

I frowned. Who the hell did that dick think he was?

GoblinKing: *Don't be so unfriendly, Chuck. It's been just us for a while. I, for one, welcome new blood.*

"That's Phin! That one is Phin." I beamed while pointing at the screen. "See, he wants me here."

ChuckShurley: *You know what they say. Four's company, five is overcrowded.*

Xcept4Bunnies: *Literally no one says that.*

"That Chuck guy doesn't seem to like you," Riley said with a frown.

He didn't. Not that I cared, but I didn't know what I was doing here. I couldn't only talk to Phin, but he was the only reason I was there.

"This is useless." I closed the lid and reached for my phone before I lost my nerve. It rang three times before Phin picked up.

"Hello?"

"Phin, it's Nash. We're meeting tomorrow. Be ready, early."

"Nash, I—"

"Be ready," I barked and then hung up the phone like a coward. I didn't look at Riley or Wyatt, though I felt their amusement as I inhaled the rest of my food, dropped the dish in the sink, and stomped to my room.

But not before I heard Riley's joking whisper, "They grow up so fast, don't they?"

Yeah, okay, I was acting like a hormonal teen. I also didn't like that Phineas had this part of him that was obviously important but that I completely didn't understand. I knew how I felt when he was with me, though, and how awful it felt to be away from him. And for as confusing as he'd been, I thought he felt the same. He was scared of something, but he didn't need to be. I'd protect him from the world.

I stomped into the bathroom and splashed water over my face, staring at my scruffy reflection. I needed a shave, and then tomorrow, I'd prove to Phin that the safest place for him was in my arms.

10

PHINEAS

Nash called again to specify we should meet at the coffee shop. Then he called once more to make sure I had a way of getting *to* the coffee shop.

He'd seemed odd. I thought he was angry about what happened at the station. Maybe he didn't want me at his place of work without his permission and I'd overstepped my bounds? But he also wasn't shy. If I had irritated him, he would tell me. Wouldn't he?

With all my unanswered questions, I was a bundle of nerves by the time I got to the cafe.

I spotted Nash through the shop windows from down the block. His dark head was down, looking at something on the table. Watching him without his knowledge sent a secret thrill through me, like I'd seen something I wouldn't normally be privy to. His face lifted as if his name had been called, and our eyes locked. My knees buckled, and I stumbled. Catching myself, I gave him a shaky smile.

Even the air between us felt different: thicker, more charged. Had I ruined everything by stopping by the station unannounced? More importantly, didn't I want to ruin everything? Leaving Nash would be easier if he didn't look at me the way he did now with that knowing sexy smirk and tight jawline that I just wanted to lick.

Now that I was at the cafe door, about to enter into the same enclosed space with him, I couldn't remember why I'd ever wanted to stop seeing him.

Nash waved me over, indicating a second coffee cup sitting at his table. I wondered what he'd ordered for me.

"Hey," I said, giving him a wide, round wave. "Thanks for..." I had been going to thank him for meeting me, but he'd called me. My brain blanked. "...being here."

Nash grinned, and it did wicked things to my body. I'd started tingling at my first glimpse of him, and that wasn't stopping. Every time I saw Nash, it felt like I was witnessing his physical perfection and rugged charm for the first time.

"I called you. Thank *you* for being here." His words sounded like they held more meaning than simple gratitude. Was he teasing me? Something seemed different about the way he watched me. He was always a big, opposing presence, but this time, he seemed more aware of it than ever.

Truthfully, he hadn't given me the choice to decline when he'd called. I wasn't going to bring that up now. I was too busy being ecstatic that I was with him again. I sat down and eyed the paper cup.

"It's coffee, nothing weird going on," Nash said with a smile. "I had them put in a dash of cream on a hunch."

"That's perfect, thank you." I reached for the cup, glad to be doing something familiar. In the sea of uncertainty I jumped in whenever I was around Nash, doing this normal, everyday task grounded me. But I didn't know why he'd asked me here, so even after I swallowed the comforting, rich flavor, I had no idea what to say. "So..."

"I thought we'd continue your lessons," Nash said

suddenly. "After all, you fulfilled your portion of our bargain. You told me what I wanted to know."

"You gave me a lesson," I mumbled. It hurt hearing that he'd called me solely to fulfill his part of our bargain. He was only here out of a misguided sense of duty. "We're even."

His forehead wrinkled with a scowl. "We most certainly are not *even*." He flexed and leaned back, hooking his hands behind his head. His elbows stretched out on either side of him like wings. He wasn't in anyone's way, but he had an air about him that demanded to be accommodated. "I didn't even teach you a fraction of what I know."

If he was worried I wasn't appropriately impressed by his skills in seducing objects of his affection, then he worried for no reason. If I was honest, I'd confess that it was never about learning to flirt. None of this was. I'd pretended the silly crush I had on Zach was the reason, but really, I wanted to be around Nash in any way possible. At least he didn't seem aware of my crush. I couldn't handle the rejection on top of the ridicule I'd feel if I thought about him joking about me with his real friends.

I brought my coffee cup to my lips, speaking before I took a sip. "And I didn't tell you everything about me, so, like I said, we're even."

Nash sat straight, bringing his arms down from his relaxed position. His eyes narrowed on my face. "What didn't you tell me?"

Whoa. In a snap, he'd gone from casual to focused. If I could bottle just a fraction of his intensity, I'd never have a problem attracting a man again. It was intoxicating to be looked at like you were the most important thing in the world.

I didn't want it to ever stop.

"Sorry I dropped in at your work. I hope you got to your call okay."

Nash shook his head. "It's fine. Come by whenever. Now what didn't you tell me?"

I shrugged. There was plenty I wanted to share. It wasn't normally so difficult for me to keep my curse to myself, but Nash made me want to come clean about *everything*.

"No, no, you don't get to shrug and be coy. Unless you're using flirting tip number seven, which is to shrug and act coy."

I snorted. "I'm not using any tip, Nash. And I appreciate the time you've spent so far. But don't feel like you have to. I'll be moving on soon and—"

"Where are you going?" Nash asked with that same intense, furrowed brow. "For how long?"

I leaned back. Did he realize how far over the table he was leaning? "I haven't made any concrete plans yet. But since I don't have to stay in one place, I try to take advantage of that." I gave him the same script I always gave on the off chance that someone questioned why I was moving instead of just being grateful like most were.

"Because you write for a living?" he asked.

"Yeah. And I can do that from anywhere."

"So why not do that from Walkerton? Permanently? There's nothing that's making you want to stay? No one?"

Like Zach? I was over that. Since meeting Nash, I did wonder what it would've been like to settle in one spot. But I just had to remember the curse and how many that had already gotten hurt to remember staying was never a possibility. "I really like it here—"

"But that's it?"

I didn't understand this anger. The most obvious

answer was that Nash was interested in me. But if that was the case, why wouldn't he come right out and say it? He wasn't shy. Everything about his behavior had told me that when Nash Walker wanted something, he reached out and he grabbed it. If there was any interest from him toward me, it was likely because of the chase. Once he caught me, he wouldn't want me, but I knew getting closer to Nash would only end in my tears and sadness. "Why do you think I should stay?"

That was the wrong thing to say, since it made Nash immediately glower. "If you don't know, I'm not going to tell you."

Huh. That sounded like he was hurt. I didn't want to hurt Nash's feelings. How did you tell someone that you thought they were a perfect person, smoking hot as well, but in a way that made it clear you knew you didn't have a shot? There wasn't a way. I opted on changing the subject instead. "What did you want to do today? Since you still seem to think you owe me, why don't we say today's lesson will bring us even? You better make it good."

His expression never changed, expressing anything other than his displeasure. "Tell me about your writing. Do you... like it?"

I licked my lips to stall while I tried to think of how to respond to that. "I do. I'm not wildly successful or anything, but the royalties are enough to help make ends meet."

"I'd like to read all your books." He sounded so genuine I believed him.

"That would make two of you, not counting me." Seeing his confusion, I explained, "My friend Chuck is the only other person except me to have read everything I wrote. He's my unofficial editor."

"The Chuck from your chat group?" he asked.

My eyebrows lifted in surprise. "Yeah, how did you remember that?"

His cheeks went red. "I... uh... Lucky guess. So you and Chuck are close?"

I brought my shoulder to my ear. "I guess. I know you think they aren't real friends, but there are four of us who chat regularly. We met in a different room and all sort of clicked. I talk to them every day. I'm close with all of them." Except they didn't know about my healing power. Only Nash knew that.

Nash sat back. "All of them equally?"

"Yeah, I guess? Wait, do you think there is something between Chuck and me? He's straight, and he's got kids. A daughter. There's *nothing* like that going on between us. You don't have to be jea—worried." Only in my insane brain would Nash be jealous of Chuck because of me.

He crossed his arms over his chest. "I want to read your things. I can edit."

"You freelance?"

"No."

I wasn't sure what to say to that, and he didn't seem to either. We fell into an awkward silence. It probably wasn't awkward on his end, just mine. I still wasn't sure why he'd called this meeting. He made it seem like another lesson, but so far he was just asking questions about me. While I searched my brain for something to talk about, Nash tore up his napkin into tiny pieces.

"You know," I said, clearing my throat, "People say that when you tear things up like that, it means you're sexually unsatisfied." I'd read that fact on some website somewhere about interpreting body language. Thanks to my occupation and natural curiosity, I was a fount of random knowledge.

I'd expected Nash to smile, maybe do that laugh that

was really just breathing sharply and quickly through his nose. Instead, he settled his hands and straightened his spine.

Clearly, I'd struck a nerve. My brain clicked into overdrive, level one damage control. "Not that I'm the expert here about being satisfied. You've had a ton more *special friends* than I have."

He cocked his head to the side. "Is that so?"

Oh shit. I'd meant to make it better, but now I'd made it sound like I thought he was sexually promiscuous. I *did* think that, but I'd said it in a way that made it seem like a bad thing. Level two, activated. "It's cool, though. I mean, at least you have the talent to satisfy your conquests. They probably don't walk straight for a week after." *Holy shit, what the fuck am I saying?* I listened to myself speak, helpless to stop the words that kept streaming from my lips.

Nash still didn't speak. He wasn't frowning anymore, at least.

What I needed to do was concentrate on drinking my coffee. If I was swallowing, I wasn't speaking. But, now that I'd started, I was having a hard time stopping. I was on a runaway train to verbal humiliation. "I've only had sex with three people. One had to ask me my name the next morning because he couldn't remember." I tapped my chin. "I should've picked up on it when he kept calling me tiger during sex. I don't blame him. I'm not that great at kissing or... any of the other stuff."

I waited for Nash to laugh. Or, at the least, make fun of my inexperience. When he didn't, I looked up at his face, blinking rapidly against the anger I saw there. He tipped his coffee back, downing the rest before gathering the clutter that had accumulated on our table. "Change of plans. We're going back to your place." He grabbed my coffee and stood.

"We are? What were we going to do? Why are we going back?" I followed him to the door. Why hadn't he just met me at my apartment if that was what he had planned?

Nash didn't answer my questions. He barreled through the door and looked back like he would tug me along if I didn't keep up.

"What are you up to, Nash?" I asked, not entirely trusting the gleam in his eye. I didn't feel in danger, but the way he looked at me now made me nervous.

"You told me to make today's lesson a good one, so I am."

I skipped forward to his side. That sounded much tamer than his expression made our plans seem.

He waited until I was right next to him before continuing. "I'm teaching you how to kiss."

———

I WASN'T sure how we made it back. I spent the whole walk in a fog, convincing myself Nash couldn't mean what I thought he'd meant, while wondering what in the heck he could've meant instead.

But walking into my apartment cleared the fog. I was being silly. Yes, I was inexperienced, but I wasn't a bumbling, doe-eyed, spring flower. If Nash wanted to impart some kissing wisdom, we were two grown adults. We could do that. "Can I get you anything to drink? Probably not coffee. I've got juice, water..." I opened my fridge. The need to offer Nash as many options as possible grew until it was an unignorable beast inside me.

The fridge door swung closed, and I popped my head up. Nash stood on the other side, pushing it closed. "I'm not thirsty."

Had he gotten taller? Had it also gotten hotter in my

apartment? I abandoned the fridge and rushed toward the window. The windows hadn't been opened since the first day when I'd aired the place out. Even then, I didn't think this window had been one of the ones opened. It refused to budge. I peeked over my shoulder. Nash stood at the line between the kitchen and the carpeted space. He leaned on the counter, bracing much of his weight against his elbow, watching me with a smirk on his face.

"It's just a little wonky," I muttered, throwing my full weight behind opening the window while trying to make it seem like I was barely trying.

"It's not warm to me."

I refused to look at him while my cheeks blazed a bright red. "Well, you're wearing less clothes."

Technically, he *was* wearing a tank top while I wore a T-shirt.

"If you don't want to do the lesson—"

I spun around. "I do!" He smirked more, and I rushed to cover my exuberance. "I mean, you can't feel like you owe me for the rest of your life."

"Right." His smirk fell. "I need to settle our score. Come sit next to me, Phin. I can't kiss you from there."

No, he couldn't. And I wanted to be kissed. But not to learn. Because of Nash. I wanted to kiss Nash. For that reason alone, I should have put a stop to things. It wouldn't be fair to Nash. He'd be kissing me for educational purposes, and I'd be kissing him to satisfy a fantasy. I dropped my hands from the window. My shoulders drooped with indecision until a thought struck me, and I stood straight. "I should brush my teeth. Wasn't that your first lesson? Clean house, clean mouth."

I sprinted down the hallway into the bathroom and gripped the counter as I stared at myself in the mirror.

"What is your problem, Phineas Peters? He just wants to teach you to kiss. Man up! Just two bros learning to kiss. Well, Nash already knows how to kiss. He's going to teach you, Phin, and you aren't going to make this weird."

I pointed at my reflection. I'd already made the situation kind of weird.

"At the least, you won't make this *any weirder*." I grabbed my toothbrush, pleased I had the presence of mind to make sure my alibi for running away in the first place was intact. Five out of five doctors would be disappointed that I didn't brush for the entire prescribed two minutes, but after about thirty seconds, I was too excited and had to stop. I stared at myself again, feeling calmer. At least I had this space where I could hide away, unheard and unseen. "You can do this, Phin. Go out there, kiss him, and pretend you don't want more."

When I opened the door, Nash was halfway down the hallway. My heart dropped. Had he heard me? No, he was still too far down to have been able to hear through the door —unless he had some kind of super hearing. "You okay? I was coming to check on you."

"I'm fine. All brushed. Ready for... the lesson."

"Good, let's get started." He waved me back.

My toes dragged all the way to the couch. I wasn't not excited at the idea of kissing Nash; I just wasn't a stupid man. I knew what this would do, how it would make me feel. I also didn't think the same thoughts and feelings would pop up in Nash.

Like an addict, I wanted the high of his lips against mine more than I cared about the unavoidable fallout.

We sat side by side on the couch. He'd sat first, and I'd taken the other end, but he looked at the space between us with an arched eyebrow. "We're gonna need to be a little closer than that."

I licked my lips nervously. "Is that the first lesson?"

Nash leaned over. His green eyes, normally a darker forest green, glowed brightly. He never blinked or looked away. "It can be. Step one in kissing, get close enough to kiss." He scooted as he spoke until our hips nearly touched. He rotated at the waist, facing me, and I did the same, feeling the arm of the couch digging into my spine.

This close, I was even more aware of every imposing inch of him. I'd always had a thing for guys out of my league. Reg had said it was a defense mechanism. My opinion was that I was just shallow and enjoyed the muscles. But now that I'd spent a few days with Nash, I'd realized the worst possible thing. He wasn't just some dumb jock—he was an actual, real-life hero.

His face was closer now, but he didn't make another move. He lingered, watching my eyes, my lips.

Soon, the tension was too much for me to sit through silently. "What's step two? Actually, how many steps are there? I might want to take notes." I lurched forward, but Nash stopped me, pushing me back gently against the couch.

"No notes," he murmured. "And no more stalling. Step two is build-up. The perfect first kiss will happen only after the kissee has been thinking and wondering about it. Sit close, and speak quietly, gently."

He demonstrated as he spoke, and I could confirm: when his tone dipped to that low, honeyed register, a ripple of need vibrated through me.

"You'll want to already be touching them a lot. Running your hands up their arms, cupping their face."

The soft flesh of his thumb brushed over my bottom lip,

and I gasped. Instantly, I searched his face, but he didn't look at all irritated by my show of authentic emotion. "Then what?" I whispered. "You kiss?"

He shook his head, tsking me softly. "Patience. Never be in a hurry. That's step three."

He dropped his hand from my face to my shoulder, and my tongue flicked out to lick my bottom lip. "Got it."

My nostrils flared as I attempted to bring in oxygen to my deprived brain. I couldn't concentrate on anything but his lips, the way they moved closer, the way they flexed and pressed together as he spoke. Enough time had passed, so I wasn't quite as on edge. This was clearly just a lesson and—

His lips pressed against mine.

I made a noise: half surprised yelp, half wanton moan. His mouth was as perfect as I feared. The kiss was sweet but restrained. Gentle. He cupped my face, seemingly content to continue what he was doing forever. He never pushed for more and didn't stick his tongue down my throat, and I appreciated that. This was a first kiss after all, and first kisses should be sweet. Except, by the time he opened his eyes and looked at me, I *wanted* more.

"Step four," he whispered. "Get them to expect it, want it. And then wait until they aren't."

That was a good reminder—he was doing this out of duty. My heart might have been doing the worm in my chest, but his wasn't. Recognizing that fact didn't have the same icy dousing effect it had the first time. Now that I knew what it felt like to have Nash's lips against mine, I didn't care about the reason. I didn't care if I had to *pay* him just as long as I got to feel him again.

I pushed off the couch, slamming our mouths together with much less finesse. If these kisses were limited, then I was going to squeeze each one out of him for as long as I could.

Nash let me take control of the kiss, holding me with his palms against my spine. My confidence faltered for a split second, but I rose to the occasion, literally. My dick pressed against my zipper, longing to be free and join in on the fun. I poked my tongue out, running it along the seam of his lips and making his mouth open.

I let out a silent whoop of joy as I thrust my tongue in, mentally smirking at the fact that I'd done to him the same thing I'd been glad he hadn't done to me. But Nash didn't seem to mind. Not at all. His tongue joined mine, the two muscles twining and dancing together until my head spun.

When our faces separated again, panic flared. He wouldn't owe me anything after this, and I'd have no excuse for remaining near. "I couldn't heal people until after the crash. The curse wasn't so bad at first. After I moved from my aunt's, though, that changed. People started getting hurt more and more, always directly around me. I'd heal them, but got to thinking, if I wasn't there, would they have been hurt? I always felt responsible, until the day I realized... I was. I don't know why or how, but the longer I stay in a place, the more people around me experience freak accidents."

Nash didn't move away, but he did look extremely confused. "Why are you telling me this now?" he asked, not unkindly.

My gaze fell, but Nash waited patiently while I worked up enough bravery to look at him again. "Because now, I've told you more, so you owe me more. That's the way this works, right?"

Nash smiled. It wasn't a smirk or a grin, but a full-on

expression of happiness that made me forget how to breathe. "If that's how you want it," he replied.

I didn't know how I wanted it, just who. Nash.

"I want to talk about this curse more, though. What do you mean when you—"

I lunged forward, grabbing his shirt by the collar as I pressed our faces together. This time, Nash quickly took control, digging his fingers in my hair, holding my face in the exact position he wanted. He cupped my neck with his other hand, letting his thumb graze gently over my neck. I could only imagine how wildly my pulse beat against his hand. Could he feel what he did to my body? I had a hunch he could. When it came to Nash, he knew exactly what he was doing.

"Did I do step four right? Wait for when they don't expect it?"

His gaze dimmed. "Yeah, you did. That was perfect."

My stomach flipped at the compliment while I tried to think of something else I could tell him that would keep the kisses going but wouldn't make him despise me as a human.

His phone chimed in his pocket, and he pulled it out. "Sorry, I just need to check it really quick. Never know what the..." His words trailed off as he looked at what was on the screen. He knitted his eyebrows together, frowning at the screen.

"What is it?" I wasn't trying to be nosy, but his expression was too intense for me not to question it.

He angled the screen toward me. I frowned, unsure of what I was looking at for a second. There was a large metal cylinder sitting on a table. "Who's it from?"

"Aver. It's probably something meant for Branson. They're putting in an irrigation system out on the edge of Walkerton."

I smirked. "You got an unsolicited shaft pic."

He smiled and leaned back. "Normally I'm the one sending these."

That shocked me. "I thought you'd be too good for dick pics."

"And keep this beauty away from the world? No one puts baby in the corner." Nash darted his eyes my direction. "Can we both agree to forget that I just referred to my penis as *baby*?"

Laughter bubbled up in my throat. "Sure." As much as I wanted to kiss Nash forever, I was grateful to cut the tension. "Thanks for today. You really helped."

Nash's mouth pressed into a firm line. "We just kissed. There's more to being experienced."

I laughed nervously. "I think if we go any further, it turns into prostitution."

He didn't look at all perturbed by that idea.

"Have you...?"

Nash tilted his head, giving me the full force of his stare.

"Of course not. That was a silly question, I'm sorry."

"While no one should be pushed into doing something they don't want to, I also don't think sex should be such a big deal. It's simply another way people have of interacting. No one agonizes over a handshake."

I stuck my hand out. "Hi, I'm Phin. I agonize over everything."

He laughed. "Most people don't agonize over hand-shakes, then. Sex can be just as casual."

Maybe for him. After all, rain didn't mean the same thing to someone living in the desert as it did to someone living in a rain forest. When something came in abundance, it was easy to forget that, for others, it was a rarity. "So, your tip is to treat sex like it's something casual?"

"No," he barked, and I jerked back from the intensity. "That isn't what I'm saying," he continued at a lower level. "I'm saying it doesn't have to be a big deal that you panic over. Think of it more like a natural progression between two people who are attracted to each other."

Awesome. Bun was always saying how oblivious I was to the attentions of others. If sex depended on me recognizing interest coming from another person, I was in more trouble than I knew. Why couldn't this all be easier? I'd longed for mood detector skin ever since I was a confused child, unsure why my friends were acting the way they were. That was another reason why I preferred my friendships to be virtual—I was required to assume less and could investigate more before being required to answer. "Maybe I'm meant to be a solitary creature. I'm crap at reading people. And it isn't so bad. Sex with people is fun, but I've got enough skill and tools to have just as much fun on my own."

"Tools?" Nash asked, with a tone that was the verbal equivalent of perking up his ears.

Oh shit. "You know, just like the regular stuff."

"No, I don't know. What sort of tools?"

A man who had no problem getting someone else to touch his penis wouldn't waste time and money purchasing devices that mimicked the act of being touched. And my collection was... extensive. Why had I brought them up? He'd demand to see it all. And if I didn't show him, he'd just think I was way kinkier than I was.

I didn't own anything too crazy. A few plugs, my trusty dildo, and then some odds and ends that came as free gifts or had been on sale. There wasn't anything that I used with another person; it was all for personal, private use.

Nash got to his feet. "Where do you keep them?" He looked back in the kitchen like he was looking for a box marked Phin's Sex Toys.

"Nowhere!" I squealed. "I'm sorry I brought it up."

"I can sniff them out," he threatened.

Did he mean...? The blood poured from my face, and I felt a tad queasy.

"No! Not like that! I mean I'm good at finding things," Nash hurried to explain. He trod down the hallway toward my bedroom. "I just want to see, Phin. Here I was thinking you were so innocent and pure, and you've been holding out a sex dungeon full of toys."

In the back of my mind I knew this was not something friends did. I'd never had a friend demand to see my sex toy collection before...

Wait... that was a lie. Reg had asked, several times. And Bun wanted to compare dildos. But I'd never had a *guy* friend ask to see them. It wouldn't be like if we were at a store that happened to sell sex toys. Everything I had, I used. Most everything, anyway. I had a whole package of these cheap rubber cock rings that didn't really stay in place. There was a level of intimacy involved. At the same time, the only reason I didn't want to show him was because I was worried he would make fun of me. Except Nash didn't really seem like that type of guy. He teased, but never when the teasing wasn't playful.

Besides, he wasn't lying about being really good at finding things. He'd gone into my bedroom, and though he hadn't started rifling through my drawers yet, he looked ready.

"Okay, fine, I'll show you. But don't make any jokes, all right?"

He lifted his fingers in what I assumed was a scout's promise.

I stomped the rest of the way, passing him to get to my dresser, where I wrenched open the top drawer. I reached past the socks to the cardboard box I kept there. I felt a little like a kid who had been caught doing something naughty as I set the box on the bed, flipping the lid open before I stepped back. Nash took my spot, peering into the box as if he was worried something would jump out at him.

Then he saw the dildo and lunged for it.

In the right circumstances, my dildo was just what I needed. Flesh-toned and of average size, it wasn't like one of those monstrous double-headed bright purple ones. But in Nash's hand, it looked obscene. He set it down in favor of a black butt plug. That had come in a pack of threes, each different sizes. I'd graduated from the smallest size soon after trying them but still couldn't handle the large size. Of course, it was the medium plug that Nash picked up.

"You use this?" he asked without taking his eyes off the silicone toy.

"Sometimes," I shrugged. "Not as much as the other. You've seen them now. Can we—"

"Do you like wearing it?"

I blinked, unsure of how to answer the question. "Yes and no. It feels okay, I guess. I don't use any of this for long. In and out." I laughed at my self-deprecating joke, but Nash didn't join me. He just kept looking at me and then at the plug in his hand.

"What if you're in the mood? You don't ever put it in for a few hours, clean your apartment, go to the store?"

"With it in?" I squawked.

For the second time today, I didn't trust the gleam in his eyes. "Sure. With it in. No one could know. It would be your dirty secret."

This didn't seem to have anything to do with flirting tips, and my stomach flipped at the way Nash's words rumbled. My body tingled. My libido liked where this was going, but my head screamed for me to put the brakes on. "People wouldn't know?" I asked, my question little more than a puff of air.

Nash stared at the plug for a long moment. Then he looked to me. "You can experiment with me. Put it in, and I'll tell you if I notice."

There were a million reasons why that was a very bad idea. On top of that, I couldn't see how this related to flirting at all, but this whole day with Nash had been weird. I knew I could say no, put a stop to all of this, and that Nash would accept my answer. Or... I could say yes.

What was the worst thing that could happen while wearing a butt plug in front of a friend?

"Okay..."

11

NASH

Phineas had disappeared in the bathroom while I waited in his bedroom, left to wonder how everything had happened so perfectly.

Or not perfectly, if you considered the fact that I still hadn't told Phin how I felt and how I wanted things to change between us. He'd started talking about moving, and I'd latched onto anything to get that conversation to stop. Somehow, that snowballed into us making out on his couch.

My lips still tingled while my cock yearned to be free. I readjusted, ignoring the urge to fondle just a little.

I was doing a very bad thing. Despicable. Honesty was the best policy, and Phin deserved to know that my feelings for him had deepened. He might want to change his mind depending on how he felt. But I'd eavesdropped on him giving himself a pep talk in the bathroom.

He'd talked about pretending he didn't want more. That had to mean he wanted more.

Even though it did nothing to change the morality of my actions, I concentrated on that fact alone as I waited for Phin to emerge with the plug. That damn plug. I looked back at the box. It filled me with jealousy and desire. He didn't need any of those toys to get himself off, not anymore. I'd gladly take over that responsibility.

Except, due to a series of events I still didn't fully comprehend, Phineas was inside his bathroom, *inserting* the plug, and I was supposed to *not* immediately tear his clothes off? No. I was supposed to be *looking to see if it was obvious.* I didn't need to look—I already knew that damn plug was the only thing I'd be able to think of the moment he stepped out.

I was in over my head, but that had been the case since I first set eyes on Phineas. When he came out of the bathroom, I'd come clean. I'd lay it all out there, openly and honestly, and let him make his decision.

What if that scared him away, though? I lingered in the doorway, staring at the line of light shining from under the bathroom door. I imagined Phin, bent over, his nimble fingers searching for his hole. I growled, forcing my body to turn away. My wolf felt closer to the surface than normal, like I was a sneeze away from shifting. I expended more energy attempting to keep him back. Had this been what Branson had gone through? We'd all noticed the change in him when he'd met Riley. He became possessive, controlling, and protective, prompting the rest of us to circle around Riley in case he'd needed help.

This wasn't that. There were similarities between Riley and Phin, but they weren't the same. What had happened to them was unique, one of a kind. I shouldn't let it mess with my head now.

The bathroom door cracked open, and I had no problem focusing on only Phin as he walked stiffly out. He grabbed the door sill and gave me a shaky smile. "I feel silly."

Silly? I felt a lot of things, but silly wasn't one of them.

I'd shoved my hands in my pockets, balling my fingers into fists to keep from reaching for him, bending him over, and performing a full inspection. My resolve crumbled as my cock ached and my balls throbbed. I wanted to pull that plug out and replace it with my dick as I gave Phin the only flirting lessons I thought he ever needed. Flirt with me. Look at me. Smile at me.

Want me.

"What?" Phin asked, terrifying me for a split second.

My throat felt too dry to speak through. I couldn't have accidentally spoken out loud. I licked my lips to try to speak now. "I didn't say anything."

"Oh, I thought you did." He continued to cling to the sill as he looked absently up and down the hallway. "So, what's the verdict? Does this plug make my butt look big?"

I snorted. He was my sexy Phin, but he was also goofy as all hell. "I can't tell. Come out and strut the hallway."

He stepped carefully out, keeping his fingertips pressed against the wall as he walked closer, stopped a foot away, smiled and spun.

"How do you feel?" I croaked through a throat as dry as the Sahara.

"Pretty sexy, actually." Phin wiggled his ass just a little, and I couldn't stop my growl.

Thankfully, it was too soft for him to hear. I needed to get him to stop wiggling if I was going to be at all successful. But as I opened my mouth to say something to that effect, he wiggled again, and I was too busy drooling to do anything else.

"Maybe you're right. Don't they say confidence is your most important tool? I feel pretty confident." His steps changed into more of a strut, and I smiled at the tenacious display. "It's like this nephew I had. Shyest kid you'd ever met, until his mom put this backpack leash on him, and, I don't know, it gave him the boost he needed. Of course, I am just now listening to myself and hearing how inappropriate it is to relate this moment and feeling to a child, but it's happened now." He lifted his face, and I gave him mercy in the form of an understanding smirk.

I still wanted to rip his clothes off, but I was also getting caught up in his infectious excitement. I'd had no idea wearing the plug would make him feel so bold and daring. With each moment, his steps became more confident, his movements wider and full of more swagger. "Is this not how you've felt in the past when you wore it?"

"Not really."

I wanted the change in him to be because of me.

"Maybe it's you," he said, his lips spread in a wide, blinding smile. He lifted his leg like a marching soldier and strutted into the kitchen, where he made a flashy show of pouring a glass of water.

"We should go outside." I leaned my elbows on the kitchen counter. "Take your newfound confidence out in the wild."

He set the water down, frowning with his shoulders slouched forward. "I don't know..."

"It'll be fine," I said, coming up with the plan as I went. I might not have known this plug would give Phin such a boost, but I definitely wanted to keep that confidence going. "Why don't you go check the mail? I'll watch over you the whole time—"

Phin hurried around the counter toward me, hands reaching out like he was going to grab onto my collar. "But what if it falls out? What if someone sees and calls me a pervert and gets me thrown in jail? What if I fart, and the pressure causes it to shoot out of my butt in a—"

I pressed my finger to his rapidly moving lips. "First of all, that is a disgusting mental image. Second, none of that is going to happen. I'll be right here, watching you through the window the whole time. If anything bad happens, I'll be right there to fix it, okay?"

His eyebrows were still a wiggly line on his forehead, but he nodded. "Okay." He exhaled. "I can do this." He pumped his fists into the air and jogged around his sofa.

I smiled, noticing the slight pinch between his eyes, the way his lips remained parted slightly. This was turning him on. Not specifically the idea of going outside but wearing the plug. "Maybe you should stretch first, you know, to limber up." I was a very bad man.

He shrugged and bent over, abruptly shooting upright. His cheeks blazed a bright red. "Should have thought that over," he mumbled to himself before scowling at me like he knew I knew what that had done to him. "Okay, let's get this over with," he said with more squirm in his step.

I inhaled a thick plume of pheromones. Specifically, Phin's pheromones. The longer he wore the plug, the more concentrated the cloud grew. I swallowed rapidly, hiding the fact that I was literally salivating from his scent. I was on a runaway horse heading for a cliff. My actions had gone from despicable to deplorable, but there was no turning away at this point. We'd gone too far, and now there was nothing to do but blindly leap. Besides, this was helping Phin. The plug in his ass had put a pep in his step. "Go ahead," I said from the window. "I'll be watching."

He gave me one last brave, shaky smile before opening his door and heading down the hallway.

I couldn't believe it.

Phin was sexy, playful, and completely perfect. I nervously waited for him to emerge out of the apartment entrance. The mailboxes for this block were directly in front of his building on the sidewalk, and I beamed the moment I saw him tiptoe down the steps. He looked back, checking to make sure I was still there watching.

I waved and wiggled my fingers for him to keep going. He rolled his eyes but turned with a sassy sway. That decided it. When he came back in, I'd tell him everything. I'd explain how I felt and let him decide what to do with that information. Hopefully, he would decide to get naked. I'd explain that he didn't have to move, and he didn't need to worry about anyone getting hurt around him. It was my literal job to stop that from happening. Well, that and put out fires.

I was so lost in my head thinking about what I'd do when Phineas came back in that I didn't notice fucking Zach No-Brains Ballard sauntering up the street until he was nearly at the community mailbox. I growled and yanked the window open, leaning forward through the newly opened space. *Keep walking, No-Brains. Keep—*

"Hey, Glenn," Zach smiled. It was probably just a friendly smile, but to me, it looked predatory.

Zach isn't a shifter. He can't smell Phin's F-me cologne.

Phin lifted his head, noticing Zach once he was practically on top of him. No matter what happened today, we'd quit the flirting lessons and start working on situational awareness. I waited for my Phin to tuck his head down or turn away and run back up the stairs. I could be reasonably sure that Phin wouldn't—

"It's Phin, actually, not Glenn," Phin said with a friendly smile.

Zach blinked repeatedly, clearly attempting to understand the simple English that was spoken to him. "Really?

I'm sorry. Hey, Phin." He waved stupidly, and I waited for my Phin to scoff.

He laughed instead.

I gripped the sill, leaning almost completely out of the window. This was a stupid idea. It had also been all my idea.

"No worries. Hey yourself," Phin replied, sliding his mail key into the slot.

Instead of waiting for his turn, like a normal person, Zach stepped directly beside Phin with his mail key in hand.

Their shoulders touched.

I jumped out of the window.

Quickly straightening, I brushed off the branch that had snapped and snagged on my shoulder. Zach and Phin turned around at the same time, probably because it had sounded like a grown man had jumped from a third-story window into a line of decorative rhododendrons.

Phin's eyes bulged out of his head while Zach gave me a friendly smile. *Yeah right, buddy. I'm onto you.*

"Whatcha doin'?" I asked casually, sliding between Phin and Zach, forcing Zach to take a few steps back. *That's right.*

I knew I was being horribly jealous and possessive, but while Phin had that plug in, I wouldn't be able to let anyone who wasn't me get anywhere near him. Especially not Zach. I was a wolf shifter after all, an alpha. We had our limits, same as any other guy.

"Just checking the mail. Haven't seen you around the gym lately." Zach shut the small door to his mailbox and locked it.

"Looks like you have your mail now." I stared pointedly at the mail in Zach's hand before scowling.

Phin made a shocked, squeaky noise but didn't speak.

"Yeah, I do," Zach said slowly. The tips of his ears shone a bright red. "Bye, I guess."

"Bye, Zach. Nice seeing you," Phineas said brightly, leaning around me to look at him.

"Yeah, you too, *Phin*."

"Bye," I said sharply, crossing my arms. I ignored Zach's confused, hurt look—it didn't take a whole lot to confuse him—and waited for the door to close behind him before spinning around to face Phin. I wasn't sure what I'd been about to say but knew it didn't equal the anger that radiated off him. Was he pissed that I'd interrupted them? That would just be too bad.

"What was that?" he hissed.

I scowled, squeezing my arms more tightly across my chest to keep from hauling him over my shoulder. "I should ask you."

"Me? I was saying hello to the man, acting pretty normal if I say so myself. And then you came in and... how did you get down so fast anyway? I just saw you in the window."

"I jumped."

He gestured angrily in front of my face, assuming that I was lying. "Okay, fine, don't tell me. You suggested I come out here, Nash. I have to live with these people. It would be really great if you didn't make them hate me."

Why would Zach hate Phin because of me? That didn't make sense, and I was too angry to think it over rationally anyway. This game we played, it had come to a climax, and I was at my breaking point. "He's probably already forgotten."

Phineas pointed his finger at me, pressing it against my sternum as he spoke. "Stop being a dick! He isn't stupid just because he's muscular. Any more than you are!"

Was that what Phin had been doing? Using me as some

Zach substitute? "I'm sorry to burst your bubble, but Zach is nothing like me."

"I know! You at least remember my name!"

"Is that what we're doing here, Phin? Is *he* all these lessons were ever for? You better tell me right now."

Phineas threw his hands in the air. "Have you gone insane? Need I remind you all of *this* was your idea! You can't get mad at me for it now! That's entrapment and just plain..." His mouth gaped open like a fish as he searched for the right word. "That's just... rude!" He stepped around me, back up to the stairs.

I followed him, blocking his way. I wasn't thinking straight. My actions felt fueled by pure fire, not logical thought and reasoning. These days—hanging out with Phin but not being with him, tamping down my wolf side—I'd reached my boiling point, and while the best decision was probably to walk away and give us both some space, I could no sooner leave Phin's presence as I could jump to the moon. "Do you want Zach, Phineas? Tell me honestly. What is this that we're doing?"

Phin's lips twisted with frustration. "No, I don't want Zach."

"Then what do you want?"

The sun shone overhead. It was a rare clear day in this side of the world. Only puffy white clouds in the sky. A seagull flew by, cawing aggressively, but it was as if the two of us had frozen in time. Everything depended on whatever came out of Phin's mouth next.

He sighed tiredly and lifted his gaze to mine. Much of his anger had dimmed. "Isn't it obvious?"

What did that mean?

Oh.

OH.

My arms unfolded from my chest, and I lifted Phin, carrying him against my chest back into his apartment building. Driven by an animalistic desire, I climbed the steps and pushed open his unlocked door, kicking it closed. He stayed silent, sinking in my embrace until we reached his bedroom, and I set him down, safely on the bed. Already, I felt better. I also felt stupid for how I'd acted. But none of that mattered as much as the last three words Phineas had uttered to me. *Isn't. It. Obvious.*

Me. He wanted me.

I was an idiot, but a happy idiot.

Unless I was misunderstanding him now...?

His head was against his pillow, and he watched me quietly. If he hadn't just confessed his feelings for me, then this was probably really strange behavior on my part. "To be sure, you meant me, right?"

He smiled and nodded. "Yes, Nash. You. I'm sorry. I know I told you I wouldn't but—"

I balanced my weight on my hands at either side of his head. "Don't apologize."

"You aren't mad?"

"Would I have carried you to your bed if I was?" I looked at the way I had him pinned beneath me.

"Good point." His lips tugged up, nearly smiling but not quite. "What now?"

My heart felt like it had been stretched and filled with helium. I needed to be absolutely clear on this. "You weren't asking for my help so you could bag Zach?"

He shook his head, and I felt impossibly lighter. "No. I've been over that for a while."

"You want me?" It felt a little silly to be asking these sorts of questions while laying on top of him.

"Yes."

"No more flirting lessons," I said, my chest rumbling. "No more crushes. I need you to be mine, Phineas. Like you should have been from the beginning."

He licked his lips. "Yours?"

Oh fuck, what if he was one of those open relationship types? I was pretty confident I'd shown him how not into sharing him I was. No reason to tiptoe around it now. If he didn't want to be mine, I'd simply have to persuade him. "Yes, mine, Phin. To touch, to kiss, to protect." I grazed my lips over his, not quite kissing as much as I teased him with the promise of my kiss. "Do you have anything to say about that?" Whatever his arguments were, it was best to get them all out now. We'd toppled right over the point of no return at about the time we'd made out on his sofa.

"Just one thing," Phin replied.

I held my breath as his smile turned dazzling.

"Finally."

Covering his lips with a growl, I cupped his nape so I could keep him exactly as I wanted. I'd already kissed him, but now everything was different. I kept my motions slow, not wanting to spook him. At last, I had him where I wanted. I smiled and pulled back to look into his face. "Finally," I whispered before kissing him again, feeling as if my body was melting over the top of him.

I wanted to cover him like a second skin. I wasn't worried about whipping my dick out and getting off. I wasn't thinking about my next steps, how I got him from kissing to naked. I lived in the moment. The only thing to matter were my lips over his. Inhaling the breath, he exhaled. We'd walked around as two separate beings for far too long. It was time we were one.

"This is real, right?" Phin whispered.

Smiling, I rubbed our noses together. "Yes, you're really here. You're really mine."

His head tilted to the side. "You really want me?"

"I *really* want you." He had to feel the proof of that fact pressing into his middle. "I have since I first saw you in your underwear."

"What?" Phin's mouth parted in shock, tilting up in the corners. "That is inappropriate for a fireman to say! I was unconscious!"

I stuck my lips out more than was necessary while rotating my hips in a circle. "Ooooo yeah you were, baby. All passed out and pliant."

He punched my chest, and I pretended it made me wince. "Nash Walker, that is so wrong."

"What's wrong is why we ever stopped kissing."

Our lips crashed together with me hurrying to kiss him and him yanking my face closer. He laughed, the joyful noise bubbling into my mouth. I swallowed his mirth gladly, slipping my tongue past his lips. He tasted like candy, not because of anything he'd consumed, but because my Phin was naturally sweet. He healed old women and little girls without a worry about what might happen to him if people found out what he could do. The fact that he'd been able to keep it a secret would be the greatest mercy ever granted to me. His ability remaining secret was the only reason he was here with me now; I was sure of it.

And from this moment on, Phineas wouldn't have to rely on mercy, I would protect him.

His body and heart, happiness, and pleasure were now my responsibility to care for and nurture. I carded my fingers through his strands, grabbing hold and pulling just enough to make him gasp. "I will never let *anything* hurt you."

Phin stiffened. "You can't promise something like that."

I snarled, forgetting in my passion to soften the noise to something less than primal. "I'm sorry." I pulled back to check for fear, but his body remained open to me, trusting. "You're wrong, Phin. I'm not like the other men you've been with."

"I believe that," he murmured.

I cupped his face in my hands. "If my heart is beating, I will protect you."

His face went slack. "Don't. Don't say something like that, Nash. Please. Just—I know you are superhuman. You're fucking perfection. I can't believe I'm here right now without the help of a crossroads demon."

I squinted like that would help me better understand what that meant.

He reached up, cupping my face at the same time. "Nash, my point is, you won't impress me by putting yourself in harm's way. Never do that for me. That's how you'll keep my heart."

I couldn't make any sort of promises. He didn't seem to realize that my ownership of his joy and safety wasn't a chore but my power. I didn't believe being an alpha meant other people needed to bow down before me. That was bullshit. But I was drawn to being a fireman for the same reason I delighted in assuming Phin's wellbeing as my duty. It made me whole in a way I'd never known I was lacking. Finding Phin was the happiest moment in my life. Keeping him would become my purpose.

"I need you to take off your pants and bend over in front of me, Phineas. I think I've gone long enough without seeing that fucking plug."

He scrambled out from under me, shocking me with his speed. His pants and underwear stretched around his lower thighs, and he stretched to his hands and knees, peeking over his shoulder. The black plug teased me, wobbling with each of his sharp breaths. "Fucking hell, Phin. You're so damn perfect." I climbed to my knees, sitting upright and taking two large handfuls of his luscious ass. I pulled the globes apart, stretching his hole as my perfect boy arched his back. "You were so dirty, Phin, wearing this outside. Is that what you are? A dirty boy?"

"Fuck that shouldn't turn me on," he muttered. "It wasn't my idea!"

I shook my head, letting my nose bump against the outer tip of his plug. "No, you're right, it wasn't. It was my idea. And you're the good boy who obeyed."

"You better not start demanding I call you daddy."

I wiggled the plug sharply, making him hiss. "I don't care what you call me as long as you call me."

Leaning forward, I kissed the fleshy swell of his ass. As lovely as the sight was, if I didn't bury my dick deep inside him in the next sixty seconds, I would fucking explode. "Deep breath. Exhale... fast now, good boy." I twisted the plug as I pulled. His ass begrudgingly released the toy, gaping greedily at the void it left behind. I wasn't sure what to call the noise I made. A growl, but high-pitched, like a hum. Whatever it was, it meant desire. I laid my tongue flat, licking a single path up his body, starting at his balls, up his slit, to his winking hole. "Mmm, fuck. Your body's a candy store."

"Smooth," he chuckled. "Too smooth, Walker. Don't you use any line on me that you rotate with your conquests."

"Don't demean yourself. We both had lives. As much as I'd like to erase every memory you have of a man who isn't me, I'll have to do what I can convincing you I'm the only man who matters instead." I gripped my erection, lining our bodies up. The thrill of my wet dream finally coming true allowed me a zap of clarity. I was always safe in the bedroom, every time. Right now, my dick leaked, dropping slowly down to Phin's waiting body. "Fuck, condom?"

Phin cursed. "None," he wailed. "I'm clean, Nash. But we both know you were a manwhore."

I didn't much like the name, but I appreciated the past tense use. I also had very good news for the both of us. I was meticulous with my testing and had been in a bit of a dry spell since the whole blessed baby thing put our lives in a spin. "I was just tested. One hundred percent clean."

We stared silently at each other. This was clearly a line the other didn't often cross.

"Have you ever gone without?" I asked.

"Never. But I don't want you to go, even to the store. I need you Nash. Now. I can't wait." He gripped his cheek, stretching himself open. "Please, Nash."

Fuck, I understood the feeling. My cock twitched like it was searching for its home. "Phin—"

"No, no, no," he chanted. "Don't *Phin* me. I'm awake, I'm sober, and I need your dick in me, bare. Now." He reached back, gripping my hip.

Whatever I'd been about to say dried in my throat, replaced by a deep growl. Phin bent his spine, straining to push his ass toward me. I thrust, burying my length to the hilt. "Fuck, Phin," I nipped his shoulder. He was already open and relaxed, but I could tell by the strain in his shoulders that he needed a moment.

"You're so much bigger than the plug," he gasped. "I can't... Oh!"

I'd reached around, stroking his dick as I began to thrust. The only solution was to bring him more pleasure. "Your body feels amazing, Phin. Your tight hole is sucking me in, holding me tighter and tighter. You were made for my dick."

His gentle mewls were my only reply. I kept his dick in my hand, rubbing my palm in circles over the tip, making him buck back. For as hard as I pounded into him, he raised his hips, urging me to go harder. I forgot any plan of going soft or gentle. My Phin didn't want his hand held; he wanted his body used by someone who knew just how to cherish it when we were done.

I rotated my hips, adding a little extra variety in my forward thrusts and massaging more of his nerve endings. His howls sharpened, and I fondled his balls. I couldn't wait to learn every trick, every secret spot. As long as I had breath in my body, my Phin would be content, satisfied.

"Nash!" he squealed. No sooner did he finish were my fingers doused with his glistening essence.

"Yes, Phin, dirty boy. You're coming all over my hand." I stroked him several more times, painting his dick with his cum. I lifted my hand to his face. "Clean me," I growled. He lunged forward, taking the first finger between his lips with an eager hum. His tongue swirled around my finger. My hips never stopped pumping. With each forward thrust, his body split open beautifully. I loved fucking Phin in a way I'd never loved anything before. My own pleasure was amazing, but hearing his cries, watching the flush of his skin in response to my touch, seeing that had me teetering on the edge.

My balls tightened, signaling my coming orgasm. "I'm going to come, Phin. Do you hear me, baby? I can pull out." *Please say no.* This was a completely new desire. I'd always wanted to come, never cared where. Until now. I wanted my seed filling him, wanted to watch it leaking from him so I could gather it with my fingers and push it back in. I'd paint his body with my jizz, write my name across his back with it. I wanted it known, to shifter and human alike. Phin was mine.

"Don't think of moving," he gasped, urging his ass back. "Stay inside. I want to feel you in me."

I ran my fingers down his spine. He was so perfect. My need pulsed once sharply in my balls before exploding up my shaft, forcing a roar from my lips as my dick opened up. I kneaded his flesh, pumping continuously. Even after my dick was empty, I thrusted.

"I don't ever want to stop." I nibbled his neck, gently biting down on his earlobe. "You're mine now, really mine." I danced my hand up and down his spine. He carried my scent. If he came across another shifter, they'd sense he'd been claimed by an alpha. None of that had ever mattered until now.

I wouldn't worry about the change. I felt too good to worry.

"Don't stop. I've got all day."

I smiled, slow and evil because I didn't have anywhere to go either. I could spend the hours exactly where I was. I pulled him close, letting our bodies settle into the mattress. We'd fuck later, make love, maybe we'd even have a few quickies—preferably with him bent over the sofa, and the kitchen counter, and up against the wall—but for now, I just wanted to cuddle.

12

PHINEAS

I WOKE FROM A DREAM. Someone was sucking my dick, and they were damn good at it too. I moaned softly and pumped my hips, hoping the dream would let me remain just a little longer. My dream dick sucker kept his tongue moving, laving over my shaft. As far as dreams went, this guy had blowjob skills I didn't personally possess.

Was that possible in a dream?

I opened my eyes, but the dream didn't fade. The mouth didn't stop. It sucked harder. "Nash," I gasped. With his tongue and lips, he brought the previous day rushing back. Nash wanted me. We'd kissed, had sex.

A whole lot of sex.

And he clearly wasn't done. I'd been fucked the night before until I literally couldn't be fucked any longer. At some point, I'd collapsed, exhausted and foggy from the sudden rush of oxytocin flooding my system. And I wasn't even sure Nash had stopped there, not that I'd minded. He had blanket consent to do whatever he wanted with me. I trusted him completely.

I knew that was crazy. We'd met for the first time not

that long ago. But I couldn't help the steady rush of faith that I felt when I thought of him.

My dick slid to its limit down his throat, and I decided I could ponder the delicacies of faith and trust some other time. For now, I only wanted to grab what I could of his hair and thrust rhythmically into his mouth. Nothing was too much for him. My thrusts got a little out of hand. With me at the helm, they were bound to. But Nash took my dick however I wanted to give it to him. Something came over me. Some sort of boldly macho man took over my actions, and as I urged Nash's head down, his nose against my pubic hairs, I held him there.

Nash made a growling sound, and I released immediately. "Sorry!"

"Don't apologize," Nash said, wiping his mouth. He kept his eyes down, almost like *he* was embarrassed. "I liked it, but when you take control like that, it's difficult for me not to rise to the challenge."

"No, no, it was too far. I practically shoved my dick down your throat." I reached for the pillow to cover my face.

Nash tugged it away. If I thought he was gorgeous during the day, that was because I'd never witnessed him in all his morning glory. His hair stuck out, likely helped along by my endless tugging. His smooth face was rough with new growth. When his head had been between my legs, his stubble had scratched against my thighs like a cat's tongue.

"Listen to me, baby. I loved it. I want you to want me as much as I want you." He stopped and cocked his head to the side, making me think he was replaying that sentence in his head to make sure it said what he'd meant. "There is a part of me that yearns to dominate, at all times, so when you take the upper hand, he sees it as a challenge he's all too joyful to rise to meet."

"You speak like you've got split personalities," I said with a laugh.

He didn't contradict me. Not right away. I stopped laughing.

"It isn't quite like that, and I will tell you *exactly* what I mean, but after I taste your cum." He dove back down, returning to my dick that hadn't softened that whole time.

We picked up exactly where we'd left off, and though I was gentler, scratching my nails lightly along his scalp instead of pulling, it wasn't long before Nash got his wish, and I was hurtling to the rafters of bliss while he swallowed every lewd drop.

"I'm surprised I have any left," I groaned, sinking into the pillow while also feeling as light as air.

"You're right." Nash popped up and kissed my lips, sharing the taste of my release. "I need to keep you hydrated. And fed." He slipped off the mattress like a seal into the ocean. "Wait there! I'll bring you breakfast."

If I didn't know better, I'd have checked for an empty bottle of *Felix Felicis* under my pillow. This was all going too well.

"Ouch!" Nash bellowed from the kitchen.

My heart jumped in my throat. I sprinted to the kitchen, my bare feet slapping against the linoleum. "What is it? What's happened?"

Nash stood in front of the fridge, the door open, several broken eggs on the ground. "Why are you up? Breakfast in bed requires you to stay in bed."

Adrenaline raced through me without an outlet.

"Your fridge was a disaster. The eggs fell out. I'm sorry. I'll buy more."

Clearly, Nash thought my reaction was due to anger. "I don't care about the eggs, Nash. You said ouch."

There wasn't a pool of blood on the floor. That should have comforted me. Instead, I searched for the real injury.

"I bumped my head bending down trying to catch the eggs. I'm fine, Phin. Everything's fine."

He spoke with a soft tone that should have lulled me out of my hypervigilance, but I couldn't let the feeling go. I'd been happy for a moment, truly and completely happy, and then he'd been hurt. That wasn't a coincidence.

"Phin, I'm fine. Stop looking at me like you're expecting me to collapse." He left the mess of cracked shells and runny yolks, herding me back down the hallway with a strong arm around my waist.

"You got hurt."

"I bumped my head. If you want to apologize for something, apologize for the state of your fridge."

"I tried to buy things without cartoons on it."

He shook with laughter. "You did a good job."

He couldn't understand my fear. How real my worries were. "Don't patronize me, Nash! You could've been... it's only a matter of time before—"

"Nothing. Before nothing, Phineas. I know you think you're cursed."

I turned to him and lifted my face, catching his gaze and holding it. "I am."

He frowned, and his eyes pinched. "This isn't my first encounter with someone who could do *extra* things. That person believed they were cursed too."

Could it be dumb luck that Nash had experience with my problem? "Who? Can they heal like me?"

"No, they have a different ability, but the point is they weren't cursed. They just had bad luck. And now, they don't."

So, not like me. At all. I didn't have bad luck. Nothing

bad happened to me personally. Nash didn't understand, and he wouldn't unless he knew the entire gory truth.

"It isn't the same." I sat down, drawing my legs tight against my chest. Nash didn't try prying the death grip I had around my knees loose, sitting beside me instead with his arm draped protectively over my shoulders. "When my parents died..."

"You can't blame yourself," Nash growled.

"I don't. And I do. I didn't know what would happen." Tears filled my eyes as I brought myself to that night. To the real events that had changed every moment of my life after. "I need you to just sit and listen, okay? I've never told anyone this, but you need to know, if you're going to understand. It may seem like what I do comes from a place of good, but it doesn't."

Nash nodded solemnly but kept his mouth closed.

"I remember a lot of the crash. Most of the crash, actually. The parts about the winding road, the rain, all true. My dad must have been going too fast, or maybe he hit a slick spot. Either way, we rolled. It was so *loud*. I didn't think anything could make that much noise. There was glass everywhere, and the smell of smoke mixed with gasoline made me throw up. But my parents were fine..."

I watched the question form on his face, but true to his word, Nash didn't ask it. I'd told him my parents died in the crash. And they had. Just not because of the crash.

"I was hurt, though. Very badly. I remember looking down and just seeing red and flesh, like hamburger spilling from me."

His arm tensed over my shoulders, and he let out a growl that I was beginning to learn wasn't a growl-like sound but an actual growl. The sound came from deep in his chest, but at least this time, it didn't scare me as much as it let me know how unhappy my story was making him. The feeling was mutual.

"I remember my mom crying as she scrambled to unbuckle me, reaching for me with these huge tears streaming down her dirty cheeks. And then my dad, trying to lift me, but it hurt too badly, and I screamed. I was dying, knew it with a clarity I haven't felt since. And I was okay with it. My mom and dad weren't hurt. They'd be okay. But something happened when they touched me at the same time. The pain lessened, and my injuries healed. I didn't know what was happening until it was too late. When the smoke cleared, I was healed, and they were both dead. That's when the Good Samaritan found us, but it was too late for my parents."

I tucked my face against my legs, my mouth bumping my knees as I spoke. "My parents had healed me, at the cost of their lives. My ability has never worked like that again. I've never been able to heal myself. Not after the first time. This power... you say it isn't a curse, but how can it be anything but one? My parents were its first victim."

"They died to protect you, Phin."

I shook my head, pushing abruptly from the mattress. I couldn't be touched, consoled. I didn't deserve it. "They had no idea what was happening. That I was sucking the life force from them. It wasn't like this was something they could do before."

"I don't know what they knew, but I know that if given the chance, they would've agreed to it. You were their child, Phineas. Your parents weren't cursed—they were lucky. They died saving their child."

I wanted to believe him, but I had so many years of nightmares—night after night of seeing my dead parents asking me why I killed them in my dreams—I couldn't.

"How are you so good with all of this? I just told you I was on death's door and my parents healed me with their life force, and you didn't bat an eye."

I expected him to laugh or make light of the moment. When he didn't do either, I looked at him more closely.

"Nash?"

"I need to tell you something—"

He was cut off by a ringing sound, not just of his phone, but a second, more urgent tone. That was his work line. Nash cursed and reached for his jeans on the floor, pulling out his phone. "Fuck, get dressed, Phin." Nash slid his pants on, looking around for his shirt. I handed it to him after finding my own.

"What is it? What's happened?" I knew someone had been hurt. I just hoped we would get there in time.

Nash's face was white. He reached around my waist, half carrying me out of the apartment. "It's Riley," he told me as we moved. He grimaced, his mouth twisting unhappily. "He's been hurt."

———

THE GRAVEL FLUNG out from under Nash's tires as he revved the engine. Even though we'd turned down his driveway, he accelerated, slamming to a stop at the front door. We'd made it before the emergency services. The front door was open, and Paul stood inside, frantically waving at us to come in.

"Branson doesn't know how it happened. Riley went out to get the grill ready for lunch and—just—boom." He had a dark smudge, ash maybe, on his cheek, and though he was obviously worried, he kept his voice even.

"Paramedics are coming," Nash told him. "Make sure there isn't something they'll see that they shouldn't."

Paul grimaced. "That's the thing. When he got hurt, he shifted. We can't bring him back."

Shifted? What the hell did that mean?

"Who called 9 1 1?"

"I did. I'm sorry! The explosion was so loud. I thought we were being attacked. I called them before I even knew Riley was hurt."

Nash looked to me with a face of indecision. "Phin, maybe you should wait..."

He'd told me he had secrets. Maybe this was one of them. I didn't care. I pushed past him. "No. He's hurt. I'll help him. Where is he?"

I ran into Aver next, who looked over my head to Nash.

"Let him in. He can help," Nash told Aver, but he remained where he was.

"You know what this would mean, Nash," Aver said.

Frustration welled inside me while the two big bad men spoke in covert sentences over my head. "Look, I don't care about your secret club. After this, I'll pretend I don't know again, but Nash is right. If Riley is hurt, I *will* help him." The longer they made me wait, the harder it would be. My abilities had their limits. If a person was too far gone, I couldn't do anything.

Aver still didn't budge, so I tried a new tactic.

"Move," I snarled.

"He's not breathing!" Branson yelled from deeper inside the house.

That got Aver to move. I rushed in the direction of Branson's tortured shout, finding him in the kitchen. The last time I'd been in this house, it had been full of laughter and joy. Now, Bran Jr. was crying in the corner while a huge dog lay on its side on the counter. Large swaths of fur had been burnt off, leaving tortured, blistering skin behind. If this was what had happened to their dog, I couldn't imagine the shape Riley was in. "Where's Riley?"

"That is Riley," Nash said cautiously. He picked up the dog's leg as if he was checking its pulse.

The dog was... *what*?

"Why did you bring him?" Branson muttered angrily.

I'd forgive his rudeness, considering what was going on.

"We're shifters. That's what I was trying to tell you," Nash said quickly. "We can all turn into wolves. Riley's injuries in his human form are the exact same as they are now in his wolf form. Can you help him?"

There was a phrase I despised: nut up or shut up. It made no sense and made me slightly squeamish to picture. But if I were ever in a moment where that phrase applied, it was this one. I could either fight what I was being told and lose valuable minutes while Nash convinced me, or I could just believe what he was saying was true.

I chose the latter.

"It should work the same. Wyatt can shift like you, right?"

Nash nodded.

"I healed him no problem." He was in his human form, but I would just have to hope that didn't end up mattering.

"What do you need?" Nash asked while Branson looked ready to toss us both out.

"He can't touch him. His wounds are open. Riley will get infected—"

"Just wait," Nash said, grabbing his cousin by the neck and bringing their faces together. "You don't know what my Phin can do."

Branson didn't respond at first. Then he nodded jerkily.

I took that as the go-ahead and spread my fingers over the worst of Riley's burns. My hands heated up like two irons, and I winced at the exchange of pain. These burns were bad. This was going to really hurt.

"Look, Nash, under his hands. The skin!" Branson hovered close by, and I tried to ignore his shock, putting all my focus on the injured man-dog in front of me.

As the skin cleared, knitting together on its own, I moved working methodically over the side of his body. At his ribs, I paused. The injuries were deeper here, not just into the skin—the bones were broken as well. I closed my eyes. My hands were so hot I wouldn't have been surprised to open my eyes and see pure lava pouring from them. I relied on the others, circled tightly around us, to let me know if anything horrible like that happened.

Sweat broke across my brow as my own body began to feel like it was on fire.

Dimly, I was aware of sirens, the guys moving around me, but I kept my focus on Riley. If this all ended up being an elaborate practical joke, I'd never live it down, but I didn't think any of these guys were that good at acting.

"What are you doing?" Wyatt yelled, bursting into the kitchen from the front of the house. "They're coming!"

Nash yanked me away. I made a snarled noise of displeasure but he hugged me tightly, rubbing my back as if consoling me. "Cry," he whispered a moment before the firemen, along with Sheriff Maslow, stormed in.

"Reports said there was an explosion?" the sheriff asked, giving the dog on the counter a double take. "Why is Riley on the counter?"

The sheriff knew? I squeaked with surprise, but Nash only hugged me more tightly.

"He was knocked back," Wyatt said, reaching for the Riley dog. "Poor guy didn't know what hit him."

Branson pushed past Wyatt, knocking Wyatt's arms out of the air and replacing them with his own. He gingerly lifted the Riley dog from the counter. He was awake now and looking around, dazed and confused.

I would be too.

"Has any human been hurt?" I couldn't see with Nash pressing my face into his chest, but I thought I recognized Charles's voice from the station. "What's wrong with Phineas?"

"He really loves that dog," Nash said.

"But I thought you two just met?" Charles asked.

"What can I say? Phin's a sweet soul." Nash patted the back of my head, and I figured it was my time to shine. I sobbed loudly into his chest, beating his muscles with loose fists. Once I started, I found it easy to keep going. My skin hurt so badly I wanted to jump into the frozen water of the bay outside.

I couldn't see the other man's face, but I could imagine his confusion. He didn't push it, instead telling us he'd be with the chief at the back patio. They were inspecting the grill to see what might have gone wrong.

"No one is hurt, though?" Sheriff Maslow asked. "Where's Riley?"

"Walking," Branson replied. I peeked out under Nash's arm enough to see he'd set the Riley dog down on four paws. It rested its head on Branson's knees, where he held the baby for the dog to sniff. The Riley dog licked the baby's feet, soothing it enough so that it stopped crying.

"He didn't hear the explosion?" Sheriff Maslow asked.

Branson cleared his throat. "We have a lot of land—"

"I get it. You've got a lot of land. Maybe Riley should

look into having his hearing checked," the sheriff replied. "But it doesn't look like I'm needed here now. The fire is out, the chief will let you know about the cause, and no human has been injured. Your dog looks fine. I'm leaving."

"Thank you for all your help, Sheriff," Aver said, shaking his hand. "I know Riley had talked about wanting you over for dinner when his leave is up. I'll talk to him about it when he gets back."

The sheriff nodded. He wasn't looking at Aver, but the Riley dog. "What breed is he?"

"Husky?" Wyatt said when no one else responded.

The dog growled, and the sheriff backed away. "Weird-looking husky," he mumbled on his way out of the house.

"I vote Phin never gets an acting role again," Wyatt teased when we were alone.

"Hey!" I shouted while Nash growled over my head at his brother.

"He did amazing. And he healed your mate."

"We'll talk about how later," Branson grumbled. "Baby, stay that way for a few more minutes. I'll get rid of them. Aver..." He handed Bran Jr. to Aver before disappearing out the back patio.

I felt the stares of all three men, and one canine, on my face.

"Why is your skin so red?" Nash asked.

At the same time, Wyatt said, "I did break my leg, didn't I?" He sounded delighted at that fact.

But now that the immediate excitement was over, and Riley was healed... and *wagging his tail,* all I could feel was the pain of the exchange. Riley's burns had been deep, not to mention the broken bones, and I was experiencing the brunt of that pain all at once. I sagged against Nash, not having to act like I was too weak on my feet.

"Phineas?" Nash let me drop gently to one of the chairs around the table. Riley padded over and whined as he looked at me.

It was pure instinct to reach out and scratch behind his ears. I froze when I realized what it was that I was doing, but the Riley dog lifted his head so that it bumped into my hand again.

"Just don't scratch his butt," Aver told me as he watched his cousin through the glass door, speaking with the firemen outside. "Branson hates that."

I tried to laugh, but the pain was too much. I couldn't imagine the agony Riley had endured before we got there. The grill had exploded? That explained the burning in my throat. "Can I have some water?" I asked, unable to raise my voice above a hoarse whisper.

Wyatt was the first to hand me a glass, and I drank it greedily, audibly sighing at the refreshing cool against my sweltering skin.

I had a ton of questions, most having to do with my friend being a dog, but when I looked back up at the room, I saw I wasn't the only one who wanted answers.

Branson had returned without the firemen, and together, the four Walkers made an imposing image. I knew Nash would be on my side, but I couldn't help but wonder how happy these four would be when they found out this was all my fault.

13

NASH

PHIN'S SKIN was sweaty and red. Originally, I thought the healing tired him out, like a run around the woods, but he was clearly in pain. He hadn't been in pain when we got here.

"What's going on, Phin?" I asked once he'd finished his water.

"Can you heal anyone?" Wyatt chirped, dropping to one of the chairs at the table.

Phin clasped his hands on the table and stared at them. "I'm sorry."

Sorry? For what? He was the hero here.

Branson retrieved his baby from Aver and moved to sit on the floor in front of the table. Riley padded over, laying down with his head in Branson's lap. "You can do it, love. Just like we practiced." Branson petted Riley's head. "Deep breath. You've got this."

At least Phin wasn't looking at his hands anymore. He stared at Riley without blinking.

"He wasn't always a shifter," I said, tabling my concerns for a moment. "Riley was human and then met Branson."

"And he infected him?" Phin asked.

Bless my cousins. The only thing that kept them all from snarling at that remark was my obvious affection for Phin—and their worry for Riley. They remained silent so I could explain. "No. It isn't a sickness. This was a once-in-a-lifetime thing. None of us knew it could happen. But he's a wolf now and learning how to operate in his new body."

"Does it hurt him?" Phin asked, wincing.

I narrowed my eyes. He *was* in pain. From the healing? I bit back the growl that formed as I slowly connected the dots.

"It doesn't hurt to shift, but it can be confusing," Branson said, taking over. He looked into Riley's eyes the whole time, the two of them trying to breathe at the same rate. Synchronizing their breaths had helped Riley shift before, something he was still trying to master.

"And the baby?" Phin asked. I had to hand it to him, for, as weird as all this was, he was asking the right questions and hadn't once balked or claimed we were all insane.

"Shifter as well," Branson said proudly. "He's one hundred percent average in every other way."

The Riley dog let out a low snarl, and Branson chuckled.

"You know what I mean, babe." He patted Riley's head.

Phin looked like he might pass out—from the shock of this revelation? Or the pain? "Your turn, Phin. What's going on here? I've never noticed you having this reaction. This didn't happen when you healed the little girl."

He looked back at his hands.

The pressure in the room changed, not enough for anyone without heightened senses to detect, but enough for me to know Riley had managed to shift back.

Phin giggled sharply, slamming his hands over his

mouth. "I'm sorry, this isn't funny. I just sort of wondered about the whole clothes thing—is this a Mystique situation where he makes his clothes... I'm not saying I wanted to see him naked, but... how does that work?"

"Did he just compare us to the X-men?" Wyatt asked.

"Be quiet," I growled. "He's trying to understand and doing an amazing job."

Phin's lips turned up in a relieved smile.

"Clothing is assumed by the shifter," Aver explained. "When you shift, it becomes a part of your fur. There won't be changes in color. If you wear a striped shirt, you won't have striped fur, but if you're in bulkier outerwear, your fur may come in a little shaggier. When you shift back, it reemerges."

"That's handy," Phin said.

We all waited several more seconds, but that was all he had to say.

Riley had hugged his mate and child and rose from the floor, walking to Phin. He wrapped his arms around Phin's shoulders in a gentle hug. "Thank you. I don't know how you did that, but thank you."

The hug was a sweet gesture, but I was still tense watching Riley put his hands so close to Phin's skin. He hadn't brushed his bare flesh yet, and that seemed to be what initiated the forced truth-telling. It ended up being Phin who grabbed for Riley's hand before any of us could warn him otherwise.

Phin stiffened. His face went slack, and I lunged forward. I wasn't sure what I'd planned on doing. Maybe cover his mouth so whatever truth he'd been compelled to spill couldn't be heard. I didn't reach him in time, and even though Riley tugged his hand quickly away, Phin's mouth opened. "It hurts when I heal. I call it the exchange."

That hadn't been what I expected to hear. I let the words roll around in my head, unable to put them together in a way that didn't make me furious. "It *hurts* you?" I snarled. "Why didn't you tell me that?"

Phin didn't blink my direction. He was still focusing on Riley. "I didn't mean to say that. Why did I say that?"

"I'm sorry," Riley rushed to say as he took his spot next to Branson back on the floor. This wasn't the room for big meetings. "I honestly thought Nash might have warned you. He hates my ability so much I thought he would have said something."

I didn't hate it; I just didn't want my secrets shared without my consent. The secrets in my head weren't funny like Wyatt's—they were damning.

Aver had his phone out, looking at the screen. "Property is secure. Everyone has vacated. I'll arm the perimeter alarms, and we can all sit down at the dining table. There's room for everyone, and it looks like we have a lot of questions to answer, on both sides." He *would* sound calm and collected. He hadn't unwittingly asked Phin to *hurt himself*.

It was a good idea, and the walk to the table might give me a chance to cool down, but I was still too hot to take the suggestion. "Why didn't you tell me it hurts you?"

"Nash, he healed Riley. Why are you mad?" Branson asked.

"Because it hurt him, Branson. Look! His skin is red. How much pain are you still in?" I barked.

Phin shrugged. "It's fine. It will go away."

"It isn't fine!" I clenched my hands, feeling my claws stick into my palm. If I was partially shifting, I really did need to calm down, but I couldn't dislodge the thought from my mind. Healing hurt him.

"You need to cool down," Branson growled, getting to his feet. "Clearly he wanted to keep it a secret."

"You're just saying that because it was *your mate* that was healed," I snapped. Immediately, I knew I'd gone too far. Branson's hands around my throat was my second indication. As fired up as I was, I could've punched a hole through my cousin, but as the scuffle began, the fight whooshed from me. I deserved this pain—if not for my sin from a decade ago, then for what I'd done to Phin.

"Both of you stop it," Riley ordered. He had Bran Jr. on his hip, bouncing as he chastised us. "Grown men acting like children. Go to the table. We'll talk this out. I'm sorry for the pain I caused Phin."

Both Phin and Branson looked like they had something to say to that, but both wisely kept their mouths closed. Riley was getting spooky. If I squinted, I swore I could see Nana.

We migrated one room over. Paul helped Aver grab drinks, since apparently the Walkers couldn't have a pack discussion without refreshing beverages. He set down a tray of iced teas. "Just as Nana Walker says, a hard talk should be done with a cool drink." I hadn't realized he spent so much time with Nana. Paul always seemed to either be here or on pack lands.

I waited to see where Phin was sitting and took the seat next to him. Riley sat on his other side, shooting him appreciative looks.

"First, let me say thank you," Branson said. He sat across from Riley and reached over the table to grasp his hand. "I'm indebted to you, Phin. You healed my mate."

"Please don't thank me. It was my fault."

Branson frowned. "The chief seemed to think it was a faulty gas line in the grill. Did you make the grill?"

"No, but..." He took a deep breath.

I already knew what he was going to say, and that he was wrong, but I wouldn't stop him from speaking.

"I'm cursed. People get hurt around me. Always. I'm sorry. This is probably really shocking for you all to hear..." He looked up, clearly expecting a shocked, maybe angry response.

"Walkers have a type," Aver muttered under his breath.

"Seriously," Wyatt added with a shudder.

Phin frowned. This hadn't been the reaction he expected.

"Riley thought he was cursed too," I said. "He is the friend I was telling you about."

"Does anyone else think this is a pretty strange coincidence? Two Walker alphas meet two humans with extraordinary abilities?" Paul asked.

If anyone else had done the asking, I might have pondered the question, but since it was Paul, I only worried about these worries returning to the pack and becoming gossip. They'd been quieter than normal, delivering less presents for the blessed child each day. I wanted to keep it that way. "I'm more concerned with what you call the exchange, Phin. Explain that."

He nibbled at his bottom lip, his eyebrows dipped with worry. "It's a part of it. Every time. My hands heat up, and I heal. I can't heal sickness, cancer, or diseases, but I can heal other injuries. When I do, I feel a fraction of what the injured person felt. The deeper the injuries, the higher the pain. It isn't fun, but it's fair—"

My chest rumbled. "Fair to fucking who?"

"Nash." Aver spoke my name like a warning.

Why was I the only one angry about this? If I'd known, I never would've brought Phin. I knew him well enough to know he couldn't resist healing those around him. He hadn't thought twice with that little girl. Just like he hadn't with Riley, even though he could clearly see his burns and knew how badly it would hurt him. Why was that okay for everyone else? My frustrations grew, becoming this living, breathing shadow inside me. If Phin couldn't look out for himself, then I needed to. "No more," I demanded. "No more healing, not if it hurts you."

"You can't tell me what to do!" Phin shot back. "I'll heal if I need to."

"And if you come across someone too badly injured, then what? What happens then?"

"I don't know. If they're too far gone, nothing will happen." Phin's anger matched my own.

"And what if they aren't too far gone? You'll assume all that pain. It could kill you, Phin. That sort of shock to your body—"

"If that's what needs to happen for me to protect others, then so be it!" Phin yelled.

I jumped to my feet, every instinct in me urging me to grab Phin and run, take him to a cave where no one could hurt him, not even himself.

"Nash, breathe," Branson warned. Something about my body language must have tipped him off.

"You fucking breathe," I snarled, my gaze landing not on my cousin, but my twin. Wyatt's lips were turned down in a partial frown. I found what I always found when I looked in my brother's face—whole-hearted acceptance—but there was also worry. I sucked in, letting the air slide between my clenched teeth before exhaling. I did feel better, or at least not like I was about to run off with Phin caveman-style. I still *wanted* to but felt better equipped to restrain myself. "As my mate—"

"You're what?" Phin asked.

Fuck, fuck, fuck. That hadn't been the most graceful way of asking. I rotated around to him, trying to block the others out. If he rejected me now, I'd never hear the end of it. "I know we just... I know it's sudden, but it's what I wanted. When you talked about leaving, it scared me, Phineas. I don't know how I've gone so long without you in my life, and I don't ever want to again."

He didn't reply at first. I grasped the fact that he hadn't come out with an immediate *no way*. He sucked on his bottom lip, worrying it between his teeth before speaking. "I don't know what that means. But if it has to do with you, I know I want it."

I smiled, feeling as light as I had this morning before I knew Phin put his own body in jeopardy every time he healed another. "You'll be my mate?"

"I'll be your anything."

My soul felt like it had been attached to a yo-yo. I'd plunged to the dark depths, only to bounce back up, light as a cloud.

"I hate to interrupt," Branson said, "but are you sure that Riley is healed? His injuries won't come back?"

Riley shot his mate a dark look, saving me the trouble, but Phin didn't seem bothered. "It never has before. Once he's healed, he's healed. Unless something else happens."

"And your pain?" Branson asked.

"Already lessened," Phin replied, and my shoulders weren't the only ones that relaxed hearing that. Phin might not have known what he did today when he healed Riley, but I did. My cousins and my brother would be grateful for life. Before, they might have respected him because he was mine. Now they would because he was him.

Still, I needed to get Phin alone where I could check

every inch of him. His skin wasn't as red; that much was true. "If you're all done, I'd like to check him over."

"You aren't a doctor," Aver pointed out.

"He's going to play doctor," Wyatt added.

Riley shot them both a *be-quiet-or-I'll-poison-your-dinner* look. "Thank you again, Phineas. Truly. I thought I was..." He inhaled sharply. "Well, it was horrible. And so fast. I turned it on, clicked the pilot light, and it all went up. I think I'm only alive now because I'm a shifter."

That fact didn't sit right with any of us.

"So thank you, a hundred times over. But please don't hurt yourself for my sake again. Shifters are a tough bunch. Most of us will heal."

Except Riley had spontaneously shifted into his wolf form, so getting him help would've been difficult. It was good Phin had come when he did. I'd just make sure he never needed to again.

"I know I'm the newest member here, but I think I speak for us all when I say my home is your home. You're welcome here for as long as you would like to stay."

The others murmured their agreement, and I stood, reaching for Phin's hand. This was great and all, but my fingers ached to check him over. Aver was right. I wasn't a doctor, but I had other methods. Ones that would distract him from any pain that still lingered. I tugged Phin out of his chair. He stopped at the doorway.

"Thank you all for not hating me," he said quietly and with so much emotion clogging his throat, I could only hug him tightly.

"Of course, Phineas," Riley replied. He looked to each person that remained in the room: Paul, Wyatt, Aver, Bran Jr., and Branson. "We're a strange bunch already. You fit right in."

Phin smiled and let me pull him the rest of the way out and down the hallway. My room was at the end, and I closed the door quickly behind us before reaching for Phin's shirt.

"Whoa, whoa, whoa." Phin put his hands flat against my chest.

"I need to see," I grunted, too overcome by my alpha nature to speak in a more friendly manner. I'd claimed Phin as mine, but my wolf had claimed him long before. His care and comfort were the most important thing.

He hugged me tightly. "I'm fine, Nash, really. It's all gone now. The pain was only bad at first."

That was meant to soothe me, but it did the opposite. The pain was bad—he just admitted it. Riley had been injured severely, but not in the worst way that could happen. How much more could Phin hurt?

He'd never heal another person. I'd see to that. What had happened with Riley would be the last time. I at least knew well enough not to say as much to Phin now. He'd only fight me. But I'd make sure of it from this day forward.

"Why don't we lay down instead?" Phin asked. "I'm pretty beat now, and neither of us got a lot of sleep last night."

That was the truth. Phin had slept more than me, but even he'd only gotten a handful of hours. I'd spent most of that time watching him sleep. And napping meant holding him in my arms. "Can you sleep in that?"

"Nash Walker, you're trying to get me naked."

Yes, I was. Always. But at that moment I was more concerned with his comfort. He'd suggested the nap. That was proof enough to me of how tired he was. I laid back on my unmade bed, tugging the covers around us as Phin snuggled into my chest, finding the perfect spot to lay his head.

His fingers danced over my chest, and I growled, a happy noise that rumbled through us both.

"I like when you make that sound," Phin murmured. "Is it a wolf thing?"

"Yes."

He snuggled deeper, pressing more of his body against mine before sighing.

I enjoyed the peace. The others were murmuring to each other in the dining room. I caught enough to know they were talking about Phin and me. Suddenly, Phin lifted his head, furrowing his brow. "You know how Riley said you guys heal faster? Do you have other abilities too? Like hearing or anything?"

I petted his head, mushing his hair flat. "Shh, now, Phin. Let's sleep."

Phin stiffened but eventually relaxed into me. "I'm going to ask again when we wake up."

I didn't doubt it, and I would answer, but first we both needed to rest. Now that I'd laid down, I recognized how tired I really was. I'd planned on just watching Phin nap, but my eyelids grew heavy.

"What's happening?"

My father rushed around my room, grabbing clothes from my closet and throwing them to the bed. "We elders have come to a decision."

I sat straight, rubbing the sleep from my eyes. "Who is it? Which of us will become Alpha?"

My dad didn't answer. "You need to get dressed."

He wouldn't meet my gaze.

"Where's Wyatt?"

He flinched from my question. My father, the man who wasn't afraid of anything, flinched from a question from his eighteen-year-old son. "Your mother is bringing him."

"We're going separately?" That didn't make sense. We did everything together. I'd pulled on my pants but froze with my shirt bunched around my neck. "What do you mean? Why wouldn't we go together? Where are we going? What time is it?"

Finally, my father looked at me. I wished he hadn't. There was sorrow in his gaze, but mostly a cold determination. "This was the only way we could all agree on."

"What was? What's going on?"

He shook his head sadly, and I knew I wasn't getting answers to any of my questions. "Get dressed."

We took the town car. My father drove. He never drove, always telling us to not ever do something you could get someone else to do for you. He drove to the ceremonial fields where we accepted new members into the pack. It was pitch black outside. No morning sun shone through the trees.

"The torches are burning?" I leaned over the dash to get a better look through the trees. The torches that formed a circle around the field were only used for specific situations. Like when the pack came together to boot out a shifter causing problems. I'd never seen it happen. I'd only seen the circle used to accept new members. That clearly wasn't what was happening now.

My cousins Branson and Aver were also there. Aver looked nervously between his parents, while Branson stood like a proud statue next to his mother. I spotted Wyatt and smiled with relief. He waved, but my mom pushed his arm back down to his side.

She wouldn't look at me either.

My grandfather, Alpha Walker, was there as well.

"Where's Nana?" I asked.

"She doesn't need to be here," Delia, Branson's mother,

replied sharply. I growled at her rude tone, earning a proud look from my father.

"My mother wouldn't appreciate the lengths we've gone to attempting to secure our next heir."

I frowned at the use of the word. Packs were led by Alphas accepted by their people, not divine right. However, a Walker alpha had led the pack in Walker County since its inception.

"What are we doing here, Mother?" Branson asked with that pompous air he seemed to always carry. "I have school in the morning."

Delia squeezed his shoulder. "This is more important than schooling, Branson. This is the pack's future."

I kept my face clear—never let them know what you're thinking, that's what my father said—but inside, I was freaking out. The elders had tried to decide which of us would take control since we'd been born at the same time, or as close to it as twins could be born. Technically, if it was after midnight, it was all of our birthdays. Our eighteenth. The day we were allowed by pack law to assume control. But which of us had they chosen?

Alpha Walker cleared his throat, and we all fell silent. "Your parents have all done a tremendous job preparing each of you for rule. Perhaps this decision would be easier if they hadn't. But I cannot lead forever. No one could have foreseen Patrick dying as he did. This decision wasn't ever one I thought I'd have to make, but an Alpha does not shy away from a choice because it is difficult." He had his walking stick and used it to mark two long lines in the middle of the circle, creating a grid with four squares. "Please assume your positions."

All of us? I looked up at my father, and he nodded for me to obey. The hair on my nape stood up, and I held my breath, trying to calm my nerves. Now wasn't the time for an uncontrolled shift. It would make me seem weak, and if I was going to rule, I couldn't be weak.

I was the most qualified of us anyway. Technically, I was older than Wyatt, though the fact that we were born touching meant that in the eyes of the pack we were the same age. Aver was too sensitive to lead. He ran home to his mommy and daddy at the slightest sign of trouble, and Branson was a pompous dick. I was so sure they were about to announce me as the next Alpha, I didn't hear what Alpha Walker said until I replayed it again.

"Since a consensus cannot be reached, we have come to the conclusion that the only way we can decide is by utilizing the old traditions, Alpha by combat. The Walker alpha who remains breathing at the end will lead our people."

Instantly, my gaze changed as I sized up my cousins and brother. Wyatt would not fight me, but if I overtook Aver and Branson, perhaps that would be enough to assume the role, and then I would pardon him when I was Alpha. Adrenaline spiked through me until I finally looked up at my cousins, my twin, and saw their horrified faces...

I bolted upright with a ragged gasp, clutching my chest as I had the same dream I'd had night after night for years. It didn't come every night, not in the recent months, but enough for me to know immediately that it had been a dream. I was in my room and no longer in that circle where I'd nearly made the greatest mistake of my life.

"Nash? Nash?" Phin was there. That was new. I never had the dream when I was in bed with someone else. That had partly been the reason I'd taken to sleeping around. A stranger next to me in bed kept the familiar nightmares away.

But, for the first time, someone was there to witness my uneven gasps, the fear that felt like a cloud encompassing my body. I felt naked and seen. Except it was Phin here with me, so there was no shame, just relief that I wasn't *there* and that he was here. "I'm okay. Just a bad dream."

"Do you want to talk about it?" he asked quietly. It was dark outside. We'd slept the day away, or the sun at the least.

I told him about the events that I relived, skipping the part where I was the only one of us Walkers who had been eager to do as the elders had said. I'd wanted to rule. Wanted to be the big bad Alpha with a capital A. I explained that our parents had gathered the four of us and demanded we fight to the death, all because they couldn't decide which of us should rule. But it had never been that they *couldn't* decide, though I didn't realize that until later. They didn't want to decide. None of our parents had been willing to give up the promise of power that came with having their child chosen as Alpha.

To his credit, Phin listened without adding commentary until I was finished. He had to have had questions. I hadn't had the time before now to explain the concept of elder families or even pack hierarchy. Strange, since those two concepts had ruled my own life for so long. "Wow. That's really shitty. I'm sorry. And the four of you just left after that? Left your families and all that you knew?"

After I'd pulled my head out of my ass. "Yes. We left together. Nana eventually gave us this land, and we built our house here."

"That's amazing," Phin said, snuggling back against my chest. "You all got out. You left even when it was difficult. I'm proud of you. All of you."

I hadn't asked for his pride, but now that I had it, I'd

nurture it too. I tried to lay back down—sink into the pillow as fully as Phin had against my chest—but my legs were restless, and my breaths came more rapidly.

"Can't sleep?" Phin asked.

"Sorry, I'll be quiet. You should close your eyes a little longer. I woke you up."

Phin yawned, proving my point, but he didn't close his eyes after. His palm slid over my chest, exploring the ridges and flat planes before heading downward. "I can't heal your mind, even though I wish I could. And I can't heal your heart."

His fingers dipped beneath my waistband, and I sucked in sharply.

"But I can distract you from the pain."

Funny, I'd wanted to do the same thing for him. I knew there was no amount of sex that could make me forget the events of a decade ago, but as Phin gripped my erection, if there was anyone who could make me forget—even just for a moment—it was him.

14

PHINEAS

I MIGHT NOT HAVE HELD a lot of dicks, but I'd seen many. I was a single guy with internet. Porn was no stranger. But not even the beefiest of monster schlongs could compare to the girth I attempted to wrap my fingers around.

It wasn't that he was the largest. That would only limit the things we could do. But there was no mistaking what I held. An erect dick attached to a man who knew how to use it. Right now, though, I wanted him to lay back and simply enjoy. I was also me, though, so it wasn't long before I got into my head, sure I wasn't doing anything right.

I was determined to distract him, though, and slid to my knees so that I was crouched over him. I stroked him with my whole hand a few times, letting only my finger graze down his shaft at the end.

He hissed and jerked his hips. Clearly, that felt good. I squeezed his shaft at the base, noting how the muscles in his face twitched, the shape of his mouth as he moaned. Maybe I wasn't the one of us with unlimited sexual prowess, but I could learn. That was something I did do well. And I would. I'd learn not how to flirt or attract men—I'd learn how to make Nash happy. I parted my lips, rubbing them along Nash's shaft as he slid in my mouth.

A quiet voice nagged at the back of my head, telling me that I was only setting myself up for heartbreak. The curse had never stopped before, even if I really liked a place I'd ended up. A few of them I'd liked immensely. Probably would still be there if the weird and freak accidents hadn't driven me out.

But I didn't have to make any of those choices. Right now, I would devote everything to Nash and letting him forget the fucked-up things his parents and family did to him. I grabbed the sheet and pulled it over my bobbing head, testing the hypothesis that not being seen would make me bolder. So far, it just made the air warmer and harder to breathe.

Nash pulled the sheet back and cupped my face. "Seeing you is half the pleasure, Phineas," he murmured, rubbing my cheek softly with the rough pad of his thumb. His warm eyes were full of not only desire, but devotion, and I doubled my efforts, using my tongue to lick while my head bobbed.

I massaged his balls with my other hand, working his long dick with the other. It took some coordinating, but eventually, I had my limbs and mouth working together, a dick-sucking, stroking, fondling machine.

"Phin," Nash gasped.

No one said my name like he did. The sharp *F* sound felt more like a caress. Where I felt the caress depended on my mood. Right now, I felt it against my own dick. That gave me an idea. I had to give up one of my activities, but I needed my hand free. I felt Nash's eyes watching me, but he didn't ask any questions.

When I began stroking myself in time with my head bobs, Nash growled, the low, sexy kind. Bringing him pleasure brought me pleasure, and I was already close to orgasming. I prayed I could make him come before I did. My cheeks hollowed as I sucked, imagining I was pulling the cum from him like a straw.

Nash grunted, making sounds that weren't real words, only parts of words. He grabbed the back of my head and held me in place as the first spurt of cum splashed my tongue. I climaxed instantly while trying to swallow as he had me. I nearly succeeded before it became too much, the excess dribbling down my chin. Nash continued to cup my head. He wiped my face clean with his thumb, feeding me the extra as he gathered it on his finger.

"Thank you," Nash whispered, and I didn't think he was thanking me for the blowjob. At least, not only because of the blowjob.

Hopefully now he'd be able to rest a while longer. He pulled me back the way I'd been laying, and I settled my head against his chest a moment before his stomach rumbled. "You're hungry," I said, not as a question.

"Guess so. You?"

"I just ate."

Nash smirked. "That's what I like to hear." He kissed my nose before jumping from the bed and pulling on some pants. "Want anything? The guys are still out there." He went silent and angled his head to the side. "They're wondering if you like pickles."

"You do have super hearing!" My mouth dropped open as I thought about all the things he probably overheard me doing. Mostly, I worried he listened to me going to the bathroom. "Pee sounds are private!"

Nash laughed and smacked my ass playfully. "No one here wants to listen to that. You're safe."

He'd meant it playfully, but I couldn't help but ponder. Was I finally safe? Had I found the place I could stay? The only reason I had for wanting to believe I wasn't was because I knew how much more it would hurt when it turned out the curse was stronger than the Walkers.

———

Since it was night by the time we got up from our naps, and definitely night once we'd finished eating dinner with the others, I spent the night. The next morning, everyone acted as if my presence in the Walker home was a normal occurrence and not an odd by-product from yesterday's drama.

I was glad to see Riley, both at dinner and breakfast. His skin didn't have a mark on it, and I couldn't help the pride I felt. Yeah, it had hurt, but if the trade-off was having Riley healed, the pain was worth it. Nash and I would just have to disagree there.

Nash had something to do with Wyatt at his bar, fixing a leaky pipe or something, and I had my own work to do. I didn't want Nash thinking I was into him for his money.

Though I wasn't even sure if Nash had money. I assumed from the house and how they all lived.

Nash didn't want us to stray too far away from each other, so he went with me to my apartment, where I picked up my computer. Then he dropped me off at Rise and Grind before heading across the street to the Greasy Stump. I'd have to ask Wyatt how he came up with that name one of these days.

There it was again. Me, making plans for the undetermined future.

I cracked open my laptop, appreciating the familiar hum before my *Battlestar Galactica* emblem screensaver popped up. I smiled. Normally, the characters I watched and read about had lives so much more exciting than my own. But here I was, healing wolf-men. *Shifters.* I hadn't wanted to nerd out too hardcore in front of everyone, but I had only about a billion questions for each of them.

I was still smiling when I opened GeekGab, finding several notifications for pings and PMs. One was from Reg, and one was from Bun, and the rest were from Chuck. I scanned the first few lines of each message. My smile dropped as his obviously panicked tone increased.

ChuckShurley: *Where have you been? Neither of the girls have seen you.*

ChuckShurley: *Should I call the police where you are? Phin? Answer me please.*

ChuckShurley: *You've been acting really strange, Phineas. I'm worried. Please message me.*

I was acting weird? This was a level of friendship I hadn't seen from Chuck yet, and I didn't like it. When Nash was clingy, it was silly and sort of hot, but just the virtual version from Chuck was enough to make my skin crawl. I began to type out a reply. *Been really busy, nothing to worry about...* Did I want to reassure him? Maybe it would be better to not answer his questions about where I was and address the creepiness factor. But we'd been chatting for years, I wasn't going to let our friendship go down the drain because of a few weird messages. I deleted what I wrote, deciding to ask Bun and Reg about it instead.

"Phin, there you are." Mrs. Boxer was the last person I

expected to walk toward me, but she was, along with another old woman in a thick brown coat, her silver hair pulled back in a braid. "You weren't home last night."

I closed my laptop, letting my virtual problems stay where they belonged. "Mrs. Boxer, hi. Are you okay? You're right, I wasn't home last night. Did you need me?" When had I become so very popular?

"Oh no, just keeping an eye on you. Us single people have to stick together." She gestured to her friend. "This is Phineas Peters, the nice young man I was telling you about."

I was overjoyed to see that Mrs. Boxer did in fact have friends that weren't her children. That was one less thing I could worry about. The woman with him was a little odd, though. She hadn't spoken a word, but she stared at me like she was peering into my skull.

"You might actually know my new friends, Mrs. Boxer. Remember Nash Walker?"

The other woman pulled out one of the chairs at my table and sat down.

"Uh, please, sit..." I pulled the other chair out for Mrs. Boxer.

"Oh, I know Nash Walker," Mrs. Boxer said with a blush. That man's charm knew no bounds. "This is his great-grandmother."

Though I hadn't taken a drink, I began to cough like I had and it had gone down the wrong tube.

"Nana Walker," the other woman said, sticking out her hand.

I shook it, surprised by the firmness with which she gripped my fingers. "Hi, Mrs... Ms...?"

"Nana is fine, child."

"Nana." I smiled. I could see where Nash got some of

his brashness. But the family I'd heard of from Nash hadn't sounded like great people. Grandmother included?

"I was wondering who had my great-grandson's head in the clouds." She looked at me for a long moment. "I like you."

She didn't seem like a bad person. I remembered what Nash had said about his Nana giving them the land to live on, and my face relaxed. This was a good Walker. "Thank you. I... like you too."

"You don't have to say it back," she laughed. "Where is my great-grandson right now? I can't imagine he would let you stray very far away."

That should have made me more uncomfortable than it did. She spoke with an intimate knowledge of her great-grandson and me. Coming from her lips, it sounded... almost expected. Was she a wolf too? I couldn't imagine the woman in front of me dropping to four legs, but she would have to be, wouldn't she? Maybe shifterism was hereditary, and it skipped a generation. Wait, was shifterism a rude term? I pressed my lips together, afraid I'd suddenly say the word on accident now that it was on my mind.

"What are you two up to today?" I asked, paying careful attention to each letter as I formed it.

"Just going for a stroll," Mrs. Boxer replied. "Nana makes sure I get out of the house at least once a week."

That made me happier than I thought it would.

"You've got a dark cloud over you," Nana said.

That made me less happy.

"I do?"

She peered at me some more. "It follows you, like a shadow. You stick to my Nash. He'll take care of you." She reached out and grabbed my hand, holding my fingers as tightly as she had before. "You're important to him. To them all."

Had someone told her what I'd done for Riley? That was the only reason I could think of for her cryptic message. Unless... she could sense my curse? That would definitely be like a dark shadow. And it did follow me. I licked my lips. It would have been so easy to pacify her, making promises I wasn't sure I could keep, but for some reason, I felt like she would know if I wasn't completely honest. "I'll try. I like being around him."

"Don't try, son. Do." Nana stood, and Mrs. Boxer copied her. "We better be on our way. Don't want our muscles cooling down. Need to keep our slim figures."

Mrs. Boxer giggled like a schoolgirl before following Nana out. Neither said goodbye.

That was the strangest interaction I'd had with one of the Walkers, and considering the interactions I'd had already, that was saying something.

I spotted movement outside the shop windows and smiled, expecting to see Nana and Mrs. Boxer walking that way from the exit. It was Charles from the station, though. He caught me smiling and waved. I waved back but stood before he decided to come in too.

It didn't take me very long to pack my things. I hadn't gotten a lick of work done, but I didn't think I could. Not with how weird Chuck was being and how cryptic Nash's great-grandmother had been. Maybe I could help Nash and Wyatt. I waved to the barista, grabbing my tech before heading out.

There was a traffic jam outside the coffee shop. In Walkerton, that meant more than one car was driving by. I hung back, letting the street clear before I jaywalked. As I waited, staring at the Greasy Stump sign, I heard the couple behind me whisper between each other.

"He smells like him," the man said.

"Let's just go, John."

"Absolutely not."

There was a tap on my shoulder next. The last car had driven by, and I was clear to cross, but I turned instead, coming face to face with a man who was undoubtedly related to Nash and Wyatt. He looked like half of them both. Mixed with the woman at his side, I was confident in assuming these were his parents.

The bad Walkers.

First his great-grandma, now his parents? Was there a convention in town? Though, replaying their whispered conversation now that I had an idea who they were, led me to assume that perhaps they were here for their son specifically.

"Do you know Nash Walker?" the man asked.

I looked from him to the woman. She folded her hands in front of her, flicking her hair over her shoulders in a repetitive, nervous pattern.

It wasn't like I was going to lie. "I do. He's my friend."

The man leaned in and sniffed, his mouth turning up in a smile that was overly familiar. "Friend. Got it."

"I'm sorry, can I help you?"

"You can. Convince my sons to come home. There's a ceremony coming up that I'd like them both to be there for."

"What sort of ceremony?"

"John, you can't," the woman whispered.

"A personal family matter," John said, waving away my suspicion.

"Then you should ask Nash yourself." I turned back around, checked the street for cars, and began to cross.

John Walker moved like lightning to the space in front of me, blocking my way. "I'll pay you," he said, his eyes scanning up and down my body like he was judging me and found me lacking. "Any amount you want, name it."

I wasn't sure if I was angrier at the proof of how horrible a parent this man was or that he assumed money would get me to turn on Nash. Both made me equally mad, and I showed that anger by calmly stepping around him.

John grabbed my wrist, holding me back as he squeezed just enough so that I knew he could seriously hurt me if he wanted.

"Let go."

His fingers tightened.

His wife tugged at his arm before something on the other side of the street made her eyes bulge.

There was a loud shout, more like an animal's roar, and then John let go of my hand on his way down to the asphalt. Blood shot out from his nose while Nash pulled me behind him. "Don't touch him," he snarled.

"Nash, it's okay." I didn't like the rage that shook his voice.

He'd hit his father without a second thought. The man was still on the ground, but Nash just stared like he was trash waiting to be collected. "It isn't," Nash growled.

He turned back to me at the exact same moment I rubbed my wrist. It didn't hurt, not badly, but Nash spotted the motion, and his eyes narrowed. He growled in a way I'd never heard before. "Did he hurt you?" His words were brittle and shattered on the ground between us.

I shook my head. "No, it isn't broken or anything, just a little red. Nash—"

"He hurt you," Nash said, sounding so calm that when

he turned on his father, punching him over and over—for a split second—I thought it was a joke.

I shouted for him to stop. His mother did too, but as the seconds ticked by at a snail's pace, Nash's snarls took on a more animalistic tone. I wasn't sure if Nash was even on the sidewalk with us anymore. I felt like I was only with the wolf.

And I had no idea how to get him to stop.

15

NASH

Nᴀsʜ ʜᴀᴅ ʟᴇFᴛ ᴛʜᴇ ʙᴜɪʟᴅɪɴɢ. I knew that I need to stop, that if I didn't, my father would die. And yet my thoughts were not my own. They weren't even human. Raw, primal rage had a vice around my head. This shifter had harmed what was mine. My mate.

My mate's body had been altered at his hands. That the shifter was my father drove my wolf to the brink of insanity.

"Please, Nash, please!" That was my sweet Phineas.

I can't. I don't want to. Now that I had my father under my fists, all the hurt, pain, and rage gathered in my fingers. With each strike, my knuckles stamped it all into his skin.

"Brother!" That voice was as familiar as my own. "Nash, man, he isn't worth this. You'll lose everything! Your job, your mate, everything!"

Lose everything? How can something that feels so good put me at so much risk?

"Dammit, you stubborn dick!" I heard something I almost never did from Wyatt, the deep resonating tone of an alpha. My wolf knew it wasn't a challenge and didn't respond aggressively, but in the moment it took to recognize the twin beast in my brother, I was able to regain some clarity. My fists paused, and Wyatt pulled me back, pinning my arms loosely at my sides.

My mother dropped to his side as my father groaned and clutched his battered face.

Phineas looked at me with horror before stepping toward my father, hands outstretched like he was going to heal him.

"Don't," I growled, issuing the only actual order I'd ever spoken to him. "Don't fucking touch him."

I couldn't see into his eyes. He looked to my father, giving me his profile. "You don't mean that."

"Whatever pain I've given him, he deserves."

The smart thing would've been to stop talking, to say I lost my temper and that I was sorry. But I wouldn't lie to Phin, even if this drove him away. I'd lost my temper, that was true, but I wasn't sorry. I didn't regret it. I'd wanted to punch that fucker in the face ever since he woke me up and told me to get dressed.

Sirens wailed. Someone had called the cops. It had been a while since I'd had the chance to relax in one of Sheriff Maslow's fine rooms. This would be the first time it was for anything substantial. Before, I'd been a young punk, fresh out of the pack and looking to get disorderly.

"Come on, we'll go back to the bar. Let them come there." Wyatt tugged me back across the street.

My feet sunk into the cement, and I looked to Phin. I wouldn't order him to follow like a dog. But if he tried to stay, I didn't know what I would do. Or even if I *could* leave him here on the sidewalk with my parents. He'd never been in greater danger than he was standing so near to them.

It was my brother who recognized the problem and let me go, heading back to Phin's side. "This is scary, I get you,

Phinster. But try to take what you know already of Nash and what you know of *them* and make your decision off of that. Don't get me wrong—Nash is going to have to apologize up and down to gain your trust back, but don't make him choose your safety over his own. He'll choose you every time."

There was truth to that. I'd had chances to punch my father several times in the decade since we left and had always restrained myself. The only difference this time was Phineas, though I preferred it if Wyatt hadn't told him that. Phin would just blame himself.

Phin turned from my parents huddled at the sidewalk. A bystander had given John an ice pack, and the sirens were so loud I wondered why we were even bothering going inside.

Still, we went back across the street with me at the lead and Wyatt as the unlucky wrangler. Phineas followed behind, though, never looking up once from his feet.

Now that the adrenaline was fading, the shame spilled in. I felt none for my father, not an ounce. But Phineas was good, pure, and kind. I'd be lucky if he ever looked at me again.

Thanks to the repair work we'd been doing, Wyatt had yet to open the bar, and it looked like that would have to wait a while longer. By the time Wyatt got us both inside, sending me to pace at the other side of the room and settling Phineas in a booth near the door, the sheriff's car was outside. He'd turned off the siren, but kept the lights running. The blues and reds revolved across the wall like lights at a dance party.

"I'll get you water and fries," Wyatt said to Phin. He popped back behind the bar into the kitchen, and I attempted to look at him without him knowing I was.

That turned out to be easier than I'd expected. Phin hadn't looked up from the table once. He looked so small and confused, like his world had been tilted to its side. And I'd done the pushing. I wanted to say *I'm sorry*, but just to him. My only regrets in this were his fear, his panic. And the fact that I'd changed the way he would ever look at me.

Wyatt returned with the fries and water. He'd brought Phin a lemon-lime soda as well, claiming he needed to get some sugar in him. If he didn't look up from the table soon, I'd be taking us to the hospital. "Wait here," Wyatt said. "I'm gonna check outside. They should've been here by now." The bell over the door jingled as he stepped out.

"Phin..." I said his name and stopped. What did I say? How did I make him understand that my devotion to him was the same—my love for him was the same? He knew what my parents had done, but if our places had been switched and Phin had been the one tasked with murdering his brother, he still wouldn't have done what I did today. My Phin wasn't that type.

He also wasn't mine anymore.

Not if he wouldn't even look at me.

I continued my pacing. There was nothing between us, and yet it felt like a hundred-foot brick wall stood between where he was and me.

When Wyatt returned, I expected him to come with the sheriff and cuffs. He came alone. "Show's over, folks," Wyatt said grimly. "When questioned, the dick said he'd come to town with those injuries, that the witnesses were mistaken, and you'd done nothing."

Of *course* he did. Because now I looked like even more of a monster in front of Phin.

"How did you guys even bump into each other?" Wyatt

asked Phin before pushing the basket closer to him, a sign to start eating.

That jolted Phin enough so he at least looked up from the table. "He wanted... no... he smelled Nash on me first. Thought—*knew*—we'd been... close. He wanted me to get him to go to a party. No, a ceremony."

I scoffed. More manipulation, more scheming.

Phin narrowed his gaze at my sound. "How was your dad?" he asked Wyatt. "Is his face..."

"Already healing," Wyatt replied grimly. "Nash could've punched him harder if he wanted."

If I'd punched him any harder, my fist would've passed through his skull to the sidewalk beneath.

"And your mom?"

"Don't worry about her," Wyatt growled. "They're vile people, Phineas. And I'm not just saying this because I want you to forgive my brother."

At talk of forgiveness, Phin's shoulders tightened, and he dropped the fry.

I'd made up my mind. There was nothing I could say to make Phin trust me again, but there might be something I could do. I would have to hope this worked because if Phin left me, he'd take my heart and soul with him. "Wyatt, call Riley. Tell him to come down."

ABOUT THIRTY SILENT MINUTES LATER, Riley walked through the door with Bran. Jr. in his car seat. Wyatt must have told him what went down because he sat immediately at Phin's table, plopping the car seat on the tabletop nearest the wall.

Phin blinked several times. "You brought your baby to a bar."

Riley shrugged. "I know the owner."

How I envied that small smile Phin gave him.

"Phin has a point," Riley said over his shoulder. "What am I doing here?"

I walked slowly. I was still worried I'd spook Phin. "I want you to touch me, Riley. Use your power."

All the humor wiped from Riley's face, and he glowered. "Why? You've never wanted me to, Nash. I don't want to do anything that will make you hate me."

"I won't. I promise. But I know nothing I say will let Phin trust me. Will let him know how sorry I am that he was there to see that. How I would never act like that to anyone else in this world. But I *won't* lose him. So touch me."

Wyatt crowded in. "Brother, I don't see how confessing you wet the bed until you were twelve will help."

That wasn't my truth, but I could see how Wyatt would think my secrets were only silly or embarrassing as his had been. "Touch me, Riley. I'm asking you to. Please."

Riley sighed, looking from Phin, who hadn't spoken a word but was watching it all happen, and then back to me. "Okay. I'm with Wyatt here, but fine. If it's what you want." He pulled his sleeve back and stuck out his hand, palm up.

I grabbed it. My mouth opened, and the words burst out of me like water from a dam. "I wanted to be Alpha so much, for a few seconds, I had no problem with what they asked of us. I'd pictured killing Branson and Aver, saving Wyatt but still becoming Alpha over him. For a few seconds, I *thought about it*, until I saw the horror in my cousins' eyes, the horror I should have had. And I knew then that I'd been raised to be a monster. Everything that man touches turns to rot. And I can say I'm sorry for the fear I caused you, but I won't say I wish I could take it back.

Because I don't. I'm glad he's hurting. He isn't hurting enough. I love you, Phineas. I—"

"Stop," Phin gasped, yanking Riley's hand out from under me. Instantly, the floating daze that had all those painful words flowing from me faded. "Stop hurting yourself." Tears filled his eyes when he finally looked up at me.

I felt something I thought I'd lost on that street. Hope.

"I was so scared. You turned into something else. It was like you couldn't hear me, like I didn't exist."

He slid out of the bench seat, and I pulled him into a tight embrace. "I'm sorry I scared you, Phin. *That* is inexcusable."

He kissed me like he was beginning to forgive me, like I hadn't ruined everything. I growled and deepened the kiss, holding him tightly while exploring that familiar terrain of his mouth with my tongue. My sweet Phin. I'd almost lost him today, and I wouldn't have been able to blame anyone but myself.

"Can you say the last part again? Without being under the influence of Riley's juju?" Phin asked.

I flipped through everything that had been compelled from me, wondering what Phineas could possibly want to hear a second—oh yeah. "I love you, Phineas Peters."

"Really, PP?" Wyatt whispered in the background, followed by the sound of Riley smacking him.

Phineas smiled. It wasn't big, but it was there, and I would take it. "I love you too," he whispered. "But next time when I tell you to stop, stop. You don't get to just push me back and say you're protecting me. We're equal, Nash. You're stronger and can hear me when I pee..."

"What?!" Wyatt whispered.

"...but I'm just as invested in this, in us. If I'm going to stay..."

I attempted to not freak out at the *if*.

"Then we protect each other. Okay?"

I wanted to say whatever I needed to to get him to stay, but I couldn't make a promise I didn't intend on keeping. "If it comes to something physical—"

"If it comes to that and there is no way to avoid it, you better believe I'll step back. I'm not stupid. But I won't wait idly by. I'll grab a stick or something. Trip him when he isn't looking."

If he needed to do any of that, then I'd failed to do my job, but I wouldn't bring that up now.

"Okay, I can see that pipe isn't getting fixed today, but I would actually like to attempt to use this business I own to make money, so will you kindly take your drama else-where?" Wyatt said, waving us out the door. "I'll get you a box for your fries."

"What do I get?" Riley asked. "I drove all the way here to touch his hand."

"I'll make you a grilled cheese," Wyatt said.

Riley looked appropriately pacified by his offering.

"Wait, you guys aren't disgusted? You don't want to rush home and tell your mate I contemplated murdering him?"

Riley waved off my worry like it was nothing. "I contemplate murdering him all the time." He smiled. "You guys were kids, with really messed-up childhoods. We're lucky you all turned out as normal as you did. I understand how that moment has stuck with you, and even why you might feel shame from it, but you've already said all I needed to hear. You thought about it, for seconds. Who wouldn't? Your whole life, you guys were raised to believe individually you were the best choice for Alpha. And you've learned from that moment, changed because of it. I can't say I won't tell Branson about today, if he hasn't already heard from the small-town gossip mill, but I'm pretty sure he'll have the same reaction as I have. It's who you are now that matters. Not who you were. That's how you will always be different from your father."

A weight lifted from my shoulders that I'd carried around for so long, I'd taken it on as a part of me.

But as good as hearing Riley say that felt, it was Phineas whose opinions mattered at the end of the day. I found his eyes, warm once more.

"Ditto," he whispered, and I kissed him again, not caring that there were two men and a baby in the room with us.

When our mouths broke apart, the pheromones clouding around us could have suffocated a man.

Wyatt opened the front door, unwittingly letting in the customers who'd gathered on the sidewalk. "That's it, you two are eighty-sixed for the day. Get out of here. Go cuddle or whatever. I'll see you at home."

"I can drive you," Riley offered. "*After* I get my grilled cheese."

———

THE REST of the day was spent at home. We went for a walk with Riley along the river but for the most part stayed inside snuggling on the couch. Phin admitted he still had work to do, so when dinner came around, Riley found us in the dining room. I was looking up some fireman training while Phin typed happily on his computer.

"I made tacos if—"

Phin shut his laptop.

"—you're hungry," Riley finished with a smile. "I've just got to drain the meat, but Bran is being really fussy. Will one of you hold him? He'll just scream if I set him down."

I frowned. He should have told me earlier. I would've watched the little guy while he cooked. But, before I could offer, Phin gave him a timid, "Sure."

He stood and stretched out his arms in a way that made it clear he hadn't held many babies.

"He's getting stronger every day, but you still want to keep your hand behind his head. Little guy likes to do random impersonations of an 80's rocker."

Phin did as he was told, cradling the child in his arms. He was clearly nervous, or maybe unsure was the better word. But he kept a firm frame around Bran, who looked up at him like he was meeting a new friend. "Hey there, buddy. I'm Phineas." He paused like he was waiting for a response.

I opened my mouth to tell him Bran couldn't talk yet— all the while hesitating because I was pretty sure Phineas knew that already.

"Oh, your name is Bran? Nice to meet you," Phineas continued as though the baby had answered. "What do you like to do, Bran?"

Again, Phin paused a moment before acting as though he'd answered. "Lay around and drink bottles! I like to lay around too. I'm over the bottle part."

I snorted. My Phin enjoyed sucking on other things now, but even I wouldn't say such an inappropriate thing in front of the baby.

Riley returned minutes later, saying he was ready to take Bran back.

"Could I hold him a while longer? Maybe while you eat," Phin asked.

Riley looked like he wanted to kiss him. We all tried to do our part with Bran, but at the end of the day, Riley was the one who cared for him the most. "Oh yes, that's fine. You aren't very hungry?"

"Nah," Phin said without looking up from Bran. "We're having a good talk."

My mate was so incredibly perfect. I wished, for a split second, that something like what happened to Riley and Branson would happen to us but quickly banished that thought. Having Bran Jr. was awesome, but I hadn't forgotten the fear and uncertainty of pregnancy. Things had turned out well for Riley. That only meant they might not the next time this sort of thing happened.

And I certainly didn't want either of us to be called blessed. Riley could keep that designation.

Branson and Aver came home at the same time, both covered in mud from their day's work. They showered and eventually made their way back to the kitchen where Riley was eating, I was making Phin and myself plates, and Phin was discussing the intricacies of interdimensional travel. He claimed Bran had some interesting things to say on the matter.

Branson kissed his mate before standing with his hands awkwardly at his sides and staring at Phin. He wanted to hold his baby. I could see it in his face, but he wasn't comfortable enough to just grab him from Phin. And Phineas either was doing an outstanding job ignoring him or still hadn't noticed the nearly seven-foot wolf hovering impatiently over his shoulder.

"Why don't you pass Bran over and we can eat?" I suggested, deciding to throw Branson a bone since his mate had been the only reason my Phin was even here with me.

"Heard about your excitement," Branson said to me after he'd kissed every inch of his son's face. "And something about you wanting to kill me?"

The confusion was clearly feigned. He'd talked to Riley, I knew it.

Aver came into the kitchen then. "Me too. I told you I was sorry for using your conditioner," he joked.

How could this damning secret that I'd carried with me for years come to mean so very little?

The answer came almost immediately. Because this was my pack. "Only for a second. And not recently."

"Makes sense," Branson shrugged. "I almost had the same thought. You were an annoying little shi—punk." Branson earned an elbow in the side from Riley, who was on his second plate of tacos.

Wyatt came home last. It was a rare night when he didn't have to close. "Did anyone see this note on the door?" he asked, flashing a piece of paper for us all to see.

My spine stiffened. We hadn't armed the alarms while everyone was expected to come back.

"It wasn't there when we got home," Aver said. "What does it say?"

Wyatt unfolded the white sheet. His eyes darted across the paper before he scowled and crumpled it into a small ball. "It's nothing."

I knew that tone. That tone meant it was something. I held out my hand. "Give it to me."

"Absolutely not. You're the last person who should—"

I plucked the paper ball from his hand, holding it over my head like we weren't the same height. "You can't treat me differently because I had a momentary lapse in chill."

"Is that what we're calling it?" Wyatt asked. I spotted the anxiety lining his eyes. I'd spent so much time worrying about Phin, I hadn't paused to worry about how my brother had handled today.

"I'm sorry, Wy."

He stopped trying to grab for my hand. "You better be. I

thought you were going to jail. That they'd finally succeeded in splitting us up like they always wanted."

I was a dick for not addressing this sooner. Wyatt was just so good at hiding how he really felt. He'd needed to be here, at home, before he could let himself be vulnerable enough to show the toll today had taken. "They didn't. They won't. Not ever."

He nodded and stepped back, giving me space to unfold the paper. I'd figured it was a note from Paul, or maybe the blessed business had started up again. But it wasn't either of those things. It was my mother.

Please forgive me for relaying this message with so much cowardice. After today, I didn't think any of you wished to see me. John was wrong to approach your friend as he did. But he wasn't wrong in wanting you, Nash, Wyatt, and your cousins to be there during today's ceremony. Our pack hasn't had one in so long, and it will be a time of hope and joy. Please attend. We will not be going. None of the new pack members are being sponsored by us. Only Delia. I give you my word: John and I will not be there. Glendon and Clarice are out of town. But the pack will be there.

At some point, we elders forgot that. The pack. They are why we exist. Please go. I'll be sending Paul for your final answer. Please don't be mean to him. He's only doing as I ask.

Julie

Not *your mother*. Not *Elder Walker*. She'd signed it like we were passing acquaintances.

Aver grabbed the letter next, reading it over before passing it to Riley, who passed it to Phin, and so on. Branson had it last. He looked up when he finished. "Have any of you seen Julie Walker use the word please in her life? Here she does..." He tapped the paper as he tallied them. "Four times. That's a record."

"We can't go," Wyatt said. But when no one agreed with him, he followed it with, "Can we?"

"Eat first," Riley suggested. "No good making a choice on an empty stomach."

I didn't need to eat. The pleases were strange, and maybe they signified a change in my mother I hadn't thought possible, but Delia would be there. Alpha Walker would have to be there. I had an idea of who was swearing loyalty: Tyrone, Denise, and the others we'd found in the shack. Going meant I'd be able to check on the little girl. Phin would appreciate that too. But was I really contemplating willingly bringing my mate to a shifter ceremony on pack lands? Maybe I needed my head checked.

"It's too risky," Aver said, copying the thoughts in my head. "The only way I'd go is if Nana called right now and—"

Aver's phone rang.

"No fucking way," Branson muttered, and we were all too shocked to censor him for the baby.

Aver pulled out his phone and answered. "Hello, Nana. Yes, we know. Julie Walker sent us a note. No, Nana. Nana, it isn't that—yes, ma'am." He hung up.

"We're going?" Wyatt asked.

"We're going." Aver nodded.

For the second time in only a few months, the four of us loaded up. We had to use Aver's work vehicle. It was the only one with enough room for us, Riley, the baby, and Phin. I wondered about Branson's choice to let Riley come, but figured if he'd tried to make him stay, he'd just fight. Plus, if the pack saw how normal Bran. Jr. was—he spit up like any other baby and had diapers that would make a lesser man cry—maybe they'd cool it with thinking he was the second coming.

Paul rode ahead in a beat-up Honda. He'd been proud of the car, claiming when he pulled up that it was the first he'd ever been able to afford on his own. I couldn't muster the excitement he'd wanted. I could only see Delia's money when I looked at the banged-up four-door.

"He gets paid by the pack?" Phin asked. The fact that I had my arm draped over his shoulders like I hadn't nearly lost him earlier was a miracle.

"Not exactly. When a shifter joins a pack—voluntarily joins, not like when you are born into a pack—they swear their loyalty and service to the Alpha. Capital A Alpha, not the designation the four of us have. If accepted, an elder will then become your patron. Depending on how the elder provides for the pack, you either work for them or do work for them, like Paul does Delia." And why I could never trust him.

"So elders must be rich."

It made sense he'd come to that assumption, and elders in other packs were often wealthy like the ones here, but they didn't have to be. That we had three strong elder households was part of the reason why the pack had always agreed that a Walker needed to lead them. Elder families were provided by the Alpha in control. Unless there was a reason for them not to, relations to the chosen Alpha almost always became elders.

That was also why no one had stepped forward to assume control from our grandfather. There wasn't a single pack member prepared to assume the responsibility and care for so many people. Thinking about it gave me a headache. It was a vicious circle with no obvious answer.

I sat straighter in my seat, clamping Phin to my side as we drove through pack lands, heading for the ceremonial fields.

"Is this...?" Phin asked quietly.

"Yes," Wyatt answered him.

This was the spot our parents had brought us to. The place where we all decided that leaving the pack was our only option. It looked different now. There were still torches, but many more of them. There was music and people gathered in the circle. At our cars, heads began to turn, and when we parked, some of the people gathered there stopped speaking altogether.

"Is Nana even here?" I asked.

"There she is," Branson said. He held Riley's hand as tightly as I held Phin to my side. It went against both of our natures to bring our mates to a place that had meant danger. Right now, it looked like a place of joy.

At least Branson had claimed Riley as his omega. That would provide him with safety to anyone who still recognized us as shifters. Most of these people had referred to myself and my cousins as the disgraced ones until recently.

Paul got out of his car and waited for us to join him.

I spotted the family Phin and I had helped. I thought Tyrone waved our direction until I noticed he had eyes only for Paul. I looked Tyrone up and down. He was a solid-looking guy with biceps that could crack nuts. That he'd traveled here, to join this pack, was the only flaw I could see. It had sounded like they'd had some trouble coming here from wherever they'd left, and I would've bet Tyrone had been instrumental in his sister, niece, and mother surviving. Denise had mentioned the father of her child and the fact that he hadn't made it.

Paul waved back, but with not as much gusto. Tyrone did seem interested. Too bad for him. Paul only had eyes for my brother.

"Are those the ones you were telling us about?" Branson asked.

"Yes. The large male is Tyrone. His sister Denise, niece Tanya, and I don't know their mother's name."

"How do they seem?"

"Honestly? Better. They were thinner and dirtier before. Like they'd crawled out of a war zone to get as far as they had."

The little girl, Tanya, ran hunched over through her uncle's legs, laughing as she did. She straightened with a frown, her small eyes searching her surroundings until she saw us. Her face split open into a smile, and she ran.

Those who hadn't noticed our arrival saw us now. They also saw Tanya sprinting through them, running past Paul directly to Phineas. When she was a few feet away, she opened her arms and jumped. Phineas caught her, slamming into my chest in the process. I steadied him and stepped back, letting them have their reunion. Phin had spoken with the kid for a few minutes and had healed her cheek, but right now, they seemed like long-lost friends.

"You made it! I told Ma you would make it, and she said she wasn't certain because she'd heard some things, but you made it." She spoke quickly, but she wasn't at all hard to understand. I couldn't only imagine the types of things her mother had heard about us once they'd mingled with the pack.

"We made it," Phin replied, beaming. He looked back at the crowd she'd run from, and if he noticed any of the sour faces, he didn't let on. "We didn't miss anything?"

"No." Tanya shook her head so hard the baubles holding her braids in place pinged against her cheek. "They were waiting for the Alpha. Then after, there's a party!"

"Tutu calls it a pregame."

"Hold on there, half-pint," Tyrone said, having made his way over. He also seemed to ignore the whispers and stares. "She's telling all my secrets," he said to the rest of us. "Hi, I'm Tyrone." He stuck his hand out to Branson, who was closest, and made his way around to the others. I got a fist bump, and Phin got a nod. "I don't think I had a chance to thank you properly after the last time. You could've refused to help, but you didn't. Thank you. I don't know what your omega did to Tanya, but she didn't complain once after about her face hurting."

Riley shuffled nervously from foot to foot. Man, he was a bad liar.

"No worries. Glad to hear it," I replied. "I see you've gotten to know Paul." I nodded to Paul, who had chosen to walk back to join us rather than wait.

"Yeah, he's been really helpful." I didn't think I imagined the slightly husky tone in Tyrone's voice as he spoke of Paul. "I apologize for not asking before, but may I thank your omega?"

That question probably made no sense to Phineas. Tyrone was mistaken. I hadn't claimed Phineas as my omega. It wasn't like claiming he was my mate or swearing I would always take care of him. The title of omega was a shifter thing. Only an alpha could claim another as their omega, and since there often weren't extra alphas laying around in a pack, there weren't a lot of omegas either. The designation was for life, no matter what happened. There wasn't any divorcing or deciding you really didn't want an omega after all. Branson had claimed Riley to keep him safe. No one from the pack would touch him without permission, which was why Tyrone asked now. But it also made him a target. The surest way to hurt an alpha was to harm his omega.

"We should get over. Alpha Walker is waiting," Paul said, likely thinking he was saving me from having to correct Tyrone.

We ambled over anyway, the seven and a half of us clumped tightly together as Paul and Tyrone led the way. Tanya had run back to her mom.

Alpha Walker was there, sitting in one of two chairs inside the circle. Delia held the other chair, her eyes glittered from the torchlight as she tracked her son.

The moment we reached the crowd, standing next to Nana as she motioned for us to face the same way as everyone else, Alpha Walker stood.

"Today is a joyous day," he announced, the tone of his voice conveying no actual joy. "With each new shifter, our pack becomes stronger. Not just because our numbers grow, but because each shifter brings with them a potential that only they have. As Alpha, when I accept a shifter's pledge of loyalty, I am recognizing a shifter's potential. Will the shifters joining us stand forward?"

Tyrone joined his sister, and together they helped their mother into the open space of the circle, standing directly in front of where the Alpha and Delia sat.

When my grandfather launched into another speech about pack pride, I zoned out. Most of it was bullshit anyway. Swearing loyalty wasn't. It ensured these shifters would be cared for as long as the elders had the means to. But I knew how my parents viewed the lower members of our pack. I knew because they'd taught me to treat them like cattle, bodies to benefit off of.

Still, I couldn't get Tyrone's question out of my head. He'd assumed so readily that Phin was my omega, even though I was pretty sure I'd told Denise he absolutely wasn't. Or had I said he just wasn't blessed? Whatever I'd said, Tyrone must have seen something to convince him otherwise.

I hadn't pondered the idea of claiming Phineas in front of the pack because, ultimately, I didn't give a shit what they thought. But I'd liked hearing Tyrone address Phin that way.

Except, if claiming Phin as my omega made no difference between the two of us, then why should I do it? If I did, it would be for the pack's sake, not ours. I needed to get Branson's opinion.

My grandfather stopped his speech, indicating it was time for Tyrone and the others to give their pledges. Each stood forward, promising loyalty by the moon, to defend the land and its people, and to never make a choice that would knowingly harm the pack. I tried to pay attention, not because my mother had asked us to be there, but because I believed these shifters were good people and their pledge should be treated with respect.

But I couldn't stop that little voice in the back of my head that wanted me to make Phineas mine, in every way imaginable.

16

PHINEAS

I STAYED close to Nash both by preference and because if he didn't have his arm over my shoulder, he was squeezing my hand. He'd stepped back briefly when Tanya had come in for a hug, but the second he could, he swooped back in. I didn't mind. I was out of my element here, both socially and as the only human in attendance.

Riley was a shifter now after all. So was Bran Jr..

The ceremony was a solemn affair compared to the party we'd pulled up to. There was a lot of pledging, a lot of accepting of pledges, and the word loyalty was thrown around. Delia, Branson's mother, stood at one point, and Tyrone, his sister, and their mother were required to bow to her. I didn't like that part. But, after, everyone clapped, and Tyrone smiled back at the crowd, so I took it to mean the right things had happened. I couldn't walk into a completely new culture and expect to understand everything, so I kept my opinions to myself. Nash was quiet through the whole thing, which didn't strike me as odd because everyone not in the ceremony had been quiet.

Now that it was over and people were bringing in

tables, chairs, music, and food, I'd thought Nash would speak again, but he was as quiet as he'd been.

It was obvious that none of the Walker cousins had wanted to come. Branson and Wyatt still looked like they didn't want to be here. Nana had pulled Aver away to help her grab some things from her car, and I was about to take a seat next to Riley and the baby when Nash tugged me back.

"Where are you going?" he asked, looking over my head.

"To sit next to Riley. Is that okay, Mr. Alpha?"

Nash's face jerked down to mine. "Don't make those jokes here," he said, not rudely, but I felt chastised all the same. "I'm sorry, babe. Please don't look at me like that. You don't understand the pack laws. Badmouthing the Alpha is a punishable offense on pack lands. Don't get me wrong. I could kick every ass here, but I don't want to."

I didn't want him to either. "There's no first amendment on pack lands?" I stuck my lips out in a pout.

"Only if the Alpha says there is." Nash kissed my pout. His gaze drifted again, and I lost Nash once more to the thoughts swirling in that gorgeous skull of his.

"What did Tyrone mean about that omega stuff? And touching me? Is that like being a mate?"

Nash sucked in a sharp breath. "No it isn't the same. An omega is a title that only matters within the pack."

That was a little more concise of an answer than he normally gave me. Did he not want to talk at all while we were here, or was it the fact Tyrone had called me his omega that had him impersonating a statue?

The crowd quieted, though I didn't know why. Then I saw Nash's grandfather, Alpha Walker, standing.

"I know the pack will do their best to make our new members feel welcome," he said, Delia's hand cradled in the crook of his arm. "We will leave you to it." He turned, pausing once to look in our direction. His eyes landed on me, and I was too cowardly to hold his gaze. I slid mine down, hoping he'd stop looking and leave.

He did, climbing into a sleek black car with Branson's mom. The moment the two left, the mood in the field brightened. It felt like everyone had exhaled a collective sigh of relief. Nana Walker returned from her car with Aver. They both carried cardboard boxes, and Wyatt rushed forward to take the box from Nana.

Others had already covered some of the tables with dishes of food. Clearly, this was a potluck sort of thing. "Should we have brought something?"

Nash shook his head.

Someone turned up the radio on an upbeat country song. I didn't recognize it, but country wasn't my thing. It was the perfect song for the moment, and people, young and old, started bobbing their heads and tapping their toes to the beat. Not Nash. He was my gargoyle, except the sun was down and he was still made out of stone. It wasn't a Walker cousin thing because while Branson still looked unhappy, he was at least nodding along to the song. Wyatt had already pulled Nana out to the part of the field where people had started to dance. "Nash? What's wrong?"

"I want you to be my omega," he blurted out, his face contorted, anguished.

His words said one thing, his face another. "That makes you mad?"

He did a double take. "Fuck no. But it worries me. Claiming you as my omega wouldn't change anything but how the pack views you. I've gone over ten years without caring how the pack views anything that I do. Why do I care now?"

I wished I had an answer for him. I didn't understand

the intricacies of what it all meant enough to give a helpful answer.

"Because it would protect Phin," Branson said. "We're more alike than you think, Nash. All of us are. I would've done anything if it meant Riley would be even a fraction safer. You would too. It bugs you, but it shouldn't. You're an alpha. There is a beast inside you that, for better or worse, influences your actions. It won't let you rest until you've made Phin as safe as possible."

I hadn't realized he'd been eavesdropping and couldn't tell if his message had harmed or hurt the situation. Nash's face never changed. I'd be Nash's omega—or not. Whichever would make him happiest was the option I chose.

Until he stood up and immediately climbed on top of the table.

The hush started like a wave, beginning with those closest to us and rippling out. I wasn't sure if it was the oddness of someone standing on a table that quieted them or because the person standing there was Nash, but in moments, the field was quiet. The moment was so reminiscent of what had happened when Alpha Walker stood to leave, the hairs on my arm stuck up.

"I have an announcement," Nash called out to the crowd. "This man beside me is Phineas. I claim him as my omega."

My face had to be redder than a tomato, but I didn't shy away. If Nash could do this thing, even though it made him uncomfortable, then I would be here to support him. Branson started to clap, followed by Riley's whoop of excitement. Wyatt and Aver joined, but it was when Nana began to clap that the pack clapped as well. All but Paul and Tyrone—they began to cheer early.

Soon, we were enveloped by a crowd of happy faces.

No one pushed in or tried hugging me like I'd feared. They kept a respectful distance, offering congratulations from afar. For a guy who had a thing about people and personal space, it was very nice.

Not everyone came to congratulate us, about half. The others just continued dancing like we weren't there. This was Tyrone's night anyway. Him, Denise, and their mom. I tugged on Nash's sleeve so he would drop his head down far enough for me to whisper in his ear. "Dance with me?" I asked. Hopefully, that would put an end to the congratulating and swing the party back on track.

He smirked and nodded, pulling me out to the field. "Too much peopling? I'm sorry, I didn't think about that."

"No, just the right amount. Are you okay with what just happened?"

We'd been doing a slow shuffle, but at my question. Nash's feet stopped. "I'm very okay with it. My hesitation was never because of you. You're the only part of this equation that makes sense."

I smiled, needing to hear that more than I'd known. I set my head against Nash's chest, and we swayed a few moments longer. All around us people danced, ate, laughed, and drank. I'd wondered if this was going to turn into a weird *True Blood* wolf pack situation, but so far, no one had pulled out shots of vampire blood. If I didn't know these people were shifters, I would've thought them all friends or close neighbors.

Tucking my face against Nash's chest, I yawned, hoping the angle would conceal it, but he held me a few inches away and studied my face.

"You're tired. I need to get you home. We should leave before anything horrible happens anyway."

In the distance, over the darkened treetops, there was a

loud boom followed by the unmistakable orange glow of fire.

Before I'd really worked out what had happened, Nash had us off the dance floor and found his cousins, and the four of them circled around Nana, Riley, the baby, and me, like they expected the people we were with to suddenly turn on them.

But everyone else looked as shocked as we did. A few ran into the forest, toward the explosion. I thought they were all falling into the trees, which didn't make sense until I saw they were shifting as they ran.

"What is it? What's happening?" Riley asked.

"A fire," Aver replied. "That's the direction of—"

"My son!" Nana cried out.

Her son? I couldn't think of who she was referring to until the obvious came to me. Alpha Walker was her son.

Knowing the blast may have come from their leader's home changed the moment considerably for me. I had only video games and comic books to go off of. This could be an attack. We needed to move. I opened my mouth to say as much when Nash whistled loudly.

"Everyone stop running around. Has someone called 911?"

No one answered.

"Aver, call 911 and tell them we need the firetruck here. Paul and Tyrone, you take Riley and Phin back home—"

"I can help here," Tyrone said.

"I don't doubt that, but I don't trust anyone else. Nana—"

"I'm coming with you." Her tone was as straight as her spine.

"I'm coming too!" I said.

Nash shook his head. "No—"

"Me too," Riley said.

"No," Branson growled.

But Nana grabbed our hands and tugged us from her great-grandson, breaking through their protective circle like she was a Red Rover champion. "We don't have time to argue," she mumbled, taking us to her truck.

The Walker cousins rushed to keep up. We were in the cab and driving away before she slowed to let them jump in the bed.

"Hold on," she said. "Going through is fastest."

Going through? I frowned. Going through what?

Nana gunned the truck, driving away from the gravel path we'd come in on and heading straight for the dark line where the forest grew thick. I grabbed the OS handle and hunched forward to help protect the baby in Riley's arms, while I held on for dear life.

I WASN'T sure how the guys didn't fling out or how Nana managed to narrowly miss hitting every tree we passed, but as we broke through the forest and rolled up to a large home completely engulfed in flames, we were alive, and the Walkers were still back there.

Or they had been, before they jumped out and began running toward the mansion on fire. A few people—those who had ran immediately—already had a garden hose and were trying to wet down the front door.

"We don't know where Alpha Walker is," one of them shouted. "We can't get in—it's too hot!"

Nana made a sharp noise, and I grabbed her hand. We weren't super close, but she'd once told me a dark shadow followed me, so I assumed that meant we were at least friends. "Don't worry, Nana, saving people is what Nash does."

Amazingly, the worry cleared from the old woman's expression. "You're right. It is." She sucked in a deep breath and exhaled slowly. "Come with me. They'll be needing water to drink when they come out. Food to keep their energy up."

Since we couldn't help with putting out the fire—there weren't enough hoses to go around as it was—Nana and I constructed a relief table. Some of the pack members had the foresight to bring the food and drink from the party, and we set it out for the workers.

Sirens sounded in the distance, and then I saw the lights of the firetruck. It hadn't taken them long, but no one had been able to go into the house yet. Nash dropped what he was doing and ran to the firetruck, reaching for a back compartment door before even addressing the firemen. He fit a ventilator over his head and ran, never slowing, even when he leapt through the entrance that had likely once been beautiful. Now, it was an inferno.

He's a superhero. He saves people. He didn't just jump to his death.

I tried to recall that confidence I'd had that had helped Nana, but saying Nash saved people and watching him jump into a burning building with only his mask was something else entirely.

Nana grabbed my hand this time, and though she didn't speak, she squeezed it.

The firemen had gotten into position. I spotted their chief and Paster. Krat arrived moments later in another, smaller truck. They worked like a well-oiled machine, unraveling the hose, connecting it to the water tanker, and unleashing the powerful spray against the building.

"C'mon, come on. Nash..." I mumbled, staring at the burning double doorway. "Come out. Please. Come out."

My whole body shook. All around me there were shouts and commotion, but I couldn't look away from the door.

Something snapped inside me. An imaginary patience timer had been reached, and I was done sitting and waiting. "He's hurt. He needs help. Where's a mask? I need to find him!" I lunged for the mansion, but both Nana and Paul held me back.

"You'll just put him in more danger when he needs to save your ass," Paul grunted.

He wasn't wrong, but I had to do something. My alpha had just disappeared inside a burning building.

Nash reappeared as suddenly as he'd disappeared. He wasn't alone, and I saw what had taken him so long. He had two full-grown men in his arms. Both weren't moving. He pulled them out of the doorway to the grass, where he laid them down. Chief was there with oxygen and first aid.

It looked like his boss was more worried about his health and kept trying to get Nash to take breaths, but he pushed away his chief, his eyes on me. He started toward me just as Nana and Paul let me go, and I burst forward, colliding into him in the middle of the manicured lawn.

"You scared me." I kissed his lips and every other part of his face covered with soot.

"I'm sorry," he said, kissing me back. "Alpha Walker was still breathing. His butler too. I've got to see if I can help with the house."

I didn't think it was just the smoke that made his voice tight. This was the first time I was seeing this house. That wasn't true for Nash.

"I understand. What do you need from me?"

Nash pressed his forehead to mine. "Go back to the

house, please. This is gonna take a while. We need to put the fire out and then see if we can find out how it started. The shed fire was one thing, the grill explosion another, but this is a pattern. Someone is targeting these buildings. Shifter buildings."

"You think there's an arsonist?" Branson asked.

"I more than think it," he replied grimly. To me, he said more quietly, "Please go and be where I know you'll be safe. Please."

I couldn't say no. Not when he sounded like that. I nodded. "Okay. I'll go with Riley." The baby needed to get out of here before the wind started pushing the smoke around anyway.

———

SEVERAL HOURS HAD PASSED since Paul and Tyrone had dropped Riley and me off. Nana had stayed on scene, refusing to leave her son's side. I'd helped Riley change Bran and give him a bath. He put Bran to bed in their room and turned on the baby monitor. We'd made something to eat, but neither of us had eaten much of it, choosing to sit in silence in the living room instead where we could stare at the darkened driveway outside.

"Is it always like this?" I asked Riley, hoping he would understand I wasn't complaining, just trying to mentally prepare.

"Just about," Riley replied without looking away from the window. "Not usually so fiery. Last time, it was just my crazy ex."

"You dated a shifter?" I didn't mean to sound judgmental.

"No, human."

"He came *here*?" I couldn't think of a stupider plan.

"He did." Riley smirked. "And regretted it." Riley stood suddenly. "I'm going to check on the baby." The monitor sat on the table in front of us, four green lights indicating it was on, but I understood the need to check with his own eyes. Sometimes I checked that I'd locked my front door two or three times before leaving, and that was just my apartment.

He left me to stare at my own reflection in the dark window. There were lights outside, tiny lampposts stuck into the ground that illuminated the line of the driveway, but they weren't powerful enough to illuminate much more than a few inches around them.

Anyone could be out there. Lurking. Waiting. And hadn't Riley just told me that they'd been broken into before? It could happen. I tried shaking the paranoia away but only managed to bring what Nash had said to my attention. An arsonist. A person was purposefully starting these fires? To get at the pack? Or the Walker cousins?

The baby cried, the noise pumping through the monitor, and I jumped, laughing nervously. Riley had probably accidentally woken him up when he'd checked on him. Except I didn't hear Riley's voice, no pacifying shushes or reassurances that everything would be okay. The baby just kept crying.

The hair on my nape stood up.

Riley wouldn't just stand there and let the baby cry. Which meant Riley had been incapacitated. I stood, tiptoeing toward the hallway. The light was out, the space lit up by a nightlight plugged into an outlet along the baseboard.

"Riley?" I whispered, receiving no answer. My heart pounded, and my breaths came in terrified pants.

The baby kept crying when, suddenly, there was a loud crash from outside.

I burst down the dark hallway, fear pushing me faster than I'd ran before. The hallway looked different with the lights off. Taller somehow, and when I turned the corner into Branson and Riley's room, the crib loomed feet higher than normal.

What the heck?

I walked over, my paws sinking into the carpet.

My... *what?*

17

NASH

WE'D WORKED to the first light of dawn. The moment Phineas left, I felt a tug. Like a cord that linked my body to his, growing tighter the more distance there was between us. With every hour, I grew more irritable. The others assumed I was getting tired, but with the adrenaline in me, I could run a marathon. It was being away from Phineas that made me feel so on edge.

It was best he wasn't here. The fire had been out long ago, but that was when the grueling work of picking through the charred, soggy remains began. I convinced the chief that we'd take over from here, and he must have been tired too because he agreed quickly. The moment the firemen left, the real detective work could begin. Wyatt waited for them to turn their trucks around before shifting, nose to the ground.

There were also extremely important shifter-related documents kept in the Alpha's home, like medical records for the pack, and some had chosen to let their Alpha hang onto important documents like birth certificates. Nana had the best memory for where that stuff was kept, and though we wouldn't let her go into the burned building she'd lived most of her life in, she told us where to look, and we took turns.

We worked shoulder to shoulder with the shifters. Everyone who was able had come to help. But since I sent the crew home, I was the best candidate for finding how and where the fire started. That hadn't taken long. On a hunch, I'd checked the natural gas lines, remembering what had happened with Riley. Sure enough, they'd been tampered with. The initial explosion had originated there, and the flames had quickly engulfed the historic home.

No relief could be found from finding answers. This meant, without a doubt, there was an arsonist loose in Walker County. I had ideas on that too, but I was done playing investigator. I wanted to talk everything I was thinking over with my cousins first anyway.

And I'd been away from Phineas for far too long.

Wyatt had left with Nana. She was going to stay in a vacant home on pack lands while she continued to care for Alpha Walker. Paul offered to help her. Technically, all the elders *offered* to help her, but she only accepted Paul.

There was nothing to do on scene but clean up and rebuild. Two things I wouldn't be a part of. The packs had kept me from my mate long enough. I knew he was safe, that the alarms would've gone off if something had happened. Branson had installed twice the number we'd had before since Riley's ex had broken in. But, until I saw Phineas with my own eyes, inhaled his scent, and could see for myself that he was safe, I wouldn't be able to exhale without growling.

"Go ahead," Branson said, looking at my rigid face. "I'll tie up the ends here, and Aver and I will go get the car."

I nodded once before shifting. My claws dug into the

ground, made muddy by all the water. I leapt over a puddle, landing several feet forward. Once inside the forest, I could really run. I stayed low to the ground, pushing my four legs as fast as they would move. When I found the river, I jumped over it, feeling the weight lift off me that always did when I left pack lands.

But my desire—need—to see Phin did not lessen. Though I was technically growing closer to him with every stride, the cord only tightened. By the time I broke through the tree line, spotting our home at the water's edge, I was beside myself.

The lights in the living room window glowed brightly. I'd half expected them to be asleep, but it looked like every light in the house was on. There was movement in the window—Riley. Likely, he'd heard me trip the perimeter alarm. I'd figured Branson would warn him that I was coming so he wouldn't be scared. He ran to the side, out of view, and opened the front door, waving frantically.

"Come quick!"

I pushed off with my back legs. Phin was hurt. Phin was in trouble. Phin was dead. Each stride sent another horrible thought shooting into my brain. I ran through the front door and skidded to a stop.

Phin was a wolf. I recognized him by his scent. But also by the way he cocked his head to the side curiously. I padded forward, sniffing him. He laid down in a submissive position that I didn't require, but I thought maybe it was his newfound animal instinct recognizing his alpha. I sniffed him from tail to head and back again, checking that he wasn't in pain and wasn't afraid. He seemed pleasantly curious, but not scared.

But, when this had happened to Riley, he'd taken hours to shift back. Branson had worried it wouldn't happen at all until Nana showed up. I stretched, standing on two human legs as I shifted back. "Riley, can he—"

"Isn't that cool?" Phin shouted with his human mouth. He stood beside me, having shifted as easily as I had.

I looked from Riley to Phin. Riley's face was pinched with mild irritation while Phin beamed.

"He's a freaking pro," Riley grumbled. "I'd gone to check on the baby and got distracted thinking I saw something outside. I guess in the meantime..."

Phin took over. "...I got scared and thought someone had attacked Riley. Then he knocked over a plant, and the jolt must've shifted me."

"I went back in to check on Bran, found a dog in there, turned on the lights, and he shifted back. As easy as that."

"I'm great at it," Phin piped up. "Watch!" He lowered his head, dropping to all fours. He let his paws touch the carpet for a split second before shooting back up into a standing human position.

Damn. He was fast. I smiled so hard my cheeks hurt. "You're okay?" I breathed. He looked okay, seemed okay. I still needed to hear him say it.

His smile faltered, and my heart pounded. He was hurt, angry. Upset I'd *infected* him as he called it. And how had I done that? I'd been with plenty of humans. None of them had turned into shifters. I wondered if it had something to do with not using a condom, but I'd gotten blowjobs before. It shouldn't matter which—

"What are you thinking about?" Phineas snapped. He watched my face with an intensity that was definitely new. Leaning forward, he sniffed, and his lip curled. "Who are you thinking about?"

Damn, great at shifting and at interpreting my

emotions. Some shifters could smell emotions better than others. Some, not at all. Seemed Phin could.

"No one important in my life. I'm just trying to figure out why this happened to you. To Riley. Are you... mad? You didn't ask to be a shifter."

"Are you kidding me?" Phineas asked, turning his head sharply in the direction of the driveway. "Someone's coming." He dropped down to all fours and took off out the door before I could stop him.

Branson rolled down the driveway. He spotted Phineas through the windshield, looked up to see me, and then slowed to a stop several feet away from where he normally parked.

Phineas let out a bark, and I found the thing he wasn't quite good at yet. It sounded like a puppy's yelp, not nearly as ferocious as he likely wanted. He tried again before looking back at me, one ear up, the other flopped over his eye and an expression that said, *help me out here*.

"Down boy," I said, and he growled.

"Is that Phin?" Branson asked, getting out.

"Does this mean he's pregnant?" Aver asked.

Oh shit. I hadn't thought of that. Neither had Phineas. He shifted immediately, turning into my waiting arms. Now, his eyes were wide. Not with fear, but healthy concern. "Is that what this means, Nash?"

My mouth gaped like a fish. I wanted to be able to give him an answer, something that would relieve him. But I didn't know what this meant, so it was no surprise when I heard myself say, "We need to call Nana."

"She won't leave Grandpa," Aver said, the three of us going in. Branson had hurried past to greet Riley. "Not if Phin is fine. Which he looks to be. And really good at shifting. Good job."

Phin stood a little straighter at the compliment, his steps becoming more of a strut. I tried not to be jealous that someone else had made my Phin happy. "I just think about it, and it happens. Which is weird because I used to do that a lot as a kid. Not to turn into a wolf, but something amazing. It never worked then."

When we got back inside, Riley had baby Bran on the couch. "He wakes up about this time anyway. You guys aren't usually awake," Riley explained with a yawn.

Normally, Riley got some sleep before this time too.

"I called Nana. She said she'd call back," Branson said. "Drinks?" he asked. Riley took a tea, and Phin asked for a pop, while Aver and I opted for beer. "Is the sugar good for the baby?" Branson asked.

"Now don't you start that," Riley snarled. "You let Phineas eat and drink whatever it is that he wants. You hear me, Phin? Don't let these guys bully you. You want coffee, you drink coffee."

We all knew Riley was referring to a particular time in his life when things were confusing, and we'd all gone a little crazy trying to help. He wouldn't actually advocate that Phin do anything that would harm his baby.

If he had a baby.

Why didn't that freak me out more? I wasn't sure why I even wondered. When it came to Phineas, none of my normal reactions were the same.

"Is this a for-sure thing?" Phineas asked.

"No. I don't think we've experienced this enough to know anything for sure. We've got Riley to go off of. And you're already different than he was."

"We don't need to rub it in!" Riley wailed. Clearly, he was taking Phin's natural shifter instincts a little hard. Branson returned with drinks, kissing his hand, and Riley sighed. "I am happy for you, Phineas. But before, I could say I was having a hard time because I was the only human turned shifter. Now, I can't. Is there something wrong with me?"

That was nonsense. All shifters were different. Some shifted young; some had a hard time all through their teens. There were even some that preferred their human bodies and never shifted. There was no stigma attached to whichever category you fell in. But I knew Branson would see to his mate, so I turned my attention back to the room.

"We'll need to get tests, and I want Nana to look Phin over. But while we wait for her to call, did any of you pick up anything odd around Alpha Walker's home?"

I'd sniffed every inch, coming up empty.

"Nothing. I smelled you, the firemen, and shifters, but nothing that stuck out."

I nodded. "That was my experience as well. I picked out each of the firemen, Chief, Charles, Paster, and Krat, and a ton of shifters, but no scents stuck out to me. And if it is arson, then the perpetrator would have to be someone who had been here before. They would've needed to tamper with the grill, ensuring the next time anyone used it..."

"Boom," Riley whispered.

Branson growled. "Who was at the party and on pack lands?"

Other than us, I could think of another easily. "Paul."

"'No way," Phineas interjected. "Paul? He's your guys's helper, I thought. He wouldn't hurt you."

I didn't like saying it as much as everyone didn't want to hear it, but I wouldn't blind myself because the truth was hard to look at. "He's Delia's sponsee."

"He's been nothing but helpful," Riley said. "And you've always disliked him."

"I've always disliked his connection to the pack."

"You're connected to the pack," Riley shot back.

"Not by choice," I replied more intensely than I should have, and Branson growled in warning.

"It won't do us any good to focus on one person," Phineas said quietly. He ducked under my arm, and I held him close. "I agree with Nash. We shouldn't discount anyone if we have reason to believe they are a suspect, but we'd damn our efforts just as much by focusing on one person before we know for sure it is them."

Aver nodded, looking like he wished he'd said the same thing.

"How'd you get so good at this?" I asked him, hoping he knew that was a compliment and not a veiled dig.

"I went through a mystery board game phase. You guys would really like *One Night Ultimate Werewolf,* where you have to guess who the werewolf is, and it's like that game *Mafia,* but—maybe we can talk about this another time."

I didn't want to stop my mate from sharing any excitement he held, but he was right. We had a few topics of conversation that were more important at the moment.

"I guess what we need to decide first and foremost—is this a pack issue or an us thing?" Branson asked.

Riley's mouth popped open. Clearly, he found that question callous, but I understood. If this was an us thing, we'd find out who was responsible and make them sorry. But if it was a pack thing, the smartest thing we could do was distance ourselves from the pack. Maybe the arsonist only targeted us because they thought we were more connected to the pack than we were.

"I don't see how that matters," Riley said. "Not if they need your help."

None of us Walkers answered. Riley had heard the

stories, same as Phin, and knew our history. But it was hard for someone who hadn't lived it to truly understand the damage that had occurred. It wasn't just what our parents had asked us to do that night, but every night before that. It took leaving to see how toxic the pack mentality truly was. Why should we want to preserve that?

All five of us turned when someone pulled down the driveway. We couldn't see the headlights for another second, but then I made out Paul's Honda with several bodies inside.

"This is smooth timing," I growled.

Aver pointed. "He's bringing Wyatt back."

"Likely story," I growled, heading for the front porch.

Wyatt caught sight of me and frowned but continued forward with Paul and Tyrone trailing behind.

"We aren't taking in visitors," I said when Wyatt had passed, and it was just me between Paul and the house.

Paul smiled nervously and stepped around. "Haha, Nana sent me."

I sidestepped in his way. "We'll wait for Nana to come herself."

"Nash?" Wyatt asked quietly. "What's going on?"

The others had come out as well, all but Riley, who watched through the window with the baby. They stood behind me, not quite in support but also not saying anything to contradict me. It was fine if I had to be the bad guy. Branson had said it earlier—I'd do anything to keep Phin safe.

"What's going on is there is an arsonist targeting shifter locations, and until we know more, we need to limit our interactions with the pack."

Paul didn't look angry, just sad. I steeled myself against

it. If he was here to hurt us, he was an amazing actor. "Nana is in the pack."

"A technicality. And she doesn't live on pack lands, not anymore. Plus, she's our great-grandmother, whereas you are some person who showed up as a sex offering for Branson."

Tyrone, who had remained silent and watching the exchange to that point, growled and took a defensive position. "I like you, Nash, but you need to calm down. Tonight was exciting for us all—"

I snarled. Did he think I was like a pup, shivering because there'd been a loud noise outside? "You have even less of a right to speak about this matter."

"Nash, that's enough," Branson said. "If Nana sent him—"

"She's an old woman who claims to hear things. Maybe we've all put too much stock in Nana's—" I'd known I crossed the line when the words had formed in my mouth, but I'd been helpless to stop them. But I really knew I'd crossed the line when *Paul* charged forward as if to fight for Nana's honor. Tyrone pulled him aside, forming a protective wall between us. He was over six feet of solid muscle, but so was I.

Phin grabbed my hand, squeezing my fingers in a way that had me looking down at him. His eyebrows dipped low, and he frowned. He didn't want to contradict me, but he didn't agree with my stance. Maybe I was acting overboard with Paul. But my mate's life could be on the line. What if he'd offered to grill for us? His power didn't work on himself.

But, if I was being honest, what I knew of Paul only made him less of a suspect. He'd never been happier than when he'd come to this pack. The place he came from must've been truly horrible because he delighted at the slightest compliment. He just wanted to belong.

I couldn't apologize—I still wasn't over him as a suspect —but I wouldn't fight this at after three in the morning when my mate needed to sleep anyway. I'd protect him this night and every other second until we got more answers. "Fine." I pulled Phin with me, disappearing back into the house. We stopped in the kitchen, where I looked for something to feed Phin before bed. But, thanks to his new senses, we could both hear what was going on outside. Namely, Riley trying to convince Paul to stay the night while Tyrone tried to get him to do the opposite.

"I'll be fine, Tyrone, really," Paul said.

"Come with me." Tyrone's voice never wavered, but that didn't mean he wasn't still angry.

Paul didn't answer, but I imagined he shook his head because I heard Tyrone speak again. "Fine, if you want to stay, you stay. But I won't without getting myself more in trouble. I'm new to this area. I can't afford to lose my temper."

I wanted to scoff at the idea that Tyrone thought he was a threat to me, but one look at Phin had the scoff drying up.

"I don't think it's Paul," Phineas whispered. "He's only been nice to me."

To me as well. To all of us. But I was frantic for answers. I'd claimed Phineas as my omega, and immediately after he'd turned into a wolf. And was possibly pregnant. So much was already different between Phin and Riley. I couldn't just assume the labor would be the same. And Riley's labor already hadn't been easy. By loving Phin, had I damned him?

No. I wouldn't let anything bad happen to him. I'd promised.

Eventually, Paul came in, and Tyrone must have left because when we went back into the living room, only Paul was there with Riley and Branson.

He scowled at me. I probably deserved it. "We're going to bed. Tomorrow, tests, and I'll go back to the Alpha house and see if there isn't anything we missed." I ignored the shocked expressions. I'd changed my stance since walking into the kitchen.

Clearly, I couldn't keep the pack completely out of our lives, not while there was trouble.

The best thing I could do was find the culprit and fix the trouble, and hopefully then we could all go back to ignoring the other side of the bay.

18

PHINEAS

Nash tried to leave when I was still asleep. I woke when he went into the bathroom, found the note he left me, and was waiting at the door when he came out. "Where to first?" I asked brightly. He could still order me to leave, but that would only mean we'd have to take time out of the day for me to convince him.

I wondered if this new confidence stemmed from my recent change to a creature of the paranormal, or if I was growing as a person. I tried not to show how excited I was to be able to change into a wolf. And I definitely didn't want to utter the phrase *creature of the paranormal* where any of them could hear, but to be blunt, I thought the whole thing was hecking awesome.

"Aren't you tired? Don't you want to sleep?" Nash scratched the back of his neck, rubbing his eyes after. Clearly he was tired, but he wouldn't be going back to bed. So neither would I.

"I want to be where you are."

Nash smiled. At least he didn't fight me. But he did make us wait to leave until after he'd made something for breakfast—bagel and egg sandwiches that I demanded we eat as we go.

"Should we run there?" I asked gripping the car door.

"You can't eat if you're running, babe," Nash said with a grin.

I supposed that was right. Still, I eyed my sandwich, wondering if I could open my mouth wide enough to shove the whole thing in. Nash walked around to my side, physically lifting me into his vehicle.

"You'll choke if you try. Then I'll have to save you with mouth-to-mouth, and we'll get distracted."

"Oh yes," I said while chewing. "I forgot your perversion for taking advantage of me when I need medical assistance."

Nash just winked, letting me know just how offended he wasn't.

As I settled in my seat, pulling the seatbelt over my lap, a worry struck. "What about last night? Tyrone? You don't think the shifters will be angry to see us?"

He didn't look over but stared out the windshield without blinking. "They haven't been happy to see me in years. No different now."

I didn't completely understand, but I wasn't sure I was meant to. I figured this was like the difference between being a fan of something and being in the fandom. I knew enough to play the game, but I still didn't understand all the rules. Or hacks. The only way to do that, though, was to listen and learn. "I'm with you now," I said, sliding to his side. "I'll block you from their stares."

He didn't say anything, but he wasn't frowning anymore either.

"Do you remember your first shift?" I asked, eating the rest of my breakfast.

"No, not really. I was very young. My mother used to—"

He stopped speaking so suddenly I'd worried he bit his tongue. His jaw was tight, the rigid line framing his face sharp enough to cut paper.

"You can talk about her, you know. I won't get the wrong idea. I understand what it's like to hate someone but love them." The food I had eaten rolled uncomfortably in my stomach. "I sometimes think I hate my parents. When I think how they must have known what would happen when they touched me. If I'd been given the choice, I would have wanted them to live instead. I'm not sure I was ready to face the world when I did. I've always been scared, hiding in my room instead of living in the real world." Part of that had been the curse, but I'd been so quick to assume I had one that it never occurred to me that maybe, I was just a chicken and needed a push. Funny, I hadn't blamed myself once last night for what happened to Alpha Walker. Maybe that was an oversight.

"Nash... do you think what happened... do you think it could be because of my—"

"Don't say it, Phineas," Nash growled. "I worried you would the second I saw that fireball. You are not to blame. Do you hear me?"

I nodded, but I didn't really hear him. Nash wasn't convinced anyway. "Say you understand, Phin. I need to hear it. You won't blame yourself. You won't try to fix everything on your own." He stopped and swallowed. "You won't run away to save everyone. Do you hear me?"

He couldn't stop me if I chose to, but I wasn't there in my head. I didn't really think I was to blame. I didn't even really like Alpha Walker, and it seemed like if he died, the pack would be pushed into making choices they'd allowed to grow stagnant.

"I hear you, alpha."

This time, Nash didn't chastise me. But he did look extremely pleased. "Man, I made fun of Branson so much when he tried telling us how good it felt for Riley to call him that. You can never tell him."

I could only smirk.

Once we crossed into pack lands, Nash's mood darkened. "We'll drive around, sniff at the site a little if there aren't too many people there."

We circled the entire other half of the island while Nash drove. Every once in a while, he would pull to the side of the road to let another car pass. When I asked why, he launched into an explanation of rank in the pack. "If I'd stayed, everyone would be pulling over for me," he said, not sounding like that was something he missed all that much.

I didn't get the point of it, other than to show respect. But there were so many other checks and balances in place, it seemed like overkill.

Nash didn't see anything that made him want to stop and check, and we circled back around to the Alpha's house. People had been through. There was a stack of lumber in one corner, and some of the debris had been pulled out and placed in a pile that would only grow larger.

"Do you want to look with me?" Nash asked.

I cocked my head to the side, confused, until I caught on. As wolves, he meant. Heck yeah I did. I opened my door, shifting before I stepped a human foot on the ground. Nash laughed before running around the front of the vehicle, also in his wolf form.

Being around him like this was unlike anything. I'd expected having a wolf inside me would be like hearing voices, arguing with the entities in your head. But it wasn't like that at all. I sensed my wolf, but it was more of a knowing. He was there, I was here, and so far, our wants and needs had lined up. And when I looked at Nash in this form, the wolf in me recognized his dominance. I bowed my head, fighting the urge to roll belly up.

Nash licked my muzzle and shook his head as if to say, *You don't have to worry about that.* I wasn't, not really. It was more of an instinct I had to learn how to control. He reared up on his back legs and ran forward next. There was no way I'd be left in his dust, and I sprinted to catch up, overtaking him after a few leaps and bounds.

Nash snarled and ran faster, zooming by. He ran past the house into the forest, and I followed him, planning on jumping on his back the moment I was close enough. He must not have noticed the tree he ran toward, and I was going to catch him when he skidded to a halt. Except he never slowed, and it was me who skidded to a halt right before Nash ran headfirst into the tree. He jumped at the last second, running *up* the trunk before springing off into a backflip and landing behind me.

I watched him move with fascination.

He made a chuffing noise and turned around coolly, but I wanted to try to be a ninja too, and I backed up, scratching my claws into the dirt before launching forward. I jumped and landed shoulder-first against the tree. A yelp escaped my mouth, and Nash was there in a flash, in his human form, petting me down where I'd hit the tree.

"It's okay. Branson still can't do that," Nash told me. That was information I might have wanted before I tried it.

Still, it was a good lesson. So far, I excelled at being a wolf, maybe more than I'd ever excelled as a human, but I still had things to learn and a new body to get used to.

I shifted and sniffed so that he would feel just a little sorrier before I kissed him. "Race you back," I murmured, pushing off his chest.

Nash yelled that I was a cheater. At least I'd be a victorious cheater. I would have been anyway, if Nash hadn't zoomed by, reaching the line of the property a full two seconds before me.

With the smoldering home in view, I sobered, remembering we were here for important work. Nash kept his nose to the ground, picking through the wreckage and pausing to give this or that a deeper sniff. I copied him, but there were so many new smells, and old smells that had never been so strong before, that I had to stop and wait in the yard for my head to stop spinning.

It was an overcast day, but I wasn't looking at the clouds. I was listening. The world was so much noisier as a shifter, but I practiced picking sounds and zeroing in on them. After a while of that, the noise became less chaotic and more like a song. The sharp pounding of a woodpecker, the rustle of a mouse, or the great loud roar of planes overhead.

I didn't notice Nash returning until he was right on top of me. He didn't head back for his vehicle, though. He walked by, toward the forest, and then looked over his shoulder as if to ask, *are you coming?*

I'd follow Nash Walker anywhere.

We ran to a small house. The door was open like the person inside had been expecting us or, at the least, company. Nash shifted, putting a hand out to me that clearly meant to stop and wait as he peered inside. Nana appeared behind him in the doorway and smacked Nash against the backside of his head. "That's for Paul."

"Nanaaaa," Nash said, sounding so much like he probably did as a child I had to shift so I could smile as wide as I wanted.

"There you are, Phin," Nana said, making no mention to the fact that I'd just changed from a wolf to a human.

I stood stock-still, waiting for her to give me the same treatment. She just wrapped her arms around me and brought me inside. "Come help me, dear."

I looked back for Nash, but he was already behind me, smirking despite the fact he'd just been disciplined.

Inside, the house was bare, except for some furniture, but clean. Someone must have come through recently, brushing away the cobwebs and dust. We walked by an open door where the Alpha's butler lay, his eyes closed as his chest rose and fell steadily. From the living room, you could see into the second bedroom where the Alpha lay, also asleep. His coloring had improved from the night before. It didn't seem like anyone expected anything other than a full recovery.

"His body is mending. It's his lungs I worry about."

"How can I help you?" I asked. I really didn't want to do anything that required me to interact with the Alpha. More so than any of the other elders, I saw Alpha Walker in that field so clearly. Probably because I'd seen him in the same field the night before. "Do you want me to make something?"

"Heavens no. The pack's been by a thousand times since last night, dropping off food. I just got done kicking them out."

"Did someone tell you we were coming?"

Nana nodded. "Something did."

I craned back to Nash, wondering what the heck that meant, but he just shrugged.

"You can help me by bringing me some joy. You can shift now," Nana said, sitting down.

"How did you know?"

"Don't bother," Nash said, though I noticed he was out

of reach of her arm. "She'll just tell you the spirits told her. Someone probably saw us and called her."

"Nash, your refusal to trust the unknown is unbecoming," Nana replied. "But I understand why you do it."

Nash crossed his arms over his chest. "Really? Why, then?"

"Because hope hurts. It hurts to hold it, and it hurts to lose it. But without it, my boy, life would be miserable."

Nash didn't say anything to that, probably because there was nothing that could be said. I wanted to remember every word so I could get Riley to help me stitch it on a pillow. He'd made most of the pillows in the living room and half the wall art. Riley had a knack for taking things and transforming them.

"Have you taken the test yet?" she asked, her lips stretching up. But, while she smiled, her eyes were pinched with worry. She really did need a distraction.

"We haven't," I said, decided to stop the whole *how do you know that* game. "I imagined that was on the schedule for later today."

"I thought we'd stop by the drugstore on the way back," Nash confessed.

"Do it, please. It is so much more fun when everyone knows."

That only made me wonder how many more secrets she kept hidden behind those knowing eyes.

"Why not warn me?" I asked. The question may have sounded challenging, but it was honest. "If you know so much, why not make sure those around you are ready?"

"Would it happen then?" she asked. "People often think about bad things, stopping them. But there is good in bad. Light in dark. Without mystery or uncertainty, what is life?"

Um, amazing was the first word. But I guessed I was

only saying that because I came from the other side of never knowing anything but running from it all.

"I already say more than I should. I worry about my meddling."

"Well, just keep talking in half riddles, and we'll all be okay anyway," Nash said before hopping back to avoid another smack. He bounced into the chair behind him and rubbed his hip. "You knew *that* would happen," he grumbled.

Nana sighed. I didn't like how tired she sounded.

"We can stay and help care, Nana. If you want to take a nap?"

Her eyes widened with surprise. "No, that's okay. My son can be a bit surly. And I have so few chances to care for him now as I did when he was a child." She folded her hands over her stomach and laid back, the picture of serenity.

I could only hope I loved as wholeheartedly as Nana did. And I also felt like a huge dick for what I'd thought about Alpha Walker before this. Nana was proof he couldn't be all bad.

We stayed a little while longer. Nana gave Nash a list of things to do at her property to prepare for the party, though she never mentioned which party. I left in awe, but also a little afraid of the things that woman knew.

We went to the drugstore next, and on the way out, Nash pulled me back into the grocery restroom.

"If you want a quickie, I'm pretty sure a lot of people saw us come in here together."

Nash flashed me his teeth, letting me see he wasn't against the idea. "Not a quickie. I want us to do the test. Here, where no one will be listening."

"See, it sucks to know people are listening to you pee."

"It's not because of that." Nash sat me down on the closed toilet. "When Riley tested, there was a lot of betting and joking, and I'm excited for that part, but I want this moment to just be us. Is that okay?"

Okay? That was preferable.

Nash frowned and looked back to the door. "Do you want me to wait outside while you...?"

My head twisted back and forth in an emphatic no. No way in heck I wanted to do this alone. "You don't have to hold my hand or anything, but wait here. Look, there's magazines." I pointed to a stack of two, both clearly geared toward women. "Find out if you're a winter or summer complexion while I figure out if we're having a baby." Technically, the test would do the figuring, but I ignored that part.

Nash pulled the test free from the shopping bag. He'd also bought candy—in case it was negative, he'd said. And a bottle of sparkling cider, in case it wasn't.

I opened the toilet and turned around, following the steps quickly. I hummed to get a flow going, but it wasn't as hard as it should have been to pee with someone staring at my backside. Probably because that someone was Nash. I set the test on a napkin and washed my hands.

"Now, we wait," I said.

"*Or* we watch without blinking?" Nash suggested.

His plan was better.

We didn't have to keep from blinking for long. Two little lines showed up in two separate windows, changing my life forever. "Pregnant," I whispered. The word didn't do the moment justice. I needed to scream it. And then maybe cry it because I wasn't really supposed to be pregnant, was I?

253

Nash grabbed me tightly, spinning us both in silly circles. "My mate! My pregnant mate!"

"Shh, someone will hear you." I smacked his bicep. His joy wiped away all my worry. Who cared what was supposed to happen—this *was* happening.

"I don't care," Nash replied ecstatically. His phone rang, and he frowned as he pulled it free. "It's Nana," he said, his frown clearing. "She's just telling us when and where to have your baby shower."

After all I'd witnessed of the woman, this still blew me away. Had she known or suspected? Or just hoped? Nash picked me up again, hugging me tight. I chose to only be happy now. Later, I could ponder the answers to my questions while the darker, more worried emotions rushed in. For the moment, I would just be glad that I had my alpha and that his great-grandmother, who seemed to know everything, was on our side.

———

I ROLLED OVER, wishing I could talk to the me from over two months ago. The version of me who had just found out they were pregnant, that they could shift into a wolf. Back when the world was bright and new and my feet didn't ache most of every day.

I reached for my phone to check the time, noticing a few messages from chat. Just normal Bun-Reg-Chuck banter. At least Chuck had relaxed since his last freak-out. He'd claimed that he'd been going through personal stuff that had spilled into chat and that he was sorry. I accepted his apology, but still hadn't told Nash much about what had happened. He still got weird when I talked about my chat friends.

I had faith that would change. I just had to show him how important they were to me, but also how normal we were. Like real friends, without the messy parts of seeing each other. I wasn't sure Nash understood the concept of friends, at least not my concept of it. He had his cousins and his brother, Riley, and me, and that seemed to be about it. I supposed he was friendly with his work pals, but he never wanted to hang out with them after shifts to grab beers or anything. The new guy had asked several times, but Nash had always said no.

Nash stretched. I thought he was still sleeping, but he tugged me around with a purpose to his movements. "You wake up and reach for your phone, omega? I'm jealous."

"You're always jealous," I said with a smile. Somehow, on Nash, green looked good. Probably because he never placed anger or blame on me when he was jealous. Which he often was, of everything. Yesterday, he'd confessed to feeling left out because I'd spent the day smiling at Bran Jr. while his dad attempted to go back to work for a few hours.

It was a heady feeling, being the center of someone's life. I didn't hate it.

Forgetting my phone, I nuzzled into his chest. My stomach stopped me from pushing as close as I would have liked. I'd grown as round as any person impregnated under mysterious circumstances would be. For some reason, I'd thought I wouldn't grow so large since I was a dude and all. But my belly stuck out in an unmistakably pregnant way. For the most part, I was confined to the house, only going into Walkerton with an escort and a large jacket. I'd moved my things from my apartment in town to Nash's. No one even mentioned it. That I would move in was just assumed by each of the Walkers. I'd thought at first it was because of the arsonist, but we'd made no progress on that front in weeks. There simply wasn't any evidence. In that time, I felt only welcomed.

And though we were a group of men living together under what most would call extraordinary circumstances, for the most part, life went on as usual. Nash had his shifts at the firehouse, Wyatt worked the bar, and Aver and Branson seemed to have more clients than ever. Lots of people were getting ready to entertain outside and needed their help constructing outdoor grills and patios. Riley had his projects and the baby to keep him busy at home, and now he had a few hours a week in the office—part of his reintroduction to work.

And I had my books.

All in all, we lived regular lives, if you didn't think about how there was likely an arsonist targeting us, the fact that I was pregnant, and we could all turn into wolves.

Oh, and that I hadn't seen my penis in far too many days.

Nash's hands spread over my belly, lifting my shirt. He rubbed from top to bottom, left to right. He said it was his way of saying good morning to the little guy or girl. This morning, though, his hands dipped lower, to the part of me I wasn't sure still existed.

The moment his hands gripped my dick, I knew. Yes, I had a penis, and oh my lord, it had been too long since I'd touched it.

Nash touched me now, stroking slowly, stoking the fires of my desire.

"Nash, won't you be late?" I gasped, gripping his wrist.

"I don't care," he replied with a low rumble.

"I do! It's my party today!"

We'd reached the day Nana had carved out for my baby shower before I'd even taken the test. Nash had finished her list, most of it just cleaning up clutter. She had a neighbor to tend to her animals whenever she was away.

"I'll be quick," Nash murmured, though I didn't believe him in the slightest. He wrapped all of his fingers around me, stroking with a firm grip while he used his other hand to tickle my backside, teasing as he explored deeper.

"Yes!" All the thoughts of the party or arrival times vanished, paling in comparison to Nash's touches. I flexed, clamping down on his fingers, making him groan.

"Squeeze me tight, omega," he ordered, stroking me to the brink of orgasm before abruptly stopping.

I panted and gasped. "That was rude."

Nash just chuckled, adding a second finger to the first while increasing the rate of his strokes. He kissed me, our tongues meeting and passing like old pals on the street. I could never get enough of Nash. Could never taste enough, never go deep enough. He left me content and satiated but in a way that seemed to reach no limit. There was no ceiling to his skill, and in the months since we'd become official—for lack of a better term—he'd shown me ways of orgasming that I hadn't known existed.

When I came, he held onto me. My shuddering breaths had to have tickled his ear and neck, but he kept me close, murmuring how perfect I was the entire time.

Clarity returned, brushing away the hedonistic haze, and I glanced at the clock. "I think there's enough time," I said, trying to slide to my knees.

Nash urged me back. "This isn't tit for tat, omega. Sometimes I just want to love on you."

How could I have a problem with that?

.   .   .

An hour later, I hopped out of the car with Riley and Bran Jr. Nash walked us into Nana's. She had the front room decorated with brightly colored flowers. I wasn't sure where she'd gotten them at this time of year, though I was pretty sure they hadn't been purchased from a store. Mrs. Boxer was there, the first surprise of my day.

I turned around to try to hide my belly, bumping into Nash in the process. He caught me, his gaze narrowing over my head while he searched for the cause of my panic.

"Don't stand there letting the warm out," Nana said from the kitchen.

"Mrs. Boxer is here," I said, feeling very dumb. Anyone with eyes could see that.

"Hello, Phineas. I haven't seen you since you moved out."

"I still have my lease," I replied absently. Was her eyesight so poor she couldn't see the prominent belly sticking out of me like the figurehead on a pirate ship?

"Then you have no excuse," she pouted.

Well, I could think of a few. I was pregnant now. That *excuse* came to mind pretty quickly. "I'm... sorry?"

"Apology accepted." Mrs. Boxer turned to Riley next, reaching out her arms. "Now let me hold this little niblet. As good as a sausage, he is." She pretended to eat Bran's arm, much to his delight.

I looked from Mrs. Boxer to Nana. "Are we early?" I didn't know who else I would invite, except maybe Paul.

"No," Nana said without offering more.

Nash hugged me from the back. He clasped his hands together under my belly. He had to hold me too tightly to do the same thing over my belly. "I think what he's asking, Nana, is what the heck is going on here? Is this what baby showers are?"

I wouldn't ever say what I thought so brashly, but what Nash said was basically what was going through my mind.

"The others are coming later," Nana said, brushing Nash away and tugging me forward into the kitchen. "First, we're going to make a loaf of sourdough, and after, I will send you home with your own starter. It's a tradition in my family. My grandmother passed her starter down to my mother that I will pass down to you. You aren't women, and I'm not pretending you are, but the tradition is meant to pass down to the child bearers."

"We are sure Nana isn't to blame for us all getting pregnant, aren't we?" Riley asked in a hushed tone.

I couldn't say with confidence that she wasn't.

Nana looked up, as if noticing Nash for the first time. "Get out of here. This isn't your party."

Nash grabbed his chest. "You wound me, Great-Grandmother. Besides, Phin doesn't bake. You send that home with him, and it will end up growing and becoming self-aware in the back of our fridge."

He wasn't wrong, but I wouldn't have dreamed of saying as much in front of Nana. It sounded like a sweet tradition that she hadn't had many chances to celebrate lately.

"That's not the important part," Nana said, pushing Nash out of the kitchen, while passing him something that looked suspiciously like cookies wrapped in a napkin. "Traditions aren't good because they're kept. They're good because they give us a chance to reflect. Throw it out when you get home. And when one of you pops out another, we'll make it again." She seemed pleased as punch at the idea— who was I to murder her joy?

Nash hopped around his nana and kissed me goodbye, saying he'd be back to get us in a few hours. "Cut loose if you want. I'll be the designated driver," he joked before Nana shut the door behind him.

Nana didn't end up needing much help with the bread, but I'd expected that. In the times we'd spent together, she tended to ask for help, but what she really wanted was for you to stand there while she did all the work and chatted. But Nash hadn't been wrong. I wasn't a big baker, and actually, the feel of flour under my fingernails was one of those sensations that set my teeth on edge. So I was fine with watching while Riley seemed fine with passing his baby off to Mrs. Boxer while he thumbed through a cookbook with a lot of scribbles in it.

We left the dough to rise in a covered bowl on the oven. The moment Nana finished, there was a knock on the door, and I didn't doubt that she'd planned that out. "That'll be the rest of the guests."

I didn't know who else could be coming except Paul, but when she opened the door, Tanya yanked herself from her mother's arms and ran for me. I held out my arms and winced, unsure of how to catch her with my huge belly, but Riley stepped in, lifting and spinning her before setting her back down.

"Uncle Phin is pregnant now. We must be gentle," Riley told her. She peeked around him, peering up at me.

"You got big."

I laughed. "Yes, I did. Thank you for coming to my party."

She beamed as her mom caught up. "Thank you for the invitation. We couldn't have joined a nicer pack. Every day, you all welcome us more and more." She blinked, and tears fell down her cheeks. She wiped them away so quickly I didn't think she'd meant to cry, and I patted her shoulder.

"I'm sorry, this is your day. Congratulations, really. I've never witnessed a blessed birth."

I winced, but at least Nash wasn't here to hear her. He loathed that term because of how *other* it made us seem. Anything that made us stick out, to him, only put us in more danger. "Thank you. We made bread. I don't think it will be done for hours longer, though." I shrugged.

Nana was still welcoming people in. There was Denise's mother, who made a beeline for Mrs. Baxter and claimed she was next to hold the baby. Paul was there. I'd made sure to let him know that he was still one of my very good friends, despite what had happened between him and Nash. There were a few more from the pack that I recognized by face alone and then a woman whose face I'd never forget.

Her face was sharp. Neither of her kids had inherited the intense angles of her face, save for her jawline. But her hair was as dark as theirs. She kept it short, barely kissing her shoulders, and her bangs were cut in a blunt line across her forehead. Julie Walker. If I hadn't known already she was Nash and Wyatt's mother, the green eyes would've given it away.

Riley spotted my face and looked back at the door, letting out a sharp sound. "Uh-oh," he whispered loud enough for only me to hear.

I became a deer in the headlights. Unsure of the right move. We were with Nana, and she didn't look at all surprised to see Julie, which made me think she'd been invited. But none of the Walker cousins would be happy to hear she was here. If Branson found out, he'd probably drive right down and carry Riley out—kicking and screaming if he had to.

Julie waved, the gesture as timid as her expression.

"Thank you for inviting me," she said, looking at no one person in particular. "I was so excited to hear I would have a grandson."

I covered my stomach as if blocking her from my unborn. This woman was technically my child's grand-mother, though. Was it right to keep her out of his or her life now? Nash would say yes. I wasn't so sure. I'd spent too many nights wishing my parents would come back or I'd find a set of grandparents who would spoil and love me. How could I take that chance away from my child?

She sat down in the chair across from the couch and folded her hands in her lap, tucking her legs under her.

"Okay." Nana clapped. "We're all here. Let's start the games!"

I loved games, but Nana hadn't mentioned games before. Were we going to guess what types of candy bars had been melted in diapers? I'd heard of that game before. It sounded disgusting. Other games I'd heard of involved touching or pinning things to the pregnant person. I really didn't want to do any of that.

I should've trusted Nana more.

She pulled out a tray of empty planters, a bucket of dirt, and bags of seeds without labels. She didn't seem to mind that we'd be doing this activity that required dirt in her living room. "I don't know what the seeds are—forgot to label 'em—but the flowers will be pretty all the same. Come on down. Don't be shy."

I wasn't shy, not in this home, but I did need help getting on the ground. And once I was down there, I was pretty sure Nash would have to help me get back up. The others gathered around. Tanya sat so close her crossed legs bumped into mine. "Didn't you say this is a game?" I asked, reaching for a planter. "How do we play?"

"You play by watching your flower grow," Nana said as if the answer were simple.

Riley, Paul, and I shared a grin. My gaze flitted over to Julie, and I found she was smiling as well, but stopped when our eyes met.

"Don't be shy now, dig in. After, I'll check the bread, and we can start knitting socks."

"I think she brought us here for free labor," Paul joked under his breath a few minutes later.

"I heard that," Nana barked, coming in with a tray of lemonade. "Don't worry about the dirt. I never do."

Where flour under my fingers set my teeth on edge, dirt in the same place made me smile. I worked happily, scooping dirt into my planter until it was a little more than an inch full. I reached for a pack of seeds and sprinkled some over the dirt, covering them gently.

"When are you due?" Denise asked some time later. She'd already made her own planter and was working on one for her mother since she hadn't wanted to set down baby Bran.

"No idea. We're kind of flying blind. If we go by what happened with Riley, any day now, really."

"So this pack has had *two* blessed births. That's incredible," Denise commented.

Neither Riley nor I responded to the blessed bit.

"Just one right now," I said instead. "Though I'm still not sure how this baby is getting out of me. It better happen like with Riley—inside one second, out the next."

"You're so good with shifting, you probably won't have any issues," Riley said. "You'll sneeze and poof, baby's there."

I hoped so. I didn't want to ponder the alternatives.

"Nash and Wyatt shot out of me," Julie said, patting her dirt down so it was even. She looked up, noticed us looking, and blushed. "I mean, my pregnancy wasn't the same. All nine months, I'm afraid." She sighed and smiled. "Those boys fought from the first moment they had arms and legs to hit each other with."

I wanted to ask her a million more questions. With her *and* Riley here, I could add up both of their experiences, divide it, and get the average of what I could expect. But finding more from her meant speaking directly to her. And that felt like a betrayal. What would Nash do when he found out? The truth hit me. Nash would always love me. Even if I talked to his mom when he wished I wouldn't. "This one is a wiggler too," I told her, cupping my stomach.

Tanya noticed what I was doing and reached her small brown hand toward my stomach, pulling back.

"It's okay," I said. "You can feel. The little guy or girl is doing a dance for you."

Tanya smiled and pressed her hand flat. I moved her fingers to where my hand had been. That was where she could feel it the best. "She's dancing, Mama!" Tanya shouted, getting to her feet with excitement.

I was glad when they didn't all rush to touch, and I resumed my activity, using the small pitcher to water my potential plant. "Can you tell me about your pregnancy, Mrs. Walker? I heard Wyatt came out standing on Nash's shoulders."

Julie startled but quickly smiled. "It's true. They didn't want to be separated, not for a moment." Her throat sounded tight, and she covered her mouth with her hand, seemingly forgetting it was covered in dirt. "I'm sorry." She ran to the bathroom.

Nana came in with the broom, cleaning up the small mess we'd made. "Food's ready. Then gifts," she said like a baby shower drill sergeant. "We can knit after if there's time."

Paul grinned. He could joke all he liked, but really, any other type of party wouldn't have been nearly as enjoyable. This was my kind of gathering. Someone keeping everyone on task and plenty of things to give us all something to do. Her mention of time had me looking at the clock, and I was shocked at the amount of time that had passed.

Julie came back out, and when we dished up a chili with winter vegetables and cornbread straight from the skillet, I sat next to her at the small table.

"Could you tell me what they were like?" I asked. "The boys, when they were younger?"

Julie set her spoon down and wiped her mouth. "Handfuls," she admitted with another small smile. "I swear they came out climbing, learned to walk the next day and run the next and never stopped. Nash used to have problems with shift seizures." She saw my face and explained. "When he was a toddler, he would shift uncontrollably. I tried giving him everything to stop it, but the only thing that ever worked was lavender tea. I'd slip it in his bottle with some milk." She picked up her spoon and resumed eating.

I didn't hide the fact that I was staring at her. She was more mild-mannered than I'd thought she'd be. Gentle. I wondered how much of what went on in her life was her doing. Back on the sidewalk, she'd spoken to her husband in hushed whispers. Because she was too afraid or meek to be any louder?

The only thing I had to compare her to was Delia, and that woman really liked the sound of her own voice.

"Of course, John didn't like the boys being so close. I told him it was fighting a losing battle. Some souls come out joined." That time, when she stopped speaking, she sobbed quietly. "I'm sorry."

"No need for tears. Chili isn't that bad," Nana said, and while her tone had been no-nonsense, there were tears in her eyes too.

Julie wiped her eyes, accepting a handkerchief from Mrs. Boxer before grabbing her spoon.

I waited for her to take a few bites. "How big were they? As babies, I mean."

Julie swallowed what was in her mouth. I really should've let her eat, but I was intensely aware of how limited this chance was. Would I ever get to speak to this woman in a casual setting again?

Before she could answer, the door opened, and Nash walked in. "I know I'm early, but I couldn't stay awa—" I figured about the time he spotted his mother was when his booming voice cut out. I stood, along with Riley and Paul, but Nana stayed seated, scooping another bite of chili onto her spoon and continuing to eat.

"If you can be civil, grab a chair. If not, wait outside."

Nash's scowl turned aghast for a moment before settling into a glower. He shut the door softly. "I won't be separated from my mate, not even by your command, Nana."

"I can go," Julie offered quietly. "I'll call my driver and—"

"No, please don't," I rushed to say.

She shook her head, looking at the table. "It's okay. We were just finishing here and—"

"Let's go. Phin, Riley, grab your things," Nash said. His voice wasn't sharp, and he didn't snap his fingers or anything like that, but I still wanted to headbutt him. Head as hard as his, he wouldn't feel anything if I did.

I stood, pressing my hands against his chest. "No, Nash.

I *was* having a good time talking to your mom. I didn't know you had shift seizures."

His jaw clenched tight. "Now you do. Let's go."

I rolled my eyes. Nash was being bullheaded, but really, I'd been at Nana's for hours socializing. And even though it had been easier than ever, I had been coming to my limit. But to go now felt too much like rewarding Nash's boorish behavior. "Maybe you can come to dinner sometime, Mrs. Walker," I offered, feeling like it was a fair compromise. We had Nana over all the time. And Paul.

Riley jumped in, agreeing with my suggestion.

"No." Nash didn't wait for us to ask him before issuing his decree. "Absolutely not."

"Nash, you were not raised to be so rude," Nana barked.

"Actually, I was raised to be an entitled prick, by this woman right here. So you'll have to excuse me if I—"

I pushed out of his arms, turning to those sitting uncomfortably around the table. "Thank you, everyone, for the party."

"You haven't opened your gifts," Nana growled, looking mad enough to wrestle an alligator.

"You know what they say," I told her with a smile. "Ten's company, eleven is overcrowded." I scowled at Nash, but the anger had suddenly fled from his face.

"What did you say? Just then? Is that a common saying?" Nash asked.

The question came so out of left field I didn't understand it at first. "No, I don't think so. I don't know where I picked it up. Why? Will you sit while I open my presents if I remember?"

Nash gave me a double-take. He looked to Nana, his mother, and back to me, and his face fell.

Though I'd put the space between us, I couldn't stay away from him while he looked so crestfallen.

"I'm sorry," he murmured, not seeming to care that everyone could hear us. "I didn't know she'd be here."

"I didn't either. But we've been talking. She's been telling me about your childhood. It's been nice, Nash." I kissed him softly. "Please don't make us stop."

He groaned and stepped back. "I won't, or at least, I don't want to. But I've got to check on something. A hunch, and I want to do it sooner rather than later." He sighed loudly, the sound he made when he came to a decision that he didn't all the way enjoy. "Come by tonight, for dinner," he said, and though he never addressed her, Julie bobbed her head emphatically.

"I can. I'm free," she agreed softly.

He didn't acknowledge he'd heard her. "We'll have dinner tonight. Best to get it over with. Can you open your presents then?" His gaze turned pleading. Clearly, there was something he needed to do, but he wouldn't leave me behind to do it.

"We got you diapers," Denise said from the table.

"I got you sausages," Mrs. Boxer added.

"I'll bring the rest of the presents when I come for dinner. What time, boy?" Nana asked, never minding the fact that she hadn't been expressly invited.

"Whenever," Nash said, waving his hand in the air. He threw out a number. "Seven. Doesn't make a difference. The others are going to kill me no matter what time it is at."

I frowned. This hadn't been a battle I'd thought I would wage today. The next big fight I'd expected us to have was supposed to be about my chat friends, but here I was, all but demanding Nash let his mother back into his life because she'd come to my party and knew about Nash as a baby.

There'd been a time when she'd asked her sons to do something truly heinous. Something only a bad woman would do. I trusted Nana enough to not set me up for failure, but it wasn't like I'd truly won this argument. Nash had just remembered he needed to do something more than he hated the idea of his mother coming over.

And really, that was about the best outcome I could have hoped for.

19

NASH

My PHONE RANG, and I pushed my foot on the gas. I'd dropped Phineas off at the house, and he'd protested being left behind, asking why he couldn't have stayed if I was going to leave him anyway. It was a valid question.

I had a lot to make up to my Phineas after today. But, hopefully, I'd have answers too. First, I had to drop by the firehouse to check our personnel files. I'd sent over the information to an investigator we'd worked with before, and he said he would let me know as soon as he found anything.

But until I knew, I wasn't going to say anything. We'd had a couple false alarms in the weeks prior, and I couldn't forget the whole Paul fiasco. I'd been so quick to assume the fires had been his fault. I knew they weren't now. And hopefully when I got the call, I'd know who was really to blame.

However, the person on the other end of my call wasn't the investigator—it was my brother. I didn't need to answer to know he was pissed. I'd be livid if our tables were turned. And there'd be no way he would escape a beat down.

I was already almost home, but it was better to get this over with. Maybe he'd lose some steam by the time we came head to head, and I wouldn't have to mark up that pretty face of his. I winked at that same face in the rearview mirror and picked up the phone. "This is Nash."

"I fucking know it is Nash. What the hell am I hearing?" Wyatt seethed.

"Me? My voice? Right now? This feels like a trick question."

I was pretty sure I heard his head explode. "This is funny to you? Is it? You let that viper into our home? That monster? The woman who wanted me to kill you, Nash—you want me to eat food next to her like none of that mattered?"

I squeezed my eyes closed and then remembered I was driving. "No. I mean, yes! Wyatt, man, Phineas—"

"You're hiding behind your mate?"

"No," I snarled. "But you don't understand Phineas. He sees this world like no one else can. You should look at his face when he looks at Alpha Walker. It pinches like he inhaled a captured fart. He isn't a bad judge of character."

"So now you forgive our mother and want to be her sweet little boy again?" You could cut the sarcasm with a knife.

"No, and you do know I am driving within punching distance of you right now, right? My mind hasn't changed at all. Sometimes Phineas and I disagree, and that's okay. This time will be one of those times, but I won't shut him down, Wyatt. I won't snap off whatever tenuous olive branch he extends. I love him too much to do that."

Wyatt barked out a few more choice words, none of them directed at Phin, all of them directed at me, and when my tires rolled to a stop in front of home, my ears were ringing, and he finally stopped.

"I'll give you a five-minute head start," I growled into the phone before hanging up. Ambling to the door, I pushed it open, hit instantly by a plume of delicious food smells. Damn it, I'd told the guys they didn't need to cook. I'd planned on ordering pizza or something simple. And quickly consumed.

Phin met me in the kitchen doorway. He was so fucking beautiful with that big fat stomach. I'd never call it fat to his face—he'd probably place negatives feelings to that word—but when I used it, it was with love. That extra tub meant my child was growing inside there. I didn't like the uncertainty that came with pregnancy, but I loved the way it changed his body.

I loved his not-pregnant body too. I just loved *him*. But, the last time we'd talked, we'd fought. And before that, I'd been a Grade-A dick, so I wasn't sure what I'd find when I bent down to kiss him.

He turned his face up to me with a soft smile. "Did you get your errand done?"

"Something like that," I said.

Phin raised his eyebrow. "I shouldn't trust you when you say that, should I?"

I waved at Riley, pulling something out of the fridge.

"You should always trust me." Sliding my arms around him, I cupped my hands together below his ass. "I'm sorry, Phineas. Truly. About my behavior at Nana's. I don't want to take back *what* I said, but *how* I said it. You were having a good time. I ruined it."

Phin formed his hand into a fist and bounced it softly over my heart. "Apology accepted. I know your reasons, and I don't want to be heartless here. I just wanted to talk a little longer with her. We never have to ask her over again."

Our foreheads met, and I inhaled his sweet scent. "How did I get so lucky with such an understanding mate?"

"I don't know if it's luck or if seeing Wyatt's reaction convinced me you were the tame one." Phin laughed, but the sound shook slightly.

I glared out the back patio door, still open a crack. "Did he yell at you?"

Phin slapped my chest with his open hand. "Oh no. I know that tone!"

"I told him he had five minutes. He earned this ass-kicking, baby," I said to his shocked expression. "You should have heard the mean things he said to me!"

Phineas shook his head and looked at the clock. "It's been three minutes," he called out to my backside.

I opened the patio door and peered out. "I know."

———

"I SEE HEADLIGHTS!" Phineas jumped and turned. He would have bounced off me to the floor if I hadn't caught him.

I rubbed his arms, from wrist to shoulders. I'd watched the doubt form between his eyes after we'd informed Branson and Aver who would be coming by for dinner. Aver had fussed about his parents wanting an invitation next, while Branson lectured all of us on the merits of planning these things as a group.

"I don't want to say I think it was a bad idea, only that it would've been better if we'd all had a chance to discuss it," he'd said, clearly trying to sound like the shifter version of a lovable sitcom dad.

While no one had said anything directly against Phin, that worry line had only grown. But I couldn't say much to console him. I didn't want my mother coming here, and I didn't think it was a good idea, if only because the arson attacks had stopped right about the time we'd distanced ourselves once more from the pack. Now, it felt like we were slipping right back, sinking deeper and deeper.

"I love you," Phin said, and while I loved hearing those words from him, I didn't like the hint of duress.

"Phineas, we will all survive this night. Even if she burst in, tries to make Bran Jr. a blood sacrifice, and dances on the table as an offering to Satan. Maybe we'll tease you if she does go full *Exorcist,* but I will always love you." I jerked my head back toward the other room. "The others don't get to love you like I do."

"I love you!" Wyatt shouted from the kitchen.

I growled and charged in his direction. Phin pulled me to a stop. "You've already pummeled him enough."

My mate was being kind. In the end, after I'd caught Wyatt trying to hide in a tree like a coward, we'd both emerged with as many marks. So much senseless destruction. Phin kissed the bruise on my cheek, and by then, the truck outside had parked. Phineas tugged to turn around, and I grabbed his head, keeping his face on me. "No peeking. Use your senses. Who just pulled up outside?"

He'd been frowning, but at my question, his face changed, getting that hungry look he did when he was learning something. He squinted, and I wanted to laugh and ask how that helped him hear better, but he opened his mouth. "Nana. That's Nana's truck. Did she bring your mom?"

Your mom. Just like that the humor was gone.

It would've left anyway since Nana opened the door seconds later. She wasn't one to knock. "Mmm, smells good."

"Riley and Phineas cooked," Branson said with Riley hooked to his side and Bran in his arms.

"Riley cooked," Phin corrected.

"It smells fine either way," Nana said. She stuck out her arm, guiding my mother inside.

I tried to remember if she'd ever even seen my house. Maybe from the other side of the bay.

She stepped forward. "Thank you, Phineas, and... everyone." Her hands were folded tightly at her front. She had always been thin to the point that from an early age I'd pulled back when it came to hugging her. I'd gotten strong quick, and I couldn't remember an unrestrained hug with her.

"I have everything set up in the dining room," Riley said. This was part of the plan Riley and Phin had concocted when they thought we weren't listening.

First: Suggest that we begin dinner immediately.

Second was to keep conversation to baby talk or the weather.

Too bad for them—my mother had a different idea. We circled the table, Nana sitting at one end and Riley taking the other. The rest of us sat scattered, though the seat next to my mother would remain empty.

She wasn't sitting in her seat anyway. She stood, wringing her fingers in front of her. "I thought, before we started, I'd just get the worst part out of the way. Any of you may ask me questions about why I'm here, maybe what you think my inten—" She took a shaky breath. "What my intentions are. I'm an open book. You need only ask."

"I have a question," Aver said, each letter perfectly formed. "Who did you tell that you were coming here?"

My mother shook her head. "No one. I stayed at Nana's after the party, and she drove me over here." She smiled and then quickly covered her mouth. "No one has any idea where I am."

That idea seemed to delight her more than it should

delight a woman who spent her days telling people what to do.

More than one person looked at me as if expecting me to ask the next question. I was here for Phin. The only question in my mind was *how could you?* And I didn't think that sort of thing could be answered in a quick Q&A.

Wyatt cleared his throat and stood. "I have a question." His hands were clenched at his sides, and I tensed. "Why did you want to come here?"

I breathed a sigh of relief. That wasn't a friendly question, but it wasn't as bad as it could have been.

My mother chewed on her upper lip and then the lower. Watching her now brought up a faint memory, one where she'd done that same thing, but it had made someone mad. My dad?

Stop chewing on your lips, Julie. You're not a squirrel.

That had been what my dad had said. I shook my head trying to clear the disturbing memory. People had done studies about memories and how easily they were fabricated. Had I made that up just now? Or had her presence dislodged something?

"Easy answer?" Julie replied. "I came because Phineas asked me to. We were talking at his party about you boys and what handfuls you were as children." Her smile, though still small, grew warm. Our eyes met briefly before she looked sharply away. "It doesn't look like you two have changed. Aloe vera gel should help with those bruises. John used to hate you boys leaving the house all marked up."

I grunted, not liking how quickly I'd gone from utterly despising the woman and humoring my mate to rethinking every moment of my childhood. My father had ruled our home with an iron fist. And in the years that had passed, my mother and father had sort of melded into one beast in my mind. But what if *they* weren't one beast?

"I'd say that's enough questions before dinner," Nana said in the silence that had followed.

Riley hopped up, all too thrilled to continue with their plan. "Mrs. Walker—or should I call you elder?"

"Mrs. Walker is fine, or... even Julie, if you like."

Damn why did she have to sound so hopeful that Riley would call her Julie?

"Julie." Riley nodded with a smile. "You were telling Phineas about the boys when they were babies. Any other tips for what he might be able to expect?"

Second: Keep conversation to baby talk or the weather.

Phin shot Riley a look of thanks.

"Before you answer, Julie, we've got barbecue chicken, roasted green beans, and cornbread. Not from scratch, Nana. Don't hate me." Riley said the last part like he was relaying his last message and quickly running out of oxygen.

Nana reached forward and grabbed a chicken leg with her bare hand from the platter, tearing into the flesh with her teeth. "Why would I hate you after inviting me over and cooking for me?" She took another bite, and the rest of us followed suit, dishing up, though we used the tongs Riley had set out.

"I'd say Phineas is already set up for a much easier birth," Julie said. She wasn't eating, but she'd filled her plate. "I've always had trouble keeping on weight, and pregnancy, especially with twins, was difficult." She stopped speaking so suddenly I looked over to her. She'd covered her mouth again.

I frowned. She did that a lot.

"Not that I am complaining," she said in a rush. "I ended

up in labor for hours, and those moments, alone in my room, while I spoke to you both are some of my most cherished."

"You mean when you and Father spoke to us," I said. Surely John had been in the room while my mother labored for hours?

Her head shook a fraction to the left, then right, like she wasn't sure if she'd get in trouble for answering. "John had things to do for the pack, papers to prepare. I was meant to give him an alpha after all." A sharp noise came from her mouth, like a laugh, but not. "He never forgave me for messing up that one."

As a fireman that served a wide, rural area, I was sometimes required to enter a scene knowing nothing and using the clues to assume the situation. If I were to do that now, it wouldn't take me long to connect the dots. But to do so now meant admitting that my mother had been a woman in trouble, talked down to and ordered around by her husband, left to give birth alone, shamed when we came out not as he expected. How was she supposed to control whether we were alphas or not?

"I'm sorry. I don't mean to bad-talk your father. He has his qualities. And he's taken care of me. He's kept me fed, watered, a roof over my head—"

"That's what you do for dogs," Wyatt snapped, pushing his plate back.

Our eyes met over the table, and my heart broke seeing the same confusion in his gaze that simmered in mine.

"No, really, Wyatt. He's a generous man. Maybe not kind, but—"

Wyatt's body shook. "Stop defending him!"

Just like that, Julie shut down, bringing her face down to her hands folded tightly in her lap. "I'm sorry."

Wyatt jerked back from her, blinking with his mouth

gaping open. "Don't apol—I wasn't yelling at you. I'm... not hungry." He picked up his plate and turned around.

All of us looked to Nana, who munched serenely on a green bean.

My phone rang, and if I wasn't waiting for the call I was, I would've ignored it and gone to Wyatt. I pulled it out, blocking the death glare from Nana—she hated phones at the table—and answered.

"Nash, it's me, I've got that information you wanted." My investigator friend had a clipped, no-nonsense tone.

"That was fast. Did you find anything good?" I'd asked him on a hunch, based off what Phineas had said at the party. *Ten's company, eleven is overcrowded.* That hadn't been the first time I'd heard that sort of phrase, and both times, the numbers were different. Maybe it didn't mean anything. But if it hadn't, the investigator wouldn't have called so quickly.

"I found that guy you were asking about. He saved some kid years ago. Pulled him out of the wreckage. I'll send over the articles so you can see. There's a picture from the front page of the Monterey Times."

Instantly, my current worries faded away. This silly dinner, my old anger, everything that wasn't my mate and the danger he was in crumbled. "Thank you. Send it."

At my tone, everyone at the table stopped eating and looked at me. Wyatt returned, remaining in the doorway, staring warily.

"Do you want me to keep digging? I saw something about the guy having a daughter who was sick."

"A daughter?" That fucker had mentioned having a daughter. Maybe we could call her for information.

"Yeah, deceased. Within the last couple of years. I'll go

back and bring up what I can find. I thought I saw an obituary when I ran the search for that name."

"Thanks, I appreciate it."

"Don't appreciate it—you paid me. I'm just doing my job."

He hung up, leaving me with a room of curious faces. My phone chimed, the screen filling with tiny images of an old newspaper article. "Wyatt, grab your laptop."

"Nash Walker, I let you have that call since you're a fireman, but we are eating—"

I shook my head slowly. "I know who the arsonist is."

Wyatt pulled out his laptop while Branson and Aver cleared the table. Minutes later, we circled around the screen, Nana and my mother included as I sent the pics to Wyatt's computer. He opened the first of the images.

"That's the crash," Phin gasped, pressing his face into my chest.

Damn, I should have warned him.

I was too distracted looking at the man in the picture, the man holding a tiny child-sized Phineas. He was tall, with a stocky build and dark hair. The picture was in black and white, so I couldn't tell his eye color, but I would have bet they were green.

"Isn't that the new guy at the firehouse?" Aver asked. "Charles something? I met him... at the party." His tone turned knowing. "You think he is the one?"

"The fires didn't start until he came," I said, tapping over to the picture of the article itself. "Local Good Samaritan, Charles Bracks, was in the right place at the right time to pull four-year-old Phineas Peters from a wreck that had already claimed both of his parents."

Phineas jerked his face up. "Are you guys saying Charles from the firehouse is the man who helped me from the wreck that killed my parents? And he's here now?"

"I know it's hard, but look for yourself, babe. That's his picture there. Charles Bracks. That isn't the last name he gave the firehouse."

Phineas cupped his pregnant stomach with a wince. "He followed me here? And started setting fire to things? Why?"

I shook my head and thought Phineas was shaking his head in return, except he never stopped. His head jerked back and forth, his eyes rolling while his entire body trembled. "What? What is this? What is happening?" I held him, but his shaking was so violent, he nearly tore himself from my arms.

I kicked the table, creating a gap and giving us room as the others spread out.

"He's seizing!" Riley said.

"Call the ambulance," Aver ordered.

Had the shock been too much for him? I knew it would be hard for him to see this, but I thought his thirst for knowledge would outweigh all that. Was I this wrong? Had he fallen into some kind of breakdown? I slid to the ground, all the while holding him in my arms. His arms bent in odd angles, the tendons strained so hard they stuck out like cords beneath his skin. Then his form blurred, becoming a wolf.

"Wait! He's shifting! You can't call!" It killed me to say, but what would the ambulance do for a seizing shifter other than cause more problems? I laid him down, pushing everything back around him so he wouldn't knock into something. His legs jerked, bending and unbending. This wasn't like any seizure I'd ever seen. I dropped down so my head was near his head and cupped his face lightly. My heart tightened as he continued to convulse, shifting suddenly into a human. "Nana?"

"I'm here," she said, her voice coming from close by. I couldn't look away to check. "He doesn't have a condition that would cause this? No medication?"

His form blurred, rearranging into a wolf, but no sooner had he shifted did he shift back just as suddenly. That continued, his body abruptly going from human to wolf back to human so fast he looked like a blur on the carpet.

"Phin! Phin!" With as many things as I'd seen, I'd never been as terrified than I was at that moment. My mate was in obvious pain. As a human, his jaw clenched, his mouth opening on a silent scream.

"I've seen this," a soft voice said. "Not quite as bad, but you used to have shift seizures, Nash. Just like this, from w-wolf, to boy, to wolf again." My mother was obviously terrified but lifted her chin resolutely. "Lavender. Do you have any lavender tea?"

Wyatt, Riley, and Aver ran into the kitchen while I hunched back down, putting my face in front of his.

"Careful, he might bite in his wolf form. He doesn't seem to have control," Branson said.

I ignored him. My mate could bite my face off if it meant he'd be better. If this was what I'd done as a child, my mother had nerves of steel. I was close to crying. The only thing stopping me was my sheer stubbornness that I *would* protect my mate. At the same time, we'd just discovered who our arsonist was, and the fact that he could be walking around thinking we didn't know for a single second longer was inexcusable.

Riley and the rest returned with the tea, bringing us to our next problem.

He held the steaming mug tightly in his hand. "How do we get him to drink it?"

Phin wasn't sticking to one form long enough for us to have time to bring the cup to his mouth, much less swallow. And I didn't want anything we did to make him choke. I turned to my mother.

"You never could drink it either. I'd massage it into your temples, your hands, down your spine, and your feet. Use the teabag too. You'll want to get a few more soaking, Riley," she said, and though her body trembled, she sounded confident.

I did as she instructed, ignoring the voice that had grown in the past decade that told me she was the devil and I shouldn't believe a word she said. I pressed the tea bag to Phin's temple, holding it there as he shifted rapidly. The shifts slowed to once every few seconds. "It's working."

There was more than one happy noise behind me. But we didn't have time to sit around and be happy. Not while Charles was still out there. I wouldn't leave my mate while he was like this. "Wyatt, I need you to go to the station in Walkerton."

"I'll go with him," Branson said.

"Okay, good. Charles is on shift tonight. Go pick him up. Use force if you have to. Wyatt, you call in Paster from the station. Use your me voice." No one could impersonate me like my twin. "He's on call and should be able to come in. Then call me." Hopefully by then, we'd have Phineas stable. If we didn't, I'd have to call the ambulance, wolf or no wolf.

Wyatt left immediately, and Branson followed behind after hugging Riley. I felt a flutter of uncertainty when they left. I wouldn't feel right about it until I joined them. They were both full-grown alpha wolves. Charles was a human, of that fact I was sure. A human skilled at lying. A human who had followed my mate up the west coast to Walker County. We would be stupid to think this was the first time. How long had my Phineas been chased by him without ever knowing? If Charles had ever introduced himself to Phin, he would've remembered his face. That Charles had this time didn't comfort me. A criminal didn't change their MO for fun—they did it when they were getting desperate.

Desperate for what?

Phin's shifts slowed even more. I slid my hand under his shirt, running the teabag up and down his spine, dipping it back in the tea from the mug my mother held. She watched Phineas the entire time, her forehead wrinkled with concern.

"Aver, use Wyatt's computer to log onto GeekGab. It should be in his history from a few months back. I want you to read as much of what was said between Phin's chat buddies as possible."

"Why?" Riley asked. "And for that matter, how did you know to look into Charles in the first place?"

He'd brought back the box of tea and the kettle. With an approving nod from me, my mother started on Phin's feet, using the bag to massage his soles.

"Something Phin said at the party. It's like a play on 'two's company, three's a crowd,' but he said it wrong. So did Charles a while back in the station. And Chuck that day in chat, do you remember?"

He shook his head. It was so random of a thing; I wouldn't have expected him to. It had taken Phineas saying it for me to connect the dots.

"Wait, that means you think Charles is Chuck? He's Phin's chat friend?"

I grimaced, not wanting to say it out loud. If he was able,

Phin would just accuse me of not believing that chat friends could be real. I would never say it, but this was exactly the thing I'd been worried about.

Okay, no, I hadn't been worried that Phin's friends would turn out to be lifelong stalkers, but I'd been wary of them existing at all.

Suddenly, Phin's seizures stopped. His body relaxed, and he dropped flat to the ground. His chest rose. I put my head down and heard his heart beating. "Phineas? Baby, can you hear me?"

His ribs slammed into my face as his back bowed so intensely, I thought it would break. His eyes snapped open, unfocused, staring at the ceiling before he closed them and shifted into a wolf.

"What is this, Mom? Is it the end? Is this what I did?"

She shook her head and covered her mouth. "You didn't do this part..."

He flashed twice more—human, then wolf—and I gasped. That time, when he transformed into his new animal counterpart, he wasn't alone. Not one, but two puppies snuggled into his side, eyes closed as they instinctively sought the warmth of their father's fur.

"Oh holy moon," my mom gasped. "I've never seen a blessed birth."

"We need towels," Nana said, finally sinking down to be with us. I wondered if she hadn't stayed back to give my mother a chance to help. This couldn't have been her first time seeing shift seizures, yet she'd remained mostly quiet until now.

Riley ran off to grab linens while I stroked Phineas's head. With his striking black, gray, and white coloring, he was as pretty a wolf as he was a man, but I couldn't relax until he opened those eyes. Said my name. "Phin, baby, you did it. You gave birth to twins. We have twins. Oh my god, we have twins."

He shifted slowly, morphing from wolf to man at half the speed it normally took. His eyes found me, and I stopped frowning. His gaze kept moving, sliding down to the wriggling masses at his side. "Puppies?" Too weak to raise his hand, I lifted it, settling his palm over the puppies. The moment his hand made contact, they shifted, both screaming.

"Twins," Nana announced. "One boy and one girl." She lifted both, looking them over before setting them on top of Phin's chest.

I worried he was still too weak to hold them, but it seemed having them near strengthened him by the second. He cupped the bottom of the little girl, keeping her from sliding down, and I helped him with the boy.

"I made an extra," Phin said, still in a daze.

Nana laughed, and my mother joined her, though hers was much shakier.

"I'd wondered why you got so much bigger than me," Riley said, looking surprised that he'd spoken out loud. His face turned red.

"The truth comes out," Phin mumbled, and I beamed.

If he was feeling aware enough to joke, then he was feeling better.

"What happened?" He winced like it hurt to speak.

"That'll be the dry mouth. Happened to Nash too," my mom said, standing. "I'll get you some water and ice chips."

She disappeared. Phin watched her go. "She seems better."

"She's... helping." I'd leave it at that. "I want to talk about you. You started seizing, babe. Shaking and shifting."

"I'm sorry," Phin mumbled.

"Don't apologize!" I started laughing, not because I thought the situation was extremely funny, but because I had all this pent-up nervous energy. Wiping the tears from my eyes, I cupped his face. "Don't ever do that again."

And though we both knew he hadn't had control of himself this time—and wouldn't the next time if it ever did happen—he nodded. "I promise."

My mom came back with the water and crouched to her knees to help him take careful sips.

The babies sat patiently through this, but when my mother sat back, they began to cry again.

Phineas patted them automatically, the urge to console them as ingrained as his need to breathe. "I can't believe they are on the outside of me. Is this real? Am I dreaming? I don't even remember it happening."

How odd it must feel for him to lose awareness and come to with twins. "It happened. They're real. Our children, Phineas. A son and daughter. Both alphas. I guessed overachieving runs in our genes." Sneaking a peek to my mom, she had tears in her eyes but was smiling.

Phineas had allowed me to see past the hate I'd kept in my heart for the woman of my memories and see the mother that she was. She wasn't completely forgiven, but I couldn't ever hate her as I once had.

"What are their names?" Nana asked. Thank goodness for her. While I was spacing out, coming to accept the fact that my family had tripled this evening, she'd been checking over the newborns using expertise she'd had years to perfect.

We hadn't spent a lot of time on this, deciding we would know when we saw our child for the first time. And as Phineas gazed down at his babies, I thought that had happened. He knew what they needed to be called. "Madison and Patrick."

"For Branson's father?" I asked. Of our parents, he'd been the innocent one. The few years that he'd been Alpha were remembered as the pack's golden years. He'd died when we'd all been very young.

"My father and mother. My dad was a Patrick too." Phin snuggled them both, feeling strong enough to hold them against his chest without my help. His dark crow tattoos shone brightly at his wrists. He was still a little pale from his ordeal.

"Their names are perfect, omega. Madison and Patrick Walker." I pushed away the thought of the blowback we might get from naming our alpha son after the pack's late Alpha. Pack politics had no place in this home, and even less of a place around my children. I lifted Madison, careful to keep her stable as I brought her to the spot just below my neck. She snuggled in perfectly, already asleep. "This one's gonna break hearts. But she'll have her brother to—"

"Hang on, don't go choosing for them. Maybe she doesn't want to break hearts," Phin protested, sounding even stronger. He held Patrick tight as he moved to sit up.

"You're right. I don't care what they end up wanting to do—"

"I wouldn't go that far," Nana said.

Phineas looked around. "Where are the others? What happened with Charles?"

Oh, right, the man who was targeting my omega. I hated him even more now, for cutting this perfect moment short. "Wyatt and Branson went to pick him up, and then we are going to have a chat."

"Do you really think it's him? All of this?"

All and—if I was completely right—more. "Yes. Phin, I think he might be the one—"

Though we were inside, the boom that ricocheted through the house felt as if something had exploded in the next room over. The babies screamed. Down the hall, Bran Jr. started screaming from his crib. Riley rushed to retrieve him while Nana, Aver, and I went to the back patio. It didn't take long to see the cause. The other side of the bay was burning.

Dread crept up my gut, threatening to choke me. I'd sent my brother after that man, my cousin as well. Had I sent them to their deaths? Who else could be to blame for the fire raging through the dark trees?

"The pack," Nana whispered. "You have to help them."

I shook my head at the same time as Aver. "We have to find Branson and Wyatt."

My mother joined us but would go no further than the back door. "Is it him? That man? Can you see what is burning?" Emotion made her words thick.

My phone rang, but it was Paul, not Wyatt. "What's going on?" I barked into the phone.

"Finally, one of you picks up. I couldn't get Wyatt to answer. The ceremonial fields are on fire. It felt like a bomb. Sounded like one too. The elders weren't hurt, but I'm worried about the houses closest to the blast. Some of the houses didn't hold up well against the blast. We need more strong bodies to pull people out, and I'm useless. Can you guys come help?"

No, we really couldn't. I didn't know where my brother or cousin were. My mate had just given birth to surprise twins, scaring the shit out of me in the process, and I didn't know if this blast had been coincidental timing or a retaliation.

"Please, Nash. It's the homes on the outer edges, the lower members in the pack. Everyone ran to the elders when the blast happened—no one's rushing to help them."

I thought of little Tanya and her mother. They'd all been through so much already. "Fuck!" I snarled into the air. I'd send Aver, but he didn't have my emergency response knowledge. We'd get the job done in half the time if we went together. "Fine. Aver and I will take the supplies I have and go there, but you need to come here and protect Phineas. He's given birth and... we found out who the arsonist is, so—"

"Wasn't me then?" Paul said. I liked that he was just petty enough to bring that up now. I would've done the same thing.

"No. Not you. I'm sorry, Paul. Will you come?"

"For Phin, not you. But also for you too, since you're coming to help. Tyrone already went down. So did the others. They're going door to door, flagging houses with wounded or at-risk members. Nash, please hurry. We don't have a lot of first aid supplies on hand right now."

A good Alpha would've seen those supplies replenished after all the emergencies the pack had gone through, but I didn't have time to think about that now.

I spun around, finding Nana and my mother. "Nana, we have to go."

"I heard. Don't worry about us. We will protect your mate." She folded her arms, and I didn't see a frail woman attempting to act tough—I saw a badass wise shifter who I wouldn't want to come across. I reminded myself that they would be safer here. The danger was over there, across the bay. Or it was wherever Wyatt and Branson were.

"Paul's on his way to help. We'll go to the pack," I said.

"Riley, keep calling Wyatt and Branson. We need to get a hold of them," Aver said calmly.

That was good thinking. We rushed through the kitchen. Aver split off to wait at the door with keys in his hands, while I veered into the dining room. I dropped down, helping Phineas to his feet. "Let's get you to the couch where you can be more comfortable." I'd meant to carry him, but he used me for balance and got to his feet.

"I want to come with you," he pleaded.

I'd known he would. "No, omega. You need to take care of our children and stay safe. Remember, you promised."

His eyes shone with tears. "You promised too."

If I never saw my omega cry again, it would be too soon. "The guys aren't answering. Maybe they've got him, and the fire is unrelated or was on a timer or something. I don't know. I have to figure it out. The outer houses are lower members in the pack, people that should be thought of first in these moments but aren't."

Phin's lip trembled, but he nodded. "I understand. Go. We'll be here."

I kissed him, swearing that the next time I did, this would be all behind us.

First, I just needed to figure out exactly what all *this* was.

20

PHINEAS

Nash and Aver left in a flurry of excitement that made the silence after their departure that much more noticeable. We'd diapered and clothed my babies. *My babies*. That would take some getting used to. Nana had helped give them their first meal, and then both had gone right to sleep.

"I should go," Julie said for the thousandth time. I had vague memories of the woman rubbing my feet. Riley had explained what had happened to me and how instrumental she'd been. Maybe my alpha was too kind to say the same to me, but I couldn't wait to say *I told you so*. At least, I couldn't until Riley had gone into what Nash had revealed about his suspicion around my chat friends.

He thought Chuck and Charles were the same? For that to be true... well, I'd have to be oblivious on a scale it didn't feel comfortable pondering. How could I not have picked up on something it had taken Nash only months to work out?

Because I'd assumed their intentions. That was why. I didn't fact-check everything they told me. I didn't even remember their real names half the time. Bun was always reminding me she was called Ana in her real life.

"We're needed here, and there's no one here to drive you anyway," Nana told Julie.

Julie's spine stiffened. "I can drive, Nana Walker."

"Really? I've never seen it happen. I didn't know."

Julie's cheeks went pink.

"We should all stay here," I said, checking once again that Madison and Patrick were both still breathing. I wasn't sure why they wouldn't be. I only knew I was compelled to check every other second. "Nash and the others will do their job better knowing the ones they love are safe." I had to believe that because if I didn't, I might jump right in the car with Julie.

Oddly, Julie didn't fight me. She looked down, tears falling to the carpet. "The ones they love," she whispered. Clearly, she didn't count herself as one of those people.

"I found it," Riley said, pulling Wyatt's computer over on the ottoman so we could all see the screen. "This is when Nash infiltrated your chat group. And this is Chuck saying that phrase."

"When Nash did what now?" I waved my own question away. That wasn't important right now. A years' long friendship built on lies and deception was. "Let me see that." I scrolled farther, to more recent conversations, but there was nothing that struck me as odd. It hadn't then; it didn't now.

The oddest thing for Chuck to do was when he freaked out on me a while back. I opened our PMs, scanning his apologies before noticing the green dot next to his name indicating he was online at the moment.

"You guys, Chuck is on. The man Nash thinks is Charles. He's online right now." The others circled around the couch as a car drove up outside. I closed my eyes, listening to the hum of the motor. "Paul's here." And he needed to have some work done to his car. That thing sounded like it was on its last leg.

Riley went to greet him, filling him in on all that had happened, including what we'd discovered.

"Congratulations! They're both perfect!" Paul slipped into the half circle that had formed around me. "He's online, you say?"

If there was one thing that could be said about Paul, he caught up on a situation really quickly.

I frowned at the screen. "Should I message him? If he's not Charles or the arsonist, it can't hurt. Not if we're slick about it." I tapped my fingers on the keys without pressing them enough to register.

"If we think he's dangerous, you shouldn't," Julie said. She'd gone through her moment of panic, and now she was solid again. I was liking Julie more by the second.

"But if this gives us information that can help them..." Riley had the phone to his ear. In the midst of everything, he'd been constantly calling Branson and Wyatt's phones, with no answer. That was his mate missing, after all. He kept a stiff lip, but he couldn't block the panic shining in his eyes.

"What are we discussing here? Sending this man some kind of message?" Nana asked, sounding like she'd stepped out of history.

"Don't worry, I have an idea." I typed quickly and sent the message before anyone could persuade me not to.

"What's up?" Paul read the message I'd sent.

I looked over my shoulder at him. "This way, if he isn't the arsonist, it won't seem suspicious."

Paul didn't look like he saw the beauty in my plan, but

that didn't matter because the three dots appeared, letting me know Chuck was saying something.

ChuckShurley: *Nothing much. You?*

I groaned. That wasn't exactly the full and complete confession I was hoping for, but now that I'd started, I had to keep going. "I'll tell him we just had dinner."

"I'm failing to see how any of this will help," Nana said. She lifted Patrick when he began to fuss and rocked him in her arms.

I picked up Madison. She wouldn't like laying without her brother. "I don't know. I thought maybe he'd say something again that would help us."

This had been a stupid plan, and what if Chuck and Charles weren't the same person? Then this was a stupid plan *and* a waste of time.

"He's typing," Paul said.

We all waited with bated breaths. He'd probably tell me something about a new tax trick he'd figured out. He'd been on me to get started on my taxes for weeks. But, when the message finally populated, it didn't have anything to do with taxes.

ChuckShurley: *I suppose you want to know why Wyatt and Branson aren't answering their phones?*

The blood drained from my face, and Nana snarled.

"Wyatt?" Paul growled. "What is he saying about Wyatt?"

"They both went to pick him up," Riley told him. "I'd say this is your proof, Phineas."

How nice it must have been for the others to retain the ability to speak at a time like this. I read his message again like I was trying to figure out how to read it in a way that didn't confirm my friend was actually not a friend at all.

My fingers rested on the keyboard, but I didn't want to type anything back. I didn't want Nash to be gone so soon after I'd delivered our babies. I didn't want Wyatt or Branson in trouble. And I didn't want anyone else getting hurt because of me.

I'd gone so long without thinking about it—that curse that had followed me for my life. Could my curse have a name? Was it Charles? Why?

That ended up being what I typed.

ChuckShurley: *Enough games. I'm done with all of this. Come to the station in the woods. Be prepared to leave with me. If you do, I won't hurt them.*

I didn't want to ask what he would do if I didn't. He told me anyway.

ChuckShurley: *Make no mistake, Phineas. If you don't come, their deaths will be your fault.*

"Why is he so obsessed with you?" Paul asked.

It was a valid question that I had no idea of the answer. He'd saved me once—pulled me, sobbing, from the wreckage of my parent's car. Had something happened then? Something to spur this behavior? "Call Nash," I said to Riley. I couldn't answer Paul's questions and didn't try.

"He's not answering," Riley replied moments later. He called again and put the phone on speaker.

"Hey, this is Nash Walker. Leave a message—"

Riley hung up.

ChuckShurley: *You have twenty minutes.*

"That's hardly enough time to drive to the outer station," Paul protested. He'd already slipped back on his jacket.

"What are you doing?" Riley asked him.

He looked from Riley to me as if the answer was obvious. "He has Wyatt, Branson—"

"He *said* he has Wyatt and Branson," Julie corrected him softly. "We don't actually know anything."

She wasn't wrong.

GoblinKing: *How do we know you aren't lying?*

Chuck responded almost immediately with a picture that clearly showed Branson and Wyatt, unconscious and tied to each other on a cement floor.

ChuckShurley: *The bigger they are, the harder they fall. Don't have any more rohypnol, but plenty of gasoline. Brought some marshmallows, so if you don't want to come...*

I gently squeezed Madison and kissed her forehead. If I went, there was a slight possibility that I would never see my babies again. I'd hardly seen them now. I didn't want to go to the station. I *really* didn't want to go, but how could I stay while Wyatt and Branson were hurt... killed?

"Don't tell me you're thinking about it," Nana said.

I did the unforgivable and ignored her. "Riley, keep calling Nash. You have to get a hold of him. Tell him where we went and why."

"We?" Riley asked.

"Me," Paul said, already heading to the door.

"And me," Julie added. Her chin shook, but she stood straight.

"Nash left you to be safe," Nana said. "Leaving now is spitting on that, child."

"What do we do, Nana? Wait and hope the crazy person doesn't do anything crazy? That's Wyatt, Branson—"

Riley let out the sob he'd been trying to hold.

"I'll save them," I told him, squeezing his shoulder.

"By giving yourself up?" Riley asked.

No, I didn't want to do that either. I wasn't sure how I would pull this off, but I knew I didn't have long to decide.

———

As Paul drove, I kept Chuck—or Charles, I guess—updated on our progress. I wasn't trying to be considerate. I just didn't want him to become impatient waiting.

It felt so odd, chatting with him whenever I could get a signal. It was like a regular evening, the two of us chatting. Except now he was a stalker. My stalker.

GoblinKing: *Tell me the truth—how long have you been following me?*

ChuckShurley: *How long have you had a curse?*

I gasped.

"What?" Julie asked, peering out the window.

I needed to limit my gasps at a time like this. "It was him. All along. How?"

GoblinKing: *You've been following me since I was a child? Why pull me out of the wreck if you just wanted to hurt me?*

ChuckShurley: *I would never hurt you, Phineas. Please don't say things like that. It makes my lighter finger twitchy.*

"How close are we?" I asked Paul.

"Five minutes."

GoblinKing: *Okay, you don't want to hurt me. You just wanted to hurt people around me?*

ChuckShurley: *I had to, in order to learn. I didn't want to hurt people, but it was the only way I knew to make you show me. I even offered to adopt you after the crash. Once I saw what you did in that car... you'd looked like road-kill ready for the pot, and then poof, you were healed. If I couldn't ask you how it was done, I needed to see so I could learn for myself.*

So many needless victims.

GoblinKing: *I didn't know you knew I could heal,*

298

Charles. You should have asked me directly. I don't know why it happens. It isn't a skill you can learn.

ChuckShurley: *You would say that. Don't bother lying now, Phin. Get here. I'm done chatting.*

His green light went red.

"Find anything out?" Paul asked at my sigh.

"Only that the man who *saved* me from the wreck that killed my parents is some whacko who thinks he can learn to heal as I can. He thought it was something he could learn. That if he saw me do it enough times..." I felt sick to my stomach. It stuck out from me like I was still pregnant. I guessed it took a little longer for that to change.

"Please don't blame yourself, Phineas," Julie said. "You've brought my boys back in my life in a way I thought I'd only dream of getting again. We're going to save them. Without offering you up as a sacrifice."

"How are you so sure?" I asked, not wanting to sound rude, but wanting to soak in even an ounce of her confidence.

"Because losing you would kill Nash, and he called me Mom today after over ten years. You won't be going with this Charles."

Would a mother's love be enough to get us through this? Maybe not, but we weren't going in with only a mother's love. We were three shifters—well, two and half, if skill was being counted. Being able to shift quickly didn't matter if I tripped over my own paws.

When Paul pulled up to the station in the middle of the forest, he cut the headlights. Nash had mentioned this station and how he never took shifts out here when they did man it—mostly around the warmer months—because it was too close to pack lands. Now, the stone building surrounded by tall trees was dark. The bays were empty, save for two huddled masses we could see through the glass from the outside.

The left bay door began to rumble open, revealing Charles standing just inside. He tossed a can of gasoline in our direction, and it bounced sharply, like it would if it were empty.

The stench of gasoline was already filling my nose.

"Come out, Phineas," he called out in a sing-song voice. "The rest of you stay put." Behind Charles, I thought I saw Wyatt's hand move.

"Did you...?" I whispered. Charles didn't have super hearing, but I didn't even want him seeing my lips move.

"I did," Julie said. "Paul, go closer."

Paul obeyed, rolling his Honda a few feet forward until Charles flicked his fingers, lighting the lighter in his hand.

"No further, or I serve you fried Walker. How about we add that to the list of Walker things they shove down people's face when they move here? Walker flambé, sounds good."

I went through my options. He was a human; we were all shifters. We could react faster, but faster than fire? If the worst happened and they were burned. I could heal them, but I also ran the chance that I'd become too exhausted after one to heal the other. My only option was to keep him talking, and to do that, I needed to get out of the car.

"Do either of you have a plan?" I asked, opening the door.

"No," Paul said. "But I'll think of one. Walk slowly. Try to get the lighter out of his hand."

I did as he asked, moving at a snail's pace. Maybe Riley had gotten a hold of Nash. Maybe he was on his way. Even if he was, the station was near the entrance to pack lands, and the fire was clear on the other side. Driving would take time. "You mentioned you have a daughter. Nash said she died. Do you want to talk about her?"

"And help you stall while your friends think of a plan? No thank you. We'll have time to talk about her. Time to meet her."

I frowned, slowing my steps when we were only a few feet apart. "But Nash said she died. How did that happen?"

I was almost certain I saw Branson move. The drug Charles had used to knock them out was wearing off. Likely faster than he'd expected it to.

"She got sick," Charles said, shaking his head. "She just needs the right medicine. You, Phineas. I knew when I saw what you did that you could heal me—teach me how to heal her. I just needed to watch closely enough, figure out your tricks."

My heart broke for a man desperate to do anything to save his daughter. But that man was also endangering people I'd come to love. "I'm sorry she was sick. I really am. But, if you would've just asked me, Charles, I could've told you my abilities don't work on illness. Only injury. I can't heal the sick, even if I want to."

Charles shook his head over and over, reminding me of a child throwing a tantrum. "No. That's not true. I've seen what you can do. I will take you to her, and you will heal her. Plain as that, Phin."

Inside the car, I'd been terrified. Now, I was still scared, but Charles was clearly a sick man. A sick, sad man. I was sorry for the misunderstanding and angry for all those people needlessly hurt, but I wasn't terrified.

Charles might have thought he knew who I was and what I could do, but he had no idea.

"It is true. It's sad what happened to your daughter, but she's dead. Nash said she died years ago. I can't bring that back, Charles. I can't heal death. Please, just let us have Wyatt and Branson. You can go and mourn like you should have years ago."

"Don't tell me how to care for my daughter!" Charles roared. "Do you think I just kept an eye on you and chatted with you? I broke into your computer the moment I taught myself how. If you're logged into GeekGab and are at your laptop, I can hear you, Phin. Hear every disgusting thing you've done."

That wasn't a pleasant thought. He'd been listening to me? No wonder he'd gotten so angry those nights I'd disappeared at Nash's. Did that mean he knew about shifters? I couldn't remember if that had been something we'd talked about with the laptop open. Still, none of that bothered me enough to mention. Only one thing did. "Disgusting? Charles, I thought you were my friend. You should be happy I found the love of my life." In the distance, a wolf howled, and my heart leapt.

Charles acted like he hadn't heard it. "Then it's good what they say, right? Better to have loved and lost than never to have loved at all. Let's go. Time's up for your pals." He stuck out his hand, and when I didn't immediately grab it, he raised his lighter, clicking the flame on.

Behind him, Wyatt stirred. His eyelids fluttered.

I'd been forming a plan. Somehow, I was supposed to roll forward, kick his legs out from under him, and catch the lighter as it flung from his hand. But, as he taunted me with the small flame, I felt something stirring deep within me.

Nash had told me that my wolf wouldn't always be so in tune with my own thoughts, that sometimes our wants would differ. I wasn't sure this was one of those moments because the second my wolf let it be known what he wished we could do, I wanted to do it too.

I lunged, shifting midair with my mouth open. I'd been aiming for Charles's fingers, but I wasn't quite so coordinated, and my teeth found his wrist. I bit down, tasting blood. More importantly, he dropped the lighter.

I released my jaw, shifting again as I fell from him, catching the lighter before it hit the ground. As my shoulder slammed into the concrete, I groaned, rolling to my feet. I held the lighter over my head, stunned that I'd done all of that. I pumped my fist in the air. "I'm a fucking superhero!"

That was about the time my excitement faded, and I remembered Charles was there, insane and angry. And, if the shock and revulsion in his face was any indication, he had *not* known we were all shifters. He held his bleeding wrist toward his body and reached for something at his waist. "You aren't an angel at all," he muttered, having reached max-insanity levels. "You're a demon. You're all demons." He raised his other hand, showing me the gun he'd pulled from his waistband.

Some superhero I was. I hadn't even noticed he was otherwise armed. I'd been hyperfocused on the lighter.

As he raised it toward me, headlights shone over his face. Paul revved forward, and Charles swung his arm around to the oncoming vehicle, firing twice before jumping out of the way of Paul's Honda.

I yelled for Paul to stop right before he rammed into Wyatt, who blinked rapidly at the sudden growing headlights. He and Branson both looked like they were coming to.

"Where did he go?" Julie yelled.

Charles had dived in the other direction, around to the outside of the station bay doors. Paul shot out of the car, waiting for his feet to be on the ground before he shifted as Julie and I went to Branson and Wyatt.

We'd gotten them nearly untied when Wyatt flexed his arms, straining as he stretched the rest of the restraints until they snapped. Branson did the same, and they helped each other to their feet. The rohypnol Charles had given them made them wobbly, and I helped Branson to the car as Julie led Wyatt.

"What are you doing here, Mom?" Wyatt asked, but in his stunned, drugged state, he didn't sound angry. He sounded almost like a kid.

"Making sure you're safe. Like I should have done," she said back. She was a small woman, and Wyatt was really leaning on her. He seemed to notice this and tried pulling his weight up. "Don't. You're still shaky. I don't want you to fall."

He nodded, accepting that his mother would help him whether he wanted her to or not.

I'd gotten Branson in the car about the time Paul came back. "I lost him. The gas smell is masking everything. He's in the area. I just don't know where."

That was certainly troubling, but it didn't have to be if we got out of here quick. I'd been about to get back in when I heard branches snapping. Someone or something ran at us at full force. I turned to see Nash break through the trees at the other side of the road. Our eyes met, and relief washed over me. I wasn't sure when I'd left home that I would ever see him again. But Riley had gotten through to him, and he'd rushed over. I spotted Aver behind him, catching up.

I ran to my alpha. I didn't feel like I had any other choice. Paul yelled for me to stop, his engine rumbling loudly. He must have been driving toward us. I ignored him, blocking out everything that wasn't my alpha. His shirt was torn along the bottom, and he had soot over his face. I wanted him to hold me and tell me what had happened, and when he was done, I'd do the same, and we'd both be safe and back in each other's arms. He'd look down at me with a face of love, not with the fear that flashed in his gaze now.

I frowned as I ran. There didn't need to be any fear. We'd done what we needed to do. We were safe—until Charles came back.

That was when I realized Charles had already come back. That engine rumble hadn't been Paul's Honda—it belonged to one of the huge firetrucks, and it was feet from me. I wouldn't get out of the way in time, not even if I jumped, and even though I knew all of this, I still stared at Nash.

I'd made a classic mistake, celebrating before the smoke had cleared, and now I would die for it.

Nash wasn't as paralyzed as I was. He kept running, sticking his arms out when we were nearly together, but not to grab me. He pushed me with all the force of a stampeding bull, flinging me out of the way of the firetruck seconds before it struck.

Struck Nash.

I screamed. His body soared. He landed.

He didn't move.

"No!" My throat burned.

I ran past the firetruck. Charles didn't exist to me in that moment. The growls sounding behind me meant he didn't have long in this world anyway.

Dropping to my knees at Nash's side, I realized how much hope I'd carried even in those short seconds it had taken me to run to him. Hope that he hadn't been hurt as much as I feared. That he'd somehow landed in a way that had broken nothing. But he'd been flung through the air after being struck by a firetruck going full speed.

I sobbed, wanting to touch him, but not sure where I should. He bled from his nose, mouth and ears. His legs and arms were all clearly broken, and when he inhaled, something rattled.

But he was inhaling. He was alive. I could heal him if he was alive.

I pulled my sleeves up, ripping his shirt open at the front. I'd been about to set my palms against him when someone grabbed me and yanked me back.

"That will kill you. Look at him, Phineas," Wyatt snarled, tears staining his face.

What was he talking about? I *knew* this would kill me. I'd never even attempted to heal someone as broken as this. Bones, internal bleeding, brain damage. I didn't have time to list everything that was broken inside my alpha. I didn't care. He'd saved me.

"You promised you wouldn't do this, Nash," I sobbed. "You promised!"

His rattling breath was my only reply.

"Get me Julie," I told Wyatt, my voice dead.

"Phineas, she can't help him either."

How could he sound so calm while also being so sure of his brother's death? A part of me wanted to hate Wyatt in that moment, but hating him would mean expending energy I would need saving Nash. If I could save Nash.

Julie ran over, wiping blood from her cheek. Her clothes were soaked with it. I didn't have to ask her where it came from. "My son," she dropped to her knees.

I knew the kind thing would be to let her grieve, but if I was successful, she wouldn't have to. "I'm going to heal him, Julie."

"Phin—" Branson started.

"Shut up!" I snarled. "I don't have time to argue. This might not work."

"And then you'll both be dead," Wyatt snapped.

"I don't care." I swallowed, knowing I would never see my children again. No. I couldn't think like this. If this worked, they'd grow up with an amazing father. A grandmother who would protect them from anything. A family. A pack. "Tell him I had to, please, Julie. Tell him he wasn't supposed to save me. The truck should've hit me. Tell him I love him. And tell him... I don't know. Maybe don't tell him 'I told you so' about you. Not right away, anyway."

I turned from them then, blocking them out as I had before. I knew, more than any of them, that Julie would see my message reached Nash, unaltered. He'd lose a mate but get his mother back. The pressure behind my eyes made it hard to look through them, so I squeezed them shut, pressing both palms flat against Nash's chest.

He groaned and tried to move. Probably trying to get me to stop. The sweet idiot. I could never let him die. I'd thought he knew that.

My palms heated up, growing hotter than they ever had before, but Nash's body was mending, and the pain was excruciating. We'd only scratched the surface of his injuries. I fell forward when the pain in my chest became too much to bear, laying over the top of him, touching his chest from my forearms up. At some point, I started to scream, the agony too much to contain. My hands glowed, and I wondered if this was what happened when I reached the limit of my ability. Would I simply burst into flames?

That seemed ironic.

I kept at it, sweat and tears falling from my body to Nash's skin. My eyes were closed tight. I saw something bright at the end of my vision, though I wasn't actually looking at anything. Somehow I knew that in that brightness, I would find relief from the pain that consumed me. I needed to only get to it. Nash's heart pounded, stronger than it had been seconds before. He breathed, a great shuddering gasp that did not rattle. I wanted to be happy, but I felt too empty to muster the emotion. I'd given everything I had to heal Nash, and when the brightness floated closer, I fell into it.

21

NASH

"Okay, Mom. I will. Yeah, we got the cookies. And the lasagna. Riley says thanks." It was still weird calling Julie Walker "Mom" again, but the title had stuck in the two weeks that had passed since Phineas had taken a rest.

That's what Nana called his coma, taking a rest, like he would just wake up randomly when he'd decided he'd had enough. I couldn't contradict her, not even so she'd call it something else. I had to keep hope that my mate would wake up once his body healed from the trauma he'd put it through.

When he'd healed me and brought me from the brink of death.

I flinched, thinking of that night. I'd played the highlight reel in my head thousands of times. Seeing Phin, his happiness, my confusion at what was going on. Then he'd run to me and I'd been happy—until Charles had broke through the trees behind the wheel of the station's firetruck.

I still wasn't sure how Phineas hadn't noticed the truck coming, the headlights, the roar. I vowed every morning that

that day would be the day I could ask him my questions. So far, every night, I'd gone to bed a liar.

"Please bring the kids by," my mom said. In a move no one had seen coming, Julie had left our house after we'd brought Phineas back and had gone straight to her own home to pack.

She'd shown up at Nana's, who greeted her by saying, "Couch's free." Mom wouldn't tell us everything that had gone on between her and my father, but he was livid, and I could assume that anger wasn't a new thing.

I growled, popping my knuckles. It felt nice to be mad at someone who wasn't myself or Phineas for a change. I always felt bad for being angry with Phineas. We were both liars. Neither of us had intended on keeping our promises not to put ourselves in harm's way for the other.

"I will. With Phineas, when he wakes."

I could imagine her small frown. "That sounds lovely, son. I'll call you later."

I hung up and checked the clock. It was about time for my shift to begin. Grabbing a bottled water from the fridge, I went back to my bedroom. Paul was there, sitting at Phin's side, reading from a book.

"I made a needy sound as Talon rested his hand on top of my panties and then proceeded to knead my hard-on through the fabric. My hips bucked, and my cock pulsed, still confined in its lacy prison."

My eyes bulged. "What the hell are you reading to my mate?"

Paul jerked straight, dropping the book. "I didn't hear you coming." He hooked his finger around his collar.

"I can see that. What are you reading to my omega, Paul?"

He rolled his eyes and bent down to pick up the book.

He wasn't afraid of me anymore, if he ever had been. "You haven't heard of Ann-Katrin Byrde? When my next shift comes, swing by. You can listen too." He sauntered off.

I shook my head. Dammit, but I was liking that shifter more each day. I wouldn't let him know, though. Where was the fun in that? The moment I looked back at my mate, shame filled me. I'd allowed my mind to stray from him, and that was unacceptable. What Phin had done for me...

I should have been in his place. Actually, no, I should have been six feet under. Had nearly been there. Being hit by a firetruck was like... being hit by a firetruck. That my mate had felt any of that pain enraged me to the point of madness. The way we'd figured, the only reason why Phineas wasn't dead right now was because of his recent transformation into becoming a shifter. He hadn't just gained our sense of hearing and smell, but our healing and power as well. We had no doubt that the human version of Phineas would be absolutely dead right now, had he tried the same thing.

But Phineas wasn't dead. No. He was stuck somewhere in the middle. On some days, his heartbeat was steady, loud. On others, it dimmed. I couldn't get too upset at Paul for reading that story. I'd been contemplating other things I could say to get Phin to wake up. Anything to shock or arouse his system.

So far, nothing had worked.

He looked so peaceful laying in our bed. I'd slept on the floor between the bed and the cribs every night. When the babies woke in the middle of the night, I was there to feed and change them, rock them back to sleep. But we never left their dad. Not when there wasn't someone else there to be with him.

We kept shifts, each of us, even Mrs. Boxer and Denise —Tanya stayed for as long as her child brain would allow.

"So many people love you, Phineas." I sat at his side, leaning my elbows onto the bed. "I was wrong before. They can love you however they want. No way is wrong when it comes to you, mate."

Some days I spent this time begging Phineas, teasing and, when I was at my lowest, threatening him to wake up. Others, I just talked about us. How we met. How he'd been blind to how perfectly gorgeous I was for a shocking amount of time. How I followed him, wrapped around his pinky from the moment I'd seen my first cartoon rocket. "I'm so fucking glad for Elise Boxer and those sausages. That reminds me. Aver has been a little crazy about investigating Charles. Everyone grieves in their own way, as Nana says. But he got Charles's banking information. He sent Mrs. Boxer those free sausages. He knew she'd grill them inside and hoped she'd hurt herself in the process."

She had, but Phineas had been caught up in a way Charles had not expected. A way that had brought Phineas into my life.

Until the end, I believed Charles when he'd told Phin he'd never wanted to hurt him. Aver had looked up his daughter too, gleaning from hospital records Charles had packed with him. She'd been diagnosed with leukemia just before Phin's accident. Charles had kept some journals at his apartment. Most full of Phineas sightings, whether he'd healed anyone, new theories Charles had on how. We'd burned them, but not before reading every page. He'd been growing increasingly unhinged as the years passed. The biggest dip in mental stability had been when his daughter had died. He'd grown frantic, believing he still had time if he hurried.

We knew it never would have worked, but for years, Charles carried around the image of a little boy, being sewn back together seemingly by magic as his reason to never give up hope.

My cousins, Paul, and my mother had seen to that. Charles... Chuck, or whatever he wanted to be called wouldn't have hope or anything else. They'd been careful not to consume any of him, and what hadn't soaked into the ground we'd buried or thrown in the river. Everything else, from explaining his disappearance to explaining the destruction at the fire station had been a simple matter of either cleaning up or telling a story that was easy to believe.

I didn't want to think more about that man, though. He'd already taken so much from me. He wouldn't take this time too.

"You know, I told Wyatt when he was mad about Mom coming for dinner that you see the world differently. But I don't think you see it right. How could you if you believed there was a time when I could be happy living without you? I will be the father I need to be for Patrick and Madison, but I'm not whole without you, baby. Come back. Please." Emotion closed my throat.

Angrily wiping my tears, I tore Phin's shirt open, pressing my palm to his chest as he'd done me.

After being hit, I hadn't been all there, but I'd been aware enough to know what Phin had planned. I'd tried to push him off me. Tried to scream to Wyatt to try harder to get him to stop. But he'd pressed his palms to me, and I'd been healed. Why couldn't I do the same to him? If he depleted his life force to save mine, shouldn't I have that power?

I growled, yanking my hands back. I wasn't mad at Phin,

but me. I wasn't strong enough to protect him like I'd promised. Not on my own.

The front door open, and Nana announced herself to the house.

Not on my own...

"Nana! Come back here!" I didn't have Phin's power—I would've felt it before now. Besides, I didn't have it because Phineas was alive. He had his power. And Phineas couldn't heal himself. He touched someone, and that someone received his power...

"I'll skin you alive!" Nana shouted after she ran in. "I thought Phin had woken up. Boy, why did you just make me run?"

I grinned, but it dropped when Nana bent over, grabbing her knee and wheezing. "I'm sorry, I just had an idea."

She straightened, revealing she wasn't even half as winded as she pretended. "What is your idea?"

You had to love that about Nana. She wasn't asking to argue. She was asking so we could put it into action. I explained what I thought. What I hoped. That Phin's power wasn't a one-way thing. It flowed. Until now, that flow had only been tested one way. But if Phin's power flowed to me, and I sent it to Nana, maybe Nana could return it.

It was crazy. I had no reason to believe this would work, except for that I wanted it to.

"Won't hurt to try," she said, her eyes crinkling. She didn't think this would work. She was humoring me.

That was fine. She didn't think it would work—I would think it enough for the both of us. Nana was wise. She heard things. But she didn't hear everything.

This was going to work.

It had to.

While Nana rolled up her sleeves, I sat at Phin's side,

moving his arm so his hand touched the back of my forearm. "Okay, Phineas, we're going to wake up now. Just a simple circuit, from you to me, to Nana, and back to you." I looked up to Nana. She sat on Phin's other side, pressing one hand over his heart and the other arm stretched out for me to touch.

I hovered my hand over her arm. I didn't feel different with Phin's hand on me, but maybe I wouldn't feel it until it flowed out. I took a deep breath and touched Nana's arm.

Nothing happened.

I squeezed my eyes shut, holding my breath, waiting for anything, something to feel different.

"Nash, it was a good idea," Nana said, but I wasn't finished trying.

"It can't work unless the energy flows from him," I said. "Phin isn't like Riley—his power doesn't just spring from him by touch. He has to make it happen."

How did I get my unconscious mate to try to heal me?

The front door opened: the others coming in. In a while, Riley would come back to relieve me. Aver would take the last shift before I came back for the night. I'd sleep, wake up, and be forced to act as if there wasn't a gaping hole in my body for another day.

I touched Nana's arm again, laying my head down on Phin's chest. "Please, mate. I'm broken without you. I need your healing. I know you said you can't heal hearts, but I need you to try. My heart is broken, Phineas. It's broken for you, my omega."

How could I have thought I felt Phin's power earlier when the real thing was so awe-inspiring? Was this how Phin felt when he healed? This peace, calm... and oh, ouch, my hand was hot. It burned brighter. Nana winced. She was feeling it too.

She didn't move but gritted her teeth. "Keep talking, my boy. It is working, I can feel it!"

"That's right, baby, you're doing it. You're healing my heart because you are my heart. Come back to me, Phineas. Just a little more."

My hand felt like an iron, but I hung on, watching Phin's face. His mouth twitched, his eyes rolling rapidly beneath his lids. There was more movement from him than I'd seen since I opened my eyes, healed from my omega's sacrifice.

Then it stopped. The heat disappeared. Phin's face calmed once more.

His eyes opened.

He *smiled*.

"Phin!" I pulled him toward me, burying my face against his neck. I kissed him there, up to his chin and his mouth. Nana ran out and returned with Riley, Branson, and Aver. I was pretty sure they all started to cry, but I wouldn't hold it against them.

"That was strange," Phineas croaked, his words tickling my ear.

"What was, mate? Where were you? What did you see?"

He blinked, his gaze going from each person in the room until he circled back to me. He smiled. "I don't know. I don't remember. Is everyone okay? Did everyone make it out?"

I laughed, hugging him to me again. "Everyone who deserved to."

Phineas nodded. My mate wouldn't be pleased about what had happened to Charles, but he'd understand why it needed to happen. "How long has it been?"

"Over two weeks." Two weeks of torture, of watching my heart beat outside my body.

Phin's eyes bugged a little. "Reg and Bun must be so confused," he said.

I sucked in air between my teeth. "Actually, they aren't. Also, they know everything now that I told them."

That time, Phin's eyes bugged a lot. Maybe this conversation needed to wait until a little later. He'd just woken up. But his expression said we weren't leaving this topic for a later time.

"Well, you see, Aver was doing all that research because he felt sad you were in a coma."

"And I kept logging into the chat to make sure there weren't any clues we missed in your history. Which got me to wondering about your other friends," Aver added.

"So they wanted to hire another investigator," Riley butted in. "At which point I informed them how rude that was to do unless you were absolutely sure someone's safety was at risk. And that they should do what any normal person would do when they want to find out about someone. Stalk their social media."

"We did that," Aver took over, giving Riley a brotherly glare. "And then I called the investigator anyway because safety *was at stake*. Anyone, long story, your friends, those two, they're clean."

"And you decided to tell them everything then?" Phineas asked, looking very confused.

I grabbed his hand. "Well, since we knew they were clean, so to speak, and I was looking for ways to wake you up, we got to talking. Oh, and I promised them I would tell you the moment you woke up that I am a dirty tool for logging into your chat room undercover and I will never do it again."

Phineas smirked. "That sounds like them."

My heart swelled at the gentle banter. I was afraid to

blink, scared this would all go away. "They are pretty nice. And you were right. Chat friends can be real friends. But they can also be obsessed stalkers."

My Phin rolled his eyes, and I'd never been happier. "They are going to be such a handful when I get back online."

Everyone but Phineas looked at me like they were on a safari about to watch the zebra—me—be chased by the lion. "Actually, they are going to be a handful in a week when their planes land in Seattle."

"When they're what—*what?*"

I dropped down, clasping my hands like I was begging. "I'm sorry, Phineas. They are persuasive and so worried about you. I couldn't keep away people who are worried about you! Those are my favorite types of people!"

Phin's lip twitched at the corner, and I knew I would be forgiven. "Anything else happening that I should know about?"

"Just that Wyatt and I will be forever thankful to you for forcing us to see our mother. She's... well... she didn't have the role I'd thought. She isn't forgiven," I added sharply. She knew that; this wouldn't be a shock to her if she were in the room. "But she moved off pack lands, out of my father's house and in with Nana. I call them the Silver Girls." I cupped my hand around my mouth. "But you can only use that term in front of Nana. My mom found a gray hair the same day she first heard me call her that, and I think she's holding a grudge."

Phin laughed. "I think I can handle all that."

Fuck, I wasn't sure I wasn't floating off the ground, I was so damn happy. "You don't have any more questions, love?"

"Just one," Phin said. "Where are my babies?"

―――――

THE NEXT MORNING, my mom came over, and so did Paul. Wyatt had come home after closing and spending the night in the bar—he hadn't slept at home a single night while Phin had been in his coma.

But no one left. Branson and Aver cleared their day, Riley called in, and we all relaxed now that our pack was full again. Phineas hadn't stopped holding his children.

"They've just grown so much," Phin said again, growing more teary-eyed each time it was repeated.

"They haven't grown that much. But they will soon." I leaned in, giving father, daughter, and son a kiss on the forehead. "Shifter babies grow fast early."

"Yes they do," my mom muttered. Her face snapped up, noticing us looking, and her hand twitched to her mouth, but she stopped it halfway. "You boys did, anyway. I think Nash was taller than me at seven."

"Not Wyatt too?" Phineas asked.

My mom laughed. "I suppose, yes. They were identical in everything but personality. And even there they have overlap. I mean... they could have changed, in that time."

That time, when we'd been torn up by grief and hating her guts. I didn't think I could change what had happened if I could. Wyatt and I had needed that time. But we'd also been wrong in assuming our mother's equal part in it. She'd been against the challenge. Against it all. But our father could be charmingly persuasive. And when he hadn't been able to do it charmingly, Wyatt and I had presumed he'd done it in other ways. We didn't know for sure because our mother wouldn't tell us. Probably because she knew our father wouldn't be able to walk when we finished with him if we knew for sure.

"Oh, I just remembered," Wyatt said. He'd laid down on the couch, plopping his feet on Paul's lap—to his utter and extreme delight. "I really need to get those repairs done. Been waiting for you to be ready, Nash."

Helping my brother would require leaving the house, which would mean not seeing my mate for longer than a few seconds. Why would I want to do that? "Get Paul to help you."

"I will!" Paul chirped.

"Paul doesn't know dick about plumbing. Sorry, Paul." Wyatt snarled. "Just help me, man."

I grabbed one of the baby blocks and threw it. It bounced off his face. "Don't say dick in front of my babies."

"What about my baby?" Riley whispered to Branson.

Wyatt growled, flinging the pillow that had been under his head. "You just said dick in front of your babies."

I caught it before it made contact, leaping to my feet as Wyatt did the same.

Nana's sharp whistle had me pulling back, realizing I was about to fist-fight my brother in front of my own children. And Riley's.

I sat down, sure my expression was sheepish.

"I change my mind," my mom said in the silence that followed. "They haven't changed."

EPILOGUE

HOLY CRAP, it was almost two. My friends, Ms. Xcept4Bunnies and Ms. Registered_Companion were going to be in my home. In front of my face. While I was also in front of their face... faces.

"Are you sure my shirt says cool, not scary?" I asked Nash.

He stepped down from the stool he'd used to hang the streamers. I wasn't sure how to decorate for seeing longtime friends for the first time, but streamers had seemed right. "Your shirt says *what's a wolf's favorite day of the week... Moonday* and then has a cartoon laughing werewolf sitting on a moon. How, in what universe, would that be scary, omega?"

I shrugged. Some people were afraid of circles. Tiny ones, all stacked together. Maybe the moon would...

I walked back to the bedroom, deciding I had better just change my shirt if I wasn't sure. Nash followed me in. I ripped my shirt off, throwing it back at him, and stomped into the closet. "A solid color might be better," I muttered, not wanting to wake the twins. They needed every ounce of sleep before meeting a new face. Already, they were proving to be excitable. Just yesterday, I'd caught Madison literally trying to gnaw at Paul's ankle like an elderly guard dog. They weren't really mobile yet, but it was only a matter of time.

I just worried about when they grew in teeth.

Nash stepped in, forcing me deeper into the closet. I smirked.

"Yes, omega, some foreplay. I love it." He reached for my jeans.

I didn't push his hands away, but I did stop his fingers. "Shh, don't wake up the twins."

Nash shushed me with his finger to his lips and stepped back, grabbing the doorknob and shutting us in.

That hadn't been what I meant, but the doors had really good insulation and would block our voices. "Why are you talking about foreplay? The girls will be here any minute!" I whispered.

"I assumed since you smiled... You know how that turns me on." He flicked his wrist, and instantly, my pants fell to the floor.

"It isn't impressive when you do that, you know," I said. "It just reminds me of the thousands of people you've been with that let you perfect that!" I pushed him away, not really angry but enough to put a little oomph behind it.

After becoming a shifter, some of my emotions were enhanced. Jealousy, for one. I was dealing with it.

"I've told you—you're the only one that matters, baby. Those people, they aren't regrets. They just aren't you. Once I saw you, there was no one else."

"Lord, Walker, that charm." I fanned my face. "Get out of here." I couldn't resist him when he got like that. All squinty-eyed and brooding. He must have flexed in a different way too because his biceps always looked larger. Those arms, the same arms that brought me pleasure and torture, both in the bedroom.

I gulped, forcing my eyes away from his chest and up into his knowing gaze.

I saw what he had planned plain on his face. The desire brewing. "No," I laughed, making it clear it wasn't a real no. "Don't you dare, alpha. We have guests coming. Guests you invited!"

Though I'd been making some very informed and thought-out points, Nash was undeterred. He cupped my face, shielding the back of my head as he pushed me back against the wall with a soft thud. "No? But, omega, you're trapped with me. There is only one thing you can do to save yourself."

I failed to keep the smirk from my face, but only for a second. "What can I do?" I asked. "Please, I'll do anything!" This was silly. Nash knew it, and I knew it, but at the same time, playing *trapped omega barters for his life with sex* was one of our favorite games. Well, mine. Nash's favorite *was fireman saves man who is very eager to repay him*. The guy had a type.

"You can get on your knees," Nash whispered.

My heart flipped. My dick twitched. My knees hit the carpet.

"Open, omega."

My lips parted, eager to do his bidding. Every part of me was at his beck and call. His zipper slid down with a buzzing whoosh, and he didn't even pull his pants down before yanking his dick out and sliding the spongey head between my lips.

I groaned, careful to keep the sound quiet enough it wouldn't leak. Some people might be very judgy about parents getting it on in the closet while their kids slept just outside, but those people clearly didn't have twins. Or four roommates.

His dick hit the back of my throat, and he pulled back, sliding it in once more. Trapped between his hard body and the wall, my head thudded against the wall each time his dick bottomed out down my throat. Maybe the twins wouldn't hear this, but whoever was on the other side of that wall would. I reached forward, tapping and gesturing with a nod over my shoulder, all the while keeping his dick in my mouth.

Nash's face changed from the lusty alpha to his regular one. He nodded, scowling again after. "Get over here. Can't have anyone hearing you and coming to save you before I've had my way."

I tried to say, "Oh no, please will no one help me?" but it came out garbled because of Nash's dick.

For as campy as we acted, my dick was still hard and aching. I reached down to stroke myself, and Nash growled.

"No way, omega. I give you pleasure. I'm jealous of your hand, always getting to touch what's mine."

I grinned. *Jealous of a hand?* That was new. I let him lift me to my feet anyway, dropping my hand away.

Essentially, we switched places, but Nash dropped behind me, immediately diving his face between my cheeks. "My own buffet," he groaned, minutes later, when he lifted his face for air.

I panted, hanging on the edge of orgasm. "What?"

"My very own candy shop," he whispered before returning his lips to my ass.

I floated to the precipice, rising higher, feeling the wind from the abyss licking my balls. Then it all stopped. Nash stood.

I growled.

I didn't have very long to be frustrated because he pushed me forward. His hand gripped my waist, keeping me from falling as my hands flung out, catching myself on the wall. His dick was in me before I'd completely fallen, slick with the lube he kept everywhere and splitting me open in the way only Nash knew how.

I was a goner, both in lasting another second without orgasming and for him. He was my mate, my kindred spirit. Plainly said, he was the other half of my heart. He was also very naughty, so when I climaxed, he reached down to catch it, bringing his palm to his mouth like he'd caught the fountain of youth on his fingers.

He moaned with bliss, cleaning his hand before hunching forward, nibbling at my neck and shoulder. I knew what to expect then—his warmth, filling my insides. He spilled into me, and I closed my eyes against the explosions of pleasure rocketing through me.

"I love you, Phineas," he whispered even though his brain should've still been short-circuiting, blanking from what had looked like a powerful orgasm. If the amount leaking out around his dick had anything to say about it, he'd had a very strong orgasm. Still, my name, his love for me, was always on his lips, in any situation, first.

"I love you, Na—"

My phone rang, reminding me Aver said he would call me when they were turning in. *They* being my friends, who I was meeting for the very first time. In this state.

"Holy shit, Nash! They're here! They're coming! Get out, hurry." I wiggled forward, trying to get free.

"You keep forcing me away, and I'll be compelled to convince you to go a second round."

I closed my mouth because this guy could do it.

He grabbed my clothes, yanking my pink shirt striped with tiny green frogs off the hanger. "Go rinse off. I'll tell Riley to answer, rinse off myself, and we'll meet in the hallway. Ready? Break!"

We didn't do the hand thing, but we exploded into motion. I veered off into the bathroom while he went out the bedroom door. I didn't wait for the water to heat up and took the coldest shower, trying to spare my hair. I dried to a degree that was sure to get swampy later and threw my clothes on, walking through a cloud of cologne I'd spritzed before meeting Nash in the hallway. He'd put his same clothes on after his shower but hadn't bothered to not get his hair wet. It looked cool on him.

"You look good, Walker."

"Same to you, PP."

I smacked his arm, hurrying when I heard two female voice around the corner. They were voices I'd never heard but that were familiar just the same. The cadence and word choice felt so familiar. I grabbed Nash's hand, and we stepped around the corner, coming face to face with my friends.

"Hi! Hi, I'm Phineas. GoblinKing." I waved while trying to not let it be seen I was near to hyperventilating.

Riley and Aver stood with two women in the foyer. The one on the left was short and round with long curly black hair and the prettiest hazel eyes I'd ever seen. "I'm Registered Companion. Gloria. You look just like I thought."

"I guess you know who that makes me," the other, Bun—no, Ana said. Her hair was red, but then I'd known that about her. I didn't know she had such a cool retro shoulder-length haircut with short bangs.

I was so excited, but unsure. They were here in front of

me. My friends. The seconds ticked on without anyone saying anything.

Out of nowhere, Ana stuck her hand out to Gloria. "Pay up," she said.

I frowned, and they both laughed.

"We bet on whether you'd have those long hairy ears like a werewolf."

Now that I knew the joke, I could laugh along. "You really thought that, Gloria?"

She shrugged. "You're the first shifters we've met." She looked around the room, from Riley, Nash, Aver, to me. "Hopefully not the last."

I blushed, and Nash chuckled, plopping his arm around my shoulders. He knew, without me saying a word, that I'd be shy at that moment. I'd have to learn to appreciate Gloria's forwardness in real life as I had in the chat room. And I would, just like I'd gotten used to, and came to look forward to, Ana's habit of randomly spouting out poetry.

The babies started to cry, and I asked the girls to wait a moment while Nash and I went back to the bedroom. He grabbed Patrick as I scooped up Madison, and we carried them back to the oohs and ahhs of the crowd. Nash had assured me that when he'd told the girls everything, he'd meant *everything*. Apparently, it was harder than he'd thought not opening up to strangers on the internet. But neither looked shocked to see the children. Both girls rushed forward, complimenting each baby appropriately.

I'd just have to make sure Nash or I was always holding them. And tell everyone to wear tall socks.

"Your home is beautiful, Phineas. Your husband is beautiful. I'm so happy for you," Gloria said.

Ana nodded her agreement. "We're really sorry we didn't recognize what Chuck was. He'd always been more into you than us, but we thought it was a bro thing." There was actual remorse in her gaze.

"It wasn't your fault. Either of you. Any more than it was mine."

That got them both going in my defense. I relaxed into Nash's embrace, nearly completely relaxed.

Earlier, Nash and I had made a plan of attack. We'd give them time to rest. Suggest drinks, have dinner, and then give them a tour of the property, but that had been when I was nervous about meeting them and afraid I wouldn't have anything to pass the time. As we migrated to the living room, standing or sitting, whatever was most comfortable, the time flew by, full of casual conversation, tears, and laughs. I learned that Gloria had quit her job to come, but we shouldn't be impressed because she hated it anyway. Somehow, we got on the subject of spitting and Ana insisted she could spit farther than all of us, so we had to go outside to test it. Of course, bets had to be placed before that, and then there was the process of elimination. Ana hadn't been lying. By the time we finished, the others had come home. We ate and laughed some more. And though the hour grew late, I didn't feel the drain I normally felt when I was in social situations.

I felt like I was surrounded by family, by love.

Because I was.

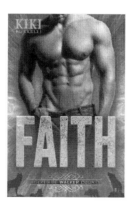

Faith: Wolves of Walker County

Chapter One
Wyatt

ANY MORE SLOW days like this one, and I was at risk of losing my mind. I needed to keep moving, both as a personality quirk and because with everything going on lately, if I didn't move, I brooded. And though the brooding only made me sexier, lately, it'd ended with me closing the bar early and getting up close and personal with a bottle of whiskey until I passed out on a table. And that just wasn't good for business.

I scanned the interior of my bar. The Greasy Stump. This building, these four walls—including the small office space upstairs—was the only thing in the world that was completely mine. Not shared with my twin or my cousins, but mine. With as cramped as things were getting at home, these hours in the bar were becoming increasingly important.

If I didn't have customers to keep me moving, I'd start thinking about the pack on the other side of the bay, how they were circling toward their own destruction. I'd think about my mother and the suffering she'd gone through on her own. I'd think about the abnormal number of blessed babies I'd witnessed in the past year. The normal number was zero. We'd had three: Riley's and then Phin's twins. I loved them all, but that shit was weird.

And I definitely didn't want to be whipped like my cousin Branson and twin, Nash. Two men, chopped down in the prime of their life to serve one man for all of eternity. They'd lucked out—Riley and Phineas were top-grade humans—but I still shuddered to think about chaining myself to one set of genitals for the rest of my life.

There was no telling what I'd miss out on, like the CILF sitting on a stool at the end of the bar top, nursing a cup of coffee. It was four in the afternoon, not so late that the cup of coffee seemed odd. I'd been in the office when he'd come in, and Jasper, my daytime bartender, had served him. Jasper was a trans man who would kick someone's face in if he caught them staring at his ass. Those had been his exact words during his interview, and I'd hired him on the spot.

Normally, I'd tell people who came in ordering coffee there was a cafe across the street that served the real stuff and save him from the battery acid we sold. I made it like my customers liked it: strong. But this customer I'd like to *fool around with* had come in when I'd been in the back, and I wasn't going to chase away someone as pretty as him.

I sauntered down the empty bar toward him. "Need a refresh?" Propping my elbow on the bar top, I balanced my chin in my hand.

The man had a small mouth with a thin upper lip. His bottom lip stuck out, slightly plumper than its companion, and curved into a smile. "You look like you need something to do. I should say yes to be kind."

The drumbeat to my internal soundtrack began to tap. I didn't dance with steps or pelvic thrusts but with my words, my gestures. "But are you kind?" I asked, letting my words linger on my lips.

He tapped the rim of his mug with a long index finger. "Some people would say no."

Interesting. I liked someone with a little intrigue.

"What about you?" the man asked. He had a frenzied restless energy about him, tapping his finger, looking up and down the bar. It didn't matter how many times he looked away when he gave me the full force of those spa-blue eyes, I knew exactly what I'd be doing tonight. And it wasn't pass out with a bottle of whiskey.

"Am I kind? Depends on who you ask, I guess." I poured him a fresh cup and pushed the dish of creamers toward him. He tapped them back.

"Pure, unadulterated jet fuel is how I prefer it." He

winked. His sandy brown hair and small face made the man seem tinier than he was. He lifted the mug to his lips, sending his forearms rippling. The man had some substance to him. Good. He wouldn't break easily.

The thrill of the chase simmered in me, burning to a boil. How long had it been since I'd encountered a fresh face? Accessible only by ferry, the city of Walkerton and the larger area of Walker County didn't get a lot of tourists around this time of year. "As flattering as it may be to think you came all the way here for a taste of my coffee, I don't think that's the case."

"Are you asking me what I'm doing here?" He set his cup down and leaned back so that his blue-and-white polo stretched tight over his trim chest.

"I know what you're doing here." I bat my eyelashes. "Saving me from an afternoon of boredom."

"I see." The man nodded. "So, I'm here to serve you. There isn't anyone waiting for you at home? No one depending on you?"

That was an odd question, but not the oddest, all things considered. The answer was a little more difficult. There were a ton of people depending on me.

Not solely me, but all of us, my two cousins, twin brother, and two mates. We lived together, looked after one another. It wasn't as if any of us, Riley and Phin included, had very much experience with children. Nor had we spent our lives dreaming of the day we'd have them. But the little tykes were *hashtag* blessed—as I liked to call it—and they'd come despite the odds or the lack of birth canal. I didn't want to bring all that into this conversation, though.

This conversation was supposed to block out all of that, not become the highlight. "Nope, no one is depending on me."

The corner of the man's mouth twitched. "Not even a pet?"

My smile stretched over my face. He could have no idea why that was so funny, both because I could turn into a wolf and because there was a little inside joke going that we did have a dog. I couldn't explain either of those things to this man, though. "I wouldn't mind a dog, but no. No pets depending on me either."

My head buzzed like I was the one sucking down coffee. I enjoyed every part of the hunt, but this part, where one wrong word could mean disaster, thrilled me. What did this guy have planned that he needed to know my whole evening was clear of responsibility?

"What about you?" I asked as the bell over the door chimed, indicating a new customer. Jasper was here. He'd help whoever came in while I helped myself.

"I'm a cat person."

He wouldn't be tonight. If I had my way, we'd both be howling to the moon.

"What about enemies?" the man asked. "Got any of those?"

My eyebrows squished together, following the direction of his glance. Paul and Tyrone from the pack stood behind the bar. Paul held a manila envelope while Tyrone had his smooth brown arms crossed menacingly over his chest. It certainly looked like I had enemies. But Paul was a family friend, and Tyrone had only ever been friendly with me. Judging from the looks on their faces, they weren't here to shoot the shit. They were here on pack business.

"I've got tons of enemies," I mumbled. "Excuse me for one moment. Don't move."

I slipped out from behind the bar. Paul and Tyrone slunk back into the corner, and I gestured to the table in the corner for us to sit. "What's up, guys?" Months ago, I would've been pissed that the pack had seen fit to come into my business with what was clearly *their business*, but things were murkier now.

"Elder Delia sent me," Paul said. He didn't often address his pack sponsor with her official title outside of pack lands.

I never did because Delia was a soulless demon who cared about money and power. And she was my aunt.

My curiosity sufficiently piqued, I spun a chair around and sat on it with my forearms braced over the back. "She thought you'd need muscle?" I jerked my chin to Tyrone. He hadn't taken a seat.

Tyrone was new to the packs. I didn't know a whole lot about him, other than that he always seemed to be where Paul was. Paul had joined within the year as well, but already it was hard to imagine life without him. He was friends with Riley and Phineas and was always at our house when he wasn't on pack lands.

Some days, I thought the interest he showed in me veered a little too far in the romance direction, but I saw Paul as a little brother. Firmly off-limits, and not in the forbidden, sexy sort of way where you meet up to have sex in a rest stop bathroom because no one can find out. The kind of off-limits that wasn't difficult not to cross because he was family. "What's going on, guys?"

Their somber faces told me they must at least know the nature of why they were here, if not the exact reason. Paul slid the envelope over the table like we were negotiating a contract.

"Have I been served? Give me a hint here." I didn't want to touch the goldenrod envelope. Not only did it smell like Delia, but nothing good ever came in one of those things.

"This wasn't our choice," Paul said, wrinkles lining his normally youthful face. Living under the strict rules and regulations of pack life would age a person. Except Paul seemed to thrive in that sort of environment. He landed on the island, clearly running from something—but then, that was how most new shifters joined a new pack. No one left a place that was awesome to start at the bottom of the pecking order somewhere else. "Delia is...I mean, Elder Delia—fuck, no, I don't mean that. This isn't right, Wyatt. I'm sorry."

Well, now I really needed to know what was inside that envelope. I wasn't so much afraid of the contents but really fucking curious about what could be inside that would torture Paul so much. Me, my brother, our cousins, the mates—we weren't in the pack. We were shifters, alphas all of us, but the four of us cousins had left the pack, and the other side of the island, over a decade ago and had no intentions of returning. "It's okay, Paul. It can't be that bad." I didn't like him looking so troubled. He was often put in a hard place, his loyalties to us sometimes clashing with that of the pack. But he was a tough cookie. I saw his potential.

Paul wouldn't look at me. Once he slid the paper across, his eyes remained on the table. Tyrone stood closer, nearly touching the back of his chair. Now I wasn't sure if Tyrone was there as muscle or emotional support. Not even the call of the hot and wild sitting half a room behind me could eclipse my curiosity.

I tore the envelope open, pulling the front sheet of many. It looked official, the pack's letterhead and formal seal stamped along the top. Just seeing that brought back memories of me as a kid, playing under my father's desk, coloring over the picture of a pack of wolves howling at a single moon. My mom would burst in, shooing me away. I wished

I could relive those moments with the lens I saw them through now. I would've been nicer to my mother.

I read through the legal mumbo jumbo, trying to get to the actual point of the thing. The whole thing stunk of Delia Walker, both literally and figuratively. When I got to the bottom part that was clearly an amount due, including back pack tax on my business, I burst out laughing.

"A bill? Delia Walker is sending me a bill?" One with more zeroes than I currently had laying around.

That wasn't exactly true. I had a chunk in the safe, but that money was for repairs. I'd realized I couldn't keep hoping Nash or the other guys would have time to help me fix what needed fixing in my business. I'd broken down and decided to call professionals to help with the projects. I had the money, but I certainly wasn't going to pass over thousands of dollars to the pack.

Ever since the four of us had left the pack, our parents, also known as the elders, had used every trick, bribe, and manipulation they could conjure to try to bring us back. This letter was definitely more of that.

It was annoying, and the legalese had raised my heart rate for a moment. That sort of talk always did. My bar was my pride and joy. But it wasn't real, not like how a letter from the IRS would be real. This was pack-related. I wasn't part of the pack, and my cousins weren't part of the pack, so we weren't subject to their rules.

In the end, Delia Walker had failed in causing me any real trouble and succeeded only in annoying me.

"Paul, really, take a breath, bro. I'm not mad."

"You aren't?" Paul's face cleared like wrinkles beneath a hot iron.

"Why would I be? This doesn't mean anything." It looked like it did, which was what Delia likely had been hoping for. "She can't tax my bar. My business has nothing to do with the pack."

"You aren't paying, then?" Tyrone asked gruffly. I hadn't thought he and I had beef, but apparently, we did.

I took my time looking at him, letting my gaze crawl to his face. "No. I'm not. Is that why you're here? To shake it out of me?"

His expression tightened. I looked at him not as a new shifter looking for refuge, and not as Paul's friend either, but as a foe. He was big, a shower. He held his muscles for the world to see. I might not have had his arm size, but I was an alpha. Tyrone would be fighting his nature and me at the same time. I wouldn't enjoy a fight with the man, but I wasn't worried over the outcome, either.

While I sized up Tyrone, he did the same. "No, but our orders are to return with your answer."

"Ty, we don't—" Paul got to his feet, moving between us though there was already a table there. He squeezed between the table and Tyrone. "I explained how this was complicated, remember?" he whispered.

"It really isn't," Tyrone replied, not bothering to lower his voice. He wasn't yelling, and the low country music piping in from the jukebox muffled most of what we had to say. "An elder of our pack issued an order. I'm still new, Paul. I can't afford to directly disobey like that. My sister is just now getting comfortable, my niece has stopped waking up in the middle of the night screaming, and my mom spends only a quarter of her day crying. They're healing here. I understand drama exists in this pack that has deep roots, but it isn't mine. It isn't yours, either. You put your reputation in the pack on the line for people who don't even appreciate you."

I got to my feet. I didn't mind people talking shit about

me—I was pretty awesome, and that made people jealous—but if they were going to do it to my face, I would at least be standing up. "We appreciate him."

At the same time, Paul said, "They appreciate me," but the way he said it was soft and unsure.

I circled around the table, dropping my arm over Paul's shoulders. I didn't like how sad he'd sounded or the way he stood now, hunched. That Tyrone had made him feel like that only made me dislike him. "Why don't you go running back to Delia? Tell that troll she can shove her bill right next to the stick up her butt, if there is room."

Tyrone stiffened and dropped his arms. His brown face wrinkled as he frowned. "That's disrespectful language directed at an elder. I'm required to—"

I waved away the rest of his words, feeling for a moment like I was standing in front of my cousin Aver from about fifteen years ago. He and Branson had battled for Pack Hall Monitor when we were kids. We hadn't had a lot of chances to hang out alone, for reasons that would become obvious years later when our parents asked us to kill each other, but when we did, each time ended with Aver finding issue in whatever we planned and tattling to his parents.

Tyrone sputtered, his eyes narrowing on my arm over Paul's shoulders. Did he have a problem with that? Too bad. Paul had been my honorary little brother before he'd been whatever Tyrone thought he was. "Paul, we have orders."

Orders. Rules. Laws. The Alpha's Word. I'd been stifled by all that before. Never again. "Then go. No matter what Delia says, this is my business. I own the building and the land. I also have the right to refuse service, and that means you're loitering. Get out before I sic Jasper on you."

That might have sounded like a joke, but only to people who hadn't seen Jasper in action.

"I'm going," Tyrone barked, his eyes never looking at me, just at Paul. "I'm going alone?"

Paul swayed but remained. "Yes. This wasn't right, what Delia did. I... just..."

"Fine." Tyrone turned and went out the door.

I led Paul to a stool and sat him down on it, sliding back behind the bar. "Are you hungry, bro? The special is a philly burger. I'll throw one on for you."

Paul nodded and reached for the cardboard coaster in front of him, spinning it like a coin. "I'm really sorry about that." His head ducked between his shoulders. "I didn't want to bring that to you, but she ordered me to..."

And as Delia's sponsee, Paul had his basic needs met— food, shelter, protection—specifically from her funds. It was the same as any new member when they joined a pack as an adult. Some packs had more elder households; others had fewer. That also meant Paul was Delia's to utilize in the pack how she saw fit. Today, that had been as messenger boy. The witch had to have known how that would have made Paul feel.

"No worries. Seriously. You've only had a few months to deal with them. We're all used to it." I couldn't imagine the texts I'd get back when I told the others what Delia had done. Considering her last stunt had been finding Riley's violent ex-boyfriend and flying him in to murder Riley, this felt tame. "Hey, Jasper, get this guy what he wants. I'm gonna throw him on a burger. You want anything?"

Jasper shook his head. "I was going to tell you. Sia is out of town visiting her parents until the weekend. If you need or want me to work to close today, I can."

An hour ago, I would've said *don't bother*. I needed to watch my overhead as much as possible while I was trying to save for repairs. That little white envelope sitting in the safe had grown painstakingly thicker thanks to my scrimping. Still, I hoped my plans had changed from an hour ago. "Sure, thanks, Jasper." Even though I was the boss, when I passed by my sexy customer on the way to the kitchen, I felt like a kid who'd learned it was a snow day. I couldn't let my shiny new toy leave before I'd had a chance to play with him. "Almost done with this. You ready?" I asked him.

The man shrugged. I wondered how much he'd watched. Right now, he looked preoccupied with his phone. "Ready for what?" he asked.

I gestured up and down my body. "All this."

The man laughed. "Go. I've got coffee left."

I rushed into the kitchen, sending the guys a group text after throwing Paul's patty on the grill. If I'd gotten a letter like this, then Branson and Aver must have gotten one similar for the business they started, Walker Construction. By the time I'd cooked the burger to a juicy rare—we were wolf shifters, after all—and threw on the grilled peppers and swiss cheese, the screen of my phone was full of replies.

Most of them were expressions of disbelief. I'd go through them later. I hastily slapped Paul's burger together, plopped it in a lined basket, and dumped fries on top. In my opinion, a good burger was one that fell apart halfway through eating it. When I went back out, Jasper had gotten Paul a Coke, and I set his burger down. "There you go. Just the thing to get the taste of Delia out of your mouth. Eat up."

Paul opened his mouth—I assumed to thank me—but no thanks were necessary, and I'd left my prey alone long enough. At least now I could be pretty confident he was interested. No man would've waited patiently if he wasn't. I slid the last few feet to him, holding my hands out like I was surfing or like I was Tom Cruise from *Risky Business*.

He smirked. "Smooth."

I dropped my elbow back on the bar top, but this time, I wasn't able to block the pack from my mind as easily. That just meant I needed this distraction more than ever. I put my other elbow down, cradling my chin in my hands as I took in his face. He wasn't just handsome; he was pretty, gorgeous, a looker. In fact, he was so attractive, I frowned.

"Do you now, or have you ever considered yourself, cursed?" I asked. When Branson had found Riley and Nash had found Phin, both men had felt as if a curse had followed them all their lives.

"Only by good looks."

Oh, this was going to be fun. But I wasn't done. "Do you have powers? Can you make things move with your mind? Does your touch compel people to cluck like a chicken?"

The man frowned.

I probably would too if I'd been asked that, but I couldn't mess around. I didn't need to find anyone who would make me act the way Nash and Branson acted once they found their mates. They'd lost all focus on things that had been important to them. Only their mates had mattered. I didn't want to disappear inside of someone else.

"I do have powers."

My gut dropped, but at the same time, my curiosity spiked. "What kind?"

He winked. "That's for you to find out later." He smiled, giving my body time to react.

Anticipation was the key to desire, and I was on a metaphorical edge. I might not have wanted to disappear into another person, but I wouldn't mind getting lost in one for a bit.

"Do you have any other questions?" he asked, slipping

his finger around the rim of his mug. The movement was different now, like all pretense had been wiped clean.

"Just one. What's your name?"

His spa-blue eyes sparkled. "Kansas."

Continue Reading

TRUTH: WOLVES OF WALKER
COUNTY BOOK ONE

Chapter One
Branson

"Have you gotten your invitation?" Aver asked. A low but steady beep told me he was on site, hopefully pouring the concrete to reinforce the posts for the Lanser's dock.

"Invitation? Oh, that's right. The winter solstice." The last time I'd seen Aver had been this morning when he'd left for the day. I should've gone with him, but the paperwork was already piled high. The Lanser's was a big job, and they'd opened the doors to us booking up for the rest of the season. Aver hadn't been back to check the mail.

"Don't play dumb with me, Branson. You know what invitation, just like you know why you've been running us both ragged with endless consultations these past weeks."

"We're running a construction company. I thought that was what we did."

Aver made a sound that was half growl, half snort. "You

should've seen it. Hand delivered. Gold foiled edges. The paper was heavier than a rock. Good stock."

I could only imagine the hours Aver's mother would've spent on choosing the card stock. She probably had her spies reporting back to make sure she was the Walker family with the thickest paper.

I scanned the untidy stacks of paper on my desk in the office Aver and I shared in the house we lived in with our two other cousins. Carbon copies of pastel pink, blue, and green fluttered each time a breeze blew from the cracked window. "Maybe mine was lost in the mail."

"You wish. Your mom makes mine look tame. If I know Delia Walker, she's enlisted an entire parade to bring it to your door. Oh yeah, unrelated, I'll be late tonight."

An alert popped up on my computer screen telling me the perimeter sensor alarm had been activated. I groaned.

"Uh oh, is that Mommy Dearest now? Was I right? Is it a parade? Or just a full marching band?"

I yanked open the curtain to the driveway that wound down from the main road. I couldn't see anyone coming. "I don't know. Maybe it was just a raccoon. I'll check it out later. I've got three proposals to finalize as well as updating those numbers for the Forstein addition. Maybe, if you see them, you can try and explain why the granite specially shipped in from Italy would be more than the original locally sourced stone we'd quoted them."

Between the two of us, Aver had a better way with words. His father had groomed him from a child in public speaking, in hopes that it would help him assume leadership of the wolf pack. Now, Aver lived off pack land and co-owned Walker Construction. How the mighty had fallen—according to Aver's father. "If I see them. But I doubt I will. I'll be at the club—"

"Say no more. I don't want to be roped into whatever scheme this is, and I will take no part in you playing this part."

"Things aren't that easy, Branson," Aver replied tiredly.

"It's as easy as 'Mom, Dad, I'm gay, stop setting me up with female shifters you think will lure me back to the pack.' It's what I said."

A knock at the door made me frown. I hadn't heard any of the other sensors. The perimeter alarm had gone off, but not the porch or the door. I pulled up the front door camera but didn't see anything. I'd told Aver that camera was angled too high.

"Awesome, now I get nagged at from both sides. Would you like to also criticize my other choices in life? How many beers I have at the end of the day? The many ways in which I am disappointing my family by living outside of the pack?"

I grinned, but I didn't feel any happiness from Aver's annoyance, just grim acceptance. Which I imagined he felt as well. Sometimes, it was easier to give a mouse a cookie. At least then it got them to stop asking for the whole bakery—for a while. "I'm sorry, you're right. Agreeing to a date now will get them off your backs, but not for long with the Winter Solstice Celebration approaching. Have you spoken to Nana? I have a voicemail I haven't checked from her waiting at the end of my to-do list." At this rate, I wouldn't be getting to the end of my list likely until Aver had returned from his ill-fated date.

"I have a voicemail too. I'm afraid to check it. I never know with that one. Either she wants us to come over so she can stuff us with pies and tell us we are smart and brave like when we were kids, or she needs to warn us of the latest apocalypse the stars have brought to her attention. It's a gamble I just won't take today. She probably called Wyatt too. Let him handle it."

Another knock sounded. I frowned. "Hold on, there's someone here. That sounds good, about Wyatt. If he is going to claim to be Nana's favorite, he can fend off her endless prophecies." I exited the office, not bothering to close the double doors and walked down the hallway to the front door. "I've been telling you, we need to lower the front door cameras..." I saw the vague outline of a small body through the frosted glass oval insert in the center of the door. So there had been someone there.

The figure was alone, not in a band or parade, so that knocked Aver's suggestions out of the running. I opened the door, my eyebrows lifting as my mouth dropped open.

"What is it?" Aver's voice spoke from far away. Except he was where he'd been the whole time while I'd found myself in a load of shit.

"Who sent you?" I barked, and the young man on my porch flinched.

He was short and slim with silky brown hair and blue eyes. He wore hardly anything, despite the frost on the ground that still hadn't melted from the night before.

"Do I need to come home? What is going on, Branson? Dammit! This camera is too high, I can't see anything!"

"Maybe you should. See if Dave can handle the site for the rest of the day." I slipped the phone in my pocket despite the fact that Aver was still speaking.

The young man on my porch had begun to shiver. My treatment of him could have started the trembling, or the fact that he was dressed like a virgin fit for sacrifice to an angry god. He'd recently bathed, adorning himself with so much cologne I should've smelled him long before the perimeter alarm had gone off. His shirt was white and so thin I could see through it. I imagined that was the intent. But, I couldn't ask him in or even offer him something to warm him up, not if he was sent from my mother.

And he was definitely a shifter.

"P-please, Alpha Walker—"

"Don't call me that," I snarled with more menace than this poor boy deserved. I sucked in a calming breath, shoving my fingers through my hair. "Who sent you? My mother, right?"

"Elder Delia said I wasn't to return if you weren't with me." He clasped his hands in front of his body, lowering his head so deep his chin rested against his chest.

I wished I could believe him, ask him in, give him a blanket, and then send him on his way, but Delia Walker had been trying to bring me back to the Walker family since the four of us—Aver, myself, Wyatt, and his twin brother Nash—left together at eighteen.

An act I'd followed by coming out.

Now, Aver got set up on blind dates, while I got barely legal, or possibly not at all legal, meat offerings.

My lips twisted into a scowl of disgust. I was sure the young man was very nice, and maybe, with a few years and pounds on him, he'd make some man very happy. Right now, he reminded me too much of my nephew, and when I thought of the types of things Delia, my mother, would've suggested to this kid to help him persuade me to return with him, I wanted to throw up. "What's your name?"

It was odd that I hadn't known him by scent, but maybe the cologne was blocking anything familiar about him. He was probably sixteen or seventeen now... Since it had been over ten years since myself and my cousins had left, I should have had at least an inkling of recognition.

"Paul, Al—sir."

"Paul?" I didn't remember anyone by that name from the pack families.

"Paul Tyson, sir, I wasn't born in this region. My family comes from the south."

I frowned. "Oregon?"

Paul shook his head. He wore a light coverage of makeup, and as he turned his head, dark blue splotches shadowed underneath. "Texas. I hate it there, and I'm not going back. You can turn me away, but I ain't... I'm not going back." He tugged at his shirt, covering more of his midriff and telling me he wasn't any more pleased to be in that outfit as I was to have him there.

It would have ended my problem, but I couldn't block out those bruises. "Now hold on. Don't go running. I will not be going back with you, but I can't order you into the cold. Hold on." I lifted a finger to tell him to wait while I dug in my pocket for my phone.

He jerked back, toward the door.

"No, just wait—"

"Sir, I don't mean to disrespect you, but I told you I won't go back, and I won't. I thought I'd find safety here, but if that's not the case..." His attention swung up to something behind me. His jaw slackened.

"Fucking fuck, Aver, he's alive. I'm looking at him right now," Wyatt griped into the phone as he moseyed down the stairs. Aver's call had clearly woken him at the early morning hour of eleven forty-five. He wore only holey jeans, and his shaggy hair flopped long enough to cover his eyes. "And what's this?" Wyatt crooned, coming to a stop at the bottom step. "He's got a friend." Wyatt winked.

I rolled my eyes. Wyatt would flirt with a rock. But Paul had stopped trying to run out the door.

"Wyatt, this is Paul Tyson. I was wondering if you

would wait with him while I make a call?" I stepped to the corner, never leaving the two.

Paul's gaze flitted toward me. "Who are you calling?" His tone was unmistakable. He didn't trust me.

That wouldn't change by me lying now. "The police. I know that might not be what you want, but I know the cops around here. They can help you. They won't make you go home."

"I know the sheriff," Wyatt said, but out of his mouth, the words were husky. "He's an alright guy. Can't quite keep up spotting me at the gym, but he tries."

I waited for Paul to start laughing, but the kid was lapping out of Wyatt's hand. "I'm eighteen, though..." Paul said instead in a half-hearted attempt.

Wyatt's gaze flicked to mine long enough for him to turn back to Paul and say, "Still, it's better to go by the book with these things."

I would've mentioned Wyatt had no idea what *these things* were. He was just good at dropping into a situation and assimilating to what was needed. He would've been much angrier had he known that Delia Walker had sent this kid to seduce me. As if I'd find my omega in a shifter who was still a child. She'd crossed the line this time, though. Maybe Wyatt didn't know enough to be angry, but I was livid.

"Sheriff Maslow." Jake answered on the second ring.

"Hey, Sheriff, this is Branson Walker. I may have a kid in trouble here."

"Kid? How young we talking? Are you at home? What's a runaway doing way out there?"

It wasn't like we were in the middle of the woods, but we were a few minutes out of town by car where the Lynx River emptied into Walker Bay. If Paul had come from pack lands, he'd likely run from the other side of the bay to here, but I wasn't going to tell the sheriff that. "Not sure. He doesn't seem like a bad kid, though..." I looked briefly over at the two of them. Wyatt had Paul's full attention talking about some superhero movie that had just released. "He might have been abused?" If my mother had knowingly sent an underaged male to seduce me, I wouldn't protect her. Pack pride be dammed.

"I'll be right there. This is good timing. Well—you know what I mean. That fancy hire from Seattle came in this week. He's been on my ass talking about updating our procedure and policy. I tried to tell him we don't have enough of those kinds of trouble in Walker County to have all that rigmarole." He stopped speaking suddenly and cleared his throat, making me wonder who had walked in on him. When he spoke again, his tone rang with polite authority. "Thank you for calling. We'll come up now. Keep him there, keep him calm."

I hung up, wondering how I was supposed to keep a skittish shifter kid from running, but Wyatt had that under control. His habit for flirting was an advantage at the bar he owned and operated, and, I guessed, it was an advantage when trying to keep impressionable youths from fleeing. I lingered around the border of the room, still keeping an eye, without interrupting. And yes, I got a vindictive amount of pleasure seeing Delia's trap circle down the drain.

If this was the type of shifter she thought would lure me back into her clutches, then she didn't really know me at all.

Suddenly, my driveway was a parking lot. First, Aver in the white work truck with Walker Construction written in blue blocky letters on the side. Behind him was a firetruck, lights spinning but thankfully not the siren, and then Sheriff Maslow in his cruiser.

"Holy shit!" Paul exclaimed when he caught sight of them all.

"It's okay. Only one of them is here to talk to you," I said. "The rest are just nosy." I'd recommended Aver come back to the house, but that was before I realized Wyatt had been asleep upstairs. He didn't always sleep at home, choosing to crash at his bar sometimes instead. And I hadn't meant for Aver to blab to our cousin Nash. He was Wyatt's twin brother and a fireman, as well as the fourth of the Walker cousins to live in this house. And apparently, the town could spare a fire truck. "Stay here," I ordered, mostly to Wyatt.

Aver was already crunching over the gravel. "What's going on?"

At the same time, Nash hopped out of the firetruck and strode over.

"Listen, both of you. Delia sent me... a *gift*," I said with a snarl so they would understand. "He's shifter—"

"If he's shifter, why is the sheriff here?" Nash asked, hackles raised as his dark eyes flit back to where the sheriff was just now getting out of his car.

"Because he's got bruises, and I'm pretty sure Delia sent him for a specific purpose. If he's underaged, I don't care if she's my mother—I'll report her." I'd have reported her even if Paul was of age, but at that point, Paul was responsible for his own decisions in the eyes of human law, and shifter law was just about useless at a time like this. "He might have come from somewhere worse. He said he traveled here to try to join the packs and make a new life, I don't know. But I won't feel comfortable until we check it out."

The sheriff walked too closely for us to continue talking. A second man approached in step beside him. He stuck out immediately in an outfit that was probably called business casual where he came from, but on this side of the bay, he might as well have been in a tuxedo. His light blue button-up and gray wool blazer fit over a broad chest. The creases in his black slacks looked like they'd come straight off the ironing board. With an outfit like that, I expected some shiny loafers or equally impractical leather dress shoes, but I grinned at the tri-colored canvas sneakers.

"Branson." The sheriff offered his hand. I shook it, and then he turned to his partner. "This is our new representative from the Washington State Social Services, Riley Monroe."

I stuck my hand out, but the other man just nodded stiffly in my direction. He had a narrow face and sharp cheeks. His dark brown hair stuck out in a style I could only describe as artfully messy. Already, he had a dusting of facial hair shadowing his chin and jaw. There were faint dark circles beneath his deep blue eyes. A late night? Or early morning?

I pulled my hand away before the moment could get any more awkward. There were any number of reasons why he wouldn't want to shake my hand. It couldn't have been something I'd said—I hadn't spoken to the man yet. But, as the moment stretched on, I needed to say something quick. "Welcome to Walkerton."

The sheriff cleared his throat. "Mr. Monroe, this is Branson Walker."

"I was wondering when I would meet a Walker. Your name is everywhere in this area. I was sure the family wasn't far behind," Riley Monroe said. His tone was pleasant enough, but with an edge I was used to by now.

"Walker is just my last name. I'm afraid you'll have to go to the other side of the bay to meet the impressive Walkers of the family." My great-great-great-great grandfather had helped develop the island. We were one of many coastal islands located between the north-easternmost tip of Washington State and San Juan Island. Accessible from the mainland only by ferry, we lived a sheltered, quiet existence.

Most of the time.

But my ancestors hadn't been all that creative when it came to naming things. We lived in Walker County, the city was named Walkerton, and I looked out onto Walker Bay every morning.

Riley's gaze drifted to the house behind me. "I don't know, this is pretty impressive."

Pride filled me. The four of us had made this home with our own two hands. It had acted as our first symbol of independence from the packs. I rarely had a chance to show it off and had thought that the more than ten years—closer to fifteen—living in it with three other bachelors might've soiled the original feeling, but, there it was again.

I heard the door opening behind me and Riley's expression transformed. When he looked at me again, there was none of the polite friendly demeanor from before. Only judgment. His dark blue eyes narrowed, his gaze searching me with a new purpose. "Is that the child in question?" he asked, his voice all steel.

"I'm not a child!" Paul shouted back, despite the fact that Riley had spoken too quietly for Paul to have reasonably heard. He was either emotional or not used to ignoring his senses around humans.

Riley's eyebrows rose. "Nothing wrong with his hearing." He stepped by me without a glance in my direction. In fact, I got the distinct impression he hadn't looked at me on purpose.

I had no reason to care about what this stranger thought of me. I knew how bad this looked; it was one of the reasons

I'd called the police so quickly. I could've sent Paul away with some money and a ticket to the wolf packs in the next territory over. But if he'd been stopped, it would've been harder to explain my involvement at that point.

"Hello, my name is Riley Monroe. I work with Washington State Social Services." Again, Riley skipped shaking hands. Was it a city guy thing? Cold and flu season? He pulled a small, leather-bound notepad out of his pocket and began writing as he asked Paul questions.

The only thing I knew for sure was that I was too busy to be hanging around, especially if my presence was no longer required. And yet, when I turned to make my excuses to the sheriff, what I was said was, "Would you like to come inside? It might be easier for the interrogations to happen in the dining room."

I very nearly clocked myself in the face, I reminded myself so much of my mother. She was vindictive and manipulative, but she would never say a mean word—to your face. Every guest was offered food and beverages, never mind if Delia Walker didn't know how to turn tap water into tea.

Riley approached, having left Paul at the front porch. "I'm going to need a list of everyone who lives in this household. As well as the number to a Mrs..." He checked his notepad. "Delia Walker. Any reason why Paul might've gone to her home? Is she known for housing runaway youths?"

I snorted. Delia Walker was known for being one of three elder households, garden parties and always getting her way. But I was sure she would've loved being associated with something so altruistic. "Delia Walker is my mother. She lives on the other side of the bay with all the other fancy Walkers." There were four official Walker households: my grandfather, my mother, Aver's parents, and Nash and Wyatt's parents. But once we started splitting the names off, it became impossible to explain without a graph and a bottle of booze.

Riley's eyes narrowed on me again. I wished I could go back to the moment before he'd seen Paul. At least then Riley hadn't looked at me like scum. "Do you know why your mother would've sent Paul here? He's dressed extremely provocatively but claims he got the clothing from your mother."

"I can't begin to pretend I understand my mother. We aren't close, not since I moved from home."

"Hm."

I didn't trust that single noise any more than I trusted the situation at hand. Until now, I'd been pretty polite, but I wouldn't have this stranger thinking something about me that was wholly untrue. "Do I need to remind you that I called the cops here, Mr. Monroe? From my side, I found a young man, clearly down on his luck. And I called the police first. I'm not asking for any sort of reward, but I'll ask you to stop concocting whatever scheme you've decided is at work here. I want Paul safe. That is all."

Riley's eyebrows rose again, only this time, they didn't settle into suspicion. "Forgive me. I'm new and still getting the hang of things. This is unusual, but for what it is worth, Paul has not claimed to have done anything he didn't want to do. I'll need to run his identification through our systems. If he's eighteen as he claims, that changes my next steps significantly."

He was clearly attractive with a level head. That didn't entirely explain my sudden interest in the man, but I wondered if maybe it had been too long since I'd traveled out of Walker County and mingled with fresh meat. I frowned at the term. I was so out of the game, I'd practically assumed Riley's orientation. He could like women... stranger things had happened.

Riley must've assumed the expression was meant for him. "I'm only doing my job, Mr. Walker. Caring for the welfare of those unable to care for themselves."

I smiled, trying to infuse as much warmth into the expression as I could. We'd gotten off on the wrong foot. I could understand why, but I was still eager to get back on the right foot. "I understand." I pulled out my card. "When you get some answers, please let me know."

Riley took the card gingerly, carefully grasping the very corner between his thumb and pointer finger. "Walker Construction," he murmured with a small smile. His finger traced over the embossed lettering on the card, and I bit my cheek, suddenly wishing his finger would trail over me instead. "I guess it's good to be proud of your name."

Alarms rang in my head as Riley's smile turned sad. I only had about a thousand questions all piled on top of each other. But the longer I stood there, the more I noticed the sheriff standing there with Paul. They were ready to leave.

"Don't be a stranger," I called out as the three of them turned back to the cruiser.

Nash walked up behind me. "Don't be a stranger," he mimicked in a high-pitched tone. I couldn't exactly elbow him with Riley looking. I was still trying to get the man to not think the worst of me.

"Shouldn't you be doing something?" I snapped instead.

Nash's smile never wavered. It hardly ever did. He was the spitting image of Wyatt, except his black hair was close-cut in a military style. "I know what you want to be doing," he teased before shutting the door and ensuring the final word.

Wyatt and Aver waited at the porch. They'd have their own annoying taunts locked and loaded. I sighed, looking back down the driveway. This wasn't the morning I'd planned for, but it was likely the morning I deserved. I could only hope that everything with Paul checked out. And I would secretly hope that Riley was the one to call me when it did.

THANK YOU!

Thank you so much for reading Hope! I can honestly say, the moments I've spent with the Walker family have been some of my fondest. Exploring the Walker County world has been a blast and I can't wait to continue the journey with you all. I need to make a very special thank you to the lovely and talented Ann-Katrin Byrde for allowing me to use the quote from their book. Paul thanks them as well. I'd also like to thank my cover designer, Adrien Rose for being so amazing, and my editor MA Hinkle of Les Court Author Services!

About Me

Kiki Burrelli lives in the Pacific Northwest with the bears and raccoons. She dreams of owning a pack of goats that she can cuddle and dress in form-fitting sweaters. Kiki loves writing and reading and is always chasing that next character that will make her insides shiver. Consider getting to know Kiki at her website, kikiburrelli.net, on Facebook, in her Facebook fan group or send her an email to kiki@kikiburrelli.net

The Den Series

(Wolf/Coyote shifter Mpreg and MMMpreg)

Wolf's Mate Series

(Wolf/Lion Shifter Mpreg and MMF)

The Omega of His Dreams

(Non-shifter Omegaverse)

Bear Brothers

(Bear/Hybrid Shifter Mpreg and MMMpreg)

The Jeweled King's Curse

(Dragon Shifter Mpreg)

Hybrid Heat

(Hybrid/Bear Shifter Mpreg and MMMpreg)

Akar Chronicles

(Alien Mpreg)

The Kif Warriors

(Alien Mpreg)

Welcome to Morningwood

(Multi-Shifter Omegaverse)

Omega Assassins Club
(Wolf Shifter Omegaverse)

Wolves of Walker County
(Wolf Shifter Mpreg)

Wolves of Royal Paynes
(Wolf Shifter Mpreg)

Printed in Great Britain
by Amazon